SLYE TEAM BLACK OPS

DECEPTIVE TREASURES

DIANNA LOVE

Praise for
the Slye Team Black Ops Romantic Series

FATAL PROMISE

"Fatal Promise left me speechless and in awe."
~~Heathercm, Amazon

"It was a slam dunk in terms of guns, international travel, romance, killers and resolution."
~~ Goodreads

STOLEN VENGEANCE

"This is one of those books where your body tenses, you stop breathing and you just can't read fast enough."
~~ Amazon

"If you love romantic suspense, you will adore Dianna Love's latest Slye Team."
~~ IMHO reviewer

DECEPTIVE TREASURES

"This may be my favorite book in the series so far. I swear they just keep getting better and better."
~~Heather CM, Goodreads

"Complex. Ongoing series. Nonstop action. Romantic suspense."
~~ Madison Fairbanks, Amazon

KISS THE ENEMY

"A FREAKING AWESOME continuation of the Slye Team series by Dianna Freaking Love!!! She did not disappoint."
~~Goodreads

"Kiss the Enemy is a high octane thrill ride through the high stakes world."
~~ J. Cazares, Amazon

HONEYMOON TO DIE FOR

"It seems with each book this series gets better."
~~The Reading Cafe

"…constantly believable and packed with intrigue."
~~Single Title Reviews

NOWHERE SAFE

"The love story is tender, steamy, erotic, and full of electricity, and the action plot will satisfy the reader's thirst for danger."
~~IndieReads review

"Blending taut pacing with sizzling tension, a little bit of James Bond with an engaging personal drama, this is a story for suspense fans and romance readers alike."
~~Goodreads

LAST CHANCE TO RUN [prequel novel]

"I could not put this bookdown...Once again Dianna has thrilled my suspense taste buds with an extra dashof spicy romance."
~~After Hours Rendezvous

"Engrossing, thrilling and wonderfully steamy...a pitch-perfect suspense that will keep readers breathless from the first nerve-racking scene to the last shocking revelation."
~~The Romance Reviews

Dedication

For my Dianna Love Street Team who is with me all along the way. Your enthusiasm and support means the world to me. I always look forward to jumping out of my writing cave to visit with you.

Chapter One

TANNER BODINE STARED at the three heat signatures on the thermal-imaging camera and cursed.

The idea was to *not* kill anyone tonight.

I should have known this mission was rolling along too easily. Not that there had been a damned thing easy about a HAHO, or high altitude, high opening, night jump into North Korea four hours ago. Now his team crouched behind an unfinished concrete wall in the one country no one should enter without an invitation.

Definitely no American.

If he and the other three Slye team operatives got caught while they were gate-crashing Pyongyang's annual citywide April celebration, the fallout would be bad. Much worse than just having the US government deny knowledge of this mission.

Tanner's team would be painted as nothing more than mercenaries trying to kidnap two North Korean physicists for financial gain. And the world would believe that lie, since Iraq was known to pay top dollar because *their* physicists got sniped all the time.

Tanner nodded at Dingo Paddock, who angled the thermal-imaging camera so that Nick Carrera and Damian "Blade" Singleton could also watch the monkey wrench shoved into their operation.

Who was that third figure following the two physicists at a covert distance?

All three continued across the empty plaza toward the first floor of a 330-meter-tall, pyramid-shaped structure that soared through the black skies above the Pyongyang skyline. The Ryugyong Hotel.

Or better known as the Hotel of Doom because it remained a giant, unfinished money pit, under construction for twenty-four years.

Twenty. Four. Years.

Who does that?

A leader willing to spend billions on a joke of a hotel while his people starved.

Tanner lifted the Velcro flap covering the illuminated face of his watch.

Twenty-two-hundred hours, five minutes. The physicists—the packages—were right on time. So where had they picked up a tail?

It wasn't either of the two guards on duty at the hotel's front gate.

Over the last two hours and ten minutes, each guard had taken turns making a casual pass around the area once an hour. The last patrol had included a smoke break in the plaza sixteen minutes ago.

Eluding the security to reach this point had been laughably easy for his team, but who would send their best personnel to watch an empty hotel?

Hadn't some UK journalist just blogged about making it right past the standing guards a few months ago to get inside the hotel before daylight?

Yep, everything about this op had rocked along smoothly … until now.

But one uninvited guest to this party was *not* going to screw Tanner's mission.

With temps hovering around thirty, he had to cover his mouth with a gloved hand to hide the frosted air when he gave orders. His throat mic easily picked up his whispered words. "You three enter by the second access point, secure the packages and head to the rendezvous location."

If anything went FUBAR, Tanner had a backup plan, but the last thing he wanted was to divide his people. He'd volunteered to run this op because of his knowledge of North Korea.

Knowledge he'd earned as a member of Delta Force.

But the real reason he'd volunteered for tonight was to save a young girl his sister had grown up with, whose dying mother had been deported. Saving that girl hinged on a successful mission here.

Tanner added, "Give me a sixty-second head start to intercept the unidentified. We rendezvous and exit at twenty-two-thirty hours."

"Roger," echoed in Tanner's ear. He lowered his night-vision monocular into place, leaving his other eye as the only body part exposed. He wore gray wool that blended in with the locals, just like the rest of his team, all custom-made clothes to cover the gear he needed for the op.

He pushed up slowly.

The roar of a cheering crowd in the distance drew his attention for a second. Lights glowed above where a hundred and fifty thousand citizens of the Democratic People's Republic of Korea, or DPRK, filled the May Day Stadium three kilometers away to celebrate the birth of their leader's grandfather.

A packed house in the largest active stadium in the world.

That's why this op had to happen right now while so many of the DPRK military were on show for their dictator.

That and the fact that the North Korea nuclear threat finally had teeth and their pit-bull leader was ready to bite someone this week.

Not happening.

Tanner lifted his Chinese Norinco rifle and moved carefully, melding from shadow to shadow. The team carried nothing that smacked of the US or South Korea. The suppressor on his rifle was Russian. Even their clothing was made without tags and with materials sourced outside the US.

Two young men waited inside that building, ready to defect to the US and trade what they knew of Project Jigu-X.

Translated, it meant Project Earth.

Did the head Nork behind Jigu-X really believe that name would camouflage his true plans? *Live on in your dream world, buddy.*

Tanner placed one careful step after another. No one could know that his team was extracting the two physicists and delivering them to the US. Plausible deniability wasn't an option. There could be no connection whatsoever to the US government.

The State Department had cashed in on a debt Sabrina Slye—the head of Slye operations—owed another government agency to get this job done off the books, so to speak.

Sabrina could have backed out by claiming she owed the DEA, not the State Department, but she'd never leave the US exposed if she could prevent it. The op had a thirty-percent chance of success and Sabrina wouldn't ask anyone to go. In fact, she'd planned to run the op herself, but Tanner had convinced her to let him take point.

Nick, Dingo and Blade had volunteered next.

Sabrina accepted the job, but only after the State Department agreed to do a favor for Tanner once he handed over the two physicists.

Tanner had told his mother he had a plan to save Martina. He would belly crawl over hot coals to fulfill his end of this deal and then he'd use the State Department's pull to cut through red tape for what he really wanted.

The silence sharpened his senses. Tanner skirted the weak lighting and hugged pooled shadows.

Get the package, get out, echoed in his mind.

Entering North Korea had been fairly simple.

Exiting would be a challenge even with transportation waiting on them a half mile away.

He hoped it was actually there when he arrived.

The two egghead physicists in this doomed hotel better be able to provide proof that North Korea had finally developed a nuclear warhead small enough to fit on a long-range missile. If so, they would live in anonymity in the US by entering the equivalent of a super-secret WITSEC program. They'd never see their home country again, but where they were going would be Utopia compared to life here for anyone other than the elite.

The leader of this country had the ultimate zero-tolerance policy when it came to defectors and anyone accused of espionage, so Tanner hoped the two eggheads would follow orders and keep up.

He'd protect the physicists at all costs, but he couldn't allow his team to be captured. Capture meant execution for all of them.

He paused near the main entrance, then continued on to one of four access points his team had located and stepped through the opening of an unfinished window. Inside, he wove through a forest of scaffolding set up for the workers and stopped short of the vast, circular lobby.

The ceiling was hundreds of feet up.

Light from a half moon dodging clouds struggled to filter through empty space covered with glass walls.

Not enough light to bother his night vision.

Just enough to sneak around inside without it.

On the far side of the unfinished room, two figures huddled together. They were dressed in the dull colors of poor citizens who lived in portable cabins outside the hotel and worked as supplementary labor alongside the military who were building this fiasco. Intelligence reports had stated that locals would help the physicists reach this point, which appeared to have happened.

If the local people who'd played a role in this defection were discovered, they'd be executed or sent to a prison camp that made hell look like a tropical vacation.

Why would people here risk their lives to help?

He could understand the physicists' motivation. Who wouldn't want to defect to a country where they ate regularly as a minimum?

These two claimed they didn't want blood on their hands.

Scientists with a conscience.

What was the world coming to?

Tanner tamped down bitter memories of one female scientist who sure as hell hadn't possessed a conscience.

He held his position as he swept the interior visually, searching for that third bastard. His team would enter from behind the physicists, which prevented anyone from surprising them. Dingo and Nick would pull the packages out of sight without making a sound while Blade covered their six.

That initial tingle of warning riding Tanner's neck since the minute he'd seen the third heat signature clawed at him harder. *Where are you?*

There.

Moving from right-to-left as silent as a ghost, a figure circled the outer perimeter of the lobby.

He was heading toward the physicists.

Tanner mirrored that movement on this side of the lobby, keeping track of the physicists as well as the unidentified.

In less than a second, two of his team coalesced from the shadows and grasped the defectors, vanishing from sight.

So far, so good.

Tanner eased near the empty space where his men had been only seconds ago, until he was between that spot and the exit point.

He stood in shadows to the side of the path, out of sight unless that third figure also wore night vision. Tanner hadn't seen any headgear.

Keep coming this way for your special welcome, you bastard.

The unidentified was heading forward at a quicker pace. Five-foot-five, maybe five-six, light build and quiet as a ninja mouse sneaking past a cat. At six-three and just over two hundred pounds, Tanner should have no problem containing that scrawny rat.

Tension ran along the tight muscles in his neck.

He froze every muscle, waiting for the intruder to pull even with his position. At that point, he could cold cock the sucker and leave him laid on the floor, none the wiser about what was going on when he did wake up.

If the little guy fought him, Tanner's only other option would be to snap his neck.

Boot heels scuffed over grit and concrete near the main entrance, dividing Tanner's attention with a new threat entering. Dammit.

The ninja practically flew toward the team's exit point.

Tanner released his weapon to hang from the dummy cord hooked to his vest. He lunged and caught the ninja, hooking his arm around a body that weighed little more than a big kid's. His captive made a soft squeak a second before Tanner covered his mouth. The speed the guy had been moving forced Tanner to spin to handle the momentum. The minute Tanner lifted his captive off the ground, the ninja stilled.

This guy's cheek skin felt too smooth to grow whiskers.

Was it a boy? Hell, he didn't want to kill some kid.

If Tanner left him unconscious, what would the guards do to him?

He moved his arm up for a better grip and bumped into … breasts.

Are you shittin' me?

His ninja was *female*?

Who had he pissed off in a former life for this bullshit? He couldn't leave her here unconscious and vulnerable to male guards who might abuse her, but neither could he leave her to spill her guts about the physicists.

Boot heels slapped the floor where the guard walked from the entrance to the center of the vacant lobby area.

Leaning to his left, Tanner took in the guard who carried a Type 56 assault rifle, a Chinese version of Kalashnikov's AK-47.

Seconds were ticking off the clock for meeting up with his team.

He slowed his breathing to where his chest barely moved. The woman in his arms did the same. She breathed in sync with him.

Another guard entered. Dammit.

The first guard turned around, saying something in clipped Korean to the second one. Tanner could grasp enough Korean to get the gist of what they were saying, but the guards spoke too low for him to hear.

Whatever they'd discussed ended with one heading to the far side of the building and the second one turning in Tanner's direction.

Of course.

No point in going halfway when things turned FUBAR.

Taking down the guard or getting out of the building silently wasn't going to happen with this woman in his arms.

Tanner turned sideways and eased backwards into a pocket of black created by a support beam. He angled his body to shield his captive.

Why? Because of his damned ingrained instinct to protect a woman. As long as she didn't try to kill him.

If she stayed quiet, the guard should pass by without noticing them. But that warm little body of hers was pressed against the front of him, and *his* body was noticing her soft curves.

Not the time for Big John to wake up.

What the hell was this woman doing here? Following a boyfriend?

Had Shin Pang or Jae Har, the physicists, told a girlfriend goodbye?

That would have been stupid. But geniuses were not known for their common sense.

Tanner sorted through ideas for what to do with her and kept coming up with nothing his conscience would accept. First, they had to escape discovery.

That *might* have been a possibility until the guard heading his way flipped on a small penlight.

You son of a bitch.

The beam swung left and right in front of the guard's feet as he moved closer.

Tanner's ninja tensed.

That damned light swept to the left and paused on a pile of construction debris. When it did swing back to the right, the light would land on Tanner and his ninja.

Well, shit.

Toss aside his ninja and go for the guard?

Sure, that'd work. And for his follow up act, he'd pull a helicopter out of his back pocket.

Chapter Two

EVERY SECOND THUMPED in tandem with Tanner's heartbeat. Blood pounded in his ears.

He had no other choice. He'd wait until the very last moment before the guard's light reached him then he'd drop the woman and go for the guard.

If his ninja remained quiet when her feet touched the floor, Tanner might just pull this off.

If not, they were both dead.

Logic said this woman would do anything to avoid discovery, because she'd be accused of spying for the Americans if she were caught with Tanner.

The guard's light bobbed over debris and pieces of piled-up scaffolding. He stood close enough for Tanner to smell the strong odor of nicotine clinging to his gray wool uniform. His nose was flat on the end.

Somebody hit you with a frying pan, Flat Nose?

Tanner's muscles were drawn-bow taut, ready to spring into action.

A high-pitched voice crackled from the guard's radio. Flat Nose stuck his flashlight under his arm. The beam bounced as he listened to the rapid chatter Tanner could barely understand. Something about ... intruders.

Had someone seen his men?

Only if Har or Pang had made a mistake.

Very possible, considering Tanner was holding an unknown woman in his arms.

She trembled but didn't make a sound.

Tanner held his breath while the rattle of scrambled words streamed from the guard's radio. He picked up that more soldiers were on the way and some reference to shutting down the exits in the city. Sweat trickled along the inside of Tanner's collar in spite of the freezing temperature.

Would a division of ground soldiers flood this building and surrounding area any minute?

The second guard who'd searched the other side of the building marched to the center and called out to Flat Nose. After a quick exchange of words, Flat Nose joined his buddy by the door, and they walked outside.

Tanner let out a breath.

His ninja did, too, at the same time, as if their cardiovascular systems were linked.

Now. What to do with her?

He'd used up six minutes. Time to make a decision. His limited Korean would only confirm that he was American, so he said nothing as he eased his hand from her mouth, waiting to see what she'd say.

She whispered, "They know you are here for Pang and Har. They know about the defection. We must hurry."

He arched an eyebrow at her that she couldn't see. Perfectly spoken English in an angel's voice, albeit with a Korean accent. Who the hell was she?

"What do you wait for?" she hissed at him. "More soldiers will come. Pang and Har have been betrayed."

If she knew about Har and Pang's defecting, then Tanner was losing time hiding that he was American. "Who are you?"

"You must hurry or—"

Did she think this was some damn game? "Explain who you are, or I'll leave you unconscious to face the soldiers alone." He wouldn't do that to a woman but threatening anything less was wasting precious seconds.

She turned rigid as his mama's broom handle and derision saturated her words. "I should expect no more from your kind."

"What kind?"

"US military."

Just how much did she know about this op? "I'm not military and you don't know what you're talking about. Time's up."

She got the message. "I am Soo Jin. I perform research in the same center as Har and Pang. I know you are here to take them to the US to defect in exchange for information on the Project Jigu-X."

This woman clearly knew something, but in this country, she could be working for any side. "What was transmitted on the soldier's radio?"

She warned, "You waste time. When your people die, it will be your fault."

Tanner grabbed her by the throat, keeping her back to his chest. "If you've set us up, I'll kill anyone responsible for harming my men." He squeezed his fingers.

She struggled against him. "Stop. I ... came ... to help."

He eased his grip. "Why?"

Her words rushed out wrapped in fear. "I am part of the network that is helping Pang and Har escape. I came to warn them and show you the way out of the city, but if you do not hurry your men will die ... if they have not been caught already."

Was she telling the truth?

He put her down and yanked her arms behind her back, holding them with one hand, and keyed his throat mic to transmit to his team. "The package has a leak. I repeat, package has a leak. Hold position."

Dingo's voice came back. "What's wrong, mate?"

"They might be expecting us. Where are you?"

"Sixty yards from wheels. We haven't seen any movement around it."

Tanner considered her words and told Dingo. "Send someone to recon, but don't touch it."

"Stand by." Dingo and the rest of the team were half a kilometer away.

Tanner itched to move out, get out of the center of the damn city, but the op had major flaws right now. The minute he left this building, he had to know for sure where he was going and what he was doing with this captive. There was still time to make the transport, if it hadn't been compromised.

Could he unload this woman somewhere between here and meeting up with his team without leaving her in a vulnerable position *and* without leaving a leak that would sink his mission?

She'd spill her guts to the soldiers the minute she was caught. Why? Because she was a woman and a scientist.

That combination had already screwed him once. Literally *and* figuratively.

"Where are your men?" she asked just loud enough for the sound to have substance.

"Where do *you* think they are?" he countered.

She drew in a breath and released it in the long, exasperated sigh someone used when counting to ten. "I heard that a truck is waiting for you next to the metro station where Kyonghung crosses Ponghwa."

She was right, which didn't weigh in her favor since only a few people back home were supposed to know that detail.

Tanner hadn't liked the setup for traveling hidden in a transport truck since hearing about it, but the only way out of Pyongyang was through a smuggling operation.

He asked, "How do you know so much about what's going on?"

"Pang and Har belong to a secret underground group working to smuggle our people out of here. I help by passing messages that are in code, but ..."

"You broke the code," Tanner finished.

"Yes. Their boss was dragged from his office at our lab an hour ago. Soldiers demanded that he tell them where Pang and Har were. I did not know if he knew, but he started crying and said Pang and Har wanted to defect. He offered to tell them everything. One of the soldiers bragged that he had better tell what he knew, and they would compare it to the information they already had. He made it sound as if he knew more about this escape than Pang and Har's boss. Someone has betrayed them."

That could be you, darlin'.

She twisted to look over her shoulder and Tanner finally saw the face his ninja hid inside a hooded shirt. This was no kid. She had to be in her mid-twenties. The face turned up to his was more oval and narrower than the rounder shape he'd expected. She had a wide mouth instead of a puckered one, a narrow nose and sharp cheeks. In fact, the only thing that hinted at Korean in her blood was her exotic gaze that was too light to be brown.

Amerasian. A beauty.

But now he understood why she'd said the words *US military* as if she'd been sucking on a lemon. US soldiers had fathered a lot of kids in Asian countries. In Korea, mixed blood with other Asians was a step down from pure blood, but Amerasians? They weren't even considered part of the Korean population. She hadn't been simply *abandoned* by her father.

He'd marked her as an outcast in a country where she'd have no human rights.

How had she ended up working in a laboratory? And why take a risk to come here and help a Korean?

She must have sensed his suspicion and pressed her case. "What are we waiting for?"

"To hear back from my man."

Seconds were ticking away with every thump of his heart. He had to decide which way to roll with her, because the minute he stepped from here all discussion would end. "Why are you here?"

"You need me."

Like hell. "How do you figure that?"

"I know the city."

"I do, too, darlin'. If that's all you have, I don't need you."

"You know *all* the ways to leave Pyongyang?" she challenged with a gutsy load of irritation for someone in her situation.

Dingo reported, "Bad news, mate. Sandman got to our guide and the engine's gonna blow."

Shit. That meant their driver was dead and the truck was rigged with explosives.

Gunfire rattled in the distance. Maybe a few hundred yards away.

Dingo's voice shouted in Tanner's comm unit. "Shit. Taking fire. We're moving."

Decision made and he hoped he wasn't wrong. Tanner yanked the woman around. "What's the quickest way out of the city?"

"I will show you." She told him where to send his men a

kilometer north of their current position. "Tell them to wait for us next to a sculpture of a lion your size."

More gunfire popped, sounding closer this time.

Heading toward the hotel.

Tanner relayed her directions to Dingo, changing her instructions at the end. "Wait for me somewhere you can *see* the lion sculpture. If I give you the go sign when I show up, then come out to join me. If not, you know what to do." *Get out of this city any way you can,* Tanner finished silently in his mind.

"Roger."

Tanner released his ninja, aka Jin. "Head out but know that I won't hesitate to drop you with a shot if I see anything that so much as hints of a trap."

"You will thank me before this night is over," she muttered as she stepped past him.

We'll see.

Tanner kept that thought sealed behind his lips when the shouts of soldiers boomed outside the lobby entrance.

Jin was on the move, heading for the exit Tanner's team had used.

Boots thundered over the concrete floor with soldiers entering the building just as Tanner stepped through the opening in the wall and picked up his pace.

The smell of hot oil and smoke permeated the air.

His ninja turned into a black slip of energy moving deftly past the temporary residences. She found passages Tanner had to turn sideways to get through and she changed direction every hundred steps to sweep around a building or blend into a wall of shadows.

Much as Tanner didn't want to admit it, Jin moved with the stealth and cleverness he'd expect from someone on his team.

But she wasn't on his team.

She pulled up short next to tires stacked in front of a rickety looking garage that faced a main highway. She tossed her arm back, waving Tanner to hide behind the tires that reeked of the stagnant water pooled inside them.

Tanner spotted what had stalled her progress.

Two soldiers stood with their backs to them, hiding behind a tuk-tuk parked along the curb on this side of the street. They used the banged-up, three-wheeled vehicle to shield their bodies and the rifles they held ready to use.

Tanner could see why she'd chosen this point to cross the two-lane street.

No lights lined either side of this stretch.

Nice and dark for making a run to the other side, if not for the soldiers waiting for someone.

Like his team.

If soldiers hid here, more would be all along this stretch of paved road if they'd been sent to watch and hunt for defectors.

Jin turned and made hand signals that he translated as *wait here for me to distract the soldiers then you run across.*

That couldn't be right.

Did she think the soldiers would just let her pass by this time of night? Not a chance.

When he didn't move, her forehead furrowed with a question then she waved him away and mouthed the word *go.*

He shook his head and slowly reached for her arm, drawing her back several steps until they had returned to the rear corner of the building. Once he had a sheltered position where he could watch the soldiers, he leaned close to her to protect his words.

A faint floral scent distracted him for a split second, allowing her an opening to berate him.

"If you know this city so well, you know that is the best place to cross."

He ground his back molars and explained, "Wait here until *I* deal with them then I'll wave you forward."

"There will be more soldiers nearby who will hear any disturbance. I can distract those two while you run across. No noise."

He studied her eyes, searching for the lie in her words. Was she waiting for him to step out then she'd raise the alarm for the soldiers to catch him? Or did she really mean to put herself at risk to cover for him?

He wasn't sure which possibility was more disturbing. "What if they catch you?"

"They will not," she declared, but he picked up on a smidgen of uncertainty in her words.

"But they might," he argued.

"Then I will no longer be your problem."

He asked her again, "Why would you take this risk?"

She looked away and shook her head then told him, "You are so stubborn. If we reach your men safely, I will tell you why."

His gut was working overtime with figuring this one out, but until she gave him a reason to think otherwise, he was going to give her the benefit of the doubt. "Your idea is too dangerous for you. Do as I say and we'll both go together."

Her head cocked to one side as she took his measure with her next look.

And the results are?

She didn't share her assessment. Instead, she said, "Your men will trust nothing I tell them if you die."

"You've got a point, Jin, but we're wasting time here so follow my lead."

"I am not the one who retreated and lost ground," she chastised under her breath.

Saucy little pistol.

Tanner headed back toward the tuk-tuk but slowed when one of the soldiers listened to his radio and replied in a low voice. He whispered something to his partner who nodded then they marched off.

Were they gone for good?

Tanner gave it sixty seconds then moved in, watching from side-to-side. Coast was clear. He waited beside the tuk-tuk and kept scanning the area as he waved Jin forward.

She reached him, did her own recon of both directions, and nodded before slipping around the little vehicle to cross the road.

Tanner had taken a step to follow when he heard, "*Jeongji!*"

Ice ran through his veins. He did as he was told and halted, turning to find a Nork bearing down on him with another Type 56 rifle.

That must be the weapon of choice tonight.

The minute this guy called in his buddies, this game was over.

Chapter Three

ADRENALINE SWAM THROUGH Tanner's blood, but he took it as a good sign that the soldier hadn't shot him yet. That only meant they wanted Tanner alive for interrogation, the kind of questioning that involved pain inflicted in creative ways.

All he needed was an opening to disarm this Nork before the soldier used his radio to call in reinforcements. This guy was young, with little experience. His arms were shaking.

The soldier growled another order at Tanner in Korean.

Tanner just stared at him, the universal sign of not understanding.

Or it should be if it wasn't.

At that, the soldier crept closer, hands shaking on a weapon capable of cutting a man in half across the middle.

The world in Tanner's field of vision slowed to microseconds.

His hearing sharpened and the air pulsed with energy.

The skinny bastard had the bony face of the underfed. He kept biting out one order after another in a squeaky voice. Tanner understood enough to know the Nork wanted Tanner down on his knees and to put his hands behind his head. Tanner continued his mute routine until the soldier finally jabbed his weapon in the direction of Tanner's hand that rested on his rifle.

Tanner made a face he hoped conveyed understanding and released his weapon so that it dangled against his chest, holding the soldier's gaze on that hand.

He'd kept his other hand hidden next to his upper thigh where he'd been working a smoke grenade free from one of his cargo pockets. He needed both hands to activate it, but if his idea worked, actually *releasing* a smoke cloud wouldn't be necessary.

There. He had it in his hand.

The Nork kept chattering orders and Tanner used his free hand to point at the ground. "Down? That what you're saying?"

The guy nodded and jabbed his weapon toward the ground, still rattling off orders.

Tanner bent his knees as if he intended to comply. He unfolded the fingers on his shielded hand and let the impotent smoke bomb drop to the ground.

That sucker rolled toward the soldier. Hot damn.

The distraction worked like a charm, drawing the Nork's attention down to the canister.

Or it would have worked perfectly if Jin hadn't come out of the shadows from behind the soldier. *Shit.* As she darted forward, Tanner moved at the same time. Jin launched herself forward and kicked the back of the guy's knee, as Tanner swept his arm in a quick arc, shoving the rifle muzzle to the side. He cracked a vicious blow across the soldier's trigger hand.

Next, Tanner booted the guy in the nuts.

The Nork's howl of pain was cut short by the crazy woman as she wrapped her hand around to grab his mouth and nose, shove his head to the left and slam him to the ground in one of the smoothest takedowns Tanner had ever seen.

But with her mixed blood, self-defense skills made sense. She'd have to be able to handle herself to keep predators at bay if she had no one else to protect her.

Jin took a step back and spun, smashing her booted foot against the back of the soldier's head, knocking him out cold.

Damn, that was hot.

Tanner added deadly to his mental description of his ninja and snatched up his smoke grenade and the guy's rifle. "Let's go." He turned to leave.

She hissed, "Wait."

"No," he snapped.

When he paused to see what her problem was, she'd run over and jumped on the driver's seat of the tuk-tuk. "Get in."

She'd fired up the engine by the time Tanner had folded his oversized body to sit on the bench seat in the sardine can three-wheeler. She made a U turn and rolled hard on the handlebar accelerator that twisted like a motorcycle control.

Bullets pinged off the metal body.

Tanner returned fire with the stolen rifle, covering their back. Might as well use their ammo instead of his.

"Stop," she ordered.

"Why? You got a bullet proof vest under that ninja outfit?" he asked, heavy with drawl.

"Ninja? Wrong country, cowboy. We can lose them, but not if they follow your gunfire. Hold on." She spun the oversized go-cart up on two of its wheels as she rounded a corner.

Tanner leaned over her, throwing his weight to counterbalance so they didn't flip.

She glanced at him, her face an inch from his, and she sucked in a breath he didn't think had a thing to do with her NASCAR turn. The third wheel hit hard, and Tanner's head bounced against the top of the cab.

He muttered a curse and dropped back on the seat.

"Are you hurt?"

"What? You worried about me, ninja?"

She never took her eyes off the road when she said, "Of course ... you are my way out of here."

"What?"

"You asked why I am helping you. I want to leave, too."

Did she think he could just add people like a Conga line at a party? Defecting wasn't as simple as it looked in the movies.

But he finally had a believable reason for what she was doing.

The only problem was that he couldn't take her with him, but he wasn't about to admit that before he got his men and the two physicists out of here.

Chapter Four

WIND BLASTED JIN'S face until she cut back the speed on the tuk-tuk as she reached the point of picking her way through narrow alleys that led to rear entrances of two-story shacks where laundry hung on lines strung between buildings.

Places vehicles weren't meant to travel.

This American might have knowledge of Pyongyang geographically, but she knew the people and the places they could pass without challenge. He said he was not military, but he had been at one time. She'd spent much of her life studying Americans and the military, trying to figure out what made a man walk away from a woman and the two children he'd made.

The cowboy watched every door and window, but no one came out. She'd called him cowboy at first because it was so American, and because he'd used a similar stereotype for Asians by calling her "ninja," but he sounded just like the men in the two cowboy movies she'd seen—both were illegal copies she'd risked watching over the years.

Would he admit that he needed her?

Probably not. Male egos did not allow room to accept that women were of value. She didn't care what he thought of her as long as he took her with him and his team.

But his silence had not said yes when she'd told him what she wanted.

He spoke just loud enough to be heard over the engine. "Have to hand it to you, darlin'."

"What?"

He turned to her, that one uncovered eye staring out from enough headgear to be some alien warrior. An eyebrow arched at her terse, one-word question.

She held her breath, waiting for him to say he would definitely take her with Har and Pang.

To be left behind would mean her death and, eventually, her sister's death. And then the loss of many more innocent lives.

She whipped their little truck around a child's bicycle, throwing her body to the side and bumping his.

Heat flushed her skin at the contact. She shook off the silly reaction and said, "Well? What are you handing to me?"

"You might not know the city better than I do, but you *do* know the people and where to go without drawing attention. I wouldn't have risked coming through narrow areas like this, places that are prime for an ambush."

Was that a compliment? It couldn't be, could it? Not from a man. She decided saying nothing would be the wisest answer.

When she emerged in the park, she slowed her speed and drove down a narrow sidewalk.

He asked, "How far?"

"Close. Maybe one block."

He spoke as if talking to himself, but he was communicating with his men. "We're comin' in rollin'. Hold your fire."

After a brief silence as he listened to someone, he replied, "Got some help from a friendly."

Jin cut her eyes at him but said nothing while she drove the last stretch to where she parked the tuk-tuk next to the painted wood carving of a lion. It sat at the corner of an abandoned warehouse with boarded windows and junk cluttered outside.

Her passenger climbed out, his sharp eyes searching the grounds until he surveyed the area and waved his hand in that direction.

In the next moment, Har and Pang emerged with three men protecting them. Those three looked like this cowboy, smoky ghosts armed for war.

One was taller than the other two, but that was all she could make out about the men on his team since they all wore the similar muted clothes of the locals over their own gear. They all had night-vision monoculars and were armed from head to toe.

Jin stepped out of the tuk-tuk on the side facing the building and flipped on a penlight to find her way through the junk to the rotting door panel twenty feet away.

When she reached it, she called quietly, "Over here."

Her cowboy nodded that he heard her, so she pushed the panel aside and squeezed through the opening. Stale odors left from years of storing dried fish and fishing equipment assaulted her nose. Docks for the Taedong River were less than a kilometer away.

When someone pulled the panel aside to enter, Jin snapped off the penlight. She'd learned to appreciate the safety darkness offered.

Once the cowboy and his team were inside with Pang and Har, one of his team asked, "What's the plan, Bo?"

Bo? That was probably not a real name. They would not use real names here.

Fair enough. She would limit what she told them as well.

Bo said, "I've got one, but it has more holes than a sieve. She's going to show us the way out of the city."

Pang and Har stood ten feet away, but with no light on in here they couldn't see her, because she couldn't see them.

Pang piped up. "She? What she?"

She might as well answer Pang as there was no hiding from him at this point. "Jin."

"Says she's part of the network that's helping you two escape," Bo explained. "Works in your lab."

Pang would ruin her chance to leave by telling these men she was of no value to the Americans.

That would have been bad enough, but Pang said, "You would trust a woman who sleeps with our soldiers?"

With one question, that lying dog Pang had undermined all the work she'd done to gain the cowboy's trust in a short time and made her sound like a whore.

Chapter Five

TANNER CLENCHED HIS fists at Pang insinuating Jin was a slut. *Why am I so angry on her behalf?*

Maybe she *had* slept with half of the DPRK army.

But Tanner took one look at her stricken face and questioned the validity of Pang's statement. This woman had laid into a soldier who could have killed her, especially if he'd gotten a shot off with that weapon pointed at Tanner's head.

She'd have died next.

Nick, Dingo and Blade waited on Tanner's word.

There wasn't time to waste speculating about Jin's sex life. Tanner had made the decision to go with her option for escaping the city. He was sticking with it. Indecision was the quickest way to die on a mission like this one.

He pointed at Jin then realized she couldn't see anything in the dark. "Turn on your penlight, Jin, and keep it away from our faces. Get busy showing us the way out of here."

Pang made a disgusted noise in his throat, but Tanner ignored it. For now.

Har started wheezing. Blade produced an inhaler and handed it to Har.

Turning to Nick and Dingo, Tanner said, "Cover us outside."

They left without creaking the panel that pretended to be a door.

Jin turned on her tiny flashlight and stuck it between her lips. Then she started dragging rotten boards and debris off to the side.

Pang's clothes had wet spots at heavy perspiration points. He had about forty pounds more than he needed for someone five-foot-nine. That one wouldn't make a serious hike.

Pang asked, "What are you doing, Jin?"

She spoke around the flashlight. "Show you the way out."

That must not have been what Pang was looking for. His tone sharpened. "Why are you *here*?"

Standing up, she pulled the flashlight out of her mouth and answered, "Because Myong has betrayed you and the soldiers know you are both defecting."

Pang snarled, "How can that be? Who did this?"

Jin dropped the handful of garbage off to the side and turned to Tanner. "I cannot show you the way if I have to spend all night answering questions."

Tanner ordered, "No more questions, Pang."

"What? You cannot—"

"I can and will do whatever I deem necessary to get you, Har and my men out of here alive. You and Har keep quiet unless one of us asks you a question."

She stared at Tanner, clearly catching that he had not included her in the people on his exit list.

Instead of commenting on it, she grabbed the edge of a barrel that had to weigh more than she did and started to drag it out of the way.

Tanner pushed her aside. "Give me some room."

The minute he had it moved, Tanner stepped back. "Now what?"

Jin kicked dirt out of the way with the toe of her boot in a couple spots until she struck something solid. She dropped to her knees to clean off the surface of a hatch. Looking up, she said, "There are steps to a tunnel. It is connected to more tunnels that will lead us out of the city."

Or get his men trapped underground.

This just got better by the minute, but sirens were screeching outside, growing louder. Coming closer.

Nick and Dingo rushed in.

Tanner said, "She's got a tunnel exit, but we may get boxed in somewhere."

Dingo said, "If we do, we fight, mate. There's nowhere outside to go right now and the lights in the stadium are dying down."

Celebration was over.

More soldiers would be available to flood the streets. Having the largest army in the world meant no lack of manpower when needed.

Tanner dropped to his knees and wrenched hard until the hatch finally came free. He raised it and swung the dusty slab of wood all the way back to lie on the ground. Standing up, he told Jin, "Lead."

She stepped down into a black hole that swallowed her in seconds. He couldn't even hear her footsteps. If not for the small light bobbing its way downward, he'd have thought the ground had sucked her in whole.

The physicists exchanged wary looks. Those two had probably never been so close to dirt in their lives and they came from a country where women had little value.

Pang clearly had an issue with Jin.

Were they rethinking their decision to defect? Too late for that.

Dingo descended next, then Tanner waved the two packages forward with Blade right behind them.

Nick was last to step into the opening and paused next to Tanner. "You trust her?"

"Not a bit."

Nick grinned and dropped down the steps.

Tanner shook his head. He never knew how to take Nick.

Once down in the hole, Tanner pulled the hatch closed. That wouldn't slow anyone down once they found the tuk-tuk and came inside to investigate. But his booby traps would.

Tanner pulled a Claymore mine out of his kit bag and set it in the dark under the steps, pointing up. Next, he rigged a pressure switch three steps from the bottom. That should take out the steps and cause their pursuers the most trouble with one punch. The whole thing took him 90 seconds to set up.

Thirty feet in, he rigged another Claymore with a trip wire across the tunnel, then hurried to catch up to his group who waited fifty feet away. That would be enough to slow them down without caving rock walls in on top of his team. He hoped.

The tunnel smelled old and the timbers supporting the ceiling had rotten areas, but it was wide enough to walk two side-by-side. He maneuvered to the front and put his hand on Jin's back to get her started forward.

Her muscles tightened under his fingers.

Not the reaction of a woman used to *any* man's touch.

Tanner dropped his hand. She took off and he stayed at her side.

If this tunnel went as far as the DMZ, which Tanner seriously doubted because those routes would be heavily guarded, his men could make the hundred-mile trek, but pudgy Pang and wheezing Har would never manage it.

There was only one given at this point.

They would run into security somewhere and his team wouldn't have the advantage if they were fighting in a tunnel.

Chapter Six

THAT CRAZY COWBOY was not going to take her with him.

Jin fanned her pitiful flashlight over the dirt floor of the tunnel and fought to draw each breath against the thick lump of disappointment lodged in her chest. She'd waited three long years for this opportunity. Not just waited but suffered every indignity her superiors had dumped on her just so she could remain close to Pang and Har.

The golden boys of Project Jigu-X.

Part of the inner circle of power forbidden to a woman.

She didn't want their power, but it would have been nice to have the same privileges when she was just as capable as those two.

But she was less than just a woman. She was Amerasian in a land where others spit upon anyone who had blood mixed with an American's.

She hurried along the uneven floor of the tunnel, careful not to stumble. A twisted ankle would mean death if she couldn't run.

She should have negotiated a deal with this Bo before he caught up with his team.

If these men were not American military, who were they?

They moved and acted like a highly skilled military team and definitely sounded American. Especially the cowboy. He was as large as a tank and clearly in charge.

Who had the United States sent to take the physicists out of here? Had this team already revealed their identity to Pang and Har?

Of course, they would have.

But not to her.

She was not part of their mission.

It didn't matter. Everyone in this tunnel depended on her right now and they were fortunate that she had no choice but to escape or face interrogation, then death.

Or worse.

For a woman, there were worse punishments than death.

Her fingers tightened on the flashlight. Pang and Har would be a problem. Pang more than Har. He hated her and, even if by some miracle she convinced the cowboy to take her with them, Pang would find a way to leave her behind.

He'd warned her that he'd make her pay for refusing his advances. Her skin crawled at the idea of being touched by Pang. He was no different than his superior who had raped a young girl. Jin was glad the soldiers had found evidence she'd planted to implicate him as a traitor.

They'd just found it too quickly and almost caught her at the lab.

The tunnel narrowed to single file, which meant she was approaching the spot for a change of direction.

The cowboy stepped in behind her, allowing her to remain in the lead. He asked, "How far does this go?"

"Not far. This will end at a sheet of metal mounted over an opening in a wall. There is a room on the other side. Once we pass through there, we find another tunnel."

"Stop before you reach the metal cover to that room and let me take the lead."

"Why?"

"In case someone's in the room."

Did he think to stand between her and a threat? She said, "The room is empty."

"I still go first."

The idea that a man would protect her stirred a funny fluttering in her chest. An American, no less. No one had ever stepped up to defend her, but this man had held her in his arms at the Ryugyong Hotel and turned his body to shield her from the guards, even when he knew nothing of her.

She had felt safe with him.

Safe had never been a word in her vocabulary. Not when it came to men.

Lack of sound sleep for months must be playing with her mind. She was no silly woman to read so much into a stranger's action.

When her light glanced off the smooth metal covering, a hole large enough for even Pang to pass through, Jin stopped. "We are almost there."

Bo touched her shoulder with a finger. "Change positions with me."

She had no choice but to flatten her back against the wall to allow him to pass through the narrow space. The cowboy turned to face her and sidestepped past, but there was still not enough room for both of them without contact.

She sucked in her breath.

He did the same and barely touched her, but the friction of his chest across the tips of her breasts sent heat shooting into her stomach. Energy raced across her skin and her pulse drummed a fast beat.

Then he was gone, striding ahead.

She needed a moment to gather her wits, then quickly fell into step behind him before anyone else tried to pass her that way. Her heart thumped faster than when she and the cowboy had faced the soldier in the Ryugyong Hotel.

When she reached the end of the path, the cowboy asked, "What's on the other side of this wall?"

"It was once a room for storing equipment when they were digging at this level, but it is no longer used after a tunnel leading to it collapsed before they could finish it."

"Collapsed?"

"Not this tunnel," she clarified. "That metal panel has been here a long time. The bolts holding it to the wall are old, but it will require two of you to push it open. There is a tall shelf on the other side to camouflage the panel. It must be pushed forward." She was telling secrets given to her during the past three years, but those secrets had been shared for the explicit purpose of aiding her escape at some point.

"How can I be sure there isn't someone on the other side?"

There shouldn't be since this area had not been used in many years, but she'd stopped depending on the way things *should be* from the minute she and her sister were sold as children.

Jin aimed her penlight at a narrow vertical opening between the panel and an eroded section of the wall on the left. "Look for yourself and decide."

He stuck his face up to the slot for a moment then stood away from the wall. "What does that room open into?"

"Another tunnel. This area has not been active in many years according to my ... sources." It grated to share so much in front of Pang, but as long as he did not know who her sources were, those friends were safe.

The cowboy ordered, "Stand back."

Only an arrogant man would not listen to her when she was the one with the information. But she understood inflated male egos. Had suffered years of them.

Stepping back, she crossed her arms and waited. The panel was one-and-a-half meters tall by one meter wide and bolted into the concrete wall.

He rammed his shoulder, and the steel gave a little bit. That had to hurt.

One of his men asked, "You want to blow it, Bo?"

He shook his head. "No, let's save the explosives until we have to use them."

Two more shoves and he jarred the panel.

Jin grudgingly admitted he was stronger than she'd thought and that was saying something for someone she considered the size of a mountain.

He peeked into the opening then stepped back, lifted his boot and rammed it into the bottom of the panel that was knee-high off the ground. The right corner shot forward then he kicked the left corner. By the time he finished attacking the panel, it hung from the only bolt still in place at the top right corner.

But that allowed enough room to force his big body through so he could shove the shelf out of the way.

Once inside, he called back, "Clear."

She took that as the signal to move and stepped through the opening he made by holding the metal back. He took her arm as she entered the storage room, guiding her to the side as if he thought she'd fall on the debris piled on the floor. She sneezed at the dust and suffered a deep breath of mildew.

The room wasn't spacious to begin with and six men filled it quickly even if two were Pang and Har.

She reached for the door and got yanked back.

"Hold it, Jin."

Swinging around, she stabbed his chest with a sharp forefinger. "Do not grab me again, cowboy."

One of his men stifled a chuckle.

"No one moves until I say so." In the tiny bit of light from her penlight, she could see Bo stare at her with that single night vision eyepiece. His uncovered eye gave her a fierce glare. Then he put his hand on the finger she poked against his chest and moved it away, but without harming her. That one eye held her gaze the whole time, warning her she was stepping dangerously close to an invisible line that marked the limit of his patience.

She kept her voice calm in spite of her own limited patience. "I know what is on the other side of that door. I know where we have to go to find a stairway. I know what to avoid. You should do as *I* say."

"That's not going to happen." He set her aside and took the lead at the door, opening it to look out. He called quietly over his shoulder, "Which direction are the steps and where do they lead?"

When she didn't answer, he turned around. "Jin."

"So now you need me? Again?"

Someone snorted and she was sure it was the taller of the two men who had watched outside the warehouse.

Bo glowered at her.

She answered only because her silence would slow them down. "The steps are to the right, a short distance away. They lead down to the rail line."

"The subway here is a hundred meters below ground."

"Yes."

"Why go that far down?"

She didn't like being that far underground in tunnels either, but she had very few options at this point, and this was the most direct passage. "You must reach the DMZ. To do that, you must go south from here, and to do that, you must travel beneath the Taedong River."

One of the cowboy's men who had an Australian accent said, "Hang on a tick. The tunnel being dug for the Pongwha Station collapsed years ago. Blokes never finished it."

She turned to him. "That is what the DPRK would have the world believe, but the tunnel *was* completed."

The glow from her penlight caught Pang's wide eyes. She couldn't tell if he was shocked or impressed, but she didn't care.

An explosion roared from the direction of the warehouse they'd left. Noise echoed through the tunnel.

Jin flinched. "What happened?"

The cowboy said, "They found the first mine I left. Everyone move out and no talking." He snatched the flashlight from her hand and flipped the light off.

"How can I—"

Long fingers grabbed her wrist and pulled her through the door into the next tunnel.

Did he expect her to run blind through here?

But shining her light would give up their position if they ran into soldiers. Plus, this man had followed her to this point on an inkling of trust. She would not argue. When she tripped over her feet, he caught her arm and kept her upright, never slowing a step.

A few minutes later, the roar of a second blast reached them. Bo didn't even flinch.

He had set a second explosive device?

She could feel the men moving behind her and hear an occasional stumble by Har or Pang.

These Americans did not stumble.

Especially the mountain dragging her along.

When they reached the end of the short tunnel, he whispered, "We're at the steps."

She opened her mouth and closed it. He was letting her know they would head downstairs next, not that he wanted her to speak.

Her fingers ached. She unclenched them, keeping her hands loose in case she fell, but the chance of that happening was slim since he had a firm hold on her.

"Step down," murmured near her ear.

She took that first step, terrified of missing a step and falling fifty feet to the next landing. Her heart practiced kickboxing against her chest.

Do not think about falling.

She could do this. She'd faced only one fear in her life that she hadn't overcome, but that one would not be an issue down here.

The cowboy's hold on her gave her confidence to move quickly down the stairs. She maintained an even spacing from one step to the next.

What if *he* slipped?

She would break her neck right along with him.

But he never hit a bump.

Voices rumbled above them, back through the tunnel they'd taken from storage room. Whatever explosive devices the soldiers hit at the warehouse had not blocked the pursuit. They would toss bodies to the side and keep moving until they caught Pang and Har.

And her.

She'd seen soldiers at her apartment. Her superiors would unleash everyone they had to stop her from escaping.

Bo whispered, "Two steps forward then down again," just as she made a step, expecting to continue down. She'd forgotten to count steps, or she'd have known where she was. The hand holding her arm changed direction and her body moved with his, but he took the next step faster than she'd anticipated.

Her boot heel caught the edge when she overshot the distance to the first step, and she fell into him.

Panic slid through her veins like ice water. She was going to knock him down this stairwell and kill both of them.

But the mountain just caught her around the waist and hauled her up against him like a sack of rice, lifting her off the floor and all the while still moving.

Footsteps thumped high up behind them.

In flailing her arms, she banged her wrist against the wall and sucked in a breath at the sharp pain.

He said, "Put your arms around me and keep them there."

Pain bit at her wrist, but she did as he said and tried not to think about hurtling blindly through a dark hole at the mercy of whatever he did. His hand held her head up against him, protecting it as he took another turn.

But that was comfort she'd have never expected. Her breathing slowed so that her chest stopped hurting with each gulped breath.

The sound of soldiers barreling down the stairs not far behind multiplied. Would they continue as one unit or divide up and find a way to cut off Jin's group?

Bo the Mountain's voice rushed out. "Which way?"

He must be close enough to the next landing to see that the tunnel went right or left.

"Right." She didn't think he could hear her, but he leaped down two steps. She held her breath in midair, then he landed and kept going.

Were they opening up their lead over the soldiers?

Shouts of the men following them grew louder.

No, we are losing ground.

Her running mountain cursed, made a hard right and took off faster.

She was slowing him down. "Put me down. I can keep up."

He didn't answer, which meant he either hadn't heard her or ignored her.

Probably the latter.

She could hear Har's raspy breathing. He had a nasally sound when he was winded, which didn't take much since he never exercised and had respiratory issues. Pang's heavy breathing had the rough rumble of a smoker ... or a predator.

She whispered, "Next left then take a right downstairs again."

Bo turned left then a fast right, swinging her body wide. Her leg bounced off the wall. She clamped her teeth to keep from making a sound.

Bo's men weren't trying to hide the noise of their boots

beating against the concrete steps now. There was no reason to with the soldiers closing in.

They kept moving like that, dropping fifty feet, turning and weaving then descending again until they'd reached the last level before the deep underground rail lines another seventy-five feet down.

At this point, the tunnel extending to the left and right had been finished with an arched metal surface running from one side of the floor to the other, wide enough for four people across. Intermittent security lights were mounted along each side of the tunnel offering enough illumination for her to see.

Jin demanded, "Put me down *now*. It's flat from here."

He lowered her to the ground, and she turned to her left. "This way."

She took off at a quick pace with the thud of six sets of footsteps close behind.

Sirens howled.

A spark of light glowed at the far end of the tunnel. Too bright, too low and too unsteady to be a ceiling fixture.

Soldiers coming toward them.

Three hundred feet away.

They blocked the route to the tunnel that led under the Taedong River.

There was one more way to go, but she had hoped to avoid it.

Bo rushed up next to her, cursed and held up his hand, ordering everyone, "Turn around."

"No!" She kept running forward, calling over her shoulder, "There will be soldiers at the other end, too. They don't see us yet."

"They *will* in another hundred feet."

She slowed, waving him forward. "We can make it. There *is* a way out and it's close."

Indecision hung in the air for all of one second before he ordered, "*Go!*"

She raced ahead, watching the bouncing lights that grew as the soldiers came toward her. She almost missed the turn to her right and skidded to a stop, swinging back to point at the tunnel. "Go there."

The cowboy waved his men, Pang and Har into the new passage.

The soldiers were closing in faster than Jin expected. Someone shouted to halt then bullets pinged, but she was snatched into the tunnel and shoved ahead. "Go and lead the way."

"What about you?"

"I'll slow them down."

Lose her mountain? Her heart fell like a brick.

She had no way to help him stop the soldiers, but neither did she want to leave this man alone to face that wall of guns coming at him.

"Get my men out of here *now*, Jin!" he roared, and she sprinted away, but she couldn't see a thing again in this dark hole.

Unlike the last primitive tunnel that had been straight, this one was a curving route with a flat dirt floor. Chewed up rocks formed the walls where workers had hacked out one section at a time by hand.

With each thud of her shoes, the ground beneath her feet gradually descended.

That was encouraging.

It should mean that she was in the correct tunnel. If so, this one led to the tunnel that had killed one hundred workers when it collapsed in 1971.

She listened for footfalls ahead of her and hoped the tunnel didn't begin to turn sooner than she'd been told, or she'd hit a wall and knock herself out at this speed.

In the next ten steps, she did hit a wall, but it was made of muscle.

He grabbed her by the arms. "Whoa. Where's Bo?"

Gunfire reverberated far away, answering his question. He muttered something about a FUBAR mission then released her.

She stepped back. "He told me to come and lead the way."

"You're doing a bang-up job so far," he growled at her in an Australian accent.

She flinched at the insinuation that they were under fire because of her.

"Where's Bo?" one of the men further inside called back.

The annoyed one next to her answered, "Buying us time, mate. Sending the guide up to you."

Then the Aussie flicked on a tiny LED flashlight that he handed to her. "Take this, keep it pointed at the ground and get up front."

She grabbed the light. What kind of team left one man to face all those soldiers alone? "What about your friend?"

An explosion boomed in the same area the gunfire had rattled and the smell of chemicals blew in on a burst of hot air.

The deadly operative snarled, "Move it. Now!"

She ground her teeth at being yelled at when she was helping these men and wormed her way to the front, ignoring Pang's muttered, "Bitch," as she passed him.

When she reached the head of the line, she took off at a fast jog, holding the light on the ground at her right. If she'd been thinking clearly, she'd have counted steps from the mouth of this tunnel, so she'd know when to expect another turn. She only knew these tunnels from secret hand-drawn maps she'd studied over and over, memorizing the number of steps from one turn to the next.

Maps from friends who knew what evil she was up against and risked much to help her leave.

Someone from the rear ordered the line to shift right, which wasn't far to move since the tunnel was barely wide enough for two of the men.

"Pick it up, Jin, they'll be right behind us as soon as they clear the bodies out of the way," her mountain ordered.

Her silly heart did a double flip of happiness at hearing his voice.

She must need rest. She should not be reacting to this man.

The tunnel gradually curved left and continued dropping in elevation.

Shouts echoed behind them. Too close. The soldiers were catching up.

"What's the plan, Jin?" her mountain asked in a calm voice that she might believe if they weren't all running for their lives.

She called up a mental picture of the map she'd studied. "We are close."

"To what?"

The ground leveled off. Gunfire reverberated through the tunnel and bullets pinged off the rock walls.

She fought panic that rose in her chest trying to choke her. *Where was that …*

"Here it is," she said just loud enough to give warning as they reached a fork in the tunnel. She took the right fork and rushed ahead, counting every step this time. The path they were on would eventually reach another turn to the secret tunnel, an alternate path that offered them a chance at evading the soldiers.

Another tunnel dug prior to the one that collapsed over forty years ago, killing so many.

The tunnel she had in mind had failed as well, but not because the structure had collapsed.

One must choose a small chance at living over sure death.

Chapter Seven

TANNER PULLED UP and stopped when Jin took a fork to the right. He wasn't going in until he could be sure all his men made it to the new tunnel.

Nick brought up the rear.

Bullets struck rock walls, ricocheting just short of the group. The Norks were shooting down the tunnel blind, hoping to hit one of them. A trophy they could bring back to their leader.

Nick was breathing hard. "We can drop a grenade, but we won't be able to go back that way.

"We can't anyhow, but a grenade might bring the walls down around us. These tunnels look like they were carved when men lived in caves."

"True." Nick took Jin's fork and Tanner fell in behind him.

Dingo's voice came through Tanner's comm set. "Jin says there's a bend in the tunnel eighty to ninety meters in. She says the soldiers should take the other fork if we aren't in view."

"Why?"

"The other tunnel has an outlet and this one's a dead end."

Then why the hell not take the other one? Not a question he could get answered now. Maybe she thought once the soldiers had passed by, his group could slip out and backtrack. But there would be more soldiers coming behind this bunch.

The ones on his heels right now would reach him in another twenty seconds.

Tanner was agile for his size, but eighty meters in twenty seconds in boots was cutting it too close to risk. Tanner gave an affirmative to follow Jin's directions and Nick kicked it into gear ahead of him.

Nick barked at Har to pick it up and get moving.

Pulling out a flash bang, Tanner backtracked toward the soldiers whose grunting and pounding boots thundered louder all the time.

He gave his men another ten seconds of lead then opened fire back toward the last turn he'd made.

Shouts and the racket of chaos answered him.

The minute it sounded as though they'd regrouped, ready to move forward, Tanner released the pins on the flash grenade and tossed it at the oncoming bodies.

He covered his ears, opened his mouth to equalize the pressure and rushed away as light exploded behind him. When he reached the turn Jin had taken with his men, Tanner shot his weapon down the path that led the wrong way. If she believed the soldiers would take that path, he wanted to give them the impression he was still running ahead of them.

The last thing he did was to pop a smoke grenade and throw it down that same tunnel to look like he'd kept running in that direction and had thrown it behind him.

That was the best he could do to decoy the soldiers in another direction.

He pumped his arms, running flat out as hard as he could. A tiny glow lit the corner of the bend. He growled, "Kill the light," and hoped his throat mic picked it up.

Thirty feet. Light blinked out.

Twenty feet. Gunshots rang out and soldiers shouted behind him, but where? Were they still in the last tunnel or had they caught up and seen him?

Ten feet.

He shortened his step to slow his speed and dove around the corner, bouncing off the rock wall.

Pain jabbed his shoulder, and he was still flying forward.

Nick and Dingo each caught an arm, using their bodies to block his forward momentum. He clenched his teeth to keep from dragging in gulps of breath and stood up on his own, freeing Nick and Dingo to handle their weapons with both hands while all three backed deeper into the tunnel.

Loud jabbering in Korean was going on far enough away it sounded like it was in the last tunnel.

Tanner waved everyone deeper behind him.

Nick stood with Tanner as Dingo and Blade backed their physicists up quietly. Even Har wasn't wheezing. No telling how much Albuterol Blade had given him to quiet that nasally chuffing.

Tanner glanced around as he continued backing up and found Jin two arm lengths away, her fingers fisted, and body tensed for attack. The only part that gave away her fear was the wide flare of her eyes.

He kept moving softly on his feet, weapon up and ready, holding his breath that this would work.

But where the hell were they going if this was a dead end?

Sweat streamed into his eyes. He blinked away the sting and felt every thump of his heart like a fist to the chest. He was the last one to step around a corner that hid his group.

Now, they waited. Moving any further risked making a sound at the wrong time.

Several sets of heavy footsteps clomped toward them.

Light flickered on the other side of the corner, then it stopped bouncing and everything went silent.

Fifteen of the longest seconds of Tanner's life passed before the light diminished and the voices retreated.

He peeked around the corner, waiting another minute for good measure, then whispered, "Clear."

Tanner let out the breath that had backed up in his lungs and sucked in a couple more deep inhales, then he swung around to Jin. He kept his voice ghost soft and hid just how pissed he was at being stuck in a dead-end route. "What's the straightest way out of here?"

"I will show you and—"

"No. You will tell me before we go anywhere else in this place."

She squared that little chin of hers, letting him know she was not intimidated even though she couldn't possibly see him without her penlight. Like that surprised him for a woman who had survived in this country to her age?

Speaking quickly, she explained, "This tunnel was a second attempt that does not go under the river."

Nick muttered, "Fuck."

Tanner agreed.

Jin tossed a glare in Nick's direction for a second then kept selling Tanner on her plan. "We have maybe twelve minutes until they reach the next turn in that tunnel where they will probably meet up with another unit of soldiers alerted by now. If we go quickly, we can make it to a point that they cannot pass."

Blade asked, "How can we get through if they can't?"

"I know the secret passage, but I can show you faster than I can explain. The longer we stay here, the less chance we have of getting out ahead of them."

Dingo piped up to point out, "I don't like it either, but we've come this far with the woman ..." His voice trailed off as in *how much worse can it get?*

Tanner knew better than to test the fates by asking that.

Nick muttered, "What the fuck? It's that or do our own version of *Butch Cassidy and the Sundance Kid* at their last stand."

Jin's face struck a totally confused expression.

Tanner considered his options, which weren't plural. He took a step toward Jin and grasped her arm so he wouldn't surprise her when he spoke close to her ear.

She tensed and backed away.

His gut clenched. Did she think he'd harm her? He might be pissed off at the situation, but he'd never injure a woman unless she attacked him or one of his men. "You and I'll take the lead."

He said for his men, "We're all in at this point. Let's see this other way."

She visibly relaxed and nodded, allowing him to move his fingers to her hand and walk her past the two physicists.

He lifted her hand to his belt next. "Hold on."

"I thought you wanted me to lead."

"Even a blind squirrel could stay on this path."

He'd gone another seventy-five meters and a ten-foot drop in elevation when his boots splashed water.

A wet tunnel? And this one was close to the river.

When the water came halfway up his shins, he paused. "Tell me we're not stuck in a flooded tunnel."

"I would be lying."

Guess he asked for that one. "Does it get any deeper?"

"Yes."

A wet tunnel could mean this passage had weak areas above, below or on one side.

He growled, "Are you *sure* you know where you're going?"

"Yes."

"Did you know this was a flooded tunnel?"

"Yes. No surveillance here."

"Better chance of a cave-in, too."

She murmured, "You are not what your people call a glass-half-full person, are you?"

Nick's voice in Tanner's ear interrupted his conversation. "We got company."

So much for twelve minutes. It might have been eight. Tanner let go of Jin's arm. "We'll have to make a stand here and fight our way out."

Jin grabbed his sleeve, tugging. "No!"

"You have no vote in this."

"Follow me thirty meters."

He heard exasperation, or panic, but he gave her his attention. "What happens then?"

"If you want to fight, it will be a better spot."

"Keep moving."

The temperature down in these tunnels felt closer to forty and the cold water about the same. As long as they kept their internal body temperature elevated by moving, he might not end up with someone dying from hypothermia. The water reached waist deep on him. That meant it was hitting the two physicists at their chests.

What about Jin?

A quick glance to his right confirmed that she was bouncing on the balls of her feet as she moved, pushing through the water.

In the next thirty meters, the tunnel split again. "Which of those tunnels goes to a higher elevation?"

"The one on the left, but we must take the one on the right.

Of course.

She slowed as the water turned her movements even more sluggish. At the fork, she said, "Come on."

Tanner grabbed her arm. "Keep going and let you lead us deeper so all they have to do is shoot us like ducks in a barrel."

"Have a little faith."

"Based on what?"

"I am here, too. I am not suicidal. Can you fight hundreds of soldiers? Do you have that much ammunition?" She made a small sound that he couldn't decipher and hushed out, "Then stay where you are and die."

She jerked away and kept moving.

Nick was bringing up the rear. His voice came through Tanner's comm set. "They're getting close enough for me to hear them talking."

"Roger," Tanner said, then ordered his team deeper into the tunnel on the right and followed Jin. He led his group into a dark void that continued losing elevation.

When he looked up, he lost all sight of Jin.

He should be able to see the outline of her black hood with his NVG.

He lunged forward, ready to go underwater and search for her, but her head popped up into view and her oval face brightened at seeing him. Water sluiced off her. She gasped a breath and said, "Stepped in a hole looking for the cable."

As if no more explanation was needed, she waved him forward to where she bobbed.

He didn't want to assign a name to the sick drop his stomach had taken at thinking she'd fallen into a hole where she'd drown.

She had one arm stretched above her head, clinging to the wall.

Tanner cupped her free arm that she'd been moving back and forth in the water to stay afloat.

She said, "Everyone must grab this cable."

His gaze tracked her other arm up to where her fingers gripped a cable bolted to the wall. The cable drooped from there to the next bolt twenty feet away where the tunnel shifted to the left.

She urged, "Quickly. We do not have much time to get out of sight."

Tanner explained to his men who brought Pang and Har up to speed. Pang looked appalled once he understood what the plan was, but that was the same expression he'd worn pretty much all night.

He did spare a moment to sneer at Jin.

What the hell? Shouldn't those two men show her some appreciation for helping them escape? Didn't Pang and Jin work together doing research?

She was an Amerasian woman, sure, but that didn't explain his negative attitude toward someone who was risking her life to find a way for him and Har to escape.

Pang was getting under Tanner's skin.

Could Har tell the State Department what they needed to know about the North Korean nuclear plans if, oops, Pang drowned?

Nick reported from the rear on the Norks closing the gap behind them. "I estimate maybe a minute until the threat reaches us."

"Get everyone up here now," Tanner whispered to the team.

The physicists passed by, and the team moved into position between them and the enemy. As soon as Nick caught up to Tanner, Jin whispered, "Everyone must be still. No water moves."

Tanner relayed that to the team.

Har started making a sniffing sound, the kind that ended in a sneeze.

Jin reached over and pinched his nose and hissed, "Silence."

Tanner hated standing still with the enemy approaching. He'd rather be proactive than reactive any day, but they were evading the soldiers one minute at a time.

This was the minute for standing quiet as a statue.

Muted noises tumbled along the tunnel walls until the first splash.

Cursing followed. Tanner knew those Korean words.

Someone didn't like getting his uniform wet. When he translated *stupid* and *suicidal*, Tanner glanced at Jin who maintained an indignant frown at everyone—even the Norks—criticizing her choices.

Once the sounds of the soldiers began to fade and it was

obvious that Jin had predicted accurately, Pang and Har's faces sagged with relief.

Tanner didn't have to look at his men to know they shared his bad feeling that the reason the soldiers walked away was because no one in their right mind would go this way. He hooked Jin's arm, drawing her close while barely disturbing the water.

She cut wary eyes at him, waiting for him to speak.

"What's next? No more surprises."

"This tunnel was abandoned when it filled with water. People I know dug another one that meets this one. The soldiers think this goes nowhere, because the water is over their heads half a kilometer from here."

"Then it's over your head, too."

"But only for sixty meters, then we reach the other tunnel and start back up to higher ground. We cannot reach the passage under Taedong now, but this will take us out of the heart of Pyongyang. The water does not go to the top of the tunnel because the original excavators kept raising the ceiling until they realized it would not work."

"Har can barely breathe. He sure as hell can't hold his breath for sixty meters."

"I have straws for breathing."

"How many?"

"Six, but I *can* hold my breath a long time and push up to gulp air when I need it. I have practiced."

She'd known there was a chance she'd have to go this way.

He was torn between admiration and suspicion. Tanner didn't know what to make of this woman, but he was finding it tougher to be angry with her for interfering when she kept coming up with options for escape.

If she hadn't, they might have been captured by now.

But she thought she was going to leave this country with them.

A lead ball of guilt landed hard in his stomach.

Tanner relayed the plan to his men then he eyed Pang and Har. "You two understand what we're going to do?"

Pang's sour expression stayed in place, but he said, "Yes."

Har nodded, then shook his head. "I cannot swim."

"No swimming required. Just hold on to the cable and if you slip, don't make a lot of noise. Nick will pull you up. You won't drown."

For that he got another confused yes, and it came without a bit of confidence.

Tanner took the lead this time, so he'd know when the water was too deep for them. Jin was right beside him, then Dingo, Pang, Blade, Har and Nick.

The silence hung thick, interrupted only by an occasional splash.

Just as Jin had said, they reached the spot where the water would rise above the heads of everyone except him and maybe Nick. The cable that sagged from point to point was already underwater, which meant their three North Koreans would have to use the straws to breathe.

Jin passed one out to everyone then handed the last one to Tanner.

He pushed it back at her. "I'm fine."

"No, you will not be fine. It is over your head soon."

"I'll get air."

"No. You will use the straw."

His men were busy getting Har and Pang situated so Tanner dropped his face down to Jin's and spoke for her ears. "You will do as I say."

"Not if it means you dying."

He was taken aback by her fierce tone. He'd expect that from one of his three sisters or his mother, but not this young woman. He quipped, "If I do, you won't have to listen to me order you around anymore."

"You are stubborn man."

"Pot?"

"What?"

He fought a laugh. "Never mind." She wouldn't get the pot-meet-kettle reference. She was going to continue to fuss so he compromised. "I'll use the straw—"

"Good."

"But I carry you so you can keep your head above water. And if you say no, then I'm going without the straw." That wasn't much of a threat if she was only blowing smoke about keeping him alive.

"Okay."

What did it mean that she agreed so quickly? That she cared? He brushed off the ridiculous thought. He was the hated American and even she'd said she needed him alive to get her out of this country.

A woman with an ulterior motive.

Now *that* he understood.

But he still had to give her a grudging respect for toughing her way through everything to this point. The DPRK would be vicious with any Americans captured while helping a local defect, but the local involved would face far worse. This government made examples of anyone who betrayed them and punished every person in their family plus future generations. Sent entire families to the labor camps for the rest of their lives.

Nick gave the nonverbal thumbs up to move out.

Tanner turned Jin to face him and picked her up.

She stuck the straw toward his mouth and poked him in the cheek.

He said, "You keep it until I tell you I need it. You'll be able to hold it for me."

"Do not step in a hole."

Bossy thing. "Yes, ma'am."

Her lips drew up on one side. Almost a smile.

He'd like to see a real smile and see her eyes in daylight. She huffed at him. "Are you moving your feet?"

"Yep." So slowly and carefully she must not feel the water curling past her body. She shivered and he pulled her to him.

That turned her stiff as his mama's ironing board.

Screw it. She was freezing. Her teeth were chattering.

"Hook your legs around me."

When she didn't do it fast enough, he wrapped an arm around her bottom, hoisting her up until her legs came around him. Damn. Now he was glad for the cold water, because Big John was thinking of braving the situation for her. Tanner thought of mucking out stables back on his mama's ranch.

Anything to discourage growing a bulge in his pants.

Once he got moving along, Jin put her hands on his shoulders and stared at his face.

Water crept higher up his chest.

Her gaze flipped past him to look behind then came back to settle on his face. "Your men have tiny lights on their heads."

"That's for Pang and Har to see them."

"Why don't you have one?"

"You don't need to see me." But he felt like she was looking through him even in this inky darkness. The water now reached his shoulders.

"Pang and Har are slowing your men."

"My men'll handle them."

That unwavering gaze pushed through the darkness, touching his face. He could feel the intensity of her thoughts and how she worked to keep them wrangled into place.

He asked, "Who helped you figure all this out?"

"Friends who will be in danger if you know their names."

Fair enough. "Where's your family, Jin?"

"My mother is dead. My sister is ... not here."

That could mean anything, even that her sister had been sent to a prison camp. If that was the case, she was wise not to mention it and draw attention to herself or she might end up there, too.

"What about your father?" Tanner had a pretty good idea what her answer would sound like.

"He did not want children when he lay with my mother, only to be satisfied."

Water reached Tanner's chin, and he lifted it to keep his lips above the surface.

He shifted Jin higher on his chest to be sure that her head stayed above his. When the water swirled around his nose, Jin leaned in to hook an arm around his neck. Her slender fingers felt from his cheek to his mouth where she put the straw at his lips. He sucked in the tip and dropped his chin back to a comfortable position, drawing her closer so he could lift her higher.

That put her breasts in his face.

She was wearing that damn ninja outfit, but it didn't hide the pair of sweet tatas hugging his cheeks. He was drawing hard on the straw and his body was enjoying the warmth of hers tucked around him. Of all the dangers he'd expected on this trip, fighting off a woody hadn't been one.

His foot bumped a rise in the ground that pushed his head up into an air pocket. Water cascaded down the sides of his face.

She leaned back slightly.

That movement slid her hips up against him, and he wished like hell that the seven-by-ten-inch titanium plate in his body armor was gone.

He ground out a pained sound.

She peered hard and felt blindly for his face with her hand. "Are you okay?"

Not even. One more brush of her so close and he'd have a helluva time walking. He growled, "I'm good. Just be careful with your head."

She ducked, which brought her face down next to his.

Close enough to kiss.

What the hell kind of thought was that?

One instigated by the bulge stretching the seam on his zipper.

The bottom dropped off beneath Tanner's next step.

He gulped a breath of air and his foot landed deep enough underwater to bring Jin beneath the surface with him.

Cupping each side of her ribcage, he lifted fast before he considered how far he'd shoved her in his rush to get her to air.

She stopped short and bounced.

Dammit. He'd been taking short steps to avoid a sudden change, but now he widened his stride and pushed up through the surface on his third one. As he blew air out of his mouth along with the straw, he held her away from him a few inches and looked up at her face. "Did I hit your head?"

"I bumped the rock. Not bad." She reached up to rub the top of her hood.

There was no way to check it in here. "I'm sorry, darlin'. I just reacted. I didn't know how deep that was or how long I'd be down there. I was afraid of drowning you."

Her eyes softened and her lips parted. She caught herself and shook off whatever thought had crossed her mind. "I am fine.

We will begin to go uphill, but it will not be as smooth as it has been to this point."

"You think that was smooth?" He chuckled.

She gave him a wry glance. "They had to push rocks down here to build the floor so that it would rise to meet the new tunnel. Do not fall."

"Why?" He couldn't help it. He had to ask again because it pushed her buttons for some reason. "Are you worried about me, ninja?"

Her eyes swam with emotions that threatened to toss him off balance again. No woman, other than those in his family, had wasted time worrying over his sorry hide. Not in many years.

Certainly not Allie. *That* scientist had cared so little she'd stomped on his heart and strolled away laughing.

In the next instant, Jin's saucy mouth was back. "Yes. I worry you will fall on top of me, and I cannot move a mountain."

He took short steps, picking his way up the rutted incline. She wasn't kidding about it getting rocky here. "So, I'm a mountain, huh?"

She looked away, embarrassed, a smile teasing her lips. "Yes, too big and thick with brains made of rocks."

But she'd been so busy bantering with him that she hadn't noticed how he'd turned her in his arms and was carrying her. Otherwise, the little hornet would demand he put her down.

She still shivered, but her teeth weren't chattering.

It took until the water had fallen to his waist before she sat up and looked around. Taking in her situation, she cocked her head at him. "Why are you still holding me?"

"Guess I like it."

He'd shocked her into silence again, but when she wiggled and demanded to be put down, he lowered her feet to the rocks.

She turned to walk and stumbled forward.

He grabbed her around the waist and lifted her to her feet, turning her to face him. "Don't get in a rush. We still have to wait on the others."

She didn't fight him. In fact, she put her hands up on his chest and every muscle inside him clenched. Just when he was sure the water had taken the starch out of his hard-on and he could walk straight again, she had to touch him.

He was in a country with a deadly dictator and his team still didn't have a clear route out, but his body evidently didn't care about *those* little insignificant details when it came to wanting a pretty woman.

Because his body wanted this one.

That just proved that there wasn't even a small brain in the little head.

Chapter Eight

JIN COULDN'T MAKE herself move with this mountain holding her arms. His hands were strong and careful at the same time.

His touch turned her body into one big mass of nerves that had apparently gone crazy, if she was thinking about the tenderness hiding in this man's gruff voice instead of the threat he represented. He'd thrown her off balance in the water and still had not said a thing about her wanting to defect.

What did that mean?

He would refuse her.

She was not on his mission plan. But how could he leave her here knowing what she'd face if she returned to the lab? By now, they had searched her research area and the sad place she called home. Going back was out of the question. She had risked all, thinking the Americans would welcome one more defector.

No, you risked all to save your sister.

She would not be left behind when Pang and Har were the only way she could locate her sister.

Jin had been so careful. How could she have come this far without negotiating a deal? It was this mountain's voice. She had yet to see his entire face, but she'd let his voice and protective actions convince her he was somehow different from all the other men she'd ever known. That he was not the kind of man who would leave her to fend for herself the way her father had left her mother.

But the longer this Bo took to confirm he was taking her with him all the way, the less she believed in that possibility.

Women should never trust men, no matter what.

This one cared only about his mission.

Her heart argued that he'd been genuinely concerned about hitting her head.

Speaking of that, between the cold and her roller coaster emotions, she'd forgotten about cracking her skull against that rock ceiling, but it was starting to hurt. When she reached up inside her hood, her fingers touched dampness too sticky to be water.

Long fingers wrapped her wrist and tugged gently. "Let me see your head."

He had the advantage of that night-vision eyepiece, and she was still moving around blind in the dark. She shook off his hand. "I am fine."

"I'll tell you when you're fine."

He was grouchy as a bear. A mountain bear.

He turned her around slowly and eased back her hood then prodded lightly at the top of her throbbing head. She hissed in pain and reached up to pull the hood back in place.

"Dammit all to hell, woman. What a mess."

She stepped out of his reach and turned on him, hands on her hips, snapping her words in the direction of his voice. "Do not curse at me. This is not my fault."

"No, it's my fault."

This man kept surprising her.

What male, especially American, would ever admit anything was his fault? Her father had not used protection when he slept with her nineteen-year-old mother, then pointed out that it was her fault she'd become pregnant and thus, getting unpregnant was also her problem.

The mountain bear grumbled, "I'll get you taken care of as soon as the others catch up."

The words were hardly out of his mouth when Har started coughing and flailing his arms. It sounded like he was thirty or forty meters back.

She had only a moment before the entire group would once again be assembled. Drawing a calming breath, she gave another try at convincing this cowboy to take her with Pang and Har. First, she reached for his arm, but her hand landed on his chest.

He moved with lightning reflexes and grabbed her wrist, firmly this time. "What do you want?"

"To talk to you."

"What were you reaching for?"

"Your arm, to gain your attention. Do you not realize I am still blind in this darkness?" He must have thought she was trying to take something off of his vest. Some of his gear or a weapon maybe. Proof that all of her efforts to help him had not won even a small bit of his trust. She clamped her lips shut to keep from ripping into him again. How many times had her mother told her that one who baits a trap with vinegar instead of honey captures only frustration? Jin had not experienced much honey from others in her life and found it difficult to play the sweet female even now.

He released her wrist. "You have my attention."

"I must go with you. I was in the lab with Pang and Har. I know much about their assignments." More than the Americans realized existed. "You may not recognize my value, but your State Department will."

Taking his time replying, he asked, "What exactly did you do?"

"Research and testing, just as they did."

"Are you saying you *are* a scientist, too?" He had not asked a question but made a grim declaration.

Why was her admission disappointing to him? "I am a researcher."

He muttered, "Potato, potahto. Same difference."

She had no idea how it had happened but admitting her background had not improved her chances of leaving with these men. Pang and Har could not arrive in the United States without her. They were Jin's only hope for locating her sister.

She'd promised her mother she would keep her sister safe no matter what. Upholding that promise might end with Jin's death, but her sister would do the same for her. Ten months apart in age, they'd been closer than twins growing up and always protected each other.

"Hold your hand out, Jin."

When his voice broke into her thoughts, she snapped out a quick, "Why?"

"Are you suspicious of everything?"

"Just as you are. Would you not be, in my shoes?"

"Point taken. I'm handing you the penlight so you can see where you're going but remember to keep the beam pointed down."

She held her hand out and the tiny flashlight landed in her palm. The moment she turned on the light and saw the others in the ambient glow, her chest relaxed with a tiny bit of relief.

Had this cowboy realized she needed something to feel back in control?

That would mean he'd shown her consideration she didn't want to assign to him.

"Take a look at her head," he told the shortest man on his team, who was still a lot taller than she was. "She hit it on the rock ceiling."

She wanted to say, *You hit my head,* but instead suggested, "I can wait until we reach the storm drain. It connects to this and is large enough for us to stop and rest."

She could see her mountain's face, or at least his one eye that stayed focused on her as he considered her words. He finally asked, "Everyone ready to move out again?"

Har's coughing sounded awful and he was shaking. "I am cold."

Blade stepped up, reached into a pocket on his vest, and pulled out a thin silver material folded in a square. He shook it open and put the covering around Har's shoulders, explaining, "That should warm you up quick once you get moving."

Pang hunched his shoulders, probably not as cold as Har with his extra body weight. He lifted his head and speared Jin with a look of contempt.

The same look she'd faced for weeks now.

But this time his gaze held something more than hate. His eyes said he'd figured out what she was up to and would not allow her to reach her goal. He did not want her to leave Korea with them and he knew what she'd face with his boss being interrogated.

At least, he did not know the real reason why she had to follow him to America.

Once again, she led the way through a tunnel that zigzagged back and forth as the floor constantly rose. They stopped three times for Har to catch his breath before she found a wooden ladder that climbed up to a grate access for the storm drain.

As usual, the cowboy scaled the ladder first and unlatched the grate in the wall of the storm drain that had been re-engineered to open *into* the tunnel area by the people she knew. If someone looked through the grate from inside the storm drain, they would only see the dirt wall two feet away, or a black hole if they looked down.

Jin was second to reach the opening. Once she stepped into the open space that was twice as tall as she was and just as wide across, her stomach turned at the stench of stagnant water six inches deep. She hurried out of the way as the other men came up next.

Pang needed help dragging his bulk through the narrow space.

She shouldn't have enjoyed his moment of panic at possibly being stuck, but even a diamond came with flaws.

She was no diamond, but she could live with hers.

As each member of Bo's team emerged from the tunnels, they went into action with little said between them. One guided Pang and Har to the side where a rectangle of two-foot-thick concrete running down one side of the drain allowed a place to sit.

The other two men set up observation points in each direction with their weapons ready.

These men worked in sync as if they read each other's thoughts. Even if she had not come along, she now believed they would have found a way out of this country. It was hardcoded in their DNA to never stop trying to succeed.

But they should realize that she'd saved them time, even if they had ended up being chased by soldiers.

Who were these men?

She'd expected a military team to take Pang and Har safely from the DPRK to the US. The fact that this team's leader had denied being military when Jin's instincts were screaming that he was, gave her plenty of reason to worry.

What if they were private operators who had nothing to do with the US government? What if they had intercepted the message intended for the US State Department and were here to kidnap Pang and Har to use for a trade?

Or to use the information promised to the Americans.

For the first time since getting grabbed in the Ryugyong Hotel, she had a moment to sort through what she'd walked into, but she couldn't turn back now.

She'd left damning evidence against Myong, Pang and Har's boss, that had been located too soon, but she would not feel bad about that. Not after she'd learned the real reason a young woman, *four* years younger than Jin, had committed suicide last year. Myong had kept the technician late one night, saying she had made mistakes in her lab tests that had to be corrected.

Then he'd raped her.

The young woman could not face her husband, so she'd sliced her wrists. As bad as that was, Jin had learned that Myong had a thirteen-year-old niece coming to live with him after her single mother had died in a freak accident. Jin suspected it had not been a true accident. Myong had always been mean to small children, but his eyes would turn lecherous when he saw a teenage girl.

He would not survive interrogation to harm another girl, but Jin was not sure just how much he knew about Har and Pang's defection.

The real surprise had been finding soldiers outside her apartment when she'd rushed home from the lab to take what she needed to leave.

The only reason the DPRK would have gone hunting Jin was because someone had tipped off the soldiers that she was not attending the ceremonies and cast suspicion on her.

But now Jin had to consider a new possibility.

Pang or Har could be working secretly with the DPRK to catch defectors. One of them might not be loyal to the secret organization that arranged this defection.

Her skin chilled at the idea that everyone present could be heading toward an ambush at any moment if one of these two physicists was not really defecting.

Should she tell her mountain or just keep her eyes open for anything unexpected?

Would anyone on this team believe her when she was not part of their mission? No.

If they were sent by the US or even another country, they would suspect *her* before casting a questionable look at Pang or Har when even she could not determine whether either of those two men was playing a role.

Her head ached with so many conflicting possibilities.

She couldn't function if she allowed fear or suspicion to drive her thoughts. For now, she would assume that this team was from the US and that the two physicists were still on task to reach America.

But she would be watching every man here with a new set of eyes and stand ready to question anything that did not sound true.

The cowboy walked up with one of his men. "Let him take a look at your head, Jin."

Did everything have to be an order? She didn't even know what to call these men. Was it too much trouble to give her a name, even a false one? "Do the rest of you have names?"

Before the mountain could snarl at her, the other man said, "I'm Blade. You already know he's Bo." Next, Blade pointed at the tall one standing guard. "He's the Italian Stallion and the other one is Dingo."

Bo the mountain let out a sound that was part sigh and part growl. "Back to your head, Jin."

She lowered her hood but sent him a warning glance about ordering her around. He wouldn't notice, though.

Blade flipped up his night-vision eyepiece and stepped over to her. He had a nice face that belonged on a doctor, but on a team like this, he would be only a medic. He reached inside his vest and pulled out a flashlight smaller than hers. "Turn around and let me take a look."

She did as instructed. This time she pulled the pin holding her hair in a knot.

Their medic made noises of concern. "You can get by without stitches, but I need to clean that and put some antiseptic on it."

"I understand," she said, giving her permission for him to proceed.

Bo stepped into view. He'd lifted his night-vision eyepiece, too, and pulled the hood back from his head as well. Dark hair sprang loose around the straps of his headgear. He had a strong jaw, something she'd always thought necessary for a man to be attractive.

Not that she considered this one attractive.

And now you are lying to yourself.

Blade touched her head with something cold that stung. She flinched.

Bo reacted by glaring over her head at Blade. "Be careful."

"Think you can do better?"

"No."

"Then shut the hell up."

She waited for the backlash from Bo, but he just rolled his eyes and shook it off. Odd. She was considering that when she lifted her gaze to check his reaction again and found him staring down at her, studying her face with great interest. His gaze shifted with concern one minute and annoyance the next.

Everything about this man confused her except for one thing.

She found no acceptance in his eyes.

He would leave her behind at the first opportunity.

Chapter Nine

A SCIENTIST.

Okay, researcher in a lab, but the same difference as far as Tanner was concerned.

He needed a shovel slapped upside his head for having a momentary attraction back in the tunnel. This Jin had shown up at the last second ready to lead him out of the city. She'd convinced him that their mission had been blown.

But the bottom line was that she wanted a free ride to America.

What if *she'd* been the one to alert the soldiers to Pang and Har's defection just to destroy Tanner's first exit strategy and undermine his faith in any other plan?

If so, that had worked brilliantly.

She'd been involved somewhere in the communication line for this extraction and must have decided that as long as Pang and Har had friends helping them, she'd jump on the same ticket out of town.

Tanner could appreciate wanting to leave this place after the atrocities the world saw committed upon these people every day, but something about the way Jin had inserted herself into this mission hadn't set well with him since he'd dragged her out of that bogus hotel.

Maybe she had nothing to do with any of the fallout tonight and just wanted to defect.

She had a sister somewhere.

If Jin were captured, her sister would end up in a prison camp even if they killed Jin, because the DPRK punished everyone related when anyone dared to break their laws.

Tanner would condemn one woman to death, and another to a life of hell if he made the wrong decision.

He dropped his gaze to Jin just as she looked up at him with soulful eyes that searched his face for answers. Her hair pooled around her shoulders and for the first time tonight, she looked desperate.

Blade started explaining to Jin how she had to keep the antibiotic on her head and the cut clean to prevent exposing it to any more germs. He glanced up at Tanner and nodded, letting him know he would do a subtle interrogation if Tanner stepped away.

That was the smart move, but Tanner's feet weren't helping him out one bit.

Blade raised both eyebrows that Tanner ignored until Dingo called over, "Bo."

When Tanner reached where Dingo kept an eye on one end of the storm drain while Nick watched the opposite direction, he clicked off his comm set to make sure Jin didn't somehow hear him through Blade's. "What's up, Dingo?"

"What do you plan to do about her, mate?"

Tanner wished he knew. "She claims she works with these two guys, and she wants to defect, too."

Dingo struck a thoughtful pose. "Pang says we're making a mistake to listen to her."

If Tanner were honest, he'd tell Dingo that he didn't care for Pang, but that might only be due to Pang's being a jerk to Jin. Why that bothered Tanner after having known those two for so little time was a mystery to him. "What reason did Pang give?"

"He says she's only a flunky and he's heard rumors that she's sleeping with soldiers all the time. He's worried that *she's* the leak."

A reasonable concern since Tanner had entertained a similar thought, but he had a tough time giving Pang any more credibility than Jin, even if the State Department had rubber stamped Pang's defection. And he'd felt Jin react to his touch in a way that called Pang a liar about her sexual activities.

Besides, the guy hadn't shared any nuclear secrets yet.

Until that happened, he was just a package to be delivered. Tanner asked, "What's your take?"

Dingo scratched his chin, with its crop of whiskers a few shades darker than his short blond hair. "She did get us out of a tight spot."

True and Tanner might be wrong to cut her any slack for that, but she'd been just as much at risk of dying. If there'd been a better alternative to the flooded tunnel, she'd have taken it.

He believed *that*, if he believed nothing else.

Blade walked up to the group. "She's good to go."

Tanner asked, "You learn anything?"

"She and her sister were raised by foster parents who are no longer in the picture. She tested high in science and languages, so she was put into an academic program at ten."

Dingo asked, "She say anything about the other two Norks?"

"Yes." Blade nodded and looked over at the pudgy physicist sitting next to Har, who still coughed and wheezed. He turned back. "She said she's just as valuable as Pang or Har, but women are given no respect in their lab beyond being assistants. She says Pang hates her because he is a ..."

"What?" Tanner prompted.

"Dwaeji."

Dingo scrunched his face. "A what?"

Tanner translated. "A pig." That fit.

Chuckling, Dingo snorted. "Because Pang doesn't miss a meal?"

"No." Blade smiled at the reference then his expression soured. "Because he tried to force himself on her and she escaped him."

Dingo stopped laughing and sent an evil look in Pang's direction.

Blade finished reporting what he'd learned from Jin. "She said Pang's been impossible to work with since she rejected him, and she fears he'll lie to make us leave her." Blade cut his eyes at Tanner. "Are we taking her, too?"

Tanner was still processing that Pang had tried to sexually assault Jin and wanted to jack the little bastard up for that, but his common sense finally showed up and reminded him that *she* could be the one lying to all of them.

Female scientist and lies had gone hand in hand before.

Not the same woman, dude.

True. But she was sure as hell hiding something. He knew it in his gut.

But his men deserved a decision so they could form the next plan of action.

Tanner spoke for his team's ears only. "Before I make a decision on Jin, I want to talk to Pang and get a read on him. While I do that and Blade deals with Har, we need to pin down where we are, Dingo."

Dingo was all over that. "I'll get our satellite position, so we aren't moving blind this time."

"Sounds good. Wait until we're further out of the city to make contact with home base," Tanner said, indicating their people back in Seoul waiting to hear from him.

When they broke up, Dingo asked Jin where the closest opening to the street level was. She pointed past Nick and explained where they were in relation to the river.

With that, Dingo took off.

Tanner motioned to Blade who had just finished administering more drugs to deal with Har's cough and sniffles. When Blade stepped up close, Tanner kept his voice low. "Get Har away from Pang without it appearing obvious that we're separating them and find out what you can from the whiny one."

"Not a problem. Har needs a quick breathing treatment. I'll tell him I want to get him under better light so I can check him over. He's eighty-percent hypochondriac. Should be no effort to get him to move."

While Blade got Har up and moving, Tanner watched Jin, who'd maintained a wide berth from everyone, especially Pang. That allowed the privacy he needed. He stepped over to sit next to Pang and commented, "She works with you, huh?"

"*For* me," Pang stressed. "She is assistant. Nothing more."

Tanner crossed his arms with his rifle hugged up against his chest. He dropped his voice to that level men used to share bedroom secrets. "You ever get a piece of that?"

Pang was very still for a moment then smirked. "Of course. Women like her will spread their legs any time for someone in my position. What else are they good for beyond giving a man pleasure? They are not as intelligent and cannot be trusted. After I had her, she slept with soldiers. I do not tolerate seconds."

Just the way Pang had said that pricked Tanner's skin.

Pang might be telling the truth, but he sounded like a sleazeball who treated women like dirt. Tanner could see this man threatening a woman who had wounded his fragile ego.

Dingo's voice called into the comm unit, "I'm heading back," alerting Nick not to shoot him.

Tanner had heard all he wanted from the *dwaeji* and slogged through the six inches of drainage sludge again to meet up with Nick and hear what Dingo had to say.

Dingo reported, "We're just under five kilometers southwest of the Ryugyong Hotel and half a kilometer from the river. She got us out of the center of the city."

When Blade joined them, Tanner asked, "What'd you find out?"

The medic frowned. "Har says Jin is little more than a messenger between the lab and the underground group helping them defect. I asked him if he trusted her, and he said he didn't know her well enough to answer that question. She stays to herself and only this week revealed herself as the contact delivering information about their escape."

Throbbing picked up behind Tanner's eyes.

Which one of the three was telling the truth? Pang and Har's stories were the closest, but Pang had said that Jin was his assistant, not a messenger.

Tanner spoke for his team's ears only. "At this point, I don't trust any one of the three of them. I said we'd deliver these guys, but that doesn't mean they can't show up in cuffs. Jin goes with us, but that could change depending on what happens between here and crossing back into friendly territory. Until we find out for sure who she is, she's under suspicion."

He paused, considering everything he'd learned just now, and added, "Don't lower your guard, but I don't want Pang harming Jin while she's in our custody. Got it?"

They all agreed, and Nick said, "Roger that."

Everyone broke apart to resume their positions for moving through the sewer.

Before leaving that spot, Tanner asked Jin where everyone could hear her answer, "Where are we?"

She eyed Dingo then her gaze slashed back at Tanner. "Your equipment does not tell you?"

"That's not what he was doing," Tanner lied.

She pointed in the direction Dingo had gone. "The river is that way. If we pass the first opening to the street, the second one is in a more secluded area where it will be very dark at this time."

Tanner nodded as if she'd just told him something he didn't know.

Everyone moved forward at a steady pace with Jin in the lead again. She walked beside Tanner, shining her tiny light onto the sludge ahead of her.

Was she telling the truth about wanting to defect or was Pang right about her being the leak? Tanner couldn't discount the physicist just because he didn't like the guy. The CIA had confirmed Pang and Har's position in the DPRK nuclear program, but there hadn't been a spit of intel that mentioned Jin.

Until someone Tanner *did* trust could establish her identity, she was an unknown entity and would be treated as such.

It took another twenty minutes to locate the manhole Jin claimed was the best place to exit the storm drain. Tanner pushed up the manhole cover and peered at the street that would be busy in any other city just after a major event.

But North Korea was a world unlike any other.

One minute a massive celebration to one man's ego, but the instant that was over all the locals scurried home and the city went silent.

Jin had been right about the lights being out in this section. That didn't stop the twitch between Tanner's shoulders.

Something was off about this entire extraction.

It could just be Jin's unexpected presence, but he had a feeling it was more than that.

He pushed up out of the hole and stepped aside to keep watch as Dingo climbed out next and called each one up behind him. Tanner sent the two physicists and Jin to hide in the shadows of nearby trees with Blade and Dingo covering them. Once they were all above ground and moved to the cluster of trees, Tanner backed away from the street, turning at the last minute to face the group.

He had to come up with a plan and fast.

Jin whispered, "What time is it?"

Dingo said, "Twenty-three, forty-seven."

She cocked her head, eyes looking away as she did the conversion.

Tanner translated, "It's thirteen minutes to midnight."

Her fine eyebrows drew tight. "We cannot stay here. A patrol comes by every half hour. We must move down the river and find a boat we can cross over with, but we will have to avoid being spotted by a river patrol."

Nick had joined the circle and stood with his arms crossed. "How far down the river to these boats?"

She said, "Seven, maybe eight kilometers."

One of the physicists grumbled at hearing that. Probably Har.

Tanner ignored them. Reaching the other side of the river wasn't the problem. It was how to get his group a hundred miles south of Pyongyang to a bridge near Panmunjom where they could cross the DMZ. The possibility for success of this mission was dropping by the minute.

The last thing he wanted to do was share what he and his team planned with any of the North Koreans, especially Jin, since he knew zip about her. He told her, "Wait over there with the other two until one of us comes to get you three."

Her eyes flared at that order.

Had he insulted her by grouping her with her co-workers? That was the least of his concerns.

The minute she was out of earshot, Nick volunteered, "I've got an idea."

When Nick offered an idea, it had equal potential to be a highly successful magic act or a major clusterfuck, but this was the kind of night that they needed to pull a rabbit out of somebody's backside.

Tanner qualified the offer by asking, "How much of Pyongyang will still be standing when we leave?"

"Is that mission critical?"

Tanner didn't have to look at Dingo or Blade to know they were thinking the same thing he was. "Not particularly."

Nick grinned. "Then this'll be fun."

Chapter Ten

JIN WATCHED BO stride toward her with a confidence she envied. What would it be like to have been born a man who had a choice in his life? She didn't know but was going to find out about having choices one day if she survived this escape.

He stopped and dropped into a squat beside where she sat. "Go with my men and do as they say."

She was wet and cold, and she'd hit her fill of orders, but she'd learned a long time ago that men didn't care what a woman thought. "Where are you going?"

"That's not your concern, just do as you're told."

"Perhaps I could help you with whatever you are going to do." Why did she even offer? Let the arrogant man get his head blown off. But the vision of him shot and bleeding bothered her. More than she wanted to admit. Her head should be checked for caring what happened to a man standing in the way of her getting to the US.

"I don't need your help."

She asked, "What will you do if you are caught or shot?" Clearly her head had not been checked, because she did care.

His eyes lit with the devil. He leaned down so close only she could hear his words. "Worried about me again, Jin?"

She crossed her arms and gave him a look she hoped sliced through his cockiness. "Of course, I am."

When his lips twitched with the start of a smile, she added, "You are my way out of here. Even a cowboy knows a live horse is of more use than a dead one."

He huffed out a growl and stood. "Just stick close to my men. They won't be understanding if you step out of line."

She stood up beside him. He was not joking.

"I'll be a good little woman," she snarled.

He shook his head and walked away with the tall, dark one called the Italian Stallion.

She knew what that term meant, but that one was not as attractive as the cowboy.

What was wrong with her? How could she find that arrogant, oversized mountain attractive?

"Let's go," Dingo said, but not as an order.

She rubbed her eyes with the heels of her hands and followed him. He led their five-person group from gap to gap along the waterfront, slipping between trees, then buildings that were closed for the night. During the half-kilometer trek, she struggled not to look over her shoulder for the irritating mountain.

Only a fool would care what happened to him.

She finally looked back. And again.

Confirmed. She was a fool. Had to be exhaustion. She'd been up for most of the past two days.

When they reached the point on the Taedong River where a canal split off to the right, Dingo directed them to wait beneath the north end of the Yanggak Bridge where the tall support structure offered places to sit.

They were safe for the moment.

But only while it was nighttime.

Come daylight, they would have to find a real place to hide. This was going to take much longer than she'd expected. If someone had not located the evidence against Pang's boss so quickly, this team would have used its resources to take Pang and Har out of here by now.

The damage to their exit plan was her fault.

But only because the soldiers had been too quick. She had waited as late as she'd thought safe to plant it, but in this country, suspicion ran high, and the leader expected all his men to watch for evidence of traitors.

But mistakes sometimes had an upside. Would this team have allowed her to stay with them so long if she hadn't proved to be useful?

Doubtful.

Still, what if they did not take her ...

She'd worry about that if and when it happened. As her calculus teacher had once told her, "Worry often gives a small thing a big shadow."

Her worries had many large shadows, such as the soldiers who'd been waiting at her apartment. By now, they knew she'd either aided Pang and Har in escaping or that she was with them.

She didn't believe Pang's superior in the lab knew that she'd been the one carrying messages for this defection, or for other escapes, but it wouldn't take long for someone to make that leap.

Or torture that information from someone.

Stop wasting time on what you cannot control.

It was nice to have a place to sit while they waited, but she needed to get up and pace. Anything that would ward off the cold seeping through her damp clothes and into her skin, robbing what heat she'd gained from the last hike.

Har started coughing again.

Blade, the medic, rushed over and squatted down to give Har something once more to keep him silent.

Pang chose that moment to rise from where he'd been squatting and walk over to Jin.

Her muscles tensed automatically, ready to fight. Blade cast a look her way that would have eased her tension if not for the way he dismissed her and went back to treating Har.

Pang waited until he was close to again ask, "Why are you here?"

But his tone bordered on pleasant this time.

She wasn't sure what he was up to, so she kept her voice as soft as his, saying only, "If I were not, you would be captured right now."

"I am not so sure. Maybe you told the soldiers we were leaving."

There was a kernel of truth in what he said, but she had not betrayed the plan for their exit. She had merely planted the information about Myong so the bastard would not get his hands on a thirteen-year-old girl. She had dodged Pang's sexual advances for weeks until she'd been cornered, but she'd broken free before he could do real damage. The worst he'd dealt her since then was spewing poison about her. Pang might believe she was stupid enough to seek revenge, but her chance to get to America was too important to ruin it just because she hated him. Too much was at stake.

There were many things she wanted to shout at him. Now was not the time. She moved the conversation away from talk of soldiers and pointed out, "You give no thought to what I have had to do tonight."

He scoffed, a nasty sound from a nasty man. "If you did not betray us, then you came to save yourself. Not for me."

He was almost correct. She would not waste her life protecting him, but she would die for her sister and to prevent many other innocent people from dying. Jin had carried a grudge against American men for her whole life, but she would not hold an entire country of people at fault for one man's actions.

Jin would never agree to participate in harming others. And neither would her sister, but her sister had no idea that she would soon be manipulated to do something horrible, and that she would not live long enough to suffer regret. If she did know and could not avoid her role, she'd never forgive herself.

Pang's eyes narrowed with hatred. "I do not want you here."

Jin would no longer allow him to treat her as he had in the past. "I risked all to help you and still you antagonize me and try to make me feel lower than dirt. You should take care who you choose as an enemy."

Pang's chin went up another regal inch. "Your blood is tainted. You are less than dirt. You are nothing."

Dingo appeared almost instantly behind Pang, his exposed eye taking them in with harsh judgment. "Settle your differences later."

Pang jammed his mouth shut and glared at her as if it was her fault the operative had castigated him. As the senior physicist in his department, Pang was considered the golden one upon whom everyone showered attention and praise. He believed himself as significant as an elite and tolerated no one talking down to him.

He might need these American operatives now, but his arrogance would be in full bloom again once the time came to show what he knew.

She had warned him that she was his enemy. He should not be surprised by what she intended to do once she arrived in the US. The world would be a better place had Pang's father invested in condoms and used them.

But to keep the peace for now, Jin swallowed her disgust.

Dingo moved to step away and tensed, listening with a finger to his earpiece.

The Aussie told Blade, "They're on the way."

Did he mean Bo?

Glad to finally be somewhere with enough ambient light to see what was going on, Jin's gaze wandered to the water when the bow of a boat came into view as it passed the dock where a fishing trawler was tied up.

Blade said, "That beats walking."

Bo and his friend had found a boat? Jin started to smile until she realized what kind of boat was coming.

A DPRK patrol boat cruised down the river.

Toward her group.

Bo was insane. She had picked the wrong person to take her out of North Korea. These men would not make it beyond the next bend in the river before they were captured. Did they think they could just drive away in a stolen DPRK patrol boat?

Her mountain would die a painful death, because the military in this country would abuse them badly before accusing America of stealing their physicists.

And she would be captured with them. She kicked that thought away, prepared to argue with her rocks-for-brains mountain.

The patrol boat rumbled and belched diesel fumes as it moved slowly toward the bank near the bridge supports.

Bo stepped around the cockpit and waved them forward. The man even waved his hand like an order.

Her sense of survival warned her not to climb on that boat, but what was her second choice?

Walk away and let her sister fall victim to men like Pang?

Pang hurried past her and one sneer from him was all the

motivation she needed to rush over and take Bo's hand. He yanked her up and onboard as if she weighed nothing.

She would keep Pang in sight at all times.

As much as she hated it, she needed him.

Chapter Eleven

THE ONLY POSITIVE to stealing a patrol boat on the Taedong River was the additional weapons and ammo onboard.

The immediate downside was that Tanner's team would very likely need that firepower before they got off this tub.

He squatted on the deck to minimize his silhouette as much as possible. Propping his weapon on the transom at the back of the boat, he pointed it toward Pyongyang to cover their asses as they cruised away from the city and toward the Yellow Sea. The deck smelled of dried fish and diesel. His clothes were drying out from the tunnel diving, but not fast enough.

Damned cold air.

Dingo snuck down beside him, using the transom to prop his weapon, too. "How long before they report this missing, mate?"

"With any luck, not until daylight. We gave the two men guarding it a lights-out tap and locked them in the back of a truck that looked to be out of commission. It was parked way off to the side with weeds growing up around it." Tanner wouldn't leave someone to starve to death. The truck was close enough to the delivery area of a nearby building for someone to hear two men yelling.

That was, once they woke up, figured out how to untie each other and got their gags off.

"Har's helping Nick figure out the controls."

Tanner glanced over his shoulder to see Har wrapped up in a life jacket, translating as Nick pointed at different gauges and kept the boat at quarter speed. "Har's being Mr. Helpful because he's terrified of this thing sinking. He doesn't realize

Nick won't be cruising this slow any longer than it takes Har to explain everything on the dash."

Dingo chuckled in agreement.

Pang stood on the passenger side of the cockpit, staring out at nothing, shoulders drooped in a sulking pose. *Not a glamorous extraction like in the movies, huh?*

Cutting his gaze back at Dingo, Tanner said, "We should put those two down in the cabin."

"I'm on it." Dingo was up and gone.

Tanner watched the lights of Pyongyang shrink into the distance.

"Hold on," was all Captain Nick called out before he kicked it in the ass.

Tanner heard a shout that was too high-pitched to be male.

He flipped around and grabbed a fistful of Jin's clothing just before she would have taken a nosedive over the transom.

She locked her fingers on his arm and dropped down beside him, swinging around to face forward.

Nick cut the running lights and the boat morphed into a black ghost ship riding the waves. Jet engines rumbled even at this slow speed, but another point for stealing one of these was that jet propulsion didn't require propellers.

Loud, but dependable on this type of boat.

Jin was breathing fast by the time she settled with her back propped against the aluminum transom.

Tanner returned to his watch position, asking, "What are you doing back here?"

"Wasting my time most likely."

Why's she annoyed at me? I just kept her from going swimming. Waiting to reply paid off. She grumbled, "Your man is not a good boat captain."

"He's doing a great job."

"He does not check to see that everyone is seated before taking off and he has turned off all the lights. How will anyone see this boat?"

"First off, you were told to stay in the cabin when you boarded the boat."

She made a noise at that. "The cabin stinks. Filthy men live on this boat."

Did she mean *all* men were filthy or just the men who had operated this boat? Hmm. Tanner continued, "Number two, the lights are out specifically so no one sees us."

"What if another boat approaches?"

"We won't hit them, because they'll have their bow lights on."

"You hope."

Did she have to challenge every word out of his mouth? "I *know*. What civilian in this country wants to risk pissing off a DPRK patrol boat by running with no lights?"

What? No more questions? Mission accomplished. He ordered his gaze to stay on the water and stop darting over to see her nibbling on her bottom lip. She had sweet lips. Kissable.

But so had another scientist.

There you go, Tanner. Perfect way to kill any sexual interest.

"This is your plan for escape?" She grumbled to herself before her gaze pinned him with accusation.

"Yes." That wasn't exactly the truth, but he'd had enough of questions.

Next, she'd want to know what he planned to do about the thunderstorm that blocked out what little moonlight they'd had. This boat was tough enough to handle rough seas, but a tall-enough rogue wave in the open sea could toss a much larger craft. At this point, a fair amount of his *plan* depended on luck.

He searched beyond the wake frothing bright in his monocular and settled in for the fifty-mile ride down the river to the Yellow Sea.

They might make it that far *if* they managed to pass through the locks at the dam without any incident.

Nick had the boat cruising at thirty knots. With no delays, they'd reach the sea in about eighty minutes.

North Korea had built a dam that prevented the Taedong freshwater from mixing with the saltwater so they could use the river for irrigation. That had probably looked better on paper.

Now the contained water had no way to naturally purify itself, so the dam had not only flooded farmlands, but the water was contaminated. Just another way to screw the poor citizens trying to survive here.

"They will attack a patrol boat if they realize who has control of it, even if their own men are onboard," Jin said loud enough to remind Tanner that she was still sitting inches away.

He hadn't forgotten. His body hadn't either, despite his remembered history with Allie. Studying the night skies had done nil to send Big John back into hibernation. Weird to have this reaction to a woman just because he was sitting close to her.

"Don't you see the beauty in taking a patrol boat?" he said, smothering a smile at her scowl.

He'd never admit that he'd had the same reservation when he and Nick had found this boat shoved up against the bank. Nick had taken one look, grinned and suggested, "What better boat to drive down the middle of the Taedong River than one that belongs to the military? Who's going to bother us?"

Nobody, or maybe the entire fucking DPRK naval fleet.

Nick had made a valid point, even if a Vegas bookmaker wouldn't take this gamble for all the money in China. Tanner shrugged at Jin, who shook her head and muttered, "We're all going to die."

She huddled into herself. Had to be cold. She didn't weigh enough to keep a mouse warm, but she wouldn't admit being uncomfortable. Not when she could berate Tanner some more.

"What if you run out of fuel? Did you even check?"

"There's fuel." To be honest, he and Nick had guessed at which control indicated fuel level, but Nick and Har should have that figured out by now.

Jin wasn't done chewing on him. "What if you meet another patrol boat and they call you on the radio? What will you tell them?"

"I don't know." There were so many ifs at this point, Tanner needed a spreadsheet to keep up with them. He finally gave her his full attention, and it was loaded with irritation. "If I stop to wonder about every possible problem, I would've thought twice about bringing you with us."

Her lips opened in a small O before she snapped them shut and looked away. "I should have known better."

Better than what?

Had he hurt her feelings?

He was too freakin' tired and on edge about getting out of here for her to push him constantly. Women would forever be his downfall. He couldn't let one face a threat alone. He couldn't leave this one to face the fury of a military they'd outmaneuvered, with her help.

And he couldn't tolerate answering to anyone other than Sabrina when he was in the middle of an op, responsible for getting his team—and his own ass—out of the fire.

Jin's fingers touched his arm. "I am sorry. I am saying that this is madness. There must be a better way."

She had that right about this being madness, but Tanner had been stuck playing the only hand left on the table. *There must be a better way.* He'd heard those words before from another woman who hadn't appreciated the sacrifice he'd made.

Screw that.

If Jin didn't like the way he and his men were getting them out of Dodge, she didn't have to stay for the ride. He caught her chin with his fingers and turned her head to him to make sure she heard him. "You were the one who decided to join us. Say the word and I'll drop you off somewhere."

He knew she couldn't see his face, but he sure as hell saw the stricken look on hers. She snatched her chin from his hand, wrapped her arms around her knees and stared at nothing.

"I cannot go back."

He barely heard her words over the roar of the jet engine beneath them. The desperation in those four words slugged him and forced the truth to surface.

He'd never leave her in the middle of nowhere.

Instead of hammering on him further, she explained, "After I saw Pang's boss dragged away, I ran home. Soldiers were waiting outside my apartment. No place will be safe for me anywhere in this country, or for anyone who associates with me, if I go back. I was lucky to get away when I could."

Maybe she was telling the truth about everything, and she really did just want to defect. "So, their boss is the reason someone got to our truck."

She looked away.

Tanner's conscience played handball with his suspicions. "Jin?"

"I heard him admit that he knew Pang and Har were defecting. He said something about the truck. That was all I heard."

But she'd known the truck had been part of the exit plan and where it was parked. "How is it that you knew so many details about tonight?"

She raised that stunning gaze at him. "I told you that I carried messages."

"Who gave—" Tanner banged his elbow when the boat bumped over a wake from a craft going toward the city. He repeated, "Who gave you the messages and who did you give them to?"

"I am not told names." She looked away. Again.

Hadn't she been taught how that was the wrong body signal for telling the truth?

Evidently not. "Let me get this straight. You want me to believe you just accepted what some stranger told you to do then did whatever he or she said to do? That sounds pretty ... naïve." He exchanged stupid for naive at the last moment.

She wasn't stupid by any definition, but she was naïve.

Insulting her would shut her down faster than an antagonized clam.

But she didn't miss the subtle cut. "It is more complicated than that, cowboy. Why must you be so suspicious? You are most annoying. Your intelligence people must have been satisfied with the information they received, or you would not be here."

"We were told to confirm two defectors and extract them. We confirmed Pang and Har. Not you. I shouldn't have to tell you that you won't be treated the same as those two since your name was never in any information related to this."

Reality of her situation hit straight between her eyes, which clouded with worry. She turned away, refusing to engage any further.

It was the truth. So why did he feel like he'd broken her favorite toy?

The boat leaned into a hard curve on Tanner's side of the deck and Jin slid into him.

He caught her with one hand again.

Her face was right up next to his. Those eyes flared with an awareness that bloomed in her face and the first thing that popped into his mind came out of his mouth.

"How old are you?"

"Why do you care?"

"You don't look old enough to be doing any of this."

"I am twenty-four. How old are you?" she countered right back, then her eyes shone with mischief, and she added, "You look too *old* to be doing this."

"Thirty-one." And some days he'd agree that he was getting too old to be doing this. He put his time in at the gym when he was in a city for more than a week or two, but all the exercise in the world couldn't cure years of being knocked around, shot and cut.

She cocked her head to one side in thought. "How long have you done this kind of work?"

An innocent enough question, but this was not the time to get social with the one person on this boat who was more mystery than asset at this point. He said, "That's more than you need to know about me."

The glimmer of humor fled her gaze and the easy moment shattered. She reached with her free arm to grab hold of a ring mounted on the transom and yank herself away from Tanner.

Damn, but her little acts of defiance were sexy.

He bet she'd be a pistol in bed, too.

Whoa, cowboy. She was not someone who would end up in his bed. Even if the State Department eventually cleared her as no threat to the US, she'd disappear from existence just like Pang and Har.

With an economy of movement, she bent her knees and wrapped her arms around them again. Then shivered.

He reminded her, "It's warmer in the cabin."

"I am fine," she lied. It took a few minutes, but she decided to talk again. "Do you truly believe we can ride this boat all the way to South Korea?"

Not a chance, which was why Dingo would be in contact with their backup in Seoul.

Tanner had to trust that Logan Baklanov and Margaux Duke would come up with a way to rendezvous somewhere in the Yellow Sea without getting everyone blown to pieces by a DPRK missile. Logan ran a division of HAMR, a group of operatives around the world who were descendants of warriors from a thousand years ago. Tanner didn't care if Logan was Underdog, as long as he actually had the connections, he'd sworn to Sabrina he had.

As a former Slye team operative, Margaux played liaison between Sabrina's teams and HAMR Brotherhood when the two groups needed support from one another.

Like during a FUBAR op.

Logan was a native Russian whose family now resided in the US, but his contacts ran deep in the international market. He'd guaranteed he could have a private jet on standby to take the team, Pang and Har back to the states.

That jet wasn't worth squat right now.

"I take your silence as no," Jin said, knocking Tanner out of his thoughts.

What had she asked?

Oh, yes, if he really expected to reach South Korea with this patrol boat. He gave her another one-shoulder shrug. "We have a plan."

"The military patrols the Yellow Sea as well as this river. You may make it through here with no lights, but you will be on radar out there."

They were on radar now, but he didn't point that out.

As long as the boat maintained a natural movement, the radar couldn't pick up something suspicious like having all the running lights off. "You worry a lot for someone who risked her neck to get to this point."

"Everything in my homeland is dangerous, but nothing is as frightening as the unknown." She leaned her head back and closed her eyes, but her last words were, "Hell is empty, and all the devils are here."

Where had he heard that before?

He had a sudden urge to pull her over next to him and wrap his arm around her to keep her warm. Safe.

But suspicion worked overtime in his mind when he was on a mission. Like reminding him that Jin could be a plant from the DPRK sent to find everyone involved in this extraction.

She could also be an innocent woman fighting to survive.

This business turned him into more of a cynic every day and the longer he vacillated on the matter of Jin, the more it would drive him crazy. Just the fact that she was a scientist raised his walls against anything she said. Okay, even if she only *worked* in a lab doing research, that still pushed all his buttons because of the fiasco with Allie.

But Jin had no one in her corner, not even those two physicists she'd risked her life to help.

If what she'd said to this point was true.

Tanner needed his head unscrewed and rethreaded back on.

Allowing a crack in the walls he'd built after Allie had wrecked his mind could also allow a repeat of what he'd gone through for a *not*-so-innocent scientist.

She'd used him then walked away.

He'd thought he loved her. Clearly, he had no idea what love was and no reason to ever make that mistake again. He was happy to qualify for Bachelors Anonymous forever.

Nope. He was not going to make the mistake of letting his emotions take over his decision making again, and definitely not here where he'd be putting his men and the mission at risk.

Besides, he had another female to worry about. Martina was trapped in Mexico, and his mother and sister were sick with worry.

He needed a club to slam upside his head to stop the chatter going on inside. Jin wasn't a threat at the moment. Until she was, he'd do what he could to help her, and then he'd never see her again. Simple enough.

Tanner chewed on that for a few minutes until a fat raindrop hit his exposed cheek.

He looked up and, yep, clouds were ganging up to pound

rain bullets at them and lightning raced across the sky in the distance. A heavy storm was bearing down on them, just as Dingo had predicted.

Jin hadn't stirred. She'd get wet again.

Tanner moved his hand to touch her arm but paused when Nick slowed the engines.

Tanner stood and looked over at the cockpit where Har stood behind the wheel with Nick overseeing.

When had *that* happened? Pang had also come up from the cabin and sat in the copilot chair, shoulders hunched and surly glower in place. Nothing new there.

Tanner stepped up next to Nick. "What's up?"

Nick ran a hand over his face. "We're coming up to the Nampho Dam. I think we should let Har drive the boat through the locks. I'll turn on the running lights, but the locks are going to be lit up like Christmas. I'll be too obvious at the wheel."

Rain started coming down harder.

Tanner looked around and saw the silver emergency blanket Blade had given Har earlier. It was shoved up on the dash. He took it and walked to the back, planning to give it to Jin, but when he bent down to hand it to her, he realized she was asleep. He wrapped the blanket around and over her like a tent, tucking it under her feet and shoulders.

Back at the cockpit, Dingo had stepped up from the cabin with the Sat phone in his hand. He said, "Home base is working on a rendezvous."

Rain slapped the water. Bad weather moving in and a hundred miles of water or land to cross. Neither option looked promising right now.

Tanner pointed a thumb at Har's back and asked Nick, "Can he do it?"

"Sure. The locks are made wide enough for ships."

But what if Har panicked and made a mistake? That dam would be crawling with security.

Blade jumped down from where he'd come around from the bow. He swiped water off his face and held binoculars in his other hand. "Two trawlers are waiting for a ship to pass through the locks. If we're going with those fishing boats, we need to get up in line."

Har turned to everyone. He had a white-knuckle grip on the wheel and his eyes were wracked with fear.

Oh, sure, he could do this.

The storm wouldn't get a chance to sink them, because they wouldn't make it through those locks.

Chapter Twelve

"I CAN DO THIS," Har said, nodding hard in Tanner's direction.

Tanner looked through the rain-sloshed windshield where bright lights from the dam blurred. He'd never have expected Har to be the one to man up on this trip, but the guy did look determined. Har said, "Please."

Maybe he figured the fastest way to get off this boat was by helping. Tanner said, "Okay, you're driving us through the locks."

Pang made a noise of disgust and Tanner fantasized giving him a knuckle sandwich to bite down on.

Nick told Har, "Hit the running lights."

Har nodded and swung around to the dash, mumbling to himself as he flipped switches. His narrow shoulders held more confidence than Tanner had seen until now. Red and green lights lit on the right and left tip of the bow. Then white stern lights popped on.

Tanner eyed their captain and told Nick, "Har needs to dress the part. Good thing we stripped those two guards."

Nick grinned. "Found something better."

"What's that?"

He reached down under Pang's feet, because the surly physicist had done nothing but sit in the passenger seat like a toad on a log the whole time. When Nick stood up, he had a rain poncho he threw over Har's narrow shoulders. Then he stuck a cap on Har that Tanner and Nick had taken off the guards they'd locked in the truck before heisting the boat.

Har grinned.

Damn, but Tanner was starting to like the guy.

Dingo suggested to Pang that he would be safer below in the cabin.

Pang looked insulted. "No. Stinks in there."

Nick went down in the cabin and came back out with another poncho and hat that he tossed at Pang. "Then put this on, don't look up at any of the security at the dam and act like you're helping your captain."

Pang had probably been mouthy back in the lab, but he had enough sense not to pop off at Nick. He pulled on the poncho.

Dingo scrunched down between Har and the side of the cockpit, hidden in a black hole of darkness. Blade took up a mirror position in the opposite corner between Pang and the cabin wall.

Nick stood next to Har, talking him through how this would work and explaining that he intended to stand just inside the cabin where Har could talk to him.

Rain started coming down in sheets.

Thunder rumbled, but the lightning that flickered was still off to the north for now. With any luck, they'd be heading south soon.

Tanner looked around and realized Jin was still under her blanket tent.

Why wasn't she up here annoying him by now?

He crossed the deck to where she huddled. The silver blanket shielded her upper body from the downpour, but her pants had to be soaked from the water on the deck. She hadn't said a word.

In fact, that little silver lump was hardly moving.

He let his rifle hang and scooped her up.

Jin muttered an irritated sound.

She'd been sleeping all the way through that? No one could sleep through a downpour and getting soaked from the bottom up unless she was at the point of bone-weary exhaustion. He'd been there before and knew that when your body was ready to shut down it would pull the plug.

He carried her to the cockpit and navigated his way down the two steps into the cabin ahead of Nick, who ducked inside then turned his back to Tanner and started coaching Har.

Jeezus on a pogo stick. This place did reek to high heaven.

Rain beat against the roof.

The engines powered up gradually this time and the boat moved forward.

Tanner shuffled his feet to adjust his weight and maintain his balance. He should put Jin down, but she'd hate that.

And why do you care?

He shouldn't. But there was no telling when those bunks had been cleaned or what turbo-germs were living there. He'd take her back up top once they were through the locks.

As they neared the locks, Tanner bent forward to bring his head down over where he held Jin until he could reach with one of his hands to flip up his monocular.

When he straightened, he sensed a change and looked down at her.

Her eyes opened all soft and dreamy. In that moment, when her hackles were down and her face held a tender sweetness, she was so damn pretty. More than pretty.

She raised her gaze to his.

He expected her to tense up and bite his head off for handling her, but those eyes were unshielded for once. Exhaustion had sapped her energy. Lights from the dam sifted through the portholes on each side and kissed her cheek. She surprised him by taking a slow breath and lifting her fingers to touch his scruffy jaw.

She said, "You did not leave me?"

The sweet, just-woke-up gruffness in her voice jerked Big John out of his slumber. Hearing a woman's sleepy voice was a favorite of Tanner's and did not belong on this op. He clamped down his straying thoughts and considered what she'd said.

Why did she think he'd leave her?

In that unguarded moment, she'd spoken with surprise that she had not been abandoned. How often had that happened to her? He quipped, "Where would I leave you?"

She yawned and even that was adorable. "Somewhere along the river. That is why I sat next to you."

He was confused. "You sat next to me because you thought I'd toss you off?"

"No. Because I hoped you would not."

Letting her continue to wonder if she was going to be left behind any minute was nothing short of mental torture. He knew he wasn't going to boot her in the middle of nowhere. "I'll take you to the US with us."

Hope flared so brightly in her eyes he wished he'd told her sooner. She asked, "How can I be sure?"

"I give you my word, and I never give it unless I intend to keep it."

"I believe you. You know nothing about me. Why would you help me?"

He muttered, "Temporary insanity. Don't press your luck."

"Thank you." Two simple words that were tossed around a million times every day across the world but coming from Jin they carried the power of something more.

He had the feeling she rarely had a valid reason to utter appreciation for anything.

While they were on the run, Tanner would do everything in his power to keep her safe, but he'd have no say over what would happen to her once they hit US soil. He expected more questions, but she studied his face and gave a nod of acceptance then blinked and stretched, waking up more.

She looked around. "Where are we?"

He ducked his head to look out the portholes. Rain came down between the boat and the water-stained walls of the lock as Har guided them through at low throttle. "Har has us almost through the dam, then we'll head out to sea."

She grabbed an arm around Tanner's neck and jerked herself up into a sitting position, stretching to look past his shoulders. "Har? He will get us killed."

"Shh. We've got him covered. He's doing just fine so far and one of my team is coaching him, but any sound might spook him."

She swung her face to Tanner's.

Those lips were smooth and full. Kissable. What would they feel like on his? Not that he'd ever know, but yes, he wanted to and right now. Her tongue peeked out and swiped her upper lip.

Don't do that, darlin'. A man could only take so much.

They passed through the locks, safe and sound.

Nick's low voice kept assuring Har he should have his captain's license.

Tanner lost track of what Nick was saying. Lost track of everything except staring at Jin, who moved forward a tiny bit.

It wouldn't take much for her lips to touch his.

The boat lifted slightly with a wave and rolled forward.

Tanner adjusted his feet to hold his balance, but Jin hugged her arm tighter and bam, they were kissing. Her hand palmed his face. She kept up a soft pressure on his mouth. He kissed her back.

What man wouldn't? She kissed him as if this was her first time and she wanted to find out all she could in one kiss. He felt the tug from her kiss all the way to his groin. Big John was knockin' at the front door, but Tanner ignored the discomfort. He knew this would end too soon and didn't want to give up something that felt so sweet and untainted.

Then it was over as quickly as it started.

She pulled back, staring at him and breathing like she'd been swimming the last mile.

He was just as winded. His senses squawked at him. What the hell was he thinking?

Wait a minute.

Why had *she* kissed him?

Whatever the reason, it left as quickly as it had come. She went from warm and accommodating to tense. "You can put me down, cowboy."

"And miss another chance to be kissed?" The devil in his brain had taken over. That was the only possible explanation for him even admitting what had just happened. "Why did you?"

The steady rumble of the boat engines filled the silence until she finally said, "Temporary insanity."

As if to distract him from what had just happened, she warned, "We will be out in the sea where they watch on radar. If someone from my country contacts us by radio and we do not answer, they will attack and shoot bombs at us."

That wasn't exactly how naval bombardment functioned out here, but the result would be the same, so he didn't try to explain the dynamics of sea warfare.

She touched his chin, pulling his eyes to her. "I *can* stand."

He knew that but holding her had been a calm moment in the middle of this madness. Just feeling a woman against his body rattled things in his head that shouldn't be disturbed.

Lowering her feet to the floor as darkness once again shrouded the cabin, he told her, "I know it smells in here, but it's safer. And the fewer people out on the deck the better right now."

"I understand." She opened her stance and squared her shoulders, so light on her feet she had no problem keeping her balance. "I am impressed, cowboy."

After all the flack she'd given him, getting a compliment out of nowhere pulled a smile from him. "Oh, yeah? Liked that kiss, did you?"

"I was talking about your strategy. I did not think you would make it this far in the patrol boat."

"Ah. So, you did like the kiss."

She rolled her eyes.

He smiled, not wanting to let on that he'd had concerns up to this point and still harbored a few more. They weren't in the clear yet by any means, but she was right. This had gone better than he'd thought when Nick had rubbed his hands together at the idea of snagging a patrol boat.

Tanner said, "Sometimes it's better to be lucky than good."

"Perhaps you were born under the right stars and were rewarded with ability *and* luck."

Nick shouted, "Hold on!" That was the only notice anyone got before he shoved the controls forward again.

Tanner threw a hand up to grab a cabinet when the boat lurched ahead and plowed into a wave.

Jin flailed an arm and slammed into his chest hard enough to knock the breath out of her.

Tanner caught his arm around her. "Are you okay?"

She grabbed a handful of his vest and, this time, lifted her chin. The entire movement happened in seconds. She was all up in his personal space.

No complaints here.

But he could feel the muscles in her back tighten beneath

her ninja outfit. She was uncomfortable, but she hadn't pushed away yet. A gentleman would help her out of his grasp.

It wasn't that his mama hadn't raised a gentleman, but that he just couldn't find it in him to push Jin away right now. He'd spent months alone whether he was on a mission or off on his own. Part of him longed for this contact.

Another part seconded that idea, but he'd let Big John talk him into some bad decisions in the past. One had been named Allie.

Jin kept staring at him. She probably thought he intended to stay below, too. He'd made up his mind to pull his arm away when she dropped her head against his chest and moved closer.

Snuggling up for his heat?

Her shoulders softened.

If this were any other woman in any other situation, he'd take that as a sign that they were finding common ground. The kind of common ground that ended up littered with clothes.

Wrong direction, cowboy. In fact, get your hands off her and head to the deck. He could use some of the cold water busting over the bow to hit him in the face. Maybe that would bring his common sense back to the forefront.

But the boat banged into a wave and jerked sideways. Tanner held on to Jin to keep her from getting battered in the cabin and used his free arm to stabilize them.

She shook hard. Ah, hell, she was scared.

He mentally searched for something to take her mind off her fears. "If the stars are guiding us, how come they're dumping all that rain on us?"

"What?" She jerked her head back to look at him with confusion shaping her expression. Then she took in his smile as her brain caught up to what he was talking about. "I did not say the stars were guiding anything tonight, but that you may have been born under one that watches over you."

"A guardian star, huh? That'd be nice." But not something he'd ever count on. He'd been the guardian over his three sisters and mother from the age of nineteen when his father died in the military.

That's why he traveled across the globe and stuck his neck

into some nasty places to make sure the world his family lived in was safe.

Who had watched over Jin as a child? And now?

She covered her mouth and her shoulders curved as if she was going to heave. When she took a breath, she said, "I want to go up on the deck."

"The movement getting to you?"

"A little."

He'd say a lot, based on her thin voice. If he stayed down here much longer, he'd be tossing his cookies soon, too. He moved back toward the steps, drawing her with him.

"How far will we go with this boat?" Jin asked and gulped another breath.

Did she need reassurance she hadn't climbed into the Titanic?

He wouldn't paint blue skies about what would happen once she landed in the US, but he could ease her worries for now some. "Maybe another hour or two. We'll be fine until then."

Someone up top yelled, "*Shit. DPRK's on our ass!*" just as the boat lurched forward hard, proving him a liar.

Chapter Thirteen

TANNER SHOUTED AT Jin, "Grab this counter and hold on."

Then he spun and jumped up the two steps to the cockpit, moving Har over into Pang's space so Tanner could stand next to Nick. "What's going on?"

Nick fought to steer the boat with one hand and work the controls with his other one. "We had a radio call for this boat, based on what Har and I have translated on everything I found in the cockpit. I think it's another patrol boat that passed us as we left the dam, and they were headed toward Pyongyang."

"What'd they say?"

"Har said they were asking for our schedule and route." Nick kept shifting his weight with the rough water in the black sea. "We've played the 'bad connection' game for the past eight minutes, but they're demanding we reply, or they'll report us to headquarters. Har isn't familiar with the military or anything nautical, plus his English goes to hell when he's stressed so I can't understand him."

Tanner glanced at Har. Lights from the dash touched his poncho that was visibly shaking. Yep, that was pretty stressed.

Shit.

Jin pushed up next to Tanner. "I will talk to them."

Tanner looked at Nick who gave him a she's-your-problem look.

Catching their silent exchange, Jin said, "I can do no worse than Har and you two."

Nick suggested, "We need a male voice. What about Pang?"

She huffed. "He speaks as an elite. The military would never believe he is operating a patrol boat."

"But they'll believe you?" Nick challenged.

"I am good with dialects, and I have listened to the soldiers talking often."

The radio crackled with a blast of Korean.

Jin reached over for the radio mic.

Nick went for the mic at the same moment, but Tanner blocked Nick's hand and said, "Let her try. We don't have a lot of options for buying time."

Nick lifted an eyebrow then sighed. "Maybe they'll think she's a young guy and his nuts haven't dropped yet."

That was Nick logic for you.

Jin pressed the button, changed her soft female expression to a fierce frown. When she spoke, she roughed her voice and rattled something quick in Korean back at the other boat captain.

Tanner couldn't imagine her giving the other captain an ass chewing, but he understood enough to know that's exactly what she'd done.

Gutsy or off her rocker?

She released the send button and said, "I told him I was with General Jeong Yul, and we were on radio silence for a reason, and that he did not have security clearance to know why. If he continued to contact us, I would have him reprimanded."

Damn. Tanner's eyebrows had to be up at his hairline. "Did he believe you?"

"For now."

Blade leaned in. "What does that mean? Will they let us go?"

She explained, "General Yul is reported to be spending today meeting with our leader and the minister of armed forces. The captain of the other boat will have to go through channels to determine if General Yul really is at that meeting or if he is here on some secret mission."

"That's damn brilliant," Blade said.

Tanner agreed. But Jin had to go and ruin his moment of hope by adding, "However, they will very likely find out the truth in the next twenty minutes."

The boat hit a wave and jarred everyone in the cockpit.

Jin grabbed Tanner before he could get a hand on her, so she didn't go tumbling.

He looked down at her face, barely lit by the lights from the controls. She stared up at him with absolute trust, something he hadn't seen in that face until now.

Nick backed off the accelerator. "We've got to make a hard run. Everyone needs to find a place and hang on."

Blade muttered, "I better get double frequent flyer miles for this trip." Then he headed back across the deck.

Tanner turned to Har and Pang. "You two go down in the cabin in case we draw fire."

Har's thin eyes opened into round discs. Pang dipped his head, looking through the open hatch to the cabin. "Stinks."

This trip couldn't end soon enough. Tanner warned him, "That's the safest place to put you if you want to live long enough to defect. My orders are to bring you in alive. You've got ten seconds to get down there on your own or I'll tie you up and toss you down. Matters not to me, but it's happening right now."

Pang scowled and muttered something nasty then stepped down into the dark cabin. Har followed Pang.

Nick barked out, "Hurry up and put a lifejacket on, Pang. They're under the bunk."

Tanner waited on Jin, who shook her head. "I will take my chances up here. I cannot hold my stomach down there."

Technically, she wasn't their package to protect, but Tanner didn't want her harmed either. He finally moved her into the position Pang had vacated and turned her to face the windshield. "Hang on to that handrail and don't let go."

She gripped a vertical stainless-steel rod on her left and put the other hand on the dash.

Tanner stepped in behind her.

Nick stood at the controls like a tsunami ready to explode and bash anything in its way.

Blade was situated at the aft with his weapon ready.

Dingo stood on the other side of Nick where he could hold the Sat phone protected from the water. He'd been on the phone to Logan and Margaux who were in Seoul, South Korea hopefully coming up with a way to help Tanner patch up an exit plan that had sprung more holes than a gunshot skiff.

He asked Dingo, "What's the word?"

"Home base assures me they're working on a plan, but I haven't heard back from them yet."

Nick looked around and said, "Hold on to your asses," then shoved the controls forward hard.

Tanner stood behind Jin. He gripped the handrail above her grasp and bent his knees, taking the shock of pounding wave after wave. He'd only thought Nick had opened up the engines before this. Based on the battering they were taking now and the waves breaking over the bow, Nick had pushed the engine only two-thirds of the maximum speed before.

He hoped Nick understood the navigation system enough to keep them from hitting a weather buoy or an island. They ran with no lights again but should see the lights of any other vessel.

Had Nick made it twelve miles offshore to reach international water yet?

Would it really matter since North Korea didn't recognize the twelve-mile break for the international traffic lane?

Nope. Not any more than the DPRK acknowledging the Northern Limit Line, an invisible division between waters claimed by North and South Korea.

But that was the direction Tanner had told Nick to head while Dingo called in support from Logan and Margaux.

Nick rode the waves hard, the bow bashing one after another for the next sixteen minutes. That was when Tanner looked over and caught Nick's nod. He acknowledged, "We just crossed the NLL."

The radio erupted with angry shouting.

Jin's gaze snapped toward Nick and said, "They know we are not who we claim and have ordered us to stop, or they will fire on—"

"We got company," Blade shouted from the rear.

Tanner searched the dark night spread behind the boat and saw two... no, three sets of lights.

How close were they?

One set of lights increased in intensity over the next minute. That threat was coming quickly.

Dingo had his elbow hooked around the cockpit's canopy

support bar and used that hand to cover one ear. He clutched the Sat phone against his other ear, shouting, "Come back again!"

Nick pushed the controls the last tiny bit.

Tanner yelled at Dingo, "What have you got?"

"Home base has a ride on the way that has us on radar, but they're eleven minutes out."

Water exploded a hundred feet behind them. That was only a warning shot. The next one would land in the middle of the deck.

Tanner had to squeeze out another eleven minutes.

He told Jin, "Get on the radio and tell them we're stopping." She hesitated for an instant then lurched over to grab the mic with Tanner holding her arm. She started talking in that same deep voice.

Tanner gave the order for everyone to put on lifejackets and prepare to abandon ship. Then he told Nick, "Cut the speed back to where we're going just fast enough to keep the nose in the wind."

That was the first time Nick looked at Tanner the way they usually looked at Nick when he had a crazy idea. Nick laughed with an edge that held a touch of insanity to it. He yelled, "I got a feeling I'm going to be disappointed this wasn't my idea."

If Nick meant that to sound supportive, he'd failed.

Tanner was running on faith and hanging by his fingernails with this plan, but it was the only way he could see to keep his team and their guests alive for another ten minutes.

Even then, if they were spotted before the ride Logan sent showed up, they were done.

The DPRK naval unit chasing them could see this patrol boat on their radar, too, but they'd have a harder time spotting a raft.

Until daylight.

Or unless they came close enough to use high-powered spotlights.

Flipping on the interior lights in the cabin, Tanner dove past a terrified Har and silent Pang to find the hard case he'd located as soon as Nick had driven the boat away from the bank in Pyongyang. Tanner wrenched up the oversized-looking briefcase that held the life raft system.

Rated for twelve men. Hot damn, that'd work.

He hurried back up top, ordering Har and Pang to follow him. Har was moaning as loud as a cow calling to its lost calf.

Blade handed Nick a life jacket he hooked over one arm.

Nick had slowed the boat but kept it moving southeast into a whipping wind from the storm. On the radar, it should look as if this patrol boat was just holding steady against the current.

Tanner located the painter, or connection line, in the briefcase and tossed the container overboard, snatching hard on the line attached to the gas cylinder release.

The raft began inflating immediately.

He pulled it to the rocking boat and ordered Blade in first. Blade handed Tanner the last lifejacket he held and waited five seconds on the next high wave then jumped into the raft. He landed hard but was up on his feet and grabbing the side of the boat to hold the raft close as Tanner fed first Har then Pang and Jin into the raft. Dingo jumped down after handing off the Sat phone and his weapon to Tanner.

Tanner passed that all back to Dingo and counted heads to insure he and Nick were last.

Every second pounded loud in his head.

Nick had found a tie-down rope he used to lock the patrol boat wheel so that it continued to drive into the wind. Tanner took Nick's weapon and handed it to Blade who was fighting to hold the raft close to the boat.

Nick latched his life jacket closed as he stepped up next to Tanner and said, "You need to cut the raft rope and let me get this thing moving away then I'll jump over."

"No!" Tanner and Blade yelled.

Nick scowled. "Turn on a light. I'll find you."

"No!"

Dingo yelled, "Logan's people are two minutes out, tops."

Nick roared, "If we don't send this thing far enough away the chase boat'll see us as soon as they get close. What the fuck is the point of the life raft if that happens?"

"Get in the fucking raft," Tanner ordered. When Nick hesitated, Tanner said, "Now. *I'll* run the boat away from the raft."

Blade cursed.

Tanner ordered, "Move it, Nick. Dollar waitin' on a dime."

Nick leaped into the raft, falling into a mass of bodies, then Tanner passed his weapon down. He handed the line to Blade and said, "Count to ten and turn on a light."

As soon as the next wave shoved the raft away, Tanner rushed over and jammed the accelerator forward. He used the momentum of the boat flying away from him to dive off the back and started swimming toward where he thought the raft should be.

A moment of panic rushed at him. He was disoriented and not sure which way to turn with everything black.

The wet wool was dragging at him, and the damned water was freezing his balls off.

He could hear the patrol boat powering away from him.

Saltwater slapped him in the face. He dug in harder, battling the current.

"Over here!" called from his left.

He treaded water hard, pushing up to locate the light. There. Shit, he'd been swimming away from them.

The whine of the patrol boat motor was getting faint.

He tried to yell, got a mouthful of water, floundered, and started swimming again.

Then he heard Jin's high pitched and frantic call. *"Where are you, cowboy?"*

She was worried about him.

Why that made him smile when his entire day had turned into a shit storm made no sense, but he felt a burst of energy. He dug his arm strokes deeper, plowing harder through the waves.

He could swear they were tossing him backwards as fast as he moved forward.

A flickering light bounced into view.

He was getting closer, right? Or was that just wishful thinking. This would only work if the current was sending them toward him.

An explosion boomed, sending a flash of fire and pieces flying into the air.

The DPRK had sunk the patrol boat.

It had to have made a quarter of a mile in that time. Was that far enough away?

Raining debris slapped the water near him.

"This way, Bo!"

Someone on the raft had spotted him. Tanner kicked his feet hard and caught a flash of light then dove toward it, swimming hard.

"Catch," yelled from the raft.

Something hit hard close to him. Tanner reached blindly. His hand hit a life ring. He yelled, "Got it."

The line went tight as they pulled him against the waves.

He reached the raft but climbing into a raft on a rough sea with drenched clothes sounded easier than it was. He couldn't haul his sorry ass up over the side. Blade and Nick dragged him in.

His heart was hammering to the beat of a metal rock band and his skin pebbled with chill bumps. The cold dug into his body with icy claws. He shivered, but this beat being out there.

Now, if this plan would only work.

Har was wheezing like a two-pack-a-day smoker and Tanner could hear Blade trying to calm him down. Blade had probably given Har well over the acceptable dose of respiratory medicine just getting him to this point.

Tanner felt Jin's fingers on his face, but she said nothing. Just touching him as if to confirm that he was alive.

He grasped her hand and gave it a gentle squeeze then shoved up on his knees to look past Nick so he could see outside the canopy.

Lights still trailed way off behind them.

Tanner asked Dingo, "Where the hell is the cavalry?"

"They said they'd find us. I can't get a connection right now."

Heaving hard breaths, Tanner wiped saltwater off his face. The wind had pushed clouds past the half moon, which could be a plus for finding this raft as long as the DPRK wasn't the one who benefitted by that.

Nick had his rifle up and pointed toward the DPRK boats. He had to be using the scope like binoculars.

Tanner asked, "They still on our ass?"

Nick gave it a second then said, "Their lights are getting smaller. Looks like they came, they scored, and they're leaving."

That would be good news if not for floating in the middle of the Yellow Sea with no way to paddle out of here.

Everyone stayed silent for the next few minutes then Nick pulled his rifle down. "That can't be good."

Through his monocular, Tanner could see a fairwater poked up from the smooth outer shell of a submarine fifty yards out.

Lifting a rifle right now, even to innocently use the scope would be inviting an attack. He asked Nick, "Did you see who it was before you dropped the scope?"

"Russian."

Son of a bitch.

A hatch on the surface popped open and the top half of a body appeared. He spoke English with a thick Russian accent through a megaphone. "You need ride. Yes?"

Tanner leaned forward, balancing himself on the side of the raft, and squinted but couldn't make out anything about the man.

Dingo lifted his Sat phone. "'Bout time, mate. Getting rough out here." He tapped Tanner on the arm. "Looks like that's who Logan sent."

"A freakin' Russian sub?" Tanner growled.

Dingo chuckled. "Logan said that was the best he could do on short notice. The Russians and Chinese have training maneuvers underway in this area. The sub is to deliver us to a lagoon thirty miles from here where Logan will meet us with a chopper and airlift us out."

Nick rubbed his hands. "I'm in. I've never driven a Russian sub."

Tanner didn't know which gave him more reason for concern. That Nick thought they'd let him operate the thing, or that he *had* driven some other kind of sub at some point.

Tanner cupped his hands around his mouth and yelled, "Yes, we need a ride."

But how was he going to keep this from the North Koreans when Russia and Korea were chummy these days? Logan was one hell of an operator, but he was also Russian and trusted the men on that sub more than Tanner did.

Mix three escaped North Koreans, four American covert operatives and the Russian navy. What could happen?

With Tanner's luck at this point, a whole new level of FUBAR.

Chapter Fourteen

Slye headquarters, Atlanta, Georgia

SABRINA BLINKED AND realized she had her head on her arms that were crossed on her desk. She'd fallen asleep.

That was not a problem.

She purposely didn't move. She'd slept at her desk plenty of times when she had an op in progress like the one in North Korea.

But something had disturbed her sleep.

Her head was turned toward the security panel on the wall just inside her office door.

All the lights were green. Activated.

She sat up and shoved a handful of hair off her face, checked her watch and did a quick calculation. Half past noon here. Tuesday.

That made it half past one Wednesday morning in Seoul, where Margaux and Logan were stationed.

No word yet.

The office was too quiet, but there was often more activity going on at the Slye headquarters *after* regular business hours. Her assistant, Amanda, had to courier sensitive documents to Washington DC for a client and the Slye agents didn't keep normal office hours. They were here on an as-needed basis. Sabrina was in no frame of mind to deal with their corporate security clients when she hadn't slept since Tanner's team went wheels up headed to North Korea, so she'd closed the office today.

Her cell phone buzzed, and she snatched it up, not wasting the time to check the caller. "Tell me some good news."

The hesitation on the line caused her to pull the phone away and note the unknown caller ID then put it back to her ear. "Who is this?"

"Unfortunately, not the person you were hoping to hear from," Gage Laughton replied.

Disappointment and pleasure fought an old battle. "What do you want, Gage?"

"Good to talk to you, too."

She scrubbed a hand over her face. Did she have to be a bitch to him just because he wasn't here to hold her and tell her this North Korea job would work out? That she wasn't going to lose people she held closer than family?

Gage hadn't been that man in her life for over two years.

He'd wanted to be, and she missed the hell out of him, but he kept putting the agency before her.

And holding out on telling her who had screwed her and her team on the last op she'd run for the CIA.

His CIA.

But he'd tried to make it up to her since then.

She picked up a pen and tapped it in a steady rhythm against the desk. Anything to release some of the tension wicking through her. "Sorry, Gage. Been a tough couple of days. How are you?"

"I'm as good as I can be without you."

It wasn't just what he said, but the longing behind his words. "Want me to hit the repeat button and ask you if you're ready to give me the names of everyone who was involved in the UK job?"

She didn't have to qualify which CIA contract she was referencing.

Only one UK job stood between them, and he refused to share the information she needed to find the people responsible for sending her and her team to their deaths. That person had to be pissed because they'd survived, but in fairness to Gage, he was the reason no one from the agency had visited her since then.

Except him.

He sighed as if he'd hit the repeat button on his end. "Can I come in?"

He was here? Her heart did a tap dance, and it was her turn to sigh. She should tell him no. She was not in peak dealing-with-Gage shape right now and might do something stupid like give in to stripping him bare right here in her office.

But it wasn't like she was going to send him away either. Why? Because, in spite of all that still stood between them, she wanted to see Gage. "Sure, just give me a minute to clear the alarm."

"Don't get up," Gage said, then stepped around the corner from her assistant's office into Sabrina's. He rocked jeans, a Henley and leather jacket like no other man. He wasn't gorgeous. Sabrina had never gone in for pretty boys. He was coiled power concealed in handsome packaging. Lean, tough and deadly, Gage would always be top dog in a room full of alphas, and they would all recognize him as such.

He lowered his hand to his side, still holding his phone.

She thumbed hers off and slammed it down on her desk.

"Does yours work after you do that, because mine would just give up the ghost." He kept moving forward then sat in the chair that faced her desk.

"I'm firing all my security people tomorrow and putting in a new system."

"Be a waste of money and loss of ace security people."

She dropped the pen and got up to pace.

That little battle nap was all the fuel she needed to kick someone's butt. She walked across her office to the sitting area where she met with corporate clients who marveled over how well trained her security people were. They rarely realized her agents ran black ops missions to places like North Korea.

The mirror on the wall above the sofa reflected her lack of real sleep in the dark areas under her eyes and that her black hair could use a brush.

Out of an unconscious female reaction, she brushed her hand over her messy hair.

"Trust me, you look amazing."

Pulling her hand down, she turned to Gage. "Why are you torturing me, Gage?"

"Looks like you're doing a better job of that all by yourself. When was the last time you slept?"

"Ten minutes ago."

"I meant in your bed."

"Your concern for my wellbeing is noted and ignored. Why are you here?"

He stood and she went on alert.

The look he gave her questioned whether she'd forgotten that they'd once been in love with each other.

He claimed to *still* love her.

She hadn't echoed that back to him. Instead, she'd threatened to kill anyone from the CIA who came near her after the UK job.

Here's the perfect opportunity, Sabrina.

She'd put that threat back on the front burner later—once she'd made up her mind how she felt about Gage.

If she went on the riot of emotions rushing around inside her at the moment, she'd admit that she wouldn't harm even one of the brown hairs that played with his collar.

He said, "I have something to show you."

She smirked. "Heard that one before."

When he smiled, his hazel eyes twinkled.

His smile used to be the first thing she'd see coming toward her as soon as either of them returned from a mission. She'd tried to forget about things like that. But with his smile now, all those memories came flooding back.

He took his time walking toward her and she held still to keep from looking defensive or aggressive.

Defensive would bring out his protective instincts.

Aggressive would just turn him on.

Either one would not end well. *Just keep a reasonable distance between you and all will be fine.*

Holding his phone up with the screen turned toward her, he touched the screen and an image popped into view of a man looking over his shoulder at someone or something on a street.

She did a double take and reached for his phone, forgetting all about keeping any distance. "Len-fucking-Rikker?"

"Yes."

She had to fight the tremble of fury that shook her hands. She held the picture of the man she and her team had gone to the UK to rescue for the CIA. He'd walked away free in trade for her team, who'd faced being tortured for information, then killed.

Rikker had surfaced once since then during a terrorist operation in Miami, but he'd slipped through their fingers.

This man had racked up a huge debt in human life and was a major part of the reason she'd pushed Gage out of her life.

She finally realized Gage stood inches from her. Should have realized it as soon as she noticed his scent. It was like no other.

His hands covered hers that held his phone.

When she lifted her eyes, his gaze watched her closely. He said, "This came off a security cam in DC. Rikker was there four days ago. I'm showing you something no one in the agency knows about but me."

Her heart raced at just knowing that Rikker hadn't vanished completely.

Gage was trying to meet her part way by sharing this. She wanted to build her half of that bridge, but did this mean he'd finally give her the names? "What are you saying by showing me this, Gage?"

He pulled the phone from her hands and slipped it into his leather jacket. Then he reached up and cupped her face. "That I'm close and I swear I'll do everything I can to keep you in on this. The reason I've never given you the names of everyone at the agency who was involved when the UK job went down, was because I haven't found any reason to believe someone there was behind this."

She jerked out of his hold and stepped away. "Still protecting the agency?"

Anger burrowed into his gaze. "You're not listening."

"I'm listening just fine, but you're still withholding vital information."

"The only things I'm holding back are names that will get you killed if you go off on your own investigation, dammit." He ran both hands over his hair and curled his fingers into fists. He looked like he wanted to plow both of them into something hard.

Sabrina didn't fear him. Never would. No matter how deadly he was, he'd never harm her, or any innocent woman for that matter.

He walked around a minute then pulled his legendary control back out and crossed the room to her, calm once again.

She let him crowd her personal space only because she missed having him close. Screwed up, but true. She told him, "If we worked together, this wouldn't be an issue."

Lifting a hand to her face again, he brushed his fingers across her cheek, then threaded them into her hair.

Her heart was thinking about jumping out of her chest and running around the room, begging him to fix this so they could go back to what they had.

Her mind was threatening to get a transplant for the defective organ. She opened her mouth to speak, and he kissed her.

No man kissed anything like Gage.

When he kissed a woman, he wanted her to know this was the only place on earth he wanted to be at this very minute. His other hand settled at her waist and tugged her to him.

She'd spent night after night missing him, missing this, missing them. Why couldn't she beat her pride into submission and put the past behind her?

Because it hadn't just been her in the UK.

She owed it to Josh, Dingo, Blade and Tanner. They'd all been there with her. Josh had lost someone he'd cared about in that fight. Sabrina had lost her ability to trust the man she loved.

Gage stepped up the kiss, making love to her mouth. He drew her in closer and her hands went around his back. Her fingers curled tight against his leather-covered shoulders.

Too many clothes. This would be infinitely better with fewer clothes.

He slowed the kiss and whispered, "Is that important?"

"What?" Then she heard the ring and broke away, diving for her phone. She thumbed the on button as she raised the phone to her ear. "Margaux?"

"Yes."

"Hold on." Sabrina sent a look of apology at Gage.

He walked over and kissed her forehead, whispering, "I will not lose you."

Then he was gone.

Sabrina's knees turned to rubber. She sat down, drew in a breath and turned back to the only problem she *could* solve right now. "Tell me you found a way to extract the team and the packages."

"Yes, but something unexpected came up."

It was that kind of night. "What happened?"

Chapter Fifteen

Seoul, South Korea

THE MINUTE THEIR private jet lifted off from Incheon International Airport into the still dark skies over Seoul, Tanner's chest muscles finally loosened.

Zero-four-forty hours.

His team was safe.

They'd survived that goatfuck of a mission *and* climbing inside a Russian sub with two DPRK defectors in tow. And oh yeah, one uncategorized pain in his ass.

Now he was finally headed in the right direction on a Gulfstream G550 arranged to transport his team and North Korean guests home.

But Jin wasn't a guest.

She wasn't persona non grata. Yet. But maybe on her way to be.

Sabrina had blistered the airwaves when Tanner called to explain their extra passenger. She was quick to question if Jin hadn't caused the problems with their exit strategy in Pyongyang. In Sabrina Slye's mind, that put Jin squarely under the heading of enemy until proven otherwise.

Not that Tanner could argue. Or would even try with Sabrina on a tear.

He'd have been saying the same things in Sabrina's shoes if he'd assessed the situation from the other side of the world. But he'd spent time up close with Jin and, if he had to swear while hooked to a lie detector, he'd say he believed Jin wanted to defect.

The part that would register as truth would be his *belief* in what she'd told him. That, however, did not prove anything about her actions.

What if she was a trained agent? If that was the case, why had she helped them escape when she could have walked them into a trap at any point? No one had worked any harder than Jin at finding a way out of North Korea.

But something niggled at Tanner. An itch of suspicion that he couldn't let go of, something that kept him from accepting her as just a defector.

In fact, Jin *wasn't* technically a defector.

Not until the State Department decided she was eligible and no threat to the US. Things had changed significantly since the days of rubber-stamping anyone who begged to defect.

Logan Baklanov walked down the aisle from where he'd been talking to the pilots. He dropped onto the sand-colored, cushy armchair next to Tanner's matching one. The chairs would recline when they were ready to sleep. All the window shades had been pulled down to keep the interior dark once they hit sunrise.

He should be asleep like the rest of his team sprawled all over the luxury cabin, but his body hadn't hit crash point yet.

Speaking of crash, that was the wrong word to be thinking right now with the luck, or lack of, he'd had since setting foot in Pyongyang.

Logan leaned forward, elbows braced on his knees as the jet continued to climb. "You are one lucky mother," Logan said.

Were Tanner's thoughts tattooing themselves on his forehead?

He started to argue, but his men and the two physicists *had* survived the escape. Instead, he said, "Thanks to your connections. And just how did you get a Russian sub to pick us up? Especially since your entire family has relocated from Russia to the US."

"I'm doing a favor for someone in a position of authority in the Kremlin," he said cryptically. "It's a delicate matter and I'm close to repairing a blunder that will save the entire country embarrassment and a potential conflict with another government." Logan gave him a that's-what-I-do shrug.

"I thought you ran ops with your HAMR teams. Sounds like you're more a negotiator or international diplomat."

Logan didn't smile, but it was there in his eyes. "Words can often be as powerful or dangerous as a weapon. My friend had a sub in the area to begin joint maneuvers with China's navy in two days. He told me he'd let his sub give your team a ride as long as I assured him that they wouldn't have to engage the DPRK."

"That's why he didn't surface until the Korean forces turned around and headed home after blowing up our patrol boat."

"Right. They knew he was out there, but they don't want to mess with Russia or China."

"You took a helluva gamble."

"Not really," Margaux Duke argued, entering the conversation as she sat across from them on a sofa.

She smiled at him. "I told Logan that worst-case scenario, you would unleash your secret weapon and take the risk of starting a third world war."

Tanner smiled for the first time in what felt like days. "Nick?"

She nodded, grinning.

"We're all lucky that submarine captain has a sense of humor." Tanner rubbed his aching head.

Logan, who *had* been smiling at Margaux, his not-quite-fiancé-but-more-than-girlfriend, turned a dark frown on Tanner. "What the hell happened?"

"Nick tried to convince the captain to teach him how to drive the sub, but the captain just grinned at him."

"Hell." Logan shuddered.

Margaux burst out laughing and, in two seconds, Logan was back to smiling again.

She was now part of Logan's HAMR Brotherhood. From what Sabrina had told Tanner, the HAMR Brotherhood was made up of teams in places all over the world and had been all male until Logan took on Margaux. But the men on his personal team had no trouble accepting her after what they'd learned about her. She'd helped Logan escape after being tortured in a South American jungle, then she'd taken one for the team in a terrorist attack in Seattle last year. Logan did covert work for

INTERPOL sometimes and had used those contacts to create an identity for Margaux that allowed her to disappear.

Someone from her past wanted her dead.

That person had better never go up against Logan or anyone from Slye. Margaux might be part of HAMR now, but she would always belong to Sabrina's team.

Tanner recalled their last parting and asked Margaux, "How's primitive life?"

"I keep trying to explain to Logan that my idea of roughing it is a hotel without a flat screen TV," she quipped, cutting a look at Logan that caused him to smother a laugh. Margaux hated anything that smacked of camping and Logan spent as much time in a jungle or wilderness as he did in civilization.

She was one dangerous operative and more than capable of defending herself, but Logan was in a league of his own and would bring the world down on anyone who touched her. They were crazy in love, even if their relationship made no sense to Tanner.

She'd walk through fire for Logan and wanted only him, but she drew the line at walking down the aisle.

The man who figured out women would rule the universe.

The plane leveled off into cruising altitude.

Margaux scooted forward to the edge of the sofa and kept her voice down now that the engine noise was a dull drone. "What's the deal with your girl?"

Jin wasn't *Tanner's girl.*

He ignored that just as he'd been ignoring the silent figure sitting in the dark at the rear of the open cabin area. He explained, "Like I told Sabrina, Jin showed up with intel that the mission had been compromised, then had a way out of Pyongyang through the tunnels."

"That could be a stroke of luck," Margaux said, thinking out loud. "Or a set-up."

Tell me about it. That conflicting thought had bounced back and forth in his mind to the point his head should have dents from the inside.

Tanner had the time during this trip to Los Angeles, then the leg to Atlanta, to figure out what he was going to say in his report about Jin. He'd have to hand over all three North Koreans to Sabrina when he reached Slye headquarters located near the Atlanta airport. Sabrina would transfer them to the person she'd cut the deal with who was in the State Department.

Someone who did not want his identity known, so the transfer would happen in the underground offices at Slye. Street level was a corporate security business, but missions were planned for national security in the basement operations center beneath the offices.

Jin, Pang, and Har would vanish the minute Tanner handed them to Sabrina.

Once that happened, no one on his team, including him, could say a word about this trip or those three. Ever. Sabrina would bust a blood vessel if he so much as hinted at wanting to know how it turned out for Jin.

Margaux twisted to her right and stretched her long neck, staring at the back of the airplane.

Now what?

She flipped back around and told Tanner, "You going to recline her chair or make your prisoner fly the whole way sitting up?"

What kind of asshole didn't consider that?

Me, I guess.

"Thanks, Duke," Tanner muttered.

She grinned. "At your service."

It grated on him to thank her for pointing out his lack of consideration for the *prisoner*. Margaux liked to be right, and he hated to admit when she was.

Guilt jumped up and slapped him in the face.

Jin had dragged him and his team through tunnels they never would have found, and he hadn't said two words to her since landing in that life raft.

Tanner stood, feeling every minute his banged-up body had endured to get here. Jin *would* be asleep by now if he'd taken the time to check on her and get her comfortable, but he'd been avoiding any show of concern for her that might be misconstrued.

And why was he beating himself up?

They'd only been in the air about ten minutes.

He knew why. He'd intentionally been avoiding anything more than professional contact with her, and he was doing it for *her* welfare even though he couldn't point that out. His report on how she'd aided their mission would carry more weight if no one got the idea that he was sympathizing with her.

Using the tiny, ankle-high lights, he walked quietly down the center of the dark airplane to keep from disturbing the others, but they were all in deep sleep.

Blade had set up Har in the private area just past where Jin sat. Not totally private right now, since Tanner had not allowed Har to close the door. He wanted to be able to see the lump back there on a sofa.

Pang was in the front, just as gone.

Tanner had separated all three of them as soon as possible. Standard Operating Procedure.

Everyone had been given an hour in a hotel to shower and change into clothes Margaux supplied. She'd taken Jin into a separate hotel room and stood guard while Jin washed the salt and grime from her skin and hair.

Margaux had tried to engage her, but Jin gave only one-word answers.

Jin had walked out of the hotel room with her dark brown hair twisted up in a knot, giving Tanner his first good look at her. She had freckles. Not many, but that little sprinkle across her nose surprised him. He was having a hard time getting them, or the silver-blue eyes out of his mind.

Blade had checked the cut on her head and told her to keep it clean but remembering how she'd gotten the injury backhanded Tanner with another slap of guilt.

As he walked up to Jin's seat, he took in the soft, blue warm-up pants and gray sweatshirt she wore, and her slender wrists, bound by flex-cuffs. Also, standard operating procedure. She was huddled into herself. Was she still cold?

Her hands were in her lap and clenched so tightly her knuckles had lost color.

What was wrong with her?

Panic over an unknown future?

He gave an internal headshake. She was the one who'd

refused to provide more than her name being Soo Jin, no last name. Before they'd boarded the jet, he'd pulled her aside and warned her that any hesitation to share information on her part would not go well.

Her answer? "You know as much as you need to know about me."

Should he play the tough guy again and warn her how bad it would be when they reached Atlanta if she didn't cough up something the State Department would consider usable, or go the nice guy route and cajole her into giving up a few nuggets of information to see if she had anything of value to offer?

She chose that moment to lift terrified eyes that smashed any chance of his playing the tough guy.

He moved over to squat in front of her. Her face was as pale as her knuckles, and she was shaking. He asked, "What's wrong?"

She clamped her jaw, refusing to answer him.

"Look, I told you what you need to do for us to cut you some slack."

"I ..."

"You what?" He leaned close. "You can tell me."

"No."

Her breathing tripped up to hyperventilation level. He reached into a side pocket on her seat and found a bag for airsickness. Opening it up, he moved it toward her face.

She jerked back. "Get ... away from me." That came out with a gasp between each word.

"Does flying make you sick?"

Her jaw muscles kept flexing with the strain of her trying to keep quiet and struggle with every breath. "Go. Away."

"No," he said gently. "Talk to me." He had to consider that this might be nothing but a ploy to get her wrists freed.

The shaking intensified.

Her pale blue eyes were unfocused. *That* didn't look like an act. She was going to black out from not getting enough oxygen any minute now.

He lifted the bag to her face and told her to breathe into it. This time she did, over and over, but the shaking wasn't getting any better. This was a full-blown panic attack.

Tossing the bag aside, he put his fingers under her chin, turning her to face him. "Tell me what you can, Jin. I'll help you. I promise."

She looked up at him with so much fear and pain he felt it slam him in his abdomen. Her shoulders were lurching forward and back with trying to breathe. "Airplane..." More hard breathing. "Dangerous."

Ah, shit. Pteromerhanophobia. He knew the name because his sister Hannah feared flying and nicknamed her phobia terra-Hannah syndrome—as in terrified Hannah. Jin had probably never been on an airplane before now.

She shoved her bound hands to her face and rocked.

Hannah had told Tanner what not to say when someone had a panic attack, especially on an airplane.

Never say to calm down. That was like telling someone with a gash in his chest to stop bleeding.

Never tell them their fear is irrational. And he shouldn't tell them to just stop it unless he wanted a voodoo doll created in his likeness.

Just thinking of Hannah and the idea of his sister's hands bound while she panicked turned his stomach inside out.

Screw this.

Tanner dug out a pocketknife and used it to slice the flex-cuff on Jin's wrists. He'd followed protocol for transporting someone of unconfirmed identity who'd appeared unexpectedly during a mission.

There wasn't *actually* a protocol for that so much as Sabrina's order to do so. That was the only reason he'd sucked it up and handcuffed Jin.

Yep, that had killed another part of his soul.

Sabrina wasn't here right now, and this was still Tanner's operation. She could rip him a new one later.

He dropped from a squat to land on his knees and pulled Jin to him.

She was stiff at first, but her fear was so strong it apparently overrode any pride she had that would make her refuse his help after he'd handcuffed her.

He rubbed her back, whispering to her to take it easy and breathe. "Count with me. One, two, three ... something."

Not a word at first then she mumbled, "Four ... five."

She'd gasp then count a little more with him urging her on. Her breathing slowly leveled out and the shaking began to subside. He kept holding her and rubbing her back because, well, he liked it. She was warm and soft.

When was the last time he'd held warm and soft?

Too damned long ago.

Allie, the soul-eater, had screwed with his mind. After her, he'd only been interested in fast, hard and no long goodbyes. He thought too much of the nice girls his mom and sisters kept trying to pawn off on him to ever date one. A prick like he was needed to stick with the cold ones who also wanted fast, hard and *see ya, thanks for the fun.*

But the female in his arms didn't fit in either of those groups.

She'd saved their bacon and he'd handcuffed her like a criminal.

He'd be pissed too if that had happened to him.

And now she'd had to admit to a phobia in front of him, when she was not only furious with him, but probably trusted him about as much as a pet rattlesnake.

In complete conflict with Jin's initial reaction to his touching her, she turned cuddly as a baby kitten.

Where had her fury gone?

He got his answer when he heard a soft snore. Exhaustion had drained the fight out of her. He kissed her hair and picked her up, then looked around belatedly to see if anyone was watching.

A tiny reading light on a stem glowed near Margaux. She was facing in his direction, watching. He'd never hear the end of this.

She stood and walked silently through the group of dead-to-the-world bodies and came back to him. Now was not the time for verbal warfare with her.

Without a word, she opened Jin's chair to recline position and stepped away, but not without sliding a smirk at him.

Tanner placed Jin down carefully, hoping she wouldn't wake

anytime soon and have to face her fear again. He'd ask Blade to give her something to handle the last leg of this trip from Los Angeles to Atlanta. They'd stop just long enough to fuel and go.

Margaux dug around in another compartment and handed him a blanket. She could have put it on Jin herself, but no, she just held it out with a look of I've-got-your-number on her face.

He covered Jin and followed Margaux back to where Logan was sprawled across the sofa.

Margaux dug out an armful of blankets. She tossed one at Tanner then dropped one in the empty chair next to his and used the last one to cover Logan. She smoothed her hand over Logan's face with a tenderness Tanner had never witnessed when she'd been on the Slye teams.

He'd have jerked her chain over it, but it made him feel good to see her happy. She used to bust his chops constantly in the Slye team war room. It irritated the hell out of him until Tanner realized that was her version of bonding.

Until he realized how very alone she'd been.

Anything that hinted of real emotion sent her racing in the opposite direction.

The Duke, as she was affectionately known, had been one of the toughest and most dependable agents he'd ever worked with, but she'd been hollow inside. Logan changed that and gave her a chance at a real life.

Tanner would overlook any asshattery from Logan for that reason alone.

When Margaux settled across from him and shook the blanket over her legs, she lifted a face empty of all humor to Tanner. "You can't save them all, cowboy."

"What are you saying?"

"The people in trouble. I'm slowly learning that you just save as many as you can and that has to be enough."

"I know that."

Margaux's steady gaze questioned if he *accepted* that truth. She mused on it a few seconds and added, "Everything about her is suspicious."

"Yep."

"If they think she's a spy or a plant, they'll lock her up. She'll never go home, and she'll never be free in our country."

That was why Tanner felt claws ripping through his insides. Jin needed help, but there wasn't a thing he could do for her once he handed her off.

Chapter Sixteen

At the Pentagon ...

THE GENERAL LIFTED his head from reviewing the budget for another prototype stealth aircraft with some impressive capabilities. The person he'd been waiting for stood in his office doorway to report in.

He dropped his pen and leaned back. "Close the door, H.P."

H.P., which stood for Huang Phon, stepped inside and made his way to the leather chair that faced the desk. He was in the State Department and overseeing the secret mission to get two physicists out of North Korea.

Nodding politely first, H.P. began in a cultured voice gained from growing up in the US. "I have news on our project. The two physicists escaped Pyongyang, but not through the anticipated route where we could intercept them before they arrived here."

"What? Find those two and bring them in." The General slammed his palm on his desktop. "I got you this State Department position so that something like this would *not* happen."

"The contractor handling the extraction is waiting on word from her people."

"Her? Who is this contractor?"

"Sabrina Slye. She executed classified work for the CIA at one time but dropped out of sight for a while after a disagreement on her last mission for the spooks. Now she is in Atlanta, where her cover company caters to corporations and select clientele who require specialized security."

The General leaned forward and growled, "You told me you

had a way to bring them here without tying up any funds. No paperwork. Why'd you choose her outfit?"

"She owed the DEA a mission and the DEA owed us a favor. You said you didn't want the military involved, sir. Sending Sabrina's people fulfilled that requirement. I spoke to the Slye woman moments ago and she assured me that her people were bringing the two physicists out alive."

The General grunted his approval. He'd spent a fat chunk of money and favors getting H.P. into a position that afforded The General a layer between him and operations such as this one.

"What happened to the exit route we arranged, H.P.?" The smugglers were to bring the two physicists into South Korea, where The General had his man Len Rikker and a team ready to capture them and take them to a secret location where The General would put them to work. Somewhere no country would interfere.

H.P. explained, "It appears someone betrayed the plan."

Who would have done that? If the DPRK knew about the defection, the men would have been shot on sight or captured and thrown in a prison camp at minimum.

Had Wayan caught wind of this operation?

Wayan was a high-ranking Chinese dignitary, but he was also a fanatic searching for five artifacts that he—and a squirrely group known as the Orion Hunters—believed prophesized a final conflict, aka World War III.

The crap some people put their faith in was amazing.

When one of The General's associates, a CIA spook he'd activated for "special" jobs, stumbled on the Orion group two years ago, The General tapped resources with deep pockets to track down one of the five artifacts. Then he'd used that carrot to open a dialogue with Wayan and form their private, secret boy's club—Czarion.

Or it *had* been a boy's club *and* secret before that damned Chatton came strutting in out of the blue.

She possessed one of the five rare artifacts and used that to coerce her way inside Czarion, so they were now a trio. She was a British ghost who had destroyed any trail to her true identity, but he and Wayan knew she'd been MI6 at one time. Maybe still was.

And he doubted that she believed the Orion Hunter prophecy mumbo jumbo any more than he did.

Wayan *was* the true fanatic, a nutcase just dangerous enough to start a war based on a bunch of ancient writing.

"Sir? What now?" H.P. didn't know him as The General, because he wasn't actually a general. That was just a moniker he used primarily with Wayan and Chatton.

"Get your hands on those physicists as soon as they hit US soil. I don't want anyone else talking to them until I've had them questioned." Getting them to Len Rikker now would be tricky. Rikker was yet another spook—former CIA—and Wayan had paid to save him when he got captured in the UK two years back.

H.P.'s smooth forehead folded into a frown. "But, sir, they believe they're defecting."

"Of course, they're defecting," The General reassured his pussy state guy. "But I need to know this isn't a plan for North Korea to game us. Once my people have a chance to talk to them and are convinced they will provide significant information, we'll give them asylum and put them in protective custody."

H.P. was writing notes on that little notepad he carried everywhere instead of an electronic device. He said, "I see. Very good. We do need to debrief them as soon as they arrive and once, they understand protective custody they'll feel safe."

The General gave an abrupt head nod that dismissed H.P.

Debrief? Yeah, those two would be debriefed in the bowels of Quantico. He wanted to make sure the Norks had the information they claimed and had no chance of accusing the US of kidnapping them.

That would start an international conflict that would bring China and Russia into the picture.

Anything was possible when dealing with someone from the DPRK.

The physicists had no worries about being safe. They'd never walk free again to be a target since this entire operation was off the books.

There would be no one to complain to since those two were not entering this country through diplomatic channels.

Chapter Seventeen

JIN FOCUSED ON the airport runway in the distance as she came closer to Los Angeles, California where it was half past one in the morning. Soon she would be handed off without another thought.

Cast aside once again.

She forced her lungs to work past the panic and breathe. Clutching her hands together, she twisted her fingers in and out of her grip, but the shaking would not cease. The handcuffs were not tight enough to cut into her skin. Bo had checked carefully when he'd put them back on after she'd awakened.

The drug Bo's medic had given her was wearing off, allowing fear to crawl through her mind, but she would hide her weakness this time. When he'd taken her into his arms on the way here, she'd hated allowing him to see her that way, but anxiety had given over quickly to exhaustion once she allowed herself to be comforted.

In that moment, her heart had taken a step out of darkness and into the sunshine.

Between the safety of his arms and the drug he'd convinced her to take a while later, she'd spent the flight asleep and awakened ready to make a decision that weighed on her.

She *had* planned to tell Bo about the people who had controlled her life since the age of seven. The same evil organization that intended to execute a deadly plan in America. She'd made a mistake and started to believe in Bo. Until meeting him, Jin had expected to fight the organization on her own and destroy their plan by finding and freeing her sister. But after that harrowing escape from North Korea, Jin had started to believe she'd found one man she could trust. One man who absolutely was not connected to the organization she ran from. It was a gut-wrenching leap of faith, since the evil people she ran from infiltrated North Korea and other countries, including America.

She'd even forgiven Bo for handcuffing her when they'd first boarded the airplane.

That forgiveness had come too soon.

Her mother's words of warning whispered in her mind. *You must not trust men or forgive a man of any misdeed, Soo Jin. Your heart is too soft.*

But Jin had argued that every man could not be bad.

Her mother had grudgingly agreed, yet still told Jin she would not be able to judge a man's true character until she was much older.

She'd realized her mother had the right of it when Jin had awakened to find her hands bound once more. Bo had handcuffed her again, while she was in the deep, drug-induced sleep.

Was it so wrong to want someone to turn to, someone to lean on for once in her life?

Jin had been fighting to survive for so long, she didn't know how to live any other way. For a moment, she'd weakened, wanted to stop fighting, but that was not wise.

Jin had argued with their adoptive parents when her sister had been forced to give up her birth name for the more American-sounding Patty. Patty needed an American name because she had been groomed for a different job than Jin's.

That argument had cost Jin a beating.

Patty had pretended she was fine with the name, and with her life, but Jin knew the truth. Patty harbored a deep hurt over their mother's decision to trade them to the Chinese couple for money to pay for medical care, even though breast cancer was killing their pretty mother.

But Patty still believed they were sold.

Jin suffered a rush of guilt, because she'd had moments of doubt herself. They were never allowed to contact their mother again, but two years ago while attending a special class for her research, Jin had learned the truth. She met a woman she'd known as a child. That woman said Jin's mother had died eight months after Jin last saw her. But this woman had shared news that Jin could not wait to tell her sister. Their mother, when she realized she would not live, had given the money she'd received from the Chinese couple to a destitute family.

Patty would finally be able to forgive her mother.

Then she and Jin would hold their own funeral to say goodbye.

Jin's eyes burned with the threat of tears she would not let fall. The two white ribbons made of hemp to wear in their hair and two hanboks, traditional black dresses for a funeral, had been left behind. She'd scavenged them before and would find a way to obtain appropriate mourning clothes again, once she rescued Patty.

"How are you doing?"

Jin jerked up at the woman's voice and gave a knee jerk answer. "I am fine."

This woman had been the one to take her into a hotel room back in Seoul. A part of Jin, her undependable over-trusting heart, prodded her to be friendly. She needed a different ally since Bo was not consistent in his actions. He could not be trusted.

"Mind if I sit here while we land?" the woman asked. She was tall and had dark auburn hair cut in a loose style that fell around her neck and ears.

"Sit if you want." Jin's gaze slipped past the woman and landed on Bo, who was talking to one of his men.

Why did looking at him make her heart hurt?

Because she still wanted to tell him what she knew, but now that he'd handcuffed her it was clear that she'd have to wait to share anything. She would need that information to negotiate for her sister's life.

The minute she told his government what she knew, which she would do because she would not allow innocent people to die, the US government would lock Jin up.

And then she would die, because an assassin would be sent to kill the traitor and this government could not prevent it.

When the woman fell quiet after sitting down, Jin glanced at her and asked, "What will happen here?"

"We land, fuel and take off again for Atlanta."

Clammy chills covered Jin's skin at the idea of flying another few hours. She stared out the window again, trying to make the airplane land faster, and muttered, "Death would be easier."

"Our medic can give you another sedative for the next leg," the woman suggested.

"No." Jin cut her eyes at the woman and softened her tone. "Thank you, but no. I do not like drugs."

More than that, she had to be alert in case this was where she would escape.

Chapter Eighteen

THE GULFSTREAM SETTLED into its landing pattern for Los Angeles International Airport, the runway a flash of bright lights beneath black skies at two in the morning.

Tanner fought off fatigue. He should have slept, but he kept worrying about Jin. Even now, he cut a glance down the cabin at Margaux.

She'd taken the seat across from Jin to help their prisoner through the descent. Halfway here, Blade had given Jin something for anxiety after she woke in terror, flailing at the covers where her feet were entangled.

Tanner had gotten to her first and gently shaken her awake, then talked her into taking the pill Blade offered.

And it seemed *everyone* had noticed his quick attention to their tunnel-guide-turned-prisoner.

While she'd slept, he'd cuffed her again. He'd known the minute she'd been alert and had suffered a blast of guilt when— glutton for punishment that he was—he'd met her gaze that had accused him of betrayal.

Then her pale skin had turned green with her fear of flying, but one look had told him not to make the mistake of touching her.

When Margaux offered to sit out the last thirty minutes of the flight across from Jin to help her make the transition through landing, Tanner had waved her off with, "Suit yourself."

She'd muttered, "Not fooling me, cowboy," as she passed him on her way to the back.

Jin was in trouble up to her delicate neck. He wouldn't apologize or take any flack for comforting her when she'd panicked any more than he would for soothing a frightened animal.

A mild mechanical groan announced the landing gear dropping into place.

Blade came walking up from the rear compartment where he'd been for the last half hour with Har and Pang.

Blade had asked Tanner to bring Pang back to help him communicate with Har, who'd gotten airsick halfway through the flight. The three had remained in Har's area since then.

Blade grabbed the corners of armchairs and sofas to keep his balance until he dropped down beside Tanner. "We got a problem."

Four words that unleashed Tanner's adrenaline, but he kept his gut-clench reaction locked down. "What?"

"Har's still throwing up and I have no idea if he has food poisoning or what, because he isn't making any sense and doesn't have a fever. He ate the same food as Pang when we were in Seoul and during the flight."

"Maybe he's got an allergy no one put in the documents."

Blade stared off and continued talking, thinking out loud. "I went over their basic medical history as soon as we took off, and Har claimed no allergies. Pang doesn't know any personal details on Har. I can hydrate him, but his symptoms are getting worse even though I gave him a shot for his nausea. I'm not going to have enough IV to make another flight if he gets worse, and I need to stabilize him before he goes airborne again."

"You think it's real?" Sure, that sounded cold, but Tanner had learned the hard way years ago to not trust any surprise.

Sweat ran down Blade's forehead. He swiped at it. "From all I can tell, it's real or, at least, the symptoms are real. Pang translated. Har said he has an irregular heartbeat. Hell, he might be having a heart attack, but I'd need an EKG to confirm it. He'd have to be a hell of an actor to pull this off."

Tanner had to agree with Blade.

They *were* talking about Har after all.

And though they all called him "medic" on these ops, Blade got his nickname because he was actually a crazy-gifted surgeon.

Nick and Dingo walked up as the Gulfstream touched down. Tanner caught them up on the newest crisis since this mission couldn't seem to continue without one. He started issuing instructions.

"Nick, we need three vehicles and the closest Slye safe house."

Lifting a phone to his ear, Nick backed away, going to work.

Dingo was already tapping on his tablet as Blade dictated a list of medical supplies. He'd send the order ahead with Blade's credentials so it would be ready for pickup. As soon as they finished the pharmaceutical shopping list, complete with all the required authorization for the supplies, Tanner continued mapping out their new game plan.

"Dingo picks up what Blade needs and food. Nick will go ahead and clear the safe house. Blade and I'll transport our Koreans."

Nick walked up. "SUVs will be here by the time the pilot shuts down the engines. Closest safe house to LAX is about three miles away near a quiet industrial area. Not much to look at, but I've used it before. It's sound."

Tanner needed somewhere secure only for today. "I'll call Sabrina as soon as everyone is set. Wouldn't want to interrupt her bitching about this to deal with logistics."

Dingo cast a critical look back in Jin's direction. "Speaking of problem females, what are you going to do with that one?"

Like there was anything *but* questions on her destiny? Tanner only had one answer. "Hand her over to the State Department. Why? You got another idea?"

"I think something's not right about her and how she showed up."

Tanner agreed but wanted to hear the rest of Dingo's thoughts. "What're you thinking?"

Dingo's body wove slightly, adjusting as the jet slowed and turned. "That woman should be asking a ton of questions and trying to find out what happens next. She's hardly spoken to anyone, except you and a few words to Margaux."

And she was no longer talking to Tanner at all, based on the frigid looks she'd sent his way.

Dingo had just voiced the very issues banging around inside Tanner's skull, but that brought up the same concern about the other two. "I'm not so sure about Har or Pang either."

Dingo raked a hand over the wild, half-inch-long hair that stuck out all over his head. His mouth twisted up on one side. "Blade and Nick both said Har has asked questions the whole time. Pang doesn't, but he's probably getting his answers via Har's questions. You're right, though. Blade went through the usual debrief with Pang and said he didn't appear overly excited to be out of North Korea. Things are off with this bunch."

A lot of things weren't right, especially about Jin, but Margaux had made sure Jin was clean of any electronics before she gave her the warm-ups to put on. Blade had searched the two physicists.

Tanner didn't have answers and still had a job to do.

He gave his head a quick shake. "Not our problem. We deliver these three and someone else figures out the puzzle."

From the back compartment, Pang called, "He is sick again. Hurry!"

Blade took off fast as the jet rolled across the runway and paused, waiting to be told by the tower when to cross a busy section.

Nick and Dingo huddled off to the side, deciding on food and whatever else they needed. Knowing Nick, additional ammo would be on that list.

Tanner strode back to where Margaux was leaning forward over Jin, blocking his view of Jin's face.

"You two set?" Tanner was ready to be done with the headache of these three. *Keep telling yourself that, buddy.* Okay, so he wasn't ready to hand over Jin, but sometimes his job sucked. That didn't change the fact that he still had to do it.

Margaux stood and stepped to the side to face him.

Jin tilted her head back, gazing at Tanner. Why did she have to look so damned vulnerable sitting there?

"What's up, cowboy?" Margaux asked.

Glad to shift his thoughts to something that didn't eat up his insides, he gave her a head nod to follow him forward. They met Logan midship.

Tanner explained, "We've got to move to a safe house and let Blade stabilize Har."

Margaux said, "I heard him coughing up his cookies. At least Jin didn't get toilet-hugging sick. You'd have been cleaning that up. I'm no Florence Nightingale."

No truer words had been spoken. The Duke's bedside manner would start with, "Don't be a pussy," and end with, "Do I look like a fucking nursemaid?"

She did ask, "Think Har needs a hospital?"

"I hope not, but that would cap off this goatfuck of a trip."

Margaux had never met an F-bomb she wouldn't drop. She smiled with understanding. "That much fun, huh?"

The team had been running hard for two days. Between jet lag from flying in both directions and hours of adrenaline overload, Tanner felt as if he'd been shoved in a cement mixer turned on high. "Yep, more fun than any one person deserves."

Logan's mouth twisted with grim concern. "How long will you need before we can fly to Atlanta?"

"I couldn't even guess at this point. You can refuel and go on. With any luck, we can fly out by the time Sabrina sends us a ride from headquarters. I'm going to see if there's any chance we can hand those two off to the State Department here, but this is that IOU deal Slye made with the government so who knows?"

"And it's my fault Sabrina got stuck with this mission," Margaux admitted glumly, raking a hand through her auburn hair.

Tanner didn't have it in him right now to be Mr. Understanding and tell her that she'd made a mistake on a bust that anyone could have made under similar circumstances. It wouldn't change the fact that she'd blown a DEA undercover op that had been going for months. But she'd been fed bad intel by someone who'd paid a lot of money to set her up.

This was the first time Sabrina had ever been put in a position where she was forced to take a government contract she'd rather refuse, but she wouldn't hold that against Margaux or any other agent.

Logan reached over and pulled Margaux to him, kissing her

on her forehead. "Shit happens in this business, baby. You saved an entire city on that mission. Count the good with the bad."

She looked over at Tanner. "That's why he's my number one guy." There came that big Margaux grin again—the one only Logan could get out of her.

Tanner backed away to find a place where he could call Sabrina. He shifted his weight as the jet wove its way to a private terminal. When he had her on the line, he explained the latest glitch in the plans.

She was quiet for a moment, but he could hear her tapping a pen against something hard, probably her desk. "Hold on, Tanner."

He stepped aside, getting out of the way to allow Logan to pass while he waited on Sabrina. She came back on with a blast of orders. "State Department says they'll pick them up in LA."

Damn. Finally, one break.

But that meant Jin would be gone sooner than he expected. Why did that run through him like a sharp-clawed badger? "Where do we go from here?"

"I'll let them meet you at our safe house. We'll scrap that one as soon as this is done. I'm happy to give up a safe house to have all of us done with this operation now." She took a breath. "I'm sending our jet to pick you up tomorrow morning. I'll be in touch as soon as they call back to give me the identification of every person showing up for those three."

"Roger that." Tanner swallowed against the sick punch to his stomach. This whole deal had been touchy from day one and now he wouldn't even get the chance to talk about Jin with Sabrina who could, and would, use her pull with the government if he convinced her Jin just wanted to stay out of North Korea.

As soon as he had a moment alone with her at the safe house, it was time to tell Jin she'd reached the end of her rope.

Chapter Nineteen

TANNER WALKED AWAY from Logan's jet, staying close behind a pitiful-looking Har, who followed Pang and Jin. Nick and Blade flanked the Koreans on each side and Dingo led the way to one of three black Suburbans parked in a line. There was a lot to be said for being able to play the Nick card when needed.

Especially at two-thirty in the morning.

If Nick called, someone would deliver a fleet of vehicles or a 747 with the same miraculous timing.

From time to time, Nick was asked about his Carrera last name. Tanner couldn't recall any straight answer, just a patent Nick smile for a reply.

At Tanner's Suburban, he waited for Har and Pang to climb in, then reached to give Jin a hand up since she was the only one handcuffed.

She snatched her arm away and sent him a death glare.

Whatever had been behind that kiss back on the boat had disintegrated to never return the minute she'd awakened with cuffs back on her wrists.

Airplanes roared overhead and the smell of jet fuel washed through the air.

Nick and Dingo wasted no time going to their individual sport utilities.

Nothing had changed with regard to their situation. Sabrina had not called back yet and probably wouldn't for another hour. It would be later today at the soonest, if not tomorrow, before the State Department representatives showed up.

Government moving at the speed of molasses in the winter.

Blade had gotten Har stable for now, but Har still looked deathly pale.

Don't let him throw up in the Suburban. Three miles in LA could take a while. Tanner did not want to be subjected to Eau de Fresh vomit for the entire ride.

Tanner dropped his rifle and monocular headgear on the floorboard of the passenger side and climbed in, cringing at the sound of Har's dry heaving. Man, that was painful to listen to and the guy already smelled like a puke fest.

Blade jumped into the driver's seat and shut his door. Tanner drew his HK Tactical and held it ready, but low, out of sight of anyone passing by.

Nick was gone by the time Blade pulled slowly out of the airport. Tanner swung around to do a quick check on each passenger.

Two rows back, Pang was doing his standard imitation of an imposed-upon celebrity, still waiting to be treated like the legend he believed himself to be. The guy better be able to deliver. If Tanner ever found out he was a fraud, the Korean King might get his ass kicked after what Tanner and his team had been through to deliver Pang safely.

Har was next to Pang, holding an airsick bag like a safety line and looking gaunt.

Tanner finally moved his gaze to Jin who sat, fuming, in the second row behind Blade. She didn't flinch when he frowned at her. No siree. She dialed up the heat on her seething gaze for several seconds then let her disappointment punch through.

I know. I'd be angry and disappointed in your shoes too, he wanted to tell her.

She finally swiveled her head away, looking past Blade's left shoulder where local traffic and airport hotels buzzed past the window.

Shit. Tanner turned back around, fighting off the drowsiness brought on by riding in a warm van that rocked gently as Blade wormed his way slowly out of the airport area and took surface streets toward the safe house.

Taking the long way would give Nick a chance to arrive first, do a walk through and be ready to meet the Suburban when they pulled up.

Considering that no one had expected his team and the Koreans' presence at LAX or that they were on the way to one of several safe houses Sabrina had in this city, all this caution might seem like overkill.

But everyone on Tanner's team wore high-end, lightweight titanium body armor.

There was no such thing as being too careful in this business.

Cold air from the vents hit him in the face and Tanner blinked his eyes. Shit, he'd almost dozed off. Rubbing his eyes with his thumb and forefinger, he lowered his hand and sat up, shaking off the fatigue. Then he gave Blade a nod, thanking him for the air conditioning wake up.

Blade swung down a two-lane road where warehouses stood. They'd been around for over twenty years from the looks of the area. Tanner reached down to the floorboard for his monocular and slipped the head straps in place, leaving the eyepiece flipped up. Blade took a left turn between two buildings crammed up to the property lines. He drove down a potholed road for the next half-mile until the dead end.

On the left were woods and, on the right, stood a one-level brick ranch.

Just your average, three-bedroom, brick residence built in the 80s, with white shutters and a gravel driveway. The security light on a twenty-foot wooden pole at the corner of the house tossed enough light to show the boarded-up windows. The house was a little rough around the edges, but it came with a basement safe room stocked with supplies in case of an attack.

A room Tanner's three guests wouldn't see unless something went very wrong.

The house sat eighty feet back off the road with the land cleared for forty feet all around it. This had to have been a holdout piece of property —owners refusing to sell—back when the area turned industrial.

The street might look like a dead end, but Nick would already know the exit strategy from this place if he'd been here before.

Nick's black Suburban sat in the driveway, backed in.

Blade backed in, too, pausing the Suburban in front of its twin, but he kept the motor running. With the house to his left, Blade had the best line of sight to watch for Nick.

Tanner turned to the other passengers.

Har was leaning against the window, his breathing shallow. The minute he moved, he'd probably start upchucking again, but he had to be ready to move when Tanner gave the order.

"Har, you with us?"

"Yesh..."

That was as good as it would get with him. Tanner said, "You three stay seated until I come around to get you."

Jin stared out the window, but she did incline her head to acknowledge hearing him.

Pang heaved a long sigh that Tanner ignored. Pain in the ass. *The State Department can't come for you soon enough.*

The security light went out, which meant Nick had flipped the switch inside the house. He should give the all-clear next. Blade put the truck in park and turned off the engine. "Nick's waving us in."

Tanner holstered his HK. Blade flipped a switch so the interior lights wouldn't activate, and Tanner dropped his night-vision monocular over his eye as he jumped out, clipped his rifle to his vest, and hustled around the front of the truck.

Stepping out with his own monocular in place, Blade drew his CZ 75 and scanned the area around the house.

One dim light inside the small entry backlit Nick at the front door. He took a step off the porch, calling out, "Took you long enough."

Gunfire erupted.

Rifle rounds sprayed the house, breaking the storm door glass, slamming Nick backwards and taking out the light.

Chapter Twenty

TANNER DOVE FOR the ground, weapon up and returning fire just for cover.

Blade was half in and half out of the truck, ordering the three inside, "*Hit the floorboard!*"

That wouldn't be enough to protect those three. Tanner yelled at Blade, "Get 'em out of here."

He'd use the distraction of the Suburban leaving to make a run for Nick and drag him in the house.

Shit, don't let that crazy Italian be dead.

A white panel van squealed up and slammed to a stop, blocking the end of the driveway. Snatch van. *Fuck.* Deep drainage ditches ran along the road the full length of the property.

Blade dropped to the ground next to Tanner. "No way out through the yard, even with the Suburban."

Tanner needed a plan B that included a chopper, but he was fresh out of magic dust. They were both breathing hard and waiting, anticipating the next round of fire.

But no one in the van at the street was shooting.

Why not?

Tanner didn't want to shoot from his current position and draw fire toward the Suburban. He told Blade, "Okay, new plan. I'll cover the packages. You get Nick inside."

"Roger." Blade slithered beneath the Suburban, then disappeared into the dark on the other side. Tanner followed him beneath the truck, a damned tight fit. All he needed was to get stuck down here. When he reached the other side, he paused to check the tree line of undeveloped land next door, then he lifted quietly to his knees and eased the rear passenger door open.

Shooting started up again from the far side of the property where the first blast had originated. Snapping hits pinged all around, blasting the windows from Nick's truck, but not one window shattered on this one.

So, they definitely wanted these Koreans alive, huh?

That was a plus. Now he just had to get them into the house.

"Jin. Har. Pang. Out here with me and stay low."

Jin must've crawled to the passenger side, because she pushed out the door and dropped to the ground first, with Har following. Jin squatted next to Tanner, echoing his thoughts when she whispered, "They must want us alive. Stay beside me and you will be safe."

Meaning he could use her as a human shield? Was she crazy? "No. Stay down and be quiet."

"Don't be—"

"Shut. Up. Give me your hands." Tanner didn't have time to argue or be polite. Nick could be bleeding to death and Tanner had to get these three somewhere safe. He pulled out his knife and sliced through the flex-cuffs around her wrists. He would not leave her bound and at a disadvantage if she had to fight. "Come over here, Har."

Har crawled forward on his hands and knees, tears streaming down his face and shaking like a leaf in a windstorm. He paused, rocked back so he was sitting upright, and heaved once. Tanner grabbed him by the shoulders, dragging him back down.

Being sick might kill him, but not as fast as a bullet.

Pang took his sweet time getting to the door and grumbled all the way out of the truck.

Hate to inconvenience you while I save your life, dickhead.

But the good news was that no bullet had struck this Suburban yet.

Tanner told the three of them, "We're going to work our way back to the house."

Pang decided to share his unwanted insight on the situation. "They will shoot us."

If Pang didn't shut up, Tanner would save someone the bullet and do the deed himself. "Stay close to the ground and move when I tell you."

Pang argued, "We will die."

Tanner grabbed him by the throat and yanked him close with one hand. "There's a safe room in that house. All we have to do is get to it. Decide now if you want to live or die but shut the fuck up."

That silenced him.

Tanner gave the order for them to start crawling down the driveway toward the house. Har was making low howling sounds, but that couldn't be stopped. Jin led the way. They'd made it as far as Nick's truck when Tanner heard someone coming up behind him.

He whispered, "Keep moving." Then he flipped around, weapon up.

The footsteps paused.

Where was that bastard?

Gunfire blasted. He could hear it ripping up the house. *Shit. Shit. Shit.*

Tanner shoved up to get ahead of Jin and the other two, so he'd be the first to face the threat.

But when he turned to face forward, he found Pang and Har being dragged off.

Where was Jin?

Tanner took one running step toward Pang and Har.

Someone body slammed him into Nick's truck. Sharp, hard strikes pounded his face below the monocular.

Tanner roared and shoved off the truck, using his body weight to try to gain room to shoot. The bastard was even bigger than he was, and was still right on top of him, punching so fast Tanner couldn't even reach for his handgun or knife. *Fuck this.* Tanner slammed a headbutt into the giant's face, jamming his monocular headgear into the other guy and into his own skin.

Shit that hurt.

But it earned Tanner a grunt of pain from the other guy, and the split second he needed to throw his weight forward, knock the guy back a half-step, and buttstroke him across the face with the rifle.

The giant staggered and grunted again but didn't fall.

Tanner bashed him two more times, adrenaline surging

through every hit he delivered. What the hell was this guy on, to take this kind of beating? He swung again but the son of a bitch moved a hair faster. Tanner hit the truck with his weapon and shock vibrated up his arm.

"No!" shouted behind him. He risked a glance.

Someone was dragging Jin away.

A boot struck Tanner's side, the penalty for looking away.

He rammed the stock up, catching his opponent low in the jaw this time. Bone crunched. Yeah, baby. That finally knocked the bastard off balance. Tanner kicked him in the head on the way down. He landed, out cold.

Sabrina would want one of them alive. Looked like it was gonna be this one. Tanner took a split second and dropped the magazine out of the guy's rifle and flung it across the yard toward the woods, then tossed the guy's empty weapon under the Suburban, out of reach, in case he woke up too soon.

"Let ... go!" Jin's voice jerked his attention to the van where they were loading Pang and Har into the back.

The guy who had a struggling Jin in his grasp must have heard Tanner's pounding steps coming around the front of the Suburban.

The next seconds stretched and distorted like one of those warped mirror reflections at a carnival show.

Jin turned with the kidnapper as he swung around with her in front of him, lifting his weapon in a smooth arc. Fuck, Tanner couldn't shoot the guy without risking Jin.

Her face registered every emotion from shock at seeing Tanner coming for her to terrified realization that he was going to run into the line of fire.

As the rifle came level, Tanner twisted away, watching for the flash of gunfire.

Jin broke her attacker's hold in one smooth move and knocked the legs out from under him. His weapon sprayed bullets up into the air, just missing Tanner's head. She turned into a miniature cage fighter, her knees on his chest, battering the guy with a series of sharp strikes at his face and throat.

Couldn't have been over five seconds.

Tanner caught his balance and flipped around to go after her.

The guy knocked her backwards, off of him, and lunged for the van, but Jin was getting to her feet. Tanner still couldn't get a shot without risking hitting her. A spray of rounds came from the passenger-side window, and Tanner and Jin both dove for the ground.

Doors slammed on the van, then it screeched forward and spun around in the middle of the road to head back toward the warehouse area. Tanner fired up the front quarter panel and driver's-side door, not willing to risk hitting Pang or Har in the back. The rounds bounced off the surface. Armored. He stood to get the tag number, knowing full well that it'd be a stolen plate and a dead end. The van slowed long enough to pop off one last shot.

Jin dove to the side again, and Tanner dropped back to his stomach. He was sick and fucking tired of being up close and personal with this damn driveway.

That last shot went nowhere near Jin but flew past Tanner.

He looked around. They'd nailed their giant buddy who'd been struggling to his feet. *Leave no one behind who can talk.*

As the van screamed away, bouncing along the potholes in the asphalt, Tanner pushed up and ran to Jin.

Or more like, he ran to the spot where she'd landed. It was empty. "*Jin!*"

Tanner swung back and forth, searching everywhere. She couldn't be hit. They didn't shoot at her. "Jin! Where are you?"

He cursed up a storm all the way back to where he'd left the giant they'd shot.

The fucker was dead. Shit. Had they taken Jin too?

Not that quickly and silently. She was too much of a fighter.

Son of a bitch.

She'd run.

Nick. Screw all of this. Nick was hurt.

Running to the house, Tanner found a smeared trail of what had to be Nick's blood leading inside. Or was it Blade's blood, too? Tanner grabbed his head.

Nick shot and all three Koreans gone.

All. Three.

He yelled at the house, "Coming in."

Blade met him at the door, hands bloody. "I can't fix Nick. He needs a hospital now."

Fuck.

Chapter Twenty-One

A flat in Thailand ...

THE BLOODY BURNER phone woke Chatton from a power nap she'd needed after being up for four days straight tracking a Russian operative through Bangkok.

Only one person had that number.

She snatched up the phone. "What do you want, Wayan?"

"Is it not possible to show some manners at least when you answer a call?"

Not when she knew how much it infuriated him to be shown no respect. Manners were for social relationships, which she didn't encourage. Her relationship with Wayan was similar to a honey badger stalking a cobra, with her being the honey badger.

Wayan just hadn't figured that out yet.

"I have an opportunity for you."

"I'm listening." She smiled at Wayan contacting her. This had to do with The General. Those two had joined forces at some point before she'd found them and finagled her way into their midst, pissing off both of them.

Two birds. One stone. Score.

"The US just extracted a pair of North Korean physicists who were part of Project Jigu-X and suddenly decided to defect."

Way to go, US. Chatton had been digging around for information on Project Jigu-X recently, just like everyone else in the intelligence business. Even if she was no longer with MI6, her beloved UK sat too close to that buggar leading the DPRK.

Rolling over on her back, she stared at the slowly moving ceiling fan and asked, "This matters to me, how?"

"You are looking for someone."

She stilled, thinking. Yes, she was hunting the serial killer who had murdered her parents and who was systematically hunting down every Macintosh in her bloodline, but Wayan did not know that. Couldn't know that since the only way he could have found out was from her.

"I'm always looking for someone, Wayan. It's what I do. Surely you and The General have come to understand the level of skills I possess and that I'm not one to allow assets to go dormant."

"Yes, we know you are a super spy. I meant that you are looking for someone specific and this search is personal to you."

"Oh? Just who am I looking for?" she asked, dancing around the cobra to make sure he didn't gain an advantage.

"I do not know who, but that is my point. If you bring me what I want, I will find the person you are hunting."

Her pulse did a double pump at that. Wayan definitely had the kind of resources that could flush out the killer and he wasn't above mowing down everyone in his path to gain something if it held a value for him.

She must have taken too long to respond. Wayan said, "Please do not waste our time denying this. Let us move to the negotiation, shall we?"

"Fine. Make me an offer I can't refuse."

"How appropriate to use an American phrase. I want the two physicists and a woman who escaped with them. Bring them to me and I will either pay two million American dollars for them or I will find the person against whom you hold a vendetta."

This had potential.

Not the money.

She'd only joined up with The General and Wayan because she was fairly certain the murders of her family were tied to the artifact she possessed. Wayan had no idea how much she wanted to find the Macintosh killer, or he'd have demanded her artifact in trade.

She told him, "How much time do I have to deliver these three Koreans?"

"Four days."

"That's not enough time to gather intel."

"I have what you need."

"Such as?" she prompted.

"I know where they are going once they arrive in the United States. You should be able to find out who extracted them with your resources and put enough together to locate them along the way."

"Should have been US military."

"My resources tell me it was not."

Interesting. "What do you want with these three?"

"Explaining to you is not part of our agreement, but these three wished to defect to China. I am inclined to believe The General is behind this extraction just to keep them out of my hands. I do not blame the three defectors for taking the only way offered to them out of North Korea."

A benevolent Wayan? She rolled her eyes.

Still, that did sound like something The General would do. Chatton thought of the potential problems and asked, "What if the three of them get separated? Do you still want only one or two?"

"The woman is your first priority. Fail to bring her to me and our deal is off."

Even *more* interesting. What was so important about this woman? "Need a new mistress, Wayan?"

"Your mind is a dark place. This woman is too valuable to allow anyone to touch her. She will live as a queen, unlike the life she had in the DPRK. I have plenty of women and would not spend this trade on something so insignificant."

Now, *that* sounded like the Wayan she knew and despised.

This was a gamble, but one it was time to take. She had yet to determine if Wayan or the General was behind the Macintosh deaths, but The General hadn't come through on the one chance she'd given him. That left him suspect, but not convicted yet.

Now was time to find out if Wayan would deliver the killer.

She'd been watching for an opening to get closer to either one of these two. This would work brilliantly if Wayan was telling her the truth.

Big *if* there.

Chatton would find the two physicists and interrogate them first to find out if Project Jigu-X was real or not.

She'd also ferret out what made this North Korean woman so valuable.

Then it would be Wayan's turn to prove he could locate the elusive killer that she'd been unable to find, because she was handing over no one until she had proof he could deliver.

But she had a feeling he could do exactly what he claimed.

One thing about Wayan was that he took his commitments to heart. A black heart, but those usually came through no matter what. "You got a deal, Wayan. Now, tell me who they are and where they're going in the States."

Chapter Twenty-Two

TANNER PACED THE lobby of the California Hospital Medical Center, wishing he could trade places with Nick, who was in surgery. Not because he wanted to have a bullet cut out of his chest—been there, done that, got the nasty scar—but deep down he knew Nick was paying the price for a mistake he'd made. The Italian had taken at least three rounds to the chest. His body armor had held until the last one. *Thank God.*

He thumbed a number into his phone and noticed the time was closing in on noon.

"How's Nick?" Sabrina said as soon as she came on the cell phone line.

He might lie to someone else to give them a quick shot of hope, but not Sabrina. "Fifty-fifty odds right now. Depends on how close the bullet is to his lung and if they find fragmentation. Blade's monitoring everything."

"Where's Dingo?"

"Guard duty." Tanner had left Dingo outside the surgery suite, watching for anyone suspicious who might come hunting for Nick.

With Jin missing, the group that attacked them might send someone to recon or try to squeeze information out of Nick. Dingo would make sure any intruder would get his nuts handed to him for even thinking about touching an injured team member.

But who was watching over Jin?

Had she run *only* because she was afraid of an unknown future? Suspicion reared its ugly head and did the cobra side-to-side motion, waiting to strike.

"Have the LAPD backed off?" Sabrina asked, skipping ahead to just one of the problems in this catastrophe.

"LAPD's out of our hair. They're dealing with the body at the scene and were trying to call this a drug deal gone bad. Whoever you tapped at the State Department must have thrown some heavy weight at this. They were hammering us for a while, getting nothing of course, then the one in charge got a call from his boss. He was pissed, but he closed up shop and left."

"Good. We've got a hell of a mess to fix."

She might not sound nurturing, but she'd storm a terrorist camp single-handed to save one of her own, and every person on her teams knew that.

Tanner had hated to be the one to tell her about Nick, but bad as this would sound to an outsider, at least it wasn't Dingo in surgery right now. Sabrina, Dingo and Josh Carrington had history. Went all the way back to childhood together, when they'd been half-pint terrors scavenging for food on the streets of New York.

Sabrina added, "Speaking of cleaning up, I sent a crew to the safe house. It's definitely burned at this point."

No shit. Tanner had to sidestep a wheelchair that was being pushed by a hospital orderly. The woman in the chair reminded him of his grandmother.

I fucking hate hospitals. He stretched out his stride. If he wasn't so wiped-out tired, he'd jog to reach the automated glass doors. He asked, "Just to be clear, the State Department *is* leaving this in our hands, right?"

"They don't want any association with this outside of our secret agreement. In the words of my contact, Slye created this problem and Slye will fix it, or I should expect to be brought in front of a Congressional committee to explain why I brought North Koreans into this country without authority. There will be no acknowledgment of a contract ever having been executed between Slye and the Federal government."

Was there no bottom to the fallout from this? "I swear I'll find them, Sabrina."

"Not your fault, Tanner."

Oh, but he was pretty sure it was. He'd discuss that with her once this was done. "Any intel yet?"

"Nothing useful. We need eyes on the ground *out there* ASAP."

"Agreed." Tanner finally stepped outside where the sky was overcast. He sucked in a deep breath of warm spring air, pollutants and all. Anything smelled better than halls of antiseptic air right now. "But how the fu—" He eyed two kids walking into the hospital with their mom so he kept moving until he found a place where he could talk unguarded. "How did anyone find us at that house, and that quickly? The best Dingo and I can figure is that they had to already have been in position nearby, waiting before Nick showed."

"There has to be a leak in the State Department," Sabrina said in a voice that threatened someone would face a bloody death if she could get her hands on said leak right now. "I called my contact to let him know about Har and Pang being stateside and explained there'd be a delay in delivery due to Har's illness. That would have been about the time you were disembarking the jet. My contact said he'd make arrangements for his people to pick up Pang and Har at the safe house tomorrow morning. He hadn't even called back with the identification of the team he was sending when you were hit."

"Did he at least agree he had a leak when you told him about the attack?"

"No. He basically said if I delivered those Koreans safely, we could put this behind both of us." She snarled, "That bastard. I was willing to burn one of my best west-coast locations just to get the Norks off our hands and you four back here quicker."

If that was a pen Tanner heard her beating against her desk, it wouldn't last long.

He hated the regret he heard in her voice. Every move and decision she made was with the sole intent of putting her people first. It wasn't business to her, not after having her team burned in the UK a few years back when they were sent to rescue Len Rikker, some CIA puke who'd disappeared.

Tanner shuddered, remembering how close they'd all come to dying there.

How about one thought that isn't bloody right now? He kept pushing through the information they had. "Based on the leak being in the State Department, the question is, who wanted those two Koreans?"

"Or all three," Sabrina corrected. "But I haven't told anyone about the woman yet."

Bringing Jin here might have been stupid, but Tanner still couldn't see any way of leaving her to face the DPRK military.

Where the hell *was* Jin? Running. She didn't trust any of them now.

He considered who would want Pang and Har. "The only answer I come up with is North Korea."

"Me, too, but—"

"But what, Sabrina?"

"I don't know ... this is just off. All of it."

Hadn't he and Dingo said that same thing? Tanner's phone dinged with a text. "Hold on a sec."

Dingo's message read: *Surgery over. Nick in recovery. Stable.*

The tight fist squeezing Tanner's chest released. He told Sabrina, "Just got a text from Dingo. Nick's out of surgery and stable."

She murmured, "Thank God." Then the steel was back in her voice. "I've got everyone here working any contacts they have on the west coast. The minute we have a break, I'll let you know. I'll send Ryder and—"

At the risk of pissing her off even more, Tanner interrupted. "Hold up. Ryder is probably of more use to you back in Atlanta. I just need intel and someone capable of guarding Nick. There's nothing anyone else can do that Dingo and I won't already be doing. You know we'll move faster on our own." He understood how much Sabrina wanted to unleash the full power of her resources and make someone pay now, but his gut said it wouldn't help. She'd have to wait.

Just like he would, and every minute was killing him.

An ambulance siren approached from the main highway.

"Fine, I'll send White Hawk to share shifts with Blade on watching Nick." Sabrina made a noise that sounded like a tired sigh. How many hours had she spent worried over her team? Every second they'd been gone. She ended the conversation with, "Keep me posted, Tanner. Call for whatever you need, no matter what or when."

As Tanner ended the call, he realized he was scanning the

parking lot surrounding the emergency center for a threat. What was he looking for? Did exhaustion have him expecting someone to jump from behind a car with a submachine gun?

The ambulance raced up to the entrance and people went into motion. Everything seemed routine.

But he had the sensation of a spider with claws walking up his spine.

He was going to be suspicious of everything until this job was done and his entire team went home.

Alive.

He spent two hours upstairs in the waiting area with Dingo until Nick was deemed in fair condition. He'd spend the night in ICU then move to a room by morning if he kept improving. Two bullets had passed through his arm. One ripped his leg and *four* had pounded his chest. The titanium plates in his body armor had stopped all but the one. Tanner would worship at Sabrina's feet for giving her team the best high-tech gear available.

The one in his leg had been scary. Another centimeter closer to his femoral artery and they'd have zipped him up in a body bag.

"You go ahead to the hotel and grab some sleep," Tanner told Dingo as he forwarded Sabrina's text with the hotel location to Dingo's phone. "I'll cover the first shift and I'll call as soon as Sabrina has any intel."

"No," Dingo said as they both stepped out of the waiting area. "I slept on the flight back. You didn't. Every time I looked up, you were moving around."

Tanner curbed the urge to flinch at the reminder he'd been nodding off on the way to the safe house. Had he been too tired to notice signs of a threat? "I should have used that down time better."

"Stop it, mate," Dingo growled. "No one made a mistake, not even Nick. They were lying in wait for us. It was a fucking ambush. Some Fed screwed us, plain and simple. Go on and get some rest. You're more help alert. Blade's staying tonight, too. I'll call if anything changes."

He was right. But Tanner doubted he'd sleep long. His dreams had been bloody for a few years now, but this time the blood would be spewing from Nick's body as he was hit by rifle rounds and flying backwards.

When Tanner reached the parking lot, he had to think about where he'd parked the Suburban. Which row?

There it was.

He clicked the driver door open, climbed in and slumped in the seat. Everything from the past forty-eight hours hit him with the force of a steel-fisted punch. He would be content to sleep right here, right now. If he didn't get moving, that's exactly what would happen, but the team needed him rested and ready to roll.

In the next minute, he drove out of the parking lot and found the interstate, headed for the hotel. Traffic wasn't bad for almost three in the afternoon, considering this was Los Angeles. What day was it? Tuesday?

His skin prickled with warning.

Adrenaline pushed into his body from some reserve he hadn't expected to have. He always checked his mirrors for someone following, but nothing appeared out of the ordinary behind him.

He tensed, reaching toward his shoulder holster ... that was empty. He'd left his HK Tactical in the console to minimize the problems they already faced racing into a hospital with a gunshot victim. They knew they'd be searched once law enforcement arrived, and Sabrina needed time to arrange clearance for their weapons, so they all didn't end up hauled to jail.

He fingered the console as he heard the word, "Don't."

Cold metal touched his neck. A fucking gun. One of *his* fucking guns.

Worse?

The light-blue eyes full of apprehension that met his in the rearview mirror belonged to Jin.

She clutched a Glock 17 that should still be in the duffel in the rear of the SUV. She'd handled herself like a pro the two times he'd seen her fight, but Tanner wasn't staring into the cold eyes of a woman capable of gunning a man down at point-blank range.

Tanner kept one eye on the road but kept coming back to the mirror to meet her gaze. Those eyes couldn't play poker if her life depended on it. And Tanner had figured something out. She'd started all-out fighting the guy back at the safe house *only* when she thought he was going to shoot Tanner. Jin might be playing tough, but he knew she didn't want him dead.

She was terrified and probably waiting on him to make a move to take the Glock away from her. That had crossed his mind, but he dismissed the idea on two counts.

First, if he scared her, she might squeeze her fingers out of natural reaction, which would include the one fidgeting on the trigger.

Second, he might get her to talk if he let her think she had the control here.

"What the hell is going on, Jin?"

"There is much I need to tell you."

"You think?" Snarling at her was the wrong tone to take, but he'd run slap out of any good intentions. "I've got a friend who just went through surgery who's still critical, two physicists missing and the State Department wanting to stomp everyone connected to this fiasco. Yeah, there's a lot to explain, starting with why you're holding a fucking gun on me."

"I just want you to listen to me."

"Well, you've got my attention, ninja."

"I am not a ninja."

"Whatever." He yanked his gaze from the rearview mirror and changed lanes to pass a slow car. The longer he looked at her, the more he wanted to throttle her. He'd been torn up worrying about her out there alone with someone evil looking for her.

"I am sorry about your man."

"I'll tell him if he lives." He lifted a hand slowly to rub his eyes then put it back on his lap. The fact that she allowed him to even move his hands was a sign that she was not trained for this, nor was she prepared to follow through on her threat. Didn't she realize how dangerous it was to pull a gun and not be ready to use it?

Do you want to clue her in on that, asshole?

"We must—" she started.

Flashing blue and red lights raced past them. LAPD headed to another crime scene.

The gun shook against his neck. Hell.

Tanner brought her attention back to him. "We must what?"

"We must find Pang and Har."

"First off, there is no *we*, babe. I'm not stupid enough to make the same mistake twice with you." He cut his eyes at her then back to the road. "I've had some time to think on all this. Everything went to shit as soon as you showed up at the Ryugyong Hotel. Then we get to the safe house and someone's waiting to ambush us. Who are they and why are you helping them?"

"You fool. I am the one who saved you and your men. I am not helping those people."

She thought she had a right to be pissed off? He'd set her straight. "Like you showing up with Pang and Har wasn't about needing us to get you out of North Korea?"

"I did not say that."

"That's because it's the truth, something you're not acquainted with, are you?"

"I am not the liar you make me out to be."

"But you did lie about why you wanted to come here, didn't you, Jin? You had no plans to defect, right?"

"Yes and no."

"It's a yes *or* no answer," he growled, tired of playing mind games, tired of waging war with an unknown enemy and just plain tired. "You know what? I'm done." He was pretty sure someone was using a baton to pound the inside of his skull. Maybe she was innocent in all this, but he couldn't spend the time finding out. He took the next exit, slowed down and turned right. "I don't know what your game is, but I'll give you one free piece of advice. Put the gun down, turn yourself in, tell us the truth about why you're here and they may go easy on you if we get Pang and Har back."

Did she just sigh?

"Listen to me, cowboy. I have been waiting to be sure of whose side you are on before I say too much."

"I'll make that easy. I'm not on your side."

"That is too bad since you need me. Your country needs me."

That was it. He whipped onto the shoulder and shoved the gearshift into park, swinging around to face her. "So now you're going back to the defection plan? You think we need one more freakin' scientist?"

"I told you. I. Am. A. Researcher!"

"I don't fucking care."

"You should." Fire snapped in her gaze.

"The only value you have right now is if you tell us how to find Pang and Har. Beyond that, we don't need another *researcher*."

She leaned in, pushing that damned gun against his neck. "I am not just a researcher either."

"Big surprise. Another fucking lie."

The end of the gun shook against his neck, but not from fear. She yelled at him, "You don't need me to *find* Pang and Har, cowboy. You need me to *stop* them."

The way she said that raised the hairs on his arms. "What are you saying?"

Maybe it was the change in his voice to a calm tone or maybe she was terrified about more than he'd realized, but her next words came out in a shaky voice.

"They were not kidnapped. Your team did what no one in North Korea could. Pang and Har are not here to defect. You brought in two men who are part of a plan to destroy your country."

Pang and Har were terrorists. *Fuck. Me.*

Chapter Twenty-Three

JIN'S ARM ACHED even though she had it propped on the back of the cowboy's seat. "I will help you, but not if you turn me over to your government."

"You won't shoot me."

"Do not underestimate me, cowboy. We both want to save something for different reasons, but trust that my need is as great as yours." She had to make him see. Had to find a way to cut through his suspicion and make him really listen.

Now that Pang and Har were gone, locking her up would be as bad for America as it would be for her. She swallowed hard. "I was trained to fight and to withstand torture. I can assure you that if you trick me into being captured, I will tell you nothing about the people behind Pang and Har."

"In other words, you'd give aid to those willing to cause the loss of innocent lives."

That's what I'm trying to prevent, foolish cowboy. How much could she say? What would he believe? "I have never harmed an innocent person intentionally, but if you prevent me from saving the one I came here to save from dying, then your country will suffer an equal fate."

"Who're you working for?"

She shook her head and her eyes lost focus for a second. God, she wanted to close them. Her head ached from lack of sleep—and probably from not eating. From racing to escape the soldiers back home, from panic over flying, from being attacked tonight. The list just kept getting longer.

Her destiny had never been her own to choose, but suddenly she felt so small. Too small for the task ahead of her. Her stomach ached from hunger, but she could not keep food down if she tried.

Get hold of yourself and focus. She gripped the gun tighter. "I will help you, but I want your word you will not hand me over to anyone who will lock me up while we search for Pang and Har."

She started to say more but held off until she got his agreement. She needed that agreement. Had to have it. This was for his country as much as for her sister.

"Why would you accept my word?"

Because you're the only man of honor I've ever met. "You said you never give your word unless you intend to follow through. You gave it to me on the boat and you brought me here."

"You would just accept that?"

"From you? Yes."

He reached up and scratched his head, looking out at the dark night. "I can't do that. I have a duty to uphold."

Stubborn mountain. "What about a duty to protect your people?"

"That's what I'm talking about."

"You would arrest me knowing I am the only hope for stopping an attack on your country?"

"Ah, so it's a bomb, huh?"

She wished. That would be easier to stop. "No, it is not nuclear."

He shrugged. "We'll find these people. We're better at protecting national security than you give us credit for."

That was probably true, if there were more men like this cowboy. But it was not enough to risk so much on. She shook her head again. "You assume this is a normal terrorist situation."

"There are no *normal* terrorist situations," he snapped, leaning forward so quickly she sucked in a breath and jerked the gun.

That caused him to freeze and speak calmly. "Easy there."

Jin felt herself go dizzy at what she'd almost done. Her heart jumped all around in her chest. "Do *not* move like that or they will be cutting bullets out of you." She spat the words, but her voice caught, and she clamped her lips shut. What if she'd actually shot her mountain?

He studied her, that stubborn mind of his working. His eyes softened and the devil slid into his gaze to taunt her. "Would you care if you shot me, Jin?"

He was doing that on purpose to make her jumpy. It was working, but she couldn't let it. Couldn't let him be more important than her mission. "Just as I told you in the tunnels, I am only concerned because you are of no use to me dead."

"Liar."

How did he know? "I want your word."

"I still haven't heard anything to convince me."

She took a deep breath, weighing how much to give him. How much would it take to convince this man to give her a small bit of his trust? She let the breath out and hoped what she said would convince him. "Pang and Har were trained as physicists to do their duty once they were called upon. That is why they were sent here." His face drew into a hard frown, and she nodded. "All I will tell you now is that without my help you will *not* find them before they unleash something on this country. It will last a long time and your people will never recover from it."

"Jee-sus, Jin. What the hell is it?"

"You know my price and we have maybe two days before they activate their project."

"Then tell me now what is going to happen."

"Not until I have an agreement."

Those clear blue eyes of his held her gaze prisoner through the tense silence. He was also weighing a decision, just as she'd expected. Accepting his word was a risk, but everything about her plan had involved gambles and the possibility of an ultimate sacrifice.

There was a very good chance she would die within two days. She wanted to ask, *would you care if that happened, cowboy?* Of course not. She was not American. Not Korean. No one wanted a half-breed.

If not for her intelligence, she would have no value anywhere.

The cowboy scratched his chin where his skin was dark with the shadow of a new beard. "What's your dog in this race, Jin?"

"I don't understand. What dog?"

"Who is it you're doing this for?"

Giving him too much information would be dangerous. "Why is that important?"

"If you're helping a terrorist, then I won't give you my word."

Hope flared in her chest at the hint of his cooperation. "I am here to save my sister. She was brought here three years ago. She has no idea that they plan to use her, then kill her." Patty had been marked as disposable when they were children. Jin had spent many late hours sneaking around to find out anything she could after Patty had been brought to the US. Blood had frozen in Jin's veins when she'd heard the plan that included killing her sister.

Jin would find a way to protect her sister, but if she failed, and odds were good that she might, she would be stuck here and would die along with everyone else.

Either way, as the Americans would say, she was screwed. "What will it be, cowboy?"

"Here's my deal. If you can convince me we need you to find Pang and Har, I'll give you my word not to hand you over until we find them. No promises after that, because I won't be in control of what happens to you."

That should have given her relief, but one look at him told her she had no reason to celebrate. He would not break his word, but giving it was causing him anguish that she regretted.

Before she could start explaining anything, he said, "Now that we have a business deal, drop the gun so I can drive to a hotel and get some rest. You do know I could have taken it from you at any point?"

She would have lied had the truth not been so obvious after watching him in North Korea. "Yes."

Pulling the gun away from his neck, she sat back while he put the SUV in gear and drove away.

A hotel.

She hadn't thought past gaining his agreement.

The city swept past her window, blurred colors and tall buildings.

What would happen at the hotel? Would he offer her shelter

there? Would she stay there with him? And if she did, what would he want as payment?

All men expected favors from a woman, especially those who gave up anything in return. She wouldn't be so concerned right now but she'd kissed this one and hadn't forgotten the feel of his lips on hers.

Would this man take advantage of her?

No. He was not like that, plus one look at him back in Seoul after he'd shed all his combat gear and showered was all she'd needed to realize this man could have his choice of women. Yes, he had deep-blue eyes and dark brown hair she found attractive, but those physical attributes were not as appealing as his confidence.

Any woman would be drawn to a man such as him.

Even her.

Especially her. The men she'd been around had no backbone when it came to standing up for a woman or treating them as an equal. They would never have listened to her in the tunnels or brought her along when she hadn't been part of the original plan.

Confidence was attractive and this cowboy's every move and action embodied it.

She'd thought about that kiss over and over.

She shouldn't think of it—shouldn't dwell on it—after what happened to the one person she'd shown attention four years ago.

Her superiors had found out she'd become involved with a young man in her lab. When they'd met secretly at night, he liked to call himself Ben, the name he'd chosen for when they escaped to America. She'd made plans, hoping to bring her sister to live with them.

But someone had figured out that she actually cared for Ben.

She and Ben were taken to a place deep underground where she was made to watch as one of the Orion Hunters swung a sword and cut off Ben's head.

"Jin!"

Her head snapped around at the sharp order. She sucked in a gulp of air. "What?"

"Why are you breathing like you're having another panic attack?"

"I am fine." But she laid the gun down on the seat so she wouldn't accidentally discharge it.

Bo parked at the entrance to a tall hotel and said, "Guess I don't have to tell you to sit tight, ninja."

"My name is Jin. That is more than you have given me. I doubt Bo is your real name."

He had opened his door and stepped out, but he paused and stuck his head back in. "You didn't negotiate for my real name in the deal."

Then he went inside. A few minutes later he returned with a small shopping bag.

Once he parked the car, he opened the back door and without asking, reached across her to get the gun she'd used. He returned it to the duffel bag in the rear.

When she stepped out, her legs felt like cooked noodles. She held the door for a moment to gain her footing. "Where will I stay?"

"With me."

Jin searched the area around them, trying to come up with another option. She'd been hiding in the back of Bo's huge vehicle since last night, and hated the thought of more time there, but the seats were soft enough.

She was standing there, staring at the open car door when Bo put the duffel and the shopping bag down, then pulled her around to him.

She didn't have the strength in her to do anything except concede. "What?"

A balmy wind tossed a lock of hair over his forehead. He studied her with eyes that yielded no insight into his thoughts. His big hand came up to cup her cheek. "I wish I knew everything inside that head of yours, but I understand protecting someone you love. Let's call a truce and get some rest. I give you my word that you'll be safe with me."

The idea that he would harm her had never taken root, but the sincerity of his declaration tugged on her heart. If she was not careful, she would make a big mistake with this man.

She nodded. "Thank you."

They entered the hotel together, not stopping until they reached the elevator. Once inside, she asked, "What did you buy?"

"A few incidentals for you ... unless you have luggage I haven't seen?"

She'd held a gun on him, and he bought her things? What man did that?

She followed him off the elevator on the tenth floor and entered a room with two large beds and a sitting area with a desk. Her entire apartment was not this big.

She stayed next to the door after he'd closed it. He walked over to drop his duffel in the middle of one bed. He flicked a look over his shoulder at her, held her gaze, then dug into his bag.

When he walked back to her, he handed her a T-shirt. "It's clean. We both need to shower. Should be soap and shampoo in there." He held up the small shopping bag. "I told a woman in the gift shop that the airline lost your luggage with your bathroom bag and to put whatever she thought you'd need in here."

All at once, it hit her that she'd lost everything. She hadn't had much to begin with, but now she had nothing. Not even her own toothbrush. Tears stung her eyes. *Do not lose your composure over something so ridiculous.*

She felt the weight of his gaze and blinked away her moment of weakness, then lifted her eyes to his, but when the words would not come, she stepped up and hugged him.

He could have just stood there and let her take what she needed, but his arms closed around her.

To be held was such a small thing compared to all that was happening in her life, but she'd forgotten entirely what it was to be held in arms that she knew would protect her. Had not felt that since she was a tiny child.

When she finally regained her composure, she eased away and lifted her eyes to him. "Thank you for ... everything."

Warmth flitted through his expression before he locked down whatever thought had softened his gaze, but his voice had a gruff gentleness to it when he spoke. "Go on and shower so I can."

She carried the bag into the bathroom, spending a moment to take in the size and amenities offered guests. In fifteen minutes, she'd scrubbed every inch of her body, washing away not just the grime from the past twenty-four hours, but the layers of desperation that had grown on her skin over the last three years.

The cut on her scalp stung from the shower water, and later, when she dried her hair.

When she pulled on his gray, short-sleeved shirt, a hint of his scent curled around her, warming her and feeling as intimate as a lover's caress.

She wrapped her hair in a towel and walked back into the room.

He lifted a small leather bag and clothes then swung around and froze.

With a slow sweep, his gaze roamed over her from the towel around her head to the way his shirt clung to her breasts and down to her bare legs.

Heat burned away the exhaustion in his eyes. She shivered in response to the animal hunger prowling behind that gaze. Her body reacted as if he had his hands on her. She should be feeling uncomfortable under that raw perusal, not ... excited.

What was wrong with her?

Jin fidgeted with the T-shirt, unsure what to say or do. "Your turn."

That broke the moment. He grunted something and walked into the bathroom.

By the time he came back out, she sat in the middle of the empty bed and had the towel off her head. The shopping bag probably had a brush or comb in it, but she'd neglected to bring the bag out of the bathroom with her.

She'd been finger-combing her waist-length hair, but the silence pulled her attention to him.

Her cowboy wore a pair of jeans and no shirt. He'd been toweling his hair and let the towel fall around his shoulders.

Even with the reading lamp casting only a soft light over the room, there was plenty to see. His chest and arms were carved with muscle. His skin had the bronze tone of someone who spent time in the sun with his shirt off. Or did that tan go further? He had that look in his eyes again, the one that said he might pounce on her.

Would he?

What would it feel like to have his hands on her body? She hadn't shown interest in any man for over four years. Not when he would face a brutal death for returning that interest. She'd accepted the reality that she'd spend the rest of her life alone unless she ever managed to escape North Korea.

She was out of North Korea, but far from being free.

The room had felt cool just a few minutes ago, but her skin was baking under his sizzling stare. Fine, let him look all he wanted, because she was doing the same.

The silence grew until the cowboy tossed his towel aside.

She let out a pent-up breath, thankful he'd lost interest. If her skin grew any hotter, she'd have to get out of it.

But he hadn't lost interest. He was moving slowly toward her.

Now he had a look on his face like the one she'd seen before she'd kissed him on the boat. That cowboy had a sexy mouth and knew how to use those lips.

Ben had kissed like a *young* man. Sweetly and tentatively.

But this cowboy kissed like a man. Period.

Would kissing him again be so bad? No.

Stupid? Yes.

Her breasts tightened at the memory of that kiss. Her body was begging to be touched, but her body had no more sense than a rock.

The cowboy reached inside his bag, pulled out a comb, then moved to sit on the bed. *Her* bed. She froze.

He was right behind her.

So close she could feel the heat coming off him.

Her heart took off racing again.

"Calm down, Jin. I'm just going to comb your hair."

What?

She felt a small section of her hair being lifted, then the gentle tug of a comb sliding through the strands. He really was combing her hair.

She asked, "Why are you doing this?"

"I used to do it for my little sister when her hair was long."

She hadn't imagined this man with a family. Not after seeing the deadly and powerful side of him. The idea of him caring for a younger sister softened her image of him.

She closed her eyes and enjoyed the moment. Things would no doubt change tomorrow, but for the first time in many years she indulged in the joy of being touched instead of fearing it.

Who was this man really? Would he truly keep his word tomorrow? She had no choice but to risk believing in him for now. She'd never met a man before who had ever kept his word, but she was sitting in America because this man had done so when he could have left her anywhere along the way.

He asked, "Where did you learn to fight the way you do? What's that called? Didn't look like Taekwondo."

He was correct. She'd never been taught any kind of Korean martial arts. "It is called Nindokai."

She had trained long hours to excel, because she had not had a big brother like this cowboy to watch over her.

But she wasn't thinking of him as she would a brother.

Not at all.

The simple motion of the comb through her hair relaxed her. He was close, and his heat drew her. His strength.

What are you doing? She tensed and realized she was leaning against his arm. She tried to move away without being obvious, but the damage was done. He could easily think she was offering some kind of intimacy. He'd stopped combing her hair, so she twisted to look up at him.

He studied her, but she couldn't read the expression on his face. She searched for something to say, but what would it be? *I care about you. But I shouldn't. I trust you. But I don't. Leaning on you feels good. But I can't.* This man stood between her and stopping something worse than an apocalypse, but he'd protected her when he had no idea who she was.

She had yet to tell him much of the truth, and certainly not the entire truth.

One more kiss from a man of honor. A kiss like the one on the boat. She might die in the next two days. She wanted that kiss. Maybe the last she would ever have.

Lifting a hand, she touched his cheek.

He seemed torn between two thoughts, then one of them must have given up because he caught her hand and moved it to his lips to kiss.

She sat there, wanting him to touch her, but stunned at how it made her feel. He kissed her wrist then her arm until she was leaning up to meet him without realizing it.

His mouth covered hers and heat spun into a tornado, churning her insides. He ran a hand into her hair, grasping a handful and drawing her closer. She held his face, smooth where he'd shaved. His tongue slid into her mouth and tortured her with every stroke, then he kissed her with the hunger of a starved man.

The power of his mouth on hers rocked her. Her one relationship had been mild compared to the way her body yearned for this man.

His phone pinged with an alert.

He broke the kiss and dropped his forehead to hers. "Kryptonite."

She sucked in a breath and asked, "What?"

"Nothing." He eased her away from him and got up to check his phone.

He'd moved quickly, but not fast enough to hide the bulge in his jeans. Not his fault. She had reached for him.

What if his phone had not interrupted? Would he have wanted more from her? Then what?

Her conscience had more questions she didn't want to acknowledge, and she had no answer for any of it. She had a goal that was far bigger than her own wishes, so was it wrong to want a moment for herself, just once? One time that she could be happy?

She'd never had that.

Life had given her a brutal education, but the one lesson she'd learned well was that anything she had today could be taken away tomorrow. *Never pass up any chance at happiness.*

He finished reading something on his phone, placed it back

on the desk and took a breath so deep the exhale sounded cleansing. When he returned to the bed, he sat behind her and started combing her hair again as if nothing had happened, but he did say, "I don't want you to worry about spending the night here. You have your own bed to sleep in."

Her shoulders drooped. She'd let her body overrule her mind and blamed it on being so tired she should have fallen on her face already. She'd made a fool of herself with this man, *again*, and now she was too wired to sleep.

What did this cowboy think of her now after she'd kissed him again?

The constant slide of the comb through her hair lulled her, pushed her worries aside, and a few minutes later she was fighting to keep her eyelids open. Maybe *not* too wired to sleep after all.

His voice was softer when he asked, "Nindokai is ... isn't that German martial arts? Why would you choose that?"

He wanted to talk about fighting? She yawned and blinked her eyes, trying to stay awake. "Yes, it is, but that fighting style was not my decision. I have never had a choice about anything in my life." She rubbed her eyes and let another yawn overtake her. "I was taught Nindokai because my superiors felt that would give me an advantage over Koreans taught Taekwondo. They would not expect me to fight a different way."

Her body begged for sleep, but she fought it because it felt so good to have him here, combing her hair. Still, her eyelids were made of lead. She struggled to keep them open.

He kept up the questions. "If you could fight like that, why were you allowing that attacker to take you to the van?"

"What?" she murmured.

"When that guy had you at the van, you weren't fighting him at first."

She drew in a deep breath to answer. "I *wanted* to go with Pang and Har so I could find my sister."

Her muscles were slowly melting.

She never slept soundly, but she was so very tired, and he was being nice. So nice, her mountain showed he was made of honor.

"Why'd you change your mind and fight him when I came after you?" he asked, then his voice came to her from a distance. "Was it because you care about me, Jin?"

Sleep was dragging her into a dark pit. She didn't want to answer his questions. Why wouldn't he stop talking so she could sleep? She mumbled, "Yes, I care for you. He would have killed you if I had not attacked him."

Then she didn't hear another word.

Chapter Twenty-Four

TANNER CAUGHT JIN as she slumped in a boneless pile against his chest, damp hair and all.

She was out cold.

Not exactly cold. In fact, her warm little body was draped all over his very awake one.

He'd been teasing her again at the end, but her reply stunned him. *Yes, I care for you. He would have killed you if I had not attacked him.*

Earlier, in the truck, she'd said she was going after her sister. He hadn't missed that little detail, but he had to be skeptical. Couldn't afford not to be. Now though, he would lay money on a bet that the mostly-asleep Jin had told the truth a few seconds ago about why she'd been going along with the kidnapper to get into the van.

Her sister was not in some Korean prison camp, as he'd originally thought. She was here, in the US, and part of some terrorist plot.

Going with Pang and Har was the next step in Jin's delusional plan to find her sister. Did she think the physicists would just *take* her to her sister? Didn't she realize how dangerous that whole idea was?

Jin must be damned confident in her fighting skills.

But she ruined her own plans to save you.

Wasn't that a kick in the chest? He'd thought once he had her here, showered and relaxed, he could convince her to give up the information she had without going along with her deal to leave her free.

How was he going to hand her over to anyone after she'd risked losing her sister to save him?

He didn't know and he was past the point of figuring out anything until he crashed for a few hours.

If Sabrina called, he'd go at Jin again, but until then he was going to sleep and get back to full speed.

He got up and pulled back the covers, then scooped her up and settled her on the bed, pulling the thick bedspread over her. His hand got caught under all that hair. It wasn't black, but a beautiful mahogany brown. He sifted the drying strands through his fingers, then reached down and brushed it off her face.

What a dog-sucking mess she was in.

She was trying to save her sister.

But she was holding back more than she was sharing. Like the role Pang and Har were playing in an attack on the US.

Once he'd caught enough sleep to think clearly, he'd give her one shot at selling him on her value.

Allie had done a helluva sales job on him when she'd convinced Tanner to stick his neck out for her.

Unless Jin could do a better pitch job than Allie—which he seriously doubted because *that* scientist had been a master at manipulation—Jin would be headed to Atlanta tomorrow for the simple reason that Sabrina needed a bargaining chip right now.

Tanner owed Sabrina first.

Jin sighed softly.

The sound reached in and yanked hard on his heart.

Dammit, Bodine, do not let this woman get to you.

He had a bad feeling it might be too late for that warning.

Chapter Twenty-Five

Pentagon, Washington, DC

THE GENERAL STRODE down the hallway from his Pentagon office to H.P.'s. When he walked in, he shut the door softly and H.P.'s head popped up from where he'd been typing furiously on his laptop. "Yes?"

Covering the three long steps to H.P.'s desk, The General spread his hands shoulder width apart and slapped them on the desk. He leaned down, gritting his teeth at the pain in his back. Miserable doctors couldn't heal him without surgery. That was fine. The pain gave more fire to his words.

"Where are my Koreans?"

"That's not an easy question to answer."

The General kept his deep voice at a quiet level of threat. "You told me we were sending a team to pick them up last night."

"I did send people, but someone ... got there first."

"I. Know. In fact, I heard there were *three* Koreans."

H.P. was genuinely surprised. "The Slye woman said nothing about a third physicist."

"I'm not sure who—or what—the third person is, but I just got an intelligence report that a protective squad was seen escorting two Korean males and one Korean woman from a Gulfstream jet at the Los Angeles airport at the time we were being informed the physicists were stateside."

"I'm on it. I'll find out more—"

"No, I don't want to *know* more. I want all three of them brought in before someone here finds out we brought three North Koreans into this country who have knowledge of nuclear weapons design and turned them loose." The General pushed off the table. "You have twenty-four hours. Find all three or send out a unit that will make this problem go away. Are we clear?"

H.P. nodded, his face as white as his shirt.

Chapter Twenty-Six

JIN WOKE SLOWLY, feeling rested for the first time in longer than she could recall. Her nightmares had come as usual, but ended quicker than normal, or at least it seemed that way. She enjoyed waking slowly, wrapped in a firm cocoon of warmth.

Firm?

Her heart went into overdrive for a second, then she inhaled and recognized the male scent. The cowboy.

It was a rich, alive smell. She opened her eyes and blinked as her vision adjusted. Daylight slipped through the hotel curtains, just enough to see the dark hairs on the broad chest she faced.

The memory of last night caressed its way back into focus. He'd combed her hair. Lulled her into rest.

They had two beds.

Then what was she doing here, wrapped up against him?

That's when she noticed the rise and fall of each breath he took. He had her tucked up against him, arms bulging with muscles holding her so close and ... safe. She hadn't felt safe in a long time, not since she was a tiny child. Long before she was handed off to a couple who had never considered her family, only a pawn to train for their own agenda.

She was wrapped up against this big man who should be in his own bed. But she felt no fear. That was not normal. Something was wrong with her survival instincts. She should move away. Now.

Her mountain mumbled something, and she froze for a second. Was he wearing anything? She took stock of her body. Still in the T-shirt. Nothing felt different, at least physically. She moved her leg and touched cloth. He had on boxers.

Naked other than that.

She started to shift away, and her knee brushed one very awake part of his anatomy. She jerked her leg back, but her crazy body had a completely opposite reaction. Her mouth dried out at the size of him.

All of her was awake now.

What should she do? Take her time moving away so she didn't disturb him?

Does taking your time have anything to do with staying snuggled up against him?

No. Not at all.

Liar.

The truth was, she'd never felt anything like this before. Never been so close to anyone remotely like him.

One big arm was wrapped all the way around her back and hooked under her arm that rested on his shoulder. The palm of his hand dangled so close to her breast. The power and strength in this mountain of a man made her a little dizzy. Made her want.

She watched that hand, imagined it in motion. On her body.

He growled in his sleep and shifted. When he did, his palm brushed her nipple. Heat shot through her, straight to her womb.

She exhaled an involuntary little moan and moved closer, her body taking over her brain and going after what it wanted.

His hand curved around her breast as if it had invited his fingers over for a visit. She didn't have large breasts and had never thought of herself as so sensitive, but she was breathing hard just waiting, wanting him to do something. His fingers twitched, but nowhere close to where she wanted them.

For so long she'd missed being touched and feeling the comfort of human contact. But more than that, she longed to feel like a woman. She hadn't had much experience, but being pressed against him, having his hands on her body, made her remember. Yearn.

Without thinking, she kissed his chest.

He groaned and his hand closed on her breast, fingers massaging gently.

She shivered. His touch was making her wet, making her want things she shouldn't from this man. Her next breath came out on a sound of bone-deep need, and his fingers stilled along with his breathing.

He didn't say a word and neither did she for the next thirty seconds.

Should she pretend she'd been asleep?

His hand moved to her hip and stayed there. She felt a wash of shame that made her face hot. What would he think of her now? That she was the whore Pang had painted her to be?

She should be thankful he hadn't gone further, but she was fighting not to cry over the loss of his touch.

"Jin?"

"Yes?"

His deep voice was raspy from sleep. "Good morning."

It had been for a moment. She murmured something that could be interpreted as good morning with a hefty dose of embarrassment.

"I didn't mean to touch you."

"I understand." She'd said that in a brittle tone but not because she didn't believe him. Just the opposite. She'd started it *again*, and even though he was proving to be a gentleman, it didn't change the pinch of disappointment in her. *Were you trying to seduce him?* No. She hadn't meant to do that. Last night she'd felt what she thought was real desire in his kiss, and her body wanted to be desired. Her mind wanted it. All of her wanted this man's desire. But she must have imagined it.

She was a mess.

She cleared her throat and asked, "So why are you in my bed?"

"You kept having nightmares and I was exhausted. The last time I woke you, it was easier to just stay here."

"I see." She *had* been the one taking advantage of their situation, not him. Suddenly mortified, she tried to push away, but he held onto her.

"Jin?"

"What?" Now she sounded like a shrew, but she needed to go hide in the bathroom and find some of her pride. "I apologize for bothering you."

He chuckled and muttered, "You're definitely bothering me."

The man had a death wish. He should be careful. She was in an accommodating mood right now.

"Let me move, cowboy, and I will no longer impose on you."

"Jin?"

She fisted her hand. "Do not use my name again until you give me one in return."

"Look at me."

"No." If she did, he'd see the depth of her humiliation at fantasizing over him.

"Please."

Had he really said please? She wanted to ignore him, but that was the first time he hadn't ordered her to do something. She had always prided herself on being calm and patient in the face of crisis. Now would be a good time for those qualities to show up.

She took a deep breath for courage, then she turned and leaned her head back to face him.

That was a mistake.

He wasn't attractive. He was gorgeous. The rumpled hair and heavy-lidded gaze actually upped the sexy factor.

He brushed a hand over her hair. "You aren't imposing on me. Well, maybe stompin' all over my sanity, but right now you're not imposing. I like you right where you are."

And there he was, touching her again. She drank in the feeling of his hand smoothing over her hair the way a flower drank in water. He confused her. She confused herself. "You said you did not want to touch me."

"No, I said I didn't *mean* to and should have added, without your permission."

Leaning forward, he kissed her hair, then nuzzled her neck and kissed her throat. "Do I have your permission?"

She shivered, hungry all over for his touch. This was not a wise move. She said, "I thought you did not want to—"

His lips moved to kiss behind her ear. "Did not want to what?"

"Uhm, do this."

He kept kissing his way down her neck to her shoulders.

Her breasts ached, impatient for their turn.

"I love doing *this*," he whispered against her collarbone. His hand had moved back up her side and he raked a finger across the hard tip of her nipple.

She clinched her legs and shook. "We should—"

"That sounds like permission. Is it?" he asked, and the husky sound shimmered through her. He kissed her shoulder and his finger kept toying with her nipple.

She couldn't think when he surrounded her senses and held them captive. Yes, she wanted to scream yes.

Nothing had ever felt so amazing as his hands skimming beneath the T-shirt that had ridden up to her navel.

What was that awful noise dinging and dinging?

His wonderful hands stopped their exploration. He let out a frustrated sound that didn't come close to matching hers. When she opened her eyes, his face was right in front of her.

"I wish I could blame this on you," he said. "But this was my fault." His phone was vibrating and dancing across the desk. "I'm sorry."

She was working to slow her breathing. She was starting to sound like Har. "You're sorry we did this?"

His eyes filled with a tenderness that surprised her, considering the tent in his boxer shorts—she could feel the evidence poking her—and that stupid phone was having a fit.

"Don't misunderstand me, darlin'," he started. "I love touching you and kissing you, but I'm not supposed to be doing this. We haven't come to any agreement, I still don't know what your real agenda is, and only a bastard would be touching you right now with no idea how any of this is going to work out. I still have a job to do, and you have plans that you're not sharing. Even if I find out you're telling me the truth and we both end up successful, the chances of us ever seeing each other again after this are ridiculously slim."

What could she say to that? Nothing. He was right.

He ran his hand over her hair and kissed her forehead. "Now I feel even more the bastard for not finishing what I started." He shook his head in a way that seemed as though he condemned himself. "Regardless, you deserve better than that."

Extracting his body from their tangle of limbs and covers, he walked over and picked up his phone. When he finished reading and thumbing some keys, he turned to her. "I'm going to find us some food. Will you stay here while I'm gone?"

She nodded, afraid her voice might crack at the emotion tumbling through her. *You deserve better.* No man had ever told her she deserved anything good.

He dressed quickly and started out, turning back to her at the door. "One more thing, Jin."

"Yes?"

"My name's Tanner."

Then he was gone. She fell back on the bed and hugged a pillow to her. Tanner. She liked that.

It fit him. Sounded honorable, like the man.

But right now, her body hurt from wanting him and she wished he'd been just a little dishonorable instead of leaving her with this ache.

Her heart was knocking on her mind with its own concern. One it shouldn't have. Would this morning—and what had happened between them—make any difference to Tanner, or would he hand her over to someone else once she told him why Pang and Har had been sent here? Would Tanner even have a choice?

Pang considered himself a star among his competition, but he *was* replaceable.

Jin was not.

That was why once she found her sister, Jin would take her and vanish. She could admit that she would have opened herself up to Tanner and enjoyed this short reprieve from her real life, but she knew she could not stay with him.

Unlike Pang, she would be hunted to the corners of the earth and anyone close to her would be killed.

She did care about this cowboy, far too much to bring about his death.

Chapter Twenty-Seven

SUNSHINE BACKLIT THE sheer hotel curtains across the room from where Tanner stood talking to Dingo on the phone and watching Jin in the middle of one bed eating her McBreakfast. "How long before you can leave the hospital?"

"White Hawk just showed up. Nick's vitals were looking up an hour ago. He was awake for a few minutes, but they're keeping him heavily drugged. Blade is making a last check on Nick ... wait, here he comes now. We're headed your way."

Tanner told him he had the key to their room then added, "No news from Atlanta yet. As soon as you grab some sleep, we'll hit the ground running."

"Blade traded off with me for a few hours last night and I've eaten. I'm fine for now and I might have someone who can help us."

That would be nice. "Who?"

"A woman who specializes in locating people and items of exceptional value."

"She sounds expensive."

"She is, but I know her."

Dingo never talked about his private life, but just the way he said that told Tanner there was more to this than a business association. "I've got someone, too," Tanner said, his gaze locked on Jin as she handled her food with precise movements. She wore mint-green workout pants that came with a matching jacket. Beneath that, she had on a white T-shirt and socks. The sneakers he'd bought her at Wal-Mart.

art when he made the food run were a half size too large, but they wouldn't fall off.

"And who's that, mate?" Dingo asked, reminding Tanner he still had to decide if Jin was staying or not.

Until he did make up his mind, he had to keep his damn hands off her.

Tanner hedged to buy time with Dingo. He didn't want to do this over the phone. "Think it'll be easier to show you. See you in ten."

"Roger that."

Tanner dropped his phone on the desk and finished his coffee, then tossed the cup in a nearby wastebasket.

Time to be the tough guy. That would be a whole lot easier if he hadn't had his hands full of Jin this morning.

And *that* wouldn't have happened if he'd been in his own bed where he wouldn't have wakened from a dream about Jin to find his hand holding a breast his fingertips still itched to feel again.

He waited for her to finish her food before he broke out his hardass routine.

Jin packed the paper and containers left from her meal back into the bag and folded the top neatly. Everything she did was precise and organized. She sat cross-legged and raised her chin, facing him when she said, "I am ready."

But she wasn't ready. She wore her heart in her eyes for anyone to see. He'd just as soon pick on a newborn foal as lay into Jin.

Tanner stayed across the room where he hoped distance would keep him from sliding off track. He started with the first question that came to mind. "Why aren't you willing to tell us anything about the vicious attack planned on this country?"

"I did not say that!" She propped a fisted hand on each hip. "Do not twist my words."

"You said Pang and Har were here to play a role in an attack. Correct?"

"Yes."

"And you wanted to go with them. Were you going to help with this attack just to find your sister, Jin?" That thought had been badgering him since he'd left to pick up food.

"No. Once I find my sister, and she understands that I am here to help her escape, she and I will prevent the attack and hand everything over to your government."

That sounded simple and justifiable, but not the least bit realistic. "Tell me what they're going to do."

"First we must come to an agreement."

He crossed his arms. "Okay. Now's the time to give it your best shot at convincing me that I need you to locate and/or stop Pang and Har."

She folded her hands and dropped them in her lap. "The people Pang and Har belong to are well organized and very dangerous. They are capable of executing this plan."

"That's not exactly news to me since I was sent over to yank those two out to get them away from your leader."

She waved a hand in a motion that scoffed at him. "See? You do not even realize that the DPRK is not behind this. North Korea will never be as dangerous as the organization who has manipulated your intelligence operations."

Tanner took a step forward. "Who are you talking about?"

Folding her hands in her lap, she said, "Have you ever heard of the Orion Hunters?"

No fucking way. He tested her to see if this really was that bunch of fanatics. "Orion who?"

"Orion *Hunters*. They are an ancient organization who are searching for rare artifacts they believe will reveal Orion's Prophecy and bring about the final conflict."

Yep, she knew who they were, but Tanner wasn't about to let on that he did, too. "Are you're saying these people are here looking for a final conflict?"

"No. You are not listening," she chastised.

Damn, she was cute when she got her feathers ruffled. He rolled his hand in a "go on" motion. "What final conflict?"

"They believe that once they locate five specific artifacts and bring them together a message will form, or appear, that dictates a final conflict in this world. We would think of it as World War III. Now do you understand?"

All too well.

The Orion Hunters were not common knowledge, being that they were a secret society and all, but they had been on the periphery of Slye missions this past year. Czarion was another name that popped up during the same time, but no one in Slye had figured out how Czarion and Orion Hunters were connected.

Tanner was torn between believing that a band of fanatics was behind the kidnapping and attack on their safe house or throwing the bullshit flag. "Prove it's the Orion Hunters behind all this."

Her little jaw jutted out and her eyes warned that she had little tolerance for stupid questions. "If it was so easy to prove, you would have known you were being fooled, but you did not. That's why Pang and Har are here and not in your custody."

Ouch. *Thanks for shoving a blast of salt in that wound.* "What exactly was your role in this, ninja?"

She growled softly at being called ninja but did not correct him this time. "I have been trained to perform research as well as fight, but once the Hunters decided I could be trusted I was also used as a messenger. The DPRK is infested with Orion Hunters, as are other governments," she said pointedly, letting him know the US was not immune to this group. "Over the three years that I carried messages, some information was the truth and some not so much. That is how they were able to deceive your intelligence people when they needed to have Pang and Har transported safely to your country."

His team had done that all right. "What does the DPRK know of this?"

"Our leader is not an Orion Hunter. He will think Pang and Har have escaped to China, the usual way that most defect. Money will be offered for their return, but when the Chinese deny knowledge of this defection our leader will do nothing. He does not want to anger China so he will not expend a great deal of energy on finding Pang and Har."

These Hunters in North Korea were a ballsy bunch to risk getting caught by that leader. "Who put this plan into action?"

"The leaders of the Pyongyang division of Orion Hunters." As she spoke, Jin grabbed her hair, twisted it into a knot of some sort that stayed up on its own. "Once I find my sister, I will give you names, but those names will mean little because they protect themselves through many layers."

"Just how do you intend to stop Pang and Har?"

"Do we have a deal yet?"

He rolled his eyes and waved his hand. "Keep talking."

"Once I understood the Hunters had a plan in mind for the US, I spent every minute of the past three years learning all I could about them. I trained twice as hard to be someone of value to the Hunters for one simple reason—to find my sister and help her escape. They think little of women, but they never waste a resource, even an Amerasian. It was simple to convince them I was honored to have any position. When they realized I was intelligent and ... submissive—"

Tanner snorted. "As if."

"—they began to trust me and give me more responsibility."

"Why didn't you find a way to insert yourself on the original mission?"

She chuckled and the sound surprised Tanner, after seeing her so open earlier. This sound came from a part of her soul that had to harbor something dark. "I said they trusted me, not that they valued me to be of any use here. I had already made up my mind to find a way to leave with Pang and Har, but when I saw soldiers outside my apartment, any question about leaving ended then. I did not think escaping would be quite so difficult."

And it wouldn't have been if Tanner's extraction plan hadn't fallen apart. Or had it been sabotaged? *"Did* you leak the information and undermine our exit strategy?"

"No. I told you the truth. Pang's boss betrayed him." She swept her gaze away from him.

"Why would he do that?"

Her gaze returned to his and shot sparks with every word. "Pang's boss was an evil man. The soldiers found information that pointed the finger at him for Pang and Har going missing."

Tanner had a feeling she knew something about how that information ended up in the hands of the soldiers, but he didn't press it since that had no bearing on anything except the extraction. "He's probably answering questions about you right now."

"He knows nothing about me. I am invisible to him." She stared off for a moment. "It does not matter. He is dead by now."

She'd said that in a hopeful tone. Tanner shrugged. "That's a possibility."

"More than just possible." She returned her gaze to meet his. "Orion Hunters do not allow anyone who betrays them to live."

That would mean her, too.

She definitely couldn't have stayed or gone back, but the State Department might ship her home to North Korea if they didn't allow her asylum.

This was going nowhere and any minute now Dingo would—

There was Dingo's quick double rap.

Tanner stepped over, checked the peephole and opened the door with his body blocking view of the room.

Dingo was saying to Blade, "That head nurse was an earbasher all right."

"Your room's two doors down," Tanner said, offering each of them a keycard.

Blade snatched his. "Stick a fork in me. I'm done." He walked down two doors and disappeared into his and Dingo's room.

That was one person out of the way.

Tanner would rather make this decision with just Dingo. He stepped back from the door.

"We need to—" Dingo had stepped into the room and stopped. "She's back?"

Tanner shut the door. "Yep. I found her in the Suburban when I drove it here."

If Dingo had any thought on that, he didn't share it. "You told Sabrina yet?"

"Not yet."

Dingo was rarely pissed, but the perception of leaving Sabrina's ass in the wind with the government did it. "Call her. Now."

Tanner held up his hands. "I'm just as concerned about getting Sabrina out of a jam as you. We'll call her *if* you still think that's a good idea in the next few minutes."

Dingo considered that and nodded. "Explain."

Tanner filled him in on what Jin had told him about Pang and Har.

The only reaction Dingo had was a sharp lift of his eyebrow

at learning their team had smuggled terrorists into the country, then a glint of surprise at hearing about the Orion Hunters. He muttered, "I'll be gobsmacked."

If that means blown away, call me gobsmacked, too. "Jin claims she's the best chance we have at finding—and stopping—Pang and Har."

"Why?" Dingo asked in Jin's direction.

Pushing a few stray hairs off her face with both hands, she said, "The first thing you must do is find the doctor who would have treated Har or is still treating him. The Hunters would not risk losing one of the physicists."

Tanner asked, "Do you have any idea what might be wrong with him? He wasn't responding to nausea medicine."

"No, I do not know, but I would not be surprised to find that Pang had poisoned him at some point once we arrived in Seoul. He may have been told that one of them needed to pretend to be ill so that they would not leave Los Angeles before the Hunters found them."

"Pang was searched."

"All cavities? Did you notice the ring on his right hand? A simple ring but if it was hollow there would have been room to hide something."

She had a point.

Shit. Even Har's illness was part of the damn plan. Tanner asked, "No one could pretend to be as sick as Har was. You think Pang poisoned him. Why?"

"Because Pang's ego would not allow him to share his glory with anyone. He believes the Hunters will reward him greatly for this. He is too full of himself to realized they will not allow him to live any more than they will allow my sister to live once she has completed her part of this."

"Her sister's a terrorist, too?" Dingo said to Tanner as if he'd conjured these women up.

"No, she is not!" Jin answered. "She does not know what they are planning. She is a—"

Dingo and Tanner both said, "What?"

Jin's face lost its animation, and she softly reminded him, "We do not have a deal yet."

"What deal, mate?" Dingo was giving Tanner a hard stare again.

"Jin says she'll help us if we don't hand her over to the State Department while we look for Pang and Har."

"Bullshit."

Jin crossed her arms. "Then you will not find them or stop them in time."

"We can call in Homeland Security, the FBI and law enforcement everywhere to find Pang and Har," Dingo said, echoing Tanner's words from last night.

"You will only succeed in the Orion Hunters using their resources to create diversions that will divide as many forces as you call up. And you will have to go public about having kidnapped two North Korean physicists. I doubt your government will want to admit to that."

Did she know that was a hot button right now or was she just doing a damn good job of guessing? Tanner let Dingo have a go at this to see just what Tanner had been up against since last night. Maybe Dingo could figure out an angle that Tanner had missed.

"You don't want to play hardball with us," Dingo warned.

"Are all American men fools?" she asked the room at large then swung that riled gaze at Dingo. "I am offering to *help* you, if you help me. I want to find my sister before she has to do something she will not live long enough to regret. I do not trust any of you to care about what happens to her. If you want my assistance, all you have to do is allow me to remain free to search with you until we find her and stop the attack. Is that so unreasonable?"

When Dingo glanced his way, Tanner gave him a raised eyebrow look to say, "She makes a sound argument."

Not ready to agree so easily, Dingo argued, "You know your way around North Korea, but over here *we* are in familiar territory. What can you do here that we can't?"

Straightening her back, she calmly dusted nonexistent crumbs from her shirt and looked up at both of them, and Tanner knew she'd been waiting patiently to lay down her bargaining chips.

Jin said, "To begin with, I know where they would have taken

Har last night and I *also* know about your country. You have several Chinatowns in different states. The first one was here in Los Angeles. That is where the Hunters would find a doctor for Har, but it will not be just any Asian doctor. It will be one who is loyal to the Orion Hunters."

Tanner silently agreed that she had a point there. He gave her a tiny move of his head to encourage her to continue.

"Even if you have a translator, they will not know if they are speaking to a doctor who belongs to the Hunters or not. In addition to English, I can speak Korean and four more Asian languages, plus six ancient languages. If you allow me to be locked up now, I can promise you will not find Pang or Har in time."

And that was the reason Tanner had misgivings about handing her off to the State Department.

Dingo showed no reaction other than to say to Tanner, "Step outside with me, mate."

Once they were out in the hallway with the door closed, Dingo asked, "The Orion Hunters? That's who is behind this and not the DPRK?"

Tanner nodded. "If she's telling us the truth, Pang and Har are key to the attack being planned, and we don't have much time."

"We can't bring in Homeland Security until we have a specific threat and an idea of a location for it."

"That's what I figure."

Dingo scratched at a beard that had grown longer over the past three days. "This is why you haven't told Sabrina about *her*."

"Right. Sabrina's butt is in a sling already. If we tell her that we have Jin, she'll have to hand her over. I'm betting, in our shoes, she'd leave Jin free to give us a chance at finding Pang and Har. But if she did that and things go bad, Sabrina would fall on the sword before she'd let either of us take the blame for it. I'm not putting her at any further risk even if it means she cuts me loose when this is done."

Tanner hadn't considered that until the words were out of his mouth, but he'd put her in this spot. If someone landed in jail when the dust cleared, it wasn't going to be Sabrina.

Nodding, Dingo said, "Right you are, mate. I don't want her in that position either. What's your plan?"

"We have to find the doctor who treated Har or still has Har as a patient. Once we give Jin our agreement to let her stay with us, we'll start with locating that doctor."

"Think she's just going to take our word?"

Tanner didn't want to make it sound like more was going on than should be in this situation, but they were on a short time frame and Dingo needed to know that this would work. "She'll accept my word."

That met with stony silence, which Tanner expected so he explained, "I told her on the boat that I'd take her with us and, because I did bring her, she's decided to believe what I tell her if I give her my word."

Dingo's white-blond hair glowed against his tanned skin. He didn't look like anyone Tanner would normally hang out with back in Texas, but Dingo could change like a chameleon and wear a Stetson in Amarillo with the same confidence he sported punk hair in New York.

In fact, that blond wasn't his natural color. Tanner had seen the roots a few times.

Dingo said, "I believe in givin' a bloke a fair go if it makes sense, and what this Jin says does. But, if she does anything suspicious that gets me thinking she's gamin' us, I'll be the first one to cuff and stuff her in a ride to Atlanta."

"Agreed." Tanner wished that had a confident ring to it, because he knew as sure as he was standing here that Jin was hiding something.

Dingo asked, "Has she given any specifics about the terrorist attack?"

"No. Refuses to share anything until we have a deal. But she did confirm that Pang and Har were the two leading physicists on Project Jigu-X. She did say it's not a nuclear weapon, but she also says it's far worse."

"That's hard to imagine."

"Yep. I have nothing more to go on than a gut check, but I think most of what she's telling us is the truth."

"Most is something to start with." Dingo shifted his gaze

down, thinking. "They were trying to grab *her* at the safe house, too."

"Right." Tanner watched a family from the other end of the hall, but they got on the elevator. He scratched his chin and thought out loud. "Why were they after Jin?"

"I don't know. She may play a bigger role in all this than we realize."

Tanner had considered the same thing more than once since meeting her, but his judgment was tainted by another female scientist who'd colored the truth according to the picture she needed to paint.

If Dingo was having the same thought, though, maybe Tanner wasn't as jaded in his thinking after all.

Tanner checked his watch. "O-seven-twenty. I'll make the deal with her, and we can start searching for the doctor in Chinatown in another hour."

"I may have someone who can narrow that down quickly."

"You mentioned a woman earlier. She some kind of private eye for the rich?" Tanner asked, hoping Dingo would offer more.

"No. She's a little more skilled than that. Someone who could be a field agent for the CIA."

"No shit. How well do you know her?"

Dingo did that thousand-yard stare and said, "We have history."

"You need to shower and shave before you tap that resource?" Tanner chuckled.

"More like I need to wear body armor to meet with her."

Chapter Twenty-Eight

DINGO DIDN'T HURRY his steps as he walked into the park where Valene Eklund waited near an oak that had stood in that spot for many decades.

Her five-foot-four height looked taller in black boots that were snug around her calves. She wore jeans made to hug the slope of her hips and a blousy white shirt buttoned up just far enough to shield breasts he could still see in his mind. Perfect alabaster mounds beneath his dark fingers.

Large areolas that were dark pink and sweet.

Blond hair that reached her collar sprung in different wavy directions. If she had on a bathing suit and sandals, she could pull off surf bum chic, especially since she could ride a curl with the best of them. The hair and clear skin came from her Nordic father. The velvet brown eyes and thick dark brown lashes had probably come from the mother Valene wouldn't talk about.

One look at her and a man couldn't think past his dick. She was pure sex on wheels. Or on heels. His damn mind chose that moment to recall her wearing four-inch stilettos one night.

Not another shred of clothing. Just those midnight-blue shoes.

He was one sick bastard to torture himself with that image.

Seven years was a long time.

It was forty-nine years in a dog's life and even longer when it came to missing a woman.

Hard to feel bad for himself when he was the one who'd walked away. Stomped away. To say he was surprised when she'd returned his call today was an understatement of ginormous proportions. Not that she'd spent much time on the message she'd left.

Just a terse order for what time to meet her and the GPS coordinates.

"Val." He stopped six feet away. Close enough to talk.

Far enough to protect his balls.

"Does that punk haircut get you laid?"

Maybe not far enough away after all.

She had proud cheeks and the keen eyes of a raptor observing a prey and trying to decide if it was worth the flight down to kill it. Her agreeing to meet him made sense now.

She wanted to hash out their history.

Not that he didn't owe her a chance to shred him with that tongue of hers, and maybe a round of kickboxing, but that would have to wait for another time. "This is serious, Val. National security at stake."

"How's this any different than last time?"

Last time, Dingo had stirred up a mafia hornet's nest when he figured out a group from Chicago was running arms for a connection in Los Angeles.

The difference was that he had no intention of allowing Val to become a target again. Not that he ever let her know she'd been one before. She would have stormed into the middle of it and gotten herself killed.

He'd had one way to keep her safe after that.

Walk away.

The mafia group was no longer a threat, or he wouldn't be back now. "I need some help finding people fast."

She looked up, tapping her chin. "If I recall correctly, and I'm sure I do, the last time I helped you find someone I was told to 'stay the fuck out of your business and away from you'."

"I didn't ask you to do that." That was the day he'd walked to draw the dogs off her trail.

She dropped her chin along with her voice. "You didn't have to, Dingo. There was a time when we didn't need to spell everything out to each other."

I guess we are *going to get into this now.* "There were reasons, Val."

She lifted a hand. "I am not here to give you a chance to relieve your guilty conscience at treating me like some weekend bang."

"I never treated you that way," he growled, feeling the phantom ache from a blade slicing up his heart.

She ignored him, taking a step forward as she continued. "My skills are worth far more than they were before. I've had seven years to groom resources that your international intelligence people would envy, if one particular agency could operate on US soil. Not that any of you spooks care about things like rules."

Good to see her ego was as healthy as ever. "I'm not a spook."

She paused and cocked her head to one side. "Oh? What are you then? You appear and disappear like a smoke ring puffed in the wind. You're trained and armed better than a CIA agent, and here you are back again looking for intel. What do I call you ... other than a heartbreaker?"

Her eyes had lost the arrogance they'd taken on with her little speech. Her walls slipped and the pain climbed up to peek out.

Just twist that blade a little more.

He wanted to cup her face and feel her skin again, tell her how much he'd missed her. But this was not the time and the last thing he wanted to do was reconcile then walk away again.

Because he would leave the minute he had what he needed, to avoid any chance of drawing attention to her. Once had been frightening enough. He hadn't been sure he could keep her safe.

Still, he owed her the words. "I'm sorry, Val."

Pain hovered in her gaze for only a second then her walls snapped back into place. Locks slammed shut. The doors were barred. "What do you want? The clock is running, and my fee is higher than last time."

He tried to breathe past the invisible dagger in his chest. Lives were at stake. He could do this again. "I have to find a doctor in Chinatown. He treated a Korean male last night who had severe nausea."

"That's it?"

Trust was something Dingo had pieced out in tiny bits over the years to anyone other than Sabrina and Josh. But at one time, he'd trusted Val more than anyone. He hoped he still could. "The sick guy was smuggled in from North Korea yesterday because he was believed to be trying to defect and give up details on their nuclear program."

"Oh, so, someone finally realized the Norks are ahead of schedule." She huffed out a disgusted little sound.

"Anyhow, he was grabbed when he arrived, but as it turns out he's part of a terrorist op."

"Oh, gawd. Who the hell was stupid enough to allow that to happen?"

When Dingo didn't reply, Val's eyes bugged out. "You are kidding. You did this?"

"Not by myself," he defended.

"Of course not. It takes a village to do something idiotic."

"There's more to it than that." He raised his hand to stop her before she got rolling good. "Don't ask me things I can't tell you."

She leveled a look full of disgust at him. "Let's not go there."

"Do you think you can find the doctor?"

"I'm sure I can but let me guess. You need to find him today not in a week or two, right?"

"I need him yesterday."

"Then you're going to have to give me more information. Something beyond one person was sick and the other is a doctor. Why would he have to go to Chinatown?"

That was the trouble with smart women. Tough to feed them "just enough" information. Dingo glanced around. Kids still played across the lawn. A middle-aged woman walked three dogs eighty feet away.

No one was close enough to hear anything.

This couldn't be any worse a decision than keeping Jin secret from Sabrina, right? His conscience kept silent, holding out on him. "Here's the thing, Val. What I'm going to tell you has to stay secret for your own good as much as this mission. There's a group called Orion Hunters who are behind this. It's a strange bunch that's scattered over different parts of the world. The Orion group in North Korea set up this whole fiasco to get Har and another physicist into the country. Har came in deathly ill and is believed to have gone to a doctor in Chinatown who is also part of the Orion Hunter network. That's the doctor we have to find."

"We?"

Dingo held firm. The less he said the better. "If you can't do it or don't want to, just say so, but please do not mention hearing anything about the Orion Hunters."

"This sounds bad."

For the first time since walking up to her, she showed a glimpse of the woman who had held him close at night and kept the demons at bay.

The one he'd never expected to want more than life.

He rubbed his hand over his mouth. "It is bad. If we don't figure out what they have planned, it's going to kill a lot of people. The only lead we have is finding this doctor. But I don't want you to get caught in the middle of this where you could get hurt. I just need the information."

Longing waded in between them, threatening to drag them both across the last foot of space to each other. A magnetic pull that had slammed them together and into bed before Dingo had realized he'd stepped off a cliff into deep waters with her. She was an addiction he hadn't been able to give up until it was almost too late.

"Val, I wish—"

She pulled herself back into lockdown fast. "I'll find your doctor, you'll pay my fee and disappear again. We'll both be happy. As for sorry, I don't care anymore."

He actually wished she didn't so he could stop bleeding over how he'd hurt her. "Agreed."

Chapter Twenty-Nine

RED, GREEN, AND yellow neon lights outlined buildings everywhere Jin looked in Chinatown as she walked and searched. She might enjoy a visit here when she wasn't watching her last hope for freedom slip through her fingers.

Three doctors down and only one left to locate.

If this last one was not an Orion Hunter, then what?

"Keep the hood pulled snug so no one sees your face," Tanner reminded her.

She looked at him through the corner of her eye. "How close are we?"

He was studying the map on his phone and kept his voice down as they passed through the crowded streets. "That last address should be up around the next corner."

Whole dead ducks hung by their necks in windows. Pungent smells of meats and spices drifted out from the small grocery where she could see fresh fish displayed on ice.

It smelled of her childhood.

Not all bad memories.

Tanner put his hand on her back to guide her around the corner and she didn't flinch this time. She'd fought off Pang after he'd cornered her late one night in the lab, and a soldier who'd caught her walking home alone when she was younger. An Amerasian was fair game. No one would come to her rescue. She'd used her defense skills both times, not touching their faces to give them proof to show to a superior that she'd attacked them for no reason. That would result in her receiving a beating.

No, she'd bruised their egos and family jewels with one strike.

As much as Pang wanted to hurt her back, he would never

submit to having his genitals examined for proof of an attack, nor admit a woman had taken him down with one hit.

She still woke up at night fighting off phantom hands.

Not last night.

In only a few days, she'd become accustomed to Tanner's hands.

No, that wasn't it. She'd become accustomed to trusting his touch. She let Tanner leave his hand at her back and allowed herself this small pleasure of pretending to walk with someone who cared for her.

Now if she could only pretend she still carried hope that this next stop would be the one to give them a lead to Har. "Your friend could find no more doctors?"

Tanner stopped fiddling with his phone. "Four doctors fit your criteria of Korean and potentially other," he said, referencing Orion Hunter as other. "There's the place up ahead."

The sign she'd been searching for came into view, but there was no indication this doctor was an Orion Hunter follower.

Jin wiped her damp palms on her pants. What would Tanner do if she did not find the doctor?

This had been the value she offered him.

In the routine manner of their earlier stops, Tanner paused so she could walk ahead and enter alone. He would step inside fifteen seconds later, because he clearly didn't trust her to tell him the truth. But from what she'd gleaned, he only understood basic Korean words and phrases.

Inside the medical office, *pansori* music played at a low volume that suited the vocal and percussive melody. The building smelled very old, but most of this area had been rebuilt in 1938. This was the new Chinatown that had replaced the one torn down for Union Station.

A flat-faced woman with curly black-and-gray hair sat at a teak desk where she typed on a computer keyboard. She looked up when Jin walked in and waited with a placid look of interest.

Speaking in Korean, Jin asked, *"Is the doctor here?"*

The woman answered in the same native tongue. *"He is busy."*

Jin was ready to admit defeat and walk away when her gaze wandered to the window, cloudy from age. Pieces of clear tape that had turned yellow with time had been left with bits of torn paper stuck beneath the adhesive. It looked as though someone had taped a flyer up then torn the paper away, except the tape had not been left in a square pattern anywhere.

When the image took shape in her mind, she realized she stared at an angular hourglass, the body of the star pattern for Orion.

Jin turned back to the woman and said in crisp Korean, "*Tell him a Hunter requires his help.*"

The woman paled and her fingers shook.

The assistant should be rushing to find the doctor, but she was paralyzed with fear.

Why? She had no reason to fear Jin.

But she might have reason to be terrified if the Orion Hunters had shown up last night with Har.

Jin just waited silently, hoping someone did not come tearing out of the back rooms with a weapon. If she acted the least bit afraid it would be a dead giveaway that something was wrong.

Tension mounted until she snapped out, "*Find him. Now.*"

"*He ... he is not here. Busy.*"

She was clearly lying.

Jin leaned down, putting both hands on the desk to prop her weight. "*You do not want me to report you.*"

That was all it took for the woman to pick up a phone and punch numbers then say, "*You have to come here, Dr. Wong.*"

She had to repeat herself before a short, thin man emerged from the back. He had a stern face and eyes that criticized Jin for being difficult.

Or being Amerasian?

His gaze moved over to Tanner who was busy reading some pamphlet written in Chinese.

Turning pages in the wrong direction.

Dr. Wong said in biting Korean, "*You would dare to talk in front of him?*"

"*Who?*" Jin looked around as if she hadn't noticed Tanner, then she swung back to the doctor and sharpened her tone. "*Tourist? You waste my time discussing a round eye who is clueless about what we are saying?*"

"How can you be sure?"

She sighed and spoke without turning around. *"You watch the tourist to see if he shows any sign of understanding what I say."* She raised her voice but kept speaking at the doctor in Korean. *"Hey you, American man. Would you like to have sex with me tonight?"*

Dr. Wong watched Tanner closely until he finally gave up.

Jin asked, *"Convinced or will you waste more of my time?"*

The doctor's eyebrows drew tight at being chastised, but he nodded.

She crossed her arms to keep her hands from shaking. *"I must know if you were able to cure Har's illness. My Orion superiors back home want a report."*

Her words took a visible year off the doctor's life from the wan look that came over him. His voice shook slightly as he answered in a whisper. *"I know nothing about someone named Har."*

He was lying. This place was full of liars. She changed tactics. *"If he did not come here last night, there must be another Orion doctor here. Who is it?"*

With every question, the doctor became more agitated. *"I know of no other here."*

Jin took an exaggerated deep breath and released it slowly to indicate how out of patience she was growing. The action actually helped calm her nerves. *"I must also locate Orion Patty Smith. Do you have the network list?"*

The little doctor's eyes bulged behind his glasses. *"What?"*

Intimidating him was not working so she played on his emotions and prayed he had a conscience. *"It is urgent that I locate her. Please."*

Sweat ran down his face. His voice went up an octave as if she squeezed his balls. *"I'm sorry. I cannot help you ... now."*

His eyes pleaded with her to understand. Why had he said *now* with so much emphasis?

She kept her voice light. *"I was exposed to Har last night and think I'm coming down with something. When are you available to see me?"*

He swallowed and shook his head, then his eyes brightened

with a thought. *"Let me check."* He looked down at his assistant's desk and slid an appointment book over where Jin could see it. She watched as he moved his finger to tomorrow's date and stopped at a space for ten in the morning.

Clearing his throat, he said, *"I'm afraid I have no openings before Monday. Can you come back at nine o'clock?"*

But his finger was pressing so hard into the slot for 10:00 AM tomorrow that his fingernail was cutting the paper.

She nodded at him. *"Pencil me in for—"* She looked down pointedly at his finger. *"—that slot. I will return then."*

He nodded, and his finger trembled when he moved it. *"Thank you for understanding. There is only so much one man can do."*

It all sank in at once. This doctor feared for his life and his wife's.

"May Orion Hunters watch over you," Jin said, using a common signature at the end of communications, then thanked him and walked past Tanner without looking his way.

As she swung the door open, Tanner asked, "Ya'll do that needle healing? Acupuncture ..."

He caught up to her in ten steps. "Well?"

Jin considered all that had been said and shared only, "He says he knows nothing about Har."

"That wasn't an Orion Hunter doctor?" Tanner whispered.

She walked fast, her heart pounding with each step because she'd asked about her sister and the doctor agreed to tell her tomorrow at ten. Something Tanner did not need to know. "Dr. Wong is with the Hunters. He's just afraid and lying."

"That's good news." Tanner had his phone out, reading something.

She didn't understand his reaction. "Why do you think so?"

"When I saw you staring at the window, it took a minute for me to realize the pattern of the tape meant something, right?"

"Yes." She shielded her mouth with her hand when she said, "That is the hourglass shape that is part of the Orion star pattern."

"Got it. I sent Dingo a text to let him know we might be in the right place. He's been shadowing us. He slipped inside while you talked to the doctor and just texted me back. He said the patient rooms were empty and he put a tap on the phones."

That could not be good for her. "What are you going to do?"

"If Har is still in the area, Dr. Wong will probably sit tight until he thinks it's safe to go to him. The minute he does, we'll catch him and the rest of this bunch. If not and Har is already gone, we'll bring the doctor in and make him talk. He was sweatin' as bad as a whore in church on Sunday. He knows something."

She fought down the panic.

Dr. Wong would tell her nothing about Patty if he was arrested.

Chapter Thirty

HOT DAMN, THIS was going to go down faster than Tanner had anticipated.

He should have a text any minute now from Dingo, who was using his source here in Los Angeles to have the audio translated. Tanner had recorded Jin and the doctor's conversation.

Call him suspicious all you want, but he'd been duped once already by this Orion group. Jin had been pretty tightlipped on the drive to the café a block away from the doctor's office, where Tanner had decided to wait on word that the doctor had left.

A tiny Asian waitress who had to be in her fifties took his order for a cola and Jin's for hot tea. Lunch hour had this place hopping.

Once the waitress left, Tanner leaned on the forearm he'd propped on the table and kept his voice low. "Did the doctor say anything else? Like where we could find another Orion doctor?"

"No. He just said he was busy, and I was taking up his valuable time." Her gaze never caught up to his when she shared that.

Tanner's instinct was screaming *liar* even if it was lying by omission. Didn't she realize her deal with him hung by a thread right now?

His phone buzzed with an incoming text. He sat back and pulled it off the table to read the transcript of her dialogue with the doctor.

Son of a bitch.

Who the hell was Orion Patty Smith?

He shot a questioning look at Jin, who froze. *Yep, you're caught, darlin'.* Patty Smith had to be her sister. Jin hadn't mentioned asking about an Orion or that she'd agreed to come back to see the doctor.

You are so busted.

"What is wrong?" she asked.

He closed the text and placed his phone face down on the plastic tablecloth. "Why would you think something was wrong?"

"That look on your face."

"You mean a look of disappointment?"

She said nothing. He rubbed his chin, considering how much to reveal then figured there was no point in hiding what he knew. "I'm sticking my neck out to keep you from being locked up, but *your* word is obviously not worth anything."

Déjà vu all over again. Hadn't letting Allie screw him over been enough?

"I have kept my word."

"I don't think so, Jin."

"Suspicion always haunts a guilty mind."

"Who're you quoting?"

"Shakespeare."

Ah, *now* he remembered. On the boat when she'd said, *Hell is empty and all the devils are here,* he'd recognized it, but between the fatigue and the pressure his brain hadn't clicked. His little Korean troublemaker had studied English literature. Damn. She just kept getting more interesting.

And more questionable with everything she held back.

"Well," he said, "I'm not the one with the guilty mind here." He leaned in again so that only she heard his words. "You asked that doctor about your sister and agreed to go back to see him again."

Her cinnamon lips parted in shock. "I ... uh ..."

"Don't make this worse by denying it."

"I told you I was looking for my sister."

"What about agreeing to come back to see him? You didn't mention that to me. What'd you think would happen? I'm just going to let you go off on your own to hunt your sister?"

"No. I thought if he knew where my sister was that I would find her, and you would find Pang and Har."

"But you didn't plan to tell me that you were going back to see the doctor, right?"

She was tapping her fingers on the table with angry strokes, but she stopped suddenly and speared him with fury that had clearly been building for a while. "I thought if you did not find Har tonight I would tell you I believed the doctor would share more tomorrow. I was afraid to tell you now because you would arrest the doctor and he would say nothing then."

"Nice try. I don't believe you." Tanner sat back. "If he doesn't lead us to anyone tonight, he is coming in first thing in the morning. He'll talk."

She curled her fingers into tight fists. "Please, do not do that. He will talk to me. I will find out much more than you can. I will tell you everything he says."

"I guess you would, now that you know I can have anything you say translated."

"I would have told you as soon as I found out where my sister is. Think about it. I need you to take me to her."

Tanner wanted to believe her. The worry in her voice was real, but her sister was her only priority, where Tanner's was trying to protect this country. His phone hummed with a call.

He answered, "What's up?"

Dingo rushed to share what he had. "The doctor made a call to someone who didn't identify himself and spoke for less than thirty seconds. I had it translated. He said, 'Wait ten minutes, then the woman delivers the message I gave you and you come to treat my man.' I've been watching and, right as I got that translation, they both just exited, moving in opposite directions. I'll have to take the woman. The doctor is headed your way, same street but on the other side from you. He's moving in a hurry."

That meant neither he nor Dingo had backup. "Got it."

He couldn't leave Jin here, not when she could disappear in this place with little trouble. Plus, she could handle herself.

The waitress had just delivered their drinks and walked away as Tanner ended the call and stood up. He tossed plenty of cash on the table. "Let's go."

Jin stood. "Where?"

"Where I tell you to go." He caught her up close to him. "Do *not* make a sound to alert anyone, because I don't want to have to hurt you."

"You insult me. I am not here to help the Orions. And you think too much of your skills if you believe you could physically harm me."

"I'll keep that in mind." Once Tanner had them at the front door, he waited until he caught sight of the doctor. Wong hurried along the other side of the road, tossing nervous glances all around him.

Tanner told Jin, "Stay close. If you do anything or go anywhere, I haven't approved, I'll put you and your sister away forever."

That was cold, but he had to give her a threat that she'd believe and respect. If not, she'd risk her slender neck just to find information on her sister.

"I had begun to expect better from you."

His conscience took a hit at the reminder of her words from when they'd first met. He was not the kind of man who would have left her mother with a child, but if allowing her to think that would support his threat and keep her close where he could protect her, then so be it.

She warned, "You must not harm the doctor."

"Because he's a Hunter," Tanner said, dodging his way through clusters of a crowd, most of which reached his shoulder in height. He hung close to the wall to keep from standing out so much.

Jin kept pace with him and when they stopped at a street crossing, she waited until people were moving again to threaten, "If you cause the doctor to not tell me where my sister is—"

"Let me guess. Our deal is off."

Shaking her head, she let out a disgusted sound. "I should say that, but no. Our deal will continue even though you have deceived me as well."

"Didn't like that translation trick, huh?"

She ignored his comment. "What I had intended to say was that the doctor is going to give me more information than the location of my sister."

A stoplight up ahead changed, and Dr. Wong had to wait on the traffic to pass.

Tanner slowed and slashed his gaze in her direction. "What kind of information? Like what role your sister is playing in all this?"

Jin's gaze moved from Tanner to the doctor at the same moment Tanner checked his target. The doctor was turning to look around him.

"Shit."

Jin launched herself upward into Tanner's arms and kissed him.

He barely caught her, but the minute her lips hit his, he was wholly onboard. What a mouth. He could spend days getting to know these lips better. She had her arms wrapped around his neck and turned her head to the side, allowing him to deepen the kiss. That fresh scent from the hotel soap was doing crazy things to his brain.

Big John came alive and if she rubbed herself up and down his front one more time, Tanner was going to shove her up against the nearest wall and unleash all his pent-up frustration on her.

She broke the kiss, huffing short breaths.

Tanner's brain swung back around into gear. He kept an eye on Dr. Wong who stood patiently waiting for the light to change. Not much of a rule breaker, huh?

Jin stared into Tanner's eyes for a second then put her lips next to his ear, whispering quickly. "The doctor has to know someone who has the American network list for Orion Hunters. That should be of great value to you and your people even after we find Pang and Har. Yes?"

Oh, hell yes. He kept his head dipped close to hers at the same time. *Keep moving, people. Nothing to see.* Just two almost-lovers sharing a whispered secret. "Why didn't you tell me this at the café?"

"Because if you capture Har and Pang today, I had hoped you would be willing to find my sister if I had that list to offer you. The Orion Hunters have been a curse my whole life. I will do whatever it takes to help you stop them. I am sorry I did not tell you I asked the doctor about Patty, but trusting is not easy for me. Here is what you do not know because my body blocked you from seeing it. Dr. Wong pointed at his appointment book for me to return tomorrow morning at ten. Now, I have told you everything."

She'd surprised him with that admission.

Tanner would think it through later, but he was willing to accept her apology for the moment. "Thank you for sharing that."

"We can still work together?"

"Yep. Heads up. We're on the move again." He lowered her feet back to the sidewalk and took her hand. Just to stay in character that they were pretending to be a couple.

It had nothing to do with how he enjoyed touching her and wanted to keep her close.

The doctor led them through a busy Chinatown, then he darted down a narrow alley.

Tanner stopped at the corner with Jin, peeking between a gutter downspout and the wall on the left to watch his target. Dr. Wong paused halfway down, looked back and forth, then opened a door and entered the building.

Backing up a step, Tanner took in the yellowed newspapers taped over the inside of the glass window at the front of the building. A business long gone. There were two stories to the abandoned storefront. He should have risked leaving Jin at the café, because now he had to go inside this building to find out who the doctor was meeting.

She gave a half-hearted huff. "We will lose the doctor."

"No, we won't. Here's how this is going to work. You follow me down the alley. When we step inside, I'll point out somewhere for you to hide. You stay there until I come back for you. If I don't come get you in ten minutes, you return to the café and wait for me or my partner."

"The Australian."

"That one. Ready?"

"Yes."

Tanner walked down the alley towing her close behind him. He respected Jin's fighting skills, but all the moves in the world wouldn't stop a bullet, so right before they entered the building, he told her once more. "Stay close to me and do exactly as I say."

"Do not get shot, cowboy."

She didn't trust easily. Neither did he, but she'd told him about the Orion Hunter network list and the meeting with the doctor tomorrow morning in a show of trust.

He needed to give her something in return. "You can talk to the doctor tomorrow."

She smiled slowly, recognizing what he had given her. "Thank you."

The Orion Hunters killed anyone who betrayed them, but she was still willing to walk into danger at Tanner's side.

Anyone in there would have to go through him to touch her.

He kissed her quickly and before she could say a word, he pulled the door open and stepped into the black hole with her hand firmly in his grasp.

Chapter Thirty-One

JIN CLAMPED HER eyes shut as she allowed Tanner to pull her into the building. During the two seconds it took for her to adjust to the sudden darkness, she was blind to everything around her.

But not afraid because of the man who held her hand.

Just because he'd told her his name and agreed to let her talk to the doctor.

Even without her eyes, her senses clued her into her surroundings. First, she caught the smell of rot and mildew from a building left to deteriorate.

She opened her eyes. An overhead light burned further into the building, but she couldn't see past piles of ragged plastic bags. Old clothes and household goods spilled out of holes torn in the bags.

A wooden ladder missing two steps had been leaned against the side of permanent shelves that extended four feet from the exterior wall.

Tanner squeezed her fingers, drawing her attention up to him. He pointed a finger at her, then at a place to hide behind a stack of wooden pallets.

Her instincts were telling her to stay with him, but she'd agreed to do as he said and had to prove to Tanner that she could be trusted to keep her word. She nodded and moved silently to the place he'd indicated.

When she turned to watch him as he walked off, she caught a movement above his head that drew her gaze.

Two black shadows dropped straight down.

"Up," Jin yelled as she shoved away from where she hid.

Tanner twisted his head up to see what was coming and

someone grabbed Jin, swinging her around so she couldn't see Tanner.

She used the momentum of being swung around to slide her feet as though she were falling down, throwing her attacker off balance. He shifted his feet to keep steady. She clasped her hands on his arms and used that leverage to swing up, kicking her heel into his balls.

He sucked in a deep breath and howled, releasing her.

Perfect. The beauty of Ninkodai was that it was all about real-life fighting and winning and survival.

Not about style.

Grunts and fists pounded bodies behind her. She hoped Tanner was getting the best of his fight.

Jin was on her feet and battering her attacker with a series of hits that jarred her shoulders. She might as well be attacking a brick wall.

Someone shouted over where Tanner fought two people. She had to help him.

Her attacker wasn't moving quickly, but he managed to scissor his legs at hers and knocked her feet out from under her. *Never assume your opponent is down!* Herr Faust shouted in her mind. Her head bounced on the floor.

Her former Nindokai instructor would have punished her severely for that error.

She hadn't made that mistake in many years, but her worry for Tanner had distracted her. Pain shot through her head from where it had met the concrete.

Herr Faust's words shouted. *Ignore the pain. Always keep moving or prepare to meet your death.*

Jin's attacker grabbed at her, fisting the front of her shirt and yanking.

Panic rushed her brain at memories of another attack. She slammed his arms upward and lunged away from him, scrambling to get free.

The shirt tore.

That sound took her back to the one and only time she'd faced rape.

Jin had feared her instructor. Rumors claimed Herr Faust had raped and then killed two female students as examples when they lost focus and could not keep fighting.

Failure was not tolerated when training as an Orion Hunter.

One look into Herr Faust's empty eyes had been to stare at death calling, taunting. He'd pounced on her the one time she'd failed to gain her feet immediately. He'd clawed at her clothes, ripping them, threatening to rape her if she did not win that fight.

Or was it *this* fight?

Terror raced through her. Memories swamped her, pulling her under. *Herr Faust was here.* He would make good on his threat.

Jin was up and hammering her attacker over and over with rapid hits, deflecting his strikes when she could and suffering abuse from the ones she missed.

But she was not going down again.

Spinning away, she intentionally stumbled and turned, hesitating a second and breathing hard to draw him in.

The face of her instructor ghosted through her mind, taunting her at how he would enjoy her body.

Herr Faust came at her. *No, this was not her instructor.*

She shook off the confusion.

Everything slowed until she could see the telltale lead of her attacker's strike. His boot swung high for a crushing blow.

Wait ... wait ...

Instead of taking a defensive move, Herr Faust had taught her to do the unexpected.

She held her ground.

As her attacker's boot raced toward her head at a deadly speed, Jin bent backwards. She had amazed her demanding instructor by being able to bend backwards far enough to touch the floor with her fingertips, push off and whip her body up quickly.

That signature move had prevented Herr Faust from ever taking her to the ground again.

She executed it now and came up under her attacker's kick, grabbed his leg and twisted, snapping bone at the knee.

His scream of pain burned her ears.

He hit the ground face first, threatening to rape her first then kill her slowly.

Blinding rage tore through her.

You will never harm another student, Herr Faust.

She straddled his back, grabbed his head, and wrenched with a gush of energy that gave her more strength than she'd believed possible.

He stopped screaming.

The sudden silence echoed through her mind.

Adrenaline rushed through her in a tidal wave. She stepped back, staring at his body. It was wrong. Herr Faust was much bigger, and his hair had been blond.

Footsteps pounded toward her.

She spun and, out of pure instinct, raised her hands, prepared to fight.

Tanner came running around the corner like an avenging angel with blood coursing down the side of his face. "Are you okay?"

"Yes." But shaking started in her core. She'd killed a man.

He dragged her into his arms. Her hand landed against his chest where his heart was beating as fast as hers. He hugged her and breathed out, "I thought they had you."

Tanner was scared for her? That pushed a warm pulse inside her, helping to steady her, but her heart clenched at taking a life. She whispered shaky words. "I told you I could defend myself."

But she had not had to kill a man before now. Why were tears stinging her eyes? This man had attacked her.

Nausea gripped her every time she thought about twisting his neck.

Pulling back, Tanner took in her face and kissed her forehead. "You sure as hell can." Then he took her in more closely. "Are you really okay?"

She struggled to breathe. Herr Faust would have laughed at her weakness. "I ..." She licked her lips and tried again, her words barely making a sound. "I killed him."

Tanner hugged her to him again. "I'm glad you did. He would have killed you."

Swallowing was difficult. She never wanted to do that again, but she would if it meant protecting her sister. Or Tanner.

He was rubbing his hands up and down her arms. Her teeth

chattered. He said, "It's shock, darlin'. Just breathe and take it easy."

His hands were warming her skin, but the cold was deep inside. He told her, "We have to go."

She understood. "I will be fine."

He bundled her close and walked toward the door.

She stopped. "Wait. What happened to the two who attacked you?"

"Dead."

A sick feeling licked at her. "What about Dr. Wong?"

Tanner tightened his hold on her. "He's dead."

"No! I need him." She yanked against his hold. Why would they kill the doctor?

Then it dawned on her. "They used Dr. Wong to lead us here."

Tanner said, "Possibly."

They knew who she was. Knew she was here. Knew she was helping Tanner.

Trusting Tanner's plan instead of her own had ruined her and would get him killed. She should have left that first night instead of waiting for him in his Suburban, but she had been sure that trusting him would save her sister and innocent lives.

That decision had cost everything.

She jerked out of his arms and backed away. "I have nothing. No way to find my sister. We have no deal."

Chapter Thirty-Two

TANNER SHOOK HIS head at Jin. "I'm sorry about losing the lead on your sister, but we can't have this conversation here. When someone doesn't hear from the men sent here for us, those people will send more muscle."

She backed up almost to the point of stepping on the body of the man she'd fought.

The one she'd killed. Then gone into shock over.

Jin was one dangerous woman to cross and right now she was pissed as a wet hen about her sister.

Tanner hated that for her, but his mission had always overruled her personal one. "We have to go before we lose Har. He has to be at the other location." He reached for her arm, and she hugged her crossed arms tighter against her chest, stepping out of his reach.

Bone deep emotional pain had her pulling in all her defenses. She was fighting shock. This was not the time to reason with her.

He went to the door and opened it to look outside. "Let's move."

She swept past him so quickly he should be shivering from the chill in her wake.

Outside, he caught up to her and put a hand on her shoulder to stop her before they reached the street.

"Do not touch me."

"We can't go out there with your clothes ripped and me bleeding."

She seemed to finally notice the condition of her clothes. The minute he'd taken out his second attacker, Tanner had been terrified that she was gone or dead. When he'd found her with her clothes torn half off, he'd wanted to kill someone.

But she'd managed to do that on her own.

And without falling into hysterics even if she was struggling with the responsibility for someone's death. He still remembered the first time he'd had to use deadly force. It had shaken him up badly.

Jin was one helluva woman.

What had she been through in her life to be trained to kill? Whether she'd intended to or not, she had the expertise to finish someone off.

But at the moment, she was dealing with ending a life and losing the first real chance she'd had at finding her sister. Tanner wanted to wrap her up in his arms and take her back to the hotel where he could hold her and keep her safe.

His phone buzzed. He wrenched it out of his pocket, checked that it was Dingo before he answered. "We're on the way."

Dingo said, "Don't. Someone cut the woman's throat the minute she stepped through the door. I was maybe sixty seconds behind her. But I found Har."

"And?"

"He's dead, too."

Tanner reached up to rub his forehead and made the mistake of touching the cut. He dropped his hand. "Same on this end except they were waiting for us here."

"Still got Jin?"

"Yep. Let's meet back at the hotel and come up with a plan."

"I'm on my way, but right now? *She's* our plan."

Tanner knew where Dingo was going with this but hoped he was wrong. "What do you mean?"

"They clearly were waiting to grab her or kill her. She's more important to this Orion attack than she's letting on. She has to come clean or it's time to hand her to Sabrina for some answers."

Tanner had no doubt that Sabrina would get whatever they needed out of Jin, because she hadn't spent the last couple days watching Jin ride an emotional roller coaster. If Tanner was being honest with himself, he was no longer objective. Not one damn bit. This would be the time to step back and let Dingo decide what to do with her.

The minute Tanner did that, he could use his conscience for target practice because there would be nothing left of it.

Chapter Thirty-Three

NICK SMILED AT the kiss on his lips.

Wait a minute. He was in a hospital room with a Slye agent standing guard outside the door.

That hadn't been a real kiss. Just something left over from a drug-induced dream.

He opened one eye then the other one. Lights were dimmed just as he'd asked, but the room still slid sideways. He had to get weaned off the drugs soon.

Moving his good arm, the one that hadn't taken two bullets, he felt for the control to raise the head of his bed so he could sit up.

"This what you're looking for?" The control moved into his sight line from above his head.

He rolled his eyes up and to his left.

A female doctor stood in her medical whites, with an aqua-blue stethoscope hooked around her neck. Blond hair was twisted up on top of her head and hazel eyes watched him.

Narrow nose, full cheeks, and crow's feet at the corners of her eyes. He'd put that face around forty.

And not a bit of it was real, including contacts to change her eye color. He was sure of it. "When are you going to come see me as yourself?"

Those eyes twinkled. What was the real color?

She handed him the control and stepped around. "Take it slow and I'll help you."

When her arm snaked behind his shirtless back, his dick jumped. Good to know that hadn't been shot off, but any minute now the sheet was going to tell everyone that certain vital parts were intact and ready to rock. He forced his mind back to the pain he'd been in before surgery and that took the starch out of his tent rod.

"There," she said in a husky voice that sounded like what he'd heard the last time they'd met covertly. She pulled her arm away. "Now I understand why it was so hard to find you."

"I'd say it's nice to see you, babe, but I have a feeling you don't bring good news."

"Depends on how you look at things." She sat on the side of the bed, facing him.

He itched to touch her hand and knocked the idea sideways. She was here for business. "If you're here to collect that I-owe-you, I may not be able to pay up."

She smiled and he could see the telltale pull of her latex mask only because he'd been taught how to identify them by a master. "I'm not here to collect, Nick. Not yet."

Just knowing she still wanted to cash in the I-owe-you gave him reason to smile. That was the only way he'd find this woman again. She was a highly skilled operative who had done him a favor that resulted in a terrorist captured and a Slye agent saved.

"What brings you to Los Angeles then?"

"For one thing, I'm looking for something that belongs to a client, according to him."

He liked that about her. No bullshitting around what he did and who he knew. "Sounds like a threat."

"Possibly. Your team brought three Koreans into the country."

He made a noncommittal grunt.

"I've been asked to retrieve them."

She shocked him with that. He asked, "You want to take them back to North Korea?"

"Bloody hell, no." She looked appalled. "I wouldn't do that to my worst enemy."

"Who sent you for them?"

"Supposedly the country the physicists originally wanted to defect to."

Maybe that's why Pang was such a jerk. He didn't like Americans. But he hadn't asked to stay in Seoul when they'd arrived there.

China would have taken those two. Nick didn't bring that up. Instead, he pointed out, "The Koreans are gone."

No one was giving him updates with him looped out on drugs, but if Tanner and the team had found the physicists, Nick felt certain Tanner, Dingo and Blade would be hanging out to tell him.

His visitor said, "I'll hunt for the physicists, but I plan to have a talk with them before they go anywhere."

"Understood, but I need both of those physicists, too. If you find them, I have to hand them over to the State Department then if they want to apply for asylum somewhere else, they can."

She pondered on that and nodded. "I might be able to make that work, but I'm taking the woman with me when I find her."

From what Nick had seen during the trip home, Tanner wouldn't go along with that if he ever located Jin again.

She said, "You're thinking too hard."

"One of our guys has an interest in the woman's welfare."

"Then he should be happy for her to end up somewhere she'll be treated as a queen instead of landing in prison here. The group behind bringing the physicists into this country is sending professionals after her. A lot of people want this woman, or they want her dead. There's also a two-million-dollar bounty on her head, but I'm not interested in that. I've picked up intel that if she doesn't give herself up, she'll be considered a threat and your government will bury her so deep she'll never see daylight again."

That was entirely possible. "You said that was one thing that brought you to LA. What else?"

She leaned down close, and he forgot all about intel. He wanted to pull her into bed and wake up junior again. When she was a breath away from his lips, she said, "The Koreans are headed to Ogallala for some reason, but I don't know why or when. If you can come up with the why and when, I'll go find them."

Then she kissed him, just a quick touch of their lips, but enough for junior to start doing the hallelujah dance. She smiled and stood. "I'm looking forward to collecting on that debt."

He grinned. "Not as much as I'm looking forward to paying it."

"You have the number I gave you?"

"Memorized." But until now he'd doubted that it was still valid.

"Call when you have anything." She stepped toward the door.

"Hey," he called out softly.

She turned back. "What?"

"You know I'm Nick. What do I call you? Still *Talia*?"

She studied on her answer for a bit, which he understood but she wouldn't be here if she didn't trust him to some degree. He thought she'd decided not to tell him when she said, "I'll tell you ... next time."

Then she was gone.

Chapter Thirty-Four

JIN SAT ON the hotel bed with her legs crossed, giving all she had to look calm in the face of an angry Tanner.

He was still angry about her holding back information.

Well, she was too because she now had to gain a new agreement. As much as she'd wanted to strike out at Tanner—strike out at anyone for the mess she was in—once she calmed down and thought about it, she could not in good conscience blame Tanner for losing her lead to Patty.

If Jin were being honest, her fear for what the Orion Hunters would do to Tanner was now almost as strong as her need to get to Patty. Almost. She could not blame Tanner for that, either.

Her stupid heart was her problem.

A shower had helped her get her head in a better place, and now she wore the extra T-shirt he'd bought her this morning with the same warm-up pants. The pants had dirt stains at the knees, but with no hope of finding her sister that was the least of her concerns. She'd used his comb on her wet hair, and left it unbound to air-dry.

Tanner dragged the office chair away from the desk and positioned himself to face her, arms crossed and jaw rigid. "My men will be here in a few minutes. It's time to tell me everything you know about the attack that the Orion Hunters are planning."

Dragging a handful of hair away from her face, she clasped her hands in her lap. She would not give up no matter what. "First, I need a new agreement."

"I don't think our agreements are working out so well. I stuck with my part of the bargain, but we don't have a lead left to follow so I'm at the point of handing you off."

She ran her tongue over her dry lips to buy a moment to think.

Tanner's gaze tightened and zeroed in on her mouth.

Just that look was enough to send a shiver across her skin and it wasn't fear. No, this was lust.

She'd never been subject to bouts of lust before, not after the way she'd been initiated into the Orion Hunters. They wanted no virgin females floating around that someone might place a value on.

There were other rules associated with this initiation such as wearing a condom so there was no chance of pregnancy or a disease transmitted by the woman, because of course, men were above such reproach. Jin hadn't felt appreciative about the condom when she'd suffered through having her virginity destroyed with the same thought as tossing out an old shoe, but much later she was thankful to have been spared anything transmitted from the man.

That was another reason this attraction to Tanner was as unexpected as it was overpowering.

"Jin?"

"I will tell you everything I know about the attack if you promise not to discount it."

"Why would I do that?"

"I fear you will not believe that what I have to tell you is truly dangerous for your country."

"I'll have to be the judge of that."

"If I tell you, will you help me find my sister?"

He waved a hand to stop her. "We tried this your way, and it didn't work. Maybe if you'd told me everything about that doctor and what's really going on, we would have planned it differently."

"I accept responsibility for the doctor's death," she said past the lump in her throat.

Tanner unfolded his arms and sat forward, hands on his knees. He frowned, but his words were gentle. "Whoa. Those deaths today were not your fault. Not even the one you took out. That's the result of terrorists with a goal. Work with us so no one else dies."

"You cannot guarantee that."

"No, I can't." He studied her, his gaze diving inside her to wander around and make her want things. "But I can guarantee more people *will* die if we don't work together. You said yourself that one of them could be your sister."

What was she supposed to do now?

Tanner sat patiently then finally said, "You trust me, don't you?"

She held his gaze, searching for the answers in his eyes. He had kept her safe and brought her to the US just as he'd promised. He'd rushed toward her kidnapper who'd turned a loaded weapon on Tanner when Tanner could not shoot back because Jin was in the way.

Plus, he'd upheld his end of the agreement. She was the one to blame for not sharing all the information with him about the doctor. Her fear of trusting men had put her in this place.

He was right. She needed to tell them everything, because for all her bravado and threatening to share nothing if they locked her up, she would not allow innocent people to die.

She opened her mouth to answer him, but someone knocked at the door.

Tanner strode over and opened it for the medic called Blade and the Australian, Dingo.

Blade took the cushioned armchair in the corner by the desk and the Australian perched on the ottoman.

Once Tanner was seated again, he said to Jin, "From the beginning, tell us everything you know about this Project Jigu-X attack."

"Nuclear, right?" Blade said.

Jin sat up straight and prepared to tell them about the project that had turned Pang into a star for the Orion Hunters. "To begin with, as I have said, there is no *nuclear* attack planned."

Blade let out a loud sigh of relief. "Thank God."

The Australian's eyes narrowed.

Tanner sat in contemplative silence.

She continued, "Do not rush to thank anyone, because what I have to tell you is far worse than a nuclear attack."

Now they were amused? Men.

Undaunted, she sent them each a scathing reprimand with her eyes. Once that wiped away their amusement, she said,

"Pang and Har were working on Project Jigu-X, but it was not a nuclear program. That was an intentional misinformation leak. It was about seeding clouds."

Blade sat up. "What? This is all about some harebrained plan to seed clouds for rain?"

She turned to Tanner. "See? I told you no one would believe me. Do not judge this until you know everything."

Tanner gave her a nod of understanding. "I'm still listening."

Dingo's eyes judged her every word, but he said, "Go on."

"Pang led the research team to develop a special seeding plan that would be *spread by* clouds and rain, not *create* that weather. Silver iodide is a compound used for seeding." The nods she now got from all three men indicated they understood seeding, so she moved on to the specific issue.

"Depending on how the silver iodide is used in the seeding, it can instigate different meteorological reactions. Pang perfected a chemical called Jigu-X that would bond to the silver iodide particles, but it has no loyalty. Once water touches the Jigu-X, the original powder composition unites with the water, forming a new chemical. The water causes a cannibalistic reaction. By the time one drop of water with Jigu-X hits the ground, the Jigu-X causes the drop to double several times in size. It is now equal to a teaspoon of liquid. That teaspoon of liquid will separate into thousands of tiny particles, making it easy to disperse."

Blade said, "Now that we've had your chemistry lesson, what's the bottom line?"

Impatient man. She faced Tanner to gauge his reaction first. He still listened, so she continued.

"The Jigu-X is highly toxic. One particle the size of a grain of sand can kill a dog if ingested, but it takes about three days. Washing a dog in water infected with Jigu-X causes first the fur to fall out, then the skin to begin peeling off until the chemical reaches an organ and destroys the animal. Once this is in your water tables, the damage is not reversible."

"Holy mother of—" Tanner muttered. "This *is* worse than a nuclear attack."

"How do you see that?" Blade challenged Tanner's words, but

his eyes never left Jin. She met his gaze and held hers steady. This was a smart man. He was testing her. Baiting her to see if she had her story straight.

Jin said, "Our world has recovered and rebuilt from nuclear devastation. How do you repair a damaged water source where the water is dangerous whether you drink it or wash your hands in it and there is no way to purify this water?"

The Australian scrubbed his hands over his face then ran his fingers across his hair. "Where do they plan to do this seeding?"

"That I do not know. I was only privy to their work because my labs were nearby, and I was being used to send and pick up messages."

Tanner stretched his legs and leaned back, staring at the ceiling, but he spoke to her. "Why did you say the attack could be as soon as two days? Why not now or tomorrow?"

"Pang has to have time to replicate the formula and create enough Jigu-X for the seeding. I saw only the documentation of results." She'd lost her dinner over the test images of ten dogs used. Pang deserved to die a painful death if only for torturing animals. "As I understand it, once he creates the chemical and bonds it to the silver iodide particles, it is packed into canisters that go into a projectile machine of some sort."

This was the first time she'd told anyone about the seeding plan and her skin chilled as she voiced the idea of infecting a water system in a way that could never be purified.

Blade leaned forward, propping his elbows on his knees, still eyeing her with doubt. "Why would the Orion Hunters destroy any of the land if their end goal is to rule the world?"

Jin cocked her head at him, considering his question. "You do not understand the Orions. All are focused on learning the prophecy, but they do not act as one. There are many factions among them, as in any other world-wide group. Each faction races to be the first to reveal the prophecy and believes it can use that information to ensure its choice of countries will survive an apocalypse. The Orions from North Korea who are living here in America are not necessarily concerned about this country. They are also not necessarily loyal to Orions who are *from* this country. Some are, but others are not. Just as the

Orions who have grown up here have different loyalties. Some are determined that America will not fall when the prophecy comes to fruition. Some will have laid aside money and plans to move to the best location once the prophecy is revealed."

The Aussie frowned. "Could we find Orions who would work against North Korean Orions?"

"Possibly, but it is difficult to first identify these groups, then to infiltrate them."

Tanner sat up. "How does your sister fit into all this, Jin?"

She jerked at the question. How could he ask her to put a target on her sister's back? "I will tell you if you agree to help me rescue her. If you are going to arrest her for doing something she has no choice in, then I will not tell you."

"Are you sure she doesn't know?" Blade asked.

"My younger sister and I are only ten months apart. We were born near the DMZ in South Korea and traded to a Chinese couple when I was seven."

"Traded for what?" the Aussie asked.

"My mother had ovarian cancer and needed treatments."

Blade interjected, "You were sold."

Jin shook her head hard. "It was not like that. My mother could not be cured. She used the money to help another family, not herself." Jin gripped her hands tighter to keep from shaking her fist at him. "You do not know what it is like to have two children who are Amerasian. We are lower than the lowest vermin in the eyes of Koreans, north *or* south. Korasians are mixed blood, but not mixed with an American. Korasians have rights."

When none of the men so much as whispered, she continued, "Amerasians are not even recognized as human beings. My mother could not care for us and had been told she would not live another six months. Once she died, we would have been cast out on the street. When a Chinese couple asked about adopting us, my mother made a sacrifice so that someone would care for her children and take us away from the struggle in Korea."

Blade's suspicion lived in his eyes. "So...how'd you end up in *North* Korea?"

"My adoptive father..." She paused, wanting to rinse the

bitter taste from her mouth from calling him that. "Is part of the Orion Hunter network. He had someone searching South Korea for outcast children who were considered bright by their teachers. My sister and I tested very high. We were given the best education and kept together until three years ago when they brought her here."

"In other words, they trained you to be sleeper cells."

Her cheeks heated with embarrassment. Yes, she had been brought up within the Orion Hunters, but she was not a terrorist. "Everyone raised as I was received specific training that the Orion Hunters use when needed. When you think of sleeper cells, you are talking about mindless fanatics who walk into a crowd with bombs strapped to their bodies."

Dingo quipped, "And your Orion Hunters aren't just as bad?"

"They are not mine and, no, they are not just as bad. Orion Hunters are far more deadly than all those terrorists combined. I would never kill for them, and neither would my sister."

"But she's here now and part of this plan," Blade prompted. "Makes it hard to believe she isn't aware that she's being used as a weapon."

Tanner let out an exhausted sound and repeated his words from earlier. "Remember I asked if you trusted me, Jin?"

Yes, and she'd like—so very much—to trust someone. She needed help and he had wide shoulders to lean on. "I want to."

"Tell us what you know about your sister and trust me to do the right thing."

Three intense gazes focused on her.

She might as well be a mouse staring at a pack of feral cats. These men were expected to do whatever it took to protect their country, which she could appreciate. But who would protect her sister?

Jin's gaze settled on her answer. Tanner.

The time had come to choose a side and hope that he was on hers and Patty's. "My sister was given the name Patty Smith before she was brought over. You will not find papers of her defection or any record of her becoming a naturalized citizen. She would have been given documentation that proves she grew up here with one American and one Korean parent who will have lived in different parts of the country to prevent anyone knowing them too well."

When Blade's face twisted with a surly expression, Jin said, "Surely you realize that the Orion Hunters are here as well."

He just shook his head and leaned back in his chair, letting out a low whistle.

"What was your sister trained to do?" Dingo asked.

"She is a pilot. She will be the one to fly the airplane for the seeding." No one commented. Jin faced Tanner to make sure he understood just how much trust she was placing in him. "Once the seeding is completed, the Hunters will kill her. I heard that discussed when I hid to listen."

Tanner nodded and that simple gesture gave Jin some hope that one man in this room understood how painful this was and her fear of letting her sister down.

He asked, "How do we find Patty?"

"She will not be listed as simply Patty Smith. She would have been given a middle name or Patty might be her middle name or she may be married by now. The Orion Hunters spend years setting up something like this. The way to locate her is by determining where they will do the seeding."

Blade slapped the arm of his chair. "Shit, what a mess."

The Aussie asked, "I thought the Orion Hunters were all about some artifacts and the end of the world. Why are they doing this?"

"You are correct about their ultimate goal, but these are still people in positions within governments and companies. Those positions require them to maintain their power for connections and to finance their operations. If this is successful, the Orion superiors in Pyongyang will go to the leader of North Korea and tell him what was done on his behalf. These Orion superiors will then move into more powerful positions."

Facing frowns, Jin lifted her hands. "Orion Hunters believe if they are in influential positions when the truth about the final conflict is revealed, they will be able to manipulate the prophecy if their chosen country is not predicted to survive. You would be wise to search your own government for these people."

"Why is your sister the only one who can fly the airplane for this?"

"I am sure the Orions have other pilots in this country, and if something happened to Patty before the seeding flight, they would use one of them. But they chose Patty for three reasons." Jin counted off on her fingers. "Number one, she was a single female with no previous ties to the United States, so it was easy to bring her here and locate her geographically so that she is in position to be the pilot for this project. "Number two, in the three years she has been here, they will not have allowed her to form ties with anyone who is not in the Orion Hunter network, so no one will care to ask questions when she dies.

"Number three," Jin went on, "she is a female, and therefore disposable. They would not want to waste a male pilot, and they clearly said that the pilot was to be terminated after this project and it should be done to appear as an accident."

"I can see that, but why do they want *you*?" The blunt question had come from the Aussie. "Are you trained to do this seeding formula, too?"

"No. I perform lab tests on artifacts the Hunters bring to me."

"Anyone could do that. They wanted you today. Set a trap to capture you. Or kill you. Why?"

Tanner's phone buzzed and Jin pretended she waited on him to take his call before she answered.

Once he hung up, she'd have to find a way to dodge that question. She still wondered why the man who attacked her had tried to kill her, when she was far more valuable alive.

Tanner smiled while he listened to the person who had called him. "How long you going to milk a couple little ol' bullet wounds just to get pampered by hot nurses?"

That had to be Tanner's friend in the hospital. Jin's shoulders lightened at the pleasure in Tanner's voice. If he sounded that happy, his friend must be improving.

His smile disappeared. "You're shittin' me. Where'd you find that out?" As he listened, a grim change came over his face. "Thanks. We're on our way over."

Tanner's gaze shot to her, but his words were for his men. "We've got a lead on the location for the attack."

How could he know so quickly? The room spun with the fast loss of blood to her head. She put her hands out to steady herself.

What did this mean for Patty?

What does this mean for me?

Chapter Thirty-Five

TANNER WALKED TOWARD White Hawk, who leaned against the wall next to Nick's hospital room door. She had one foot propped on the wall and could be some ingénue teen with her dark hair cropped short in a jaunty style. Her jeans fit her in a comfortable way and a loose fitting pale blue T-shirt hung just past her waist, but the minute she raised her gaze, any perception of innocence disappeared.

He didn't know what those intense green eyes had seen, but it hadn't all been nice. She was pretty and wore not a speck of makeup, because she didn't need it.

"How's the patient?" Tanner asked, more to be polite to White Hawk than anything. He was careful to stay out of her personal space. She could follow a suspect with the best of them, but she got a jumpy look in her eyes sometimes when too many men surrounded her.

She cocked an eyebrow. "It's Nick. Need I say more?"

Dingo strolled up. "I'm surprised he's still here."

That brought a chuckle from her. "He might not be if Blade hadn't hidden his clothes and we weren't standing guard twenty-four-seven. At this point, we're here only to make sure he stays put until tonight."

When she smiled, White Hawk was striking.

Jin was, too, even when she didn't smile.

Guilt slunk down Tanner's neck at the image of Jin sitting alone, staring at him with eyes screaming accusations that he was letting her down. She expected to be abandoned by him and he hadn't been able to dispel that worry.

"You two going back to Atlanta?" Tanner asked to confirm the arrangements. Sabrina wanted all of her people out of this mess, but she'd settle for getting Nick home for now.

"Right. Blade's going with Nick to monitor him. I'll stay here ... if you need me," White Hawk added.

If Tanner needed people, he'd call Sabrina after White Hawk left to keep from slighting her, because he knew White Hawk preferred to work alone. "We're good. Thanks, though."

Dingo followed him into the room.

Nick sat propped up in bed, eating ... a damned fine looking hospital meal that smelled of rich sauce and seafood. He grinned and moved, then flinched.

"Be still," Dingo ordered. "And tell me that's not Coquille St. Jacques."

Nick's grin widened. "Got one of the nurses to smuggle it in, but I'm done."

Once Tanner and Dingo were on each side of Nick and he'd pushed his tray away, Tanner asked, "How did you get intel in here when even Sabrina's crew back home couldn't?"

Wiping his hands on the napkin and tossing it on the tray, Nick eased back against his pillows. "Let's just say I have an exceptional informant."

"You knew who to call and waited until now?" Dingo asked.

"I didn't call anyone."

Dingo exchanged a look with Tanner before pondering his question out loud. "Someone came in here? Past our people?"

Nick growled. "Do you want the intel or not? What have *you* got?"

Tanner lifted a hand in a signal to Dingo that they should let it go. Nick had been the only one to come up with intel on Margaux when she was captured and sitting in a South American jungle. Whoever he was tapping had international connections and had gained access to him when no one should have been able to pass through their security undetected.

Dingo said, "We know the people behind all this are that crazy Orion Hunter group."

At Nick's surprised look, Tanner added, "They were behind getting the physicists out of North Korea, and we just learned that the attack is actually a cloud seeding with poisonous particles." Tanner explained what Jin had told them.

Nick grunted. "Now the location makes sense. Their target is Ogallala Aquifer. But they're after the woman we brought, too. My contact says there's a two-million-dollar bounty for her if she's captured and the insinuation was that the person behind the bounty is Chinese with powerful political connections. From what my resource says, if the Chinese guy doesn't get her through the bounty, he'll have her deported for crimes against his government. If the second contract is to kill her, then the Orion Hunters don't want her to land in anyone else's hands."

And you left her alone at the hotel.

Fuck. Tanner's pulse shot into overdrive at the thought of anyone harming Jin. She'd handled the attack earlier today, but money like that brought out heavy-duty professionals. Tanner shut down his need to tear out of there and get back where he could watch over her. His team needed him fully on board to save his country, regardless of his own feelings.

Dingo slouched, tapping a finger on Nick's bed. "I wonder just who this Jin is and why one woman is so important," he mused.

Because Jin isn't just any woman, dammit. But that was Tanner's emotions weighing in, not his objective mission brain.

Didn't matter. He could explain why any man would want her. God knows, Tanner had since the minute he stared into her eyes, but the people after Jin wanted her for something else entirely.

Those same people would make that attack this morning look like a sparring session. Tanner's heart was beating so fast he should be setting off Nick's machines.

Nick scrunched his forehead. "Why the hell wasn't she part of the original extraction if she's so valuable? But if she's not part of the seeding attack, why should we care?"

"Because if we don't, they'll kill her," Tanner growled.

Nick and Dingo stopped focusing on the upcoming attack and turned to him. Nick spoke first. "Getting attached to her can't end well."

Dingo didn't second that verbally, but his eyes said Tanner should have kept that to himself.

Damage control time. Tanner said, "I'm not attached. She's an asset right now we need to keep alive."

"So," Dingo started and scratched his nose. "We should find a secure place and put her in lockdown."

"No." Shit. Said that too fast, too. "Let's just get out to Ogallala and start hunting for her sister."

But Dingo wasn't ready to give it up. "What are you going to tell Sabrina about how we came up with all this intel?"

Tanner ran both hands over his face. "Hell, I don't know. We'll tell her we beat it out of those three Koreans who killed the doctor."

That damn Nick grinned. "Good luck with that. Sabrina didn't fall off the turnip truck yesterday, to coin one of your country sayings. Better to tell her about Jin before Sabrina calls you to ask or sends a team to pick her up."

Tanner hated to admit Nick was right. "When Sabrina does start asking questions, you can explain how you got the strike location while in a hospital."

Nick's grin vanished and he grumbled something about how they should appreciate getting free intel.

Dingo grabbed his head. "Sabrina's going to castrate all of us as soon as she finds out we've kept her out of the loop."

Nick held up his hands. "I wasn't part of that."

Tanner leaned down. "You are now."

"You could keep Sabrina off all our backs right now by handing Jin over to her," Nick suggested. "Besides, that would put Jin somewhere safe. No one would get to her in the underground living quarters at Slye."

"He's got a point, mate," Dingo added.

A damn good one from everyone's perspective except Jin's.

She would never forgive Tanner.

Chapter Thirty-Six

IF THEY SENT her back, she would ... what?

Jin was pacing the hotel room for the thousandth time when the door opened. She'd showered and put on one of Tanner's shirts just because she liked the way it made her feel close to him.

And it fell to mid-thigh on her so that she could wear just the shirt and panties for now.

Her warm-up pants were hanging in the bathroom. They were too dirty to wear again.

Tanner walked in and he might as well have been carrying a building on his shoulders from the way he moved. He tossed his jacket on the bed and just stood there staring at her.

"Do not send me away, Tanner. I must go with you to find my sister."

"There's a bounty on your head for two million US dollars. A powerful Chinese guy. Have any idea who it is?"

What? "No. The man who raised me did not have that kind of money and he does not have a need for me. His work was done once he raised me according to the plan."

Tanner started toward her. "And what was that plan, Jin? Why are people hunting for you if you aren't a scientist or a physicist like Pang? Why would someone put that much money on your head? Why do they want you in China and North Korea? And why did that guy in Chinatown try to kill you this morning?"

When he stopped, he was standing a foot away. Close enough to reach for, but miles away so long as secrets lay between them. She'd had no one to depend on once she was taken from her mother, and never had a man around to lean on.

Her heart wanted this man to be that person, but her heart

thought she could have forever with someone when that wasn't possible.

She'd been groomed to be more than a weapon.

She was a specialized tool that every Orion Hunter wanted to possess.

Tanner searched her face for answers and finally said, "Please."

Finding her voice, she said, "I told you I spoke many languages, including ancient ones. I have a gift for languages and breaking codes. My IQ is higher than Pang's. I test all the artifacts the Orion Hunters bring me. I am expected to decipher the message once those five artifacts are joined in one spot."

She'd finally shocked Tanner. He was speechless for only a moment.

He cupped her arms, holding her near him. His gaze studied her with an intensity that shivered beneath her skin. He murmured, "That's why you had to sneak away."

"Yes. They would never let me leave. They will turn the world upside down to find me and, if I am locked somewhere they cannot free me, they will send someone to execute me rather than risk anyone else using me to decipher the message first."

Pressure built in her chest. Why didn't he say something? "Do not let them do that, Tanner."

"I won't."

Her heart sang with the hope for life those two words offered her. She lunged up into his arms and kissed him.

He caught her and for a second she thought he might set her away. Then he kissed her right back with a sweetness that threatened to drop her at the knees. He nipped at her lips then her cheek and behind her ear.

This man's mouth spoke her body's language.

She stopped thinking and started feeling. Her life had offered so few times to feel happy, but this moment with Tanner ... this was joy she could hold in her heart forever.

Urging him on, she whispered, "I want you, Tanner. So. Much."

He backed her up against a wall and started kissing her with purpose.

Happiness like she'd never felt filled her. She wrapped her arms around his neck, holding on to the one wonderful thing in her life.

She had little experience but knew what she wanted from him. She whispered, "I want more."

Lust turned his eyes stormy blue. He hooked his hands under her bottom and lifted. "Put your legs around me."

Her womb tightened and responded to the raspy sound of his voice that said he needed her as much as she needed him right now. When she lifted her legs and hooked her ankles behind him, he went right back to using that wonderful mouth on her.

His thick bulge was cupped against the heat flaring between her thighs. She moved closer, moaning at the feel of rubbing against him.

His hand reached underneath and between her legs, touching the frenzied nerves hidden behind a slip of lace and begging for attention.

The surge of heat rushed up, demanding to be satisfied.

She hooked her hands around his neck and rocked up against him. "Tanner, please, now. I want you inside me."

His hand stilled. "Wait ... Jee-sus. What am I ..."

In fact, everything stopped, except for the frantic bundle of tension that had her close to pleading. "What? No. Do not stop."

Tanner dropped his head to her and sounded miserable. "I can't do this, darlin'. I sure as hell want to, but I can't touch you like this when I have no idea what's going to happen tomorrow." He kissed her so tenderly she wanted to scream. He was breathing hard and muttering, "You're not—"

The shaking had started in her middle and fanned out. "I'm not what?"

"You're not someone I can do this with and just say goodbye."

That had to be the most wonderful thing any man had ever said to her.

She hugged herself to him, inhaling the scent of hot male. "I know I may have no tomorrow, Tanner. I know you cannot make promises about what will happen to me." She kissed his lips then his cheek and neck until he shuddered. She had to make him understand. "But I also know I want this. With you."

He closed his eyes, kissing her hair and said, "I won't let you do this and regret it later."

She was sick of men making her decisions.

Pushing up to look him in the face, she thought of all the things she'd done because someone else dictated her every action. Tanner's eyes were dark with passion. For her. This man wanted her, and she wanted him.

For once, she was going to fight for her own happiness. "I have lived my whole life according to someone else's plans. I have never been allowed to make *one* decision on my own. This, right now, is *my* decision."

A multitude of emotions rolled through his face, but would he admit to any of them? Would he accept that she would not regret this?

She placed her hand on his chest and felt the steady thump of his heart. Her voice broke. "Please, Tanner, do not take this from me."

"Not a chance." He kissed her again and there was no holding back this time. His fingers wandered all around her until they slipped beneath her shirt and found her breast.

She gasped at the contact.

His fingers grazed and played, gently pinching her nipple. Jin clenched her legs and nipped his ear then licked the spot.

She angled her head to give him more access to her neck. Her body was ready for him. "Hurry, Tanner."

He chuckled against her throat. "Not a chance."

Then his fingers brushed over her bottom and slid up between them again where he pushed the lace aside this time and touched those frenzied nerves.

With her back braced against the wall, his fingers teased the hard nipple of her breast and flicked across the aching bud. She felt every touch spiral down through her until all her senses were focused in one spot.

She gripped his shoulders and tightened her legs around him until her muscles felt ready to snap. She edged closer to a ledge where the world threatened to spin out of control if she slipped off the edge.

"Let go, darlin'. I've got you."

Tanner would not let anything bad happen to her.

With another brush of his finger, she arched, and her womb exploded with a thousand tingling shards. Light behind her eyes blinded her and she heard her voice calling out to him.

He held her the whole time, never letting her go.

When she finally slumped into him, he carried her to the bed and laid her down, covering her with his body. He kept kissing her while her mind realigned with the rest of her.

His hands smoothed hair back off her face. He kissed her lips, taking his time and she never wanted that kiss to end. It was a kiss that told her this was more to him than just pleasure. That this was special. *She* was special.

When he lifted up, he said, "That was the most beautiful thing I've ever witnessed."

Why hearing that about her orgasm made her smile, she had no idea, but it did. Running a finger down the shirt he still wore, she said, "Is that all I get?"

His eyes darkened and he pushed her shirt up until he slid it off her body. "You may kill me, but I'll have a smile on my face when I go."

She laughed and the next thing she knew he was undressed and had located a condom.

Eyeing the part he intended to cover with that, she asked, "Are you sure it will ... fit?" She wasn't necessarily talking about the condom being large enough.

He finished rolling the condom on and dropped down to rest his weight on his forearms. He stroked a finger along her cheek. "Having second thoughts?"

She smiled at him. "Not a chance."

He laughed, a deep, hearty sound that she wanted to hear again and again. Then he began kissing his way down to her panties and she stopped smiling.

When he ripped the lace away and put his mouth in the center of her wet heat, she gasped first at the bold move and next at the tension that started building again.

Her fingers curled into the bed covers, twisting them as he

gently spread her legs for more access and took her on another frantic race for satisfaction. She was close, so close.

Her body bowed. She begged.

He reached up and tweaked her nipple, shooting her off that ledge again.

"You're so damned adorable," Tanner said when he moved back up to kiss her again.

Then he was sliding inside her and, oh yes, there *was* more.

He cupped her bottom and pushed deep then pulled out, taking his time. She'd waited a long time for a moment like this and couldn't take putting it off any longer.

"Slow was nice, Tanner. Now faster would be nicer."

"Yes, ma'am." But this time his words had been guttural and sounding as if that was just what he'd been waiting to hear. He rocked into her again and again.

She lifted her legs and hooked them around him and drove his next stroke deep inside. She trembled at the feel of him.

He was moving faster, driving in and out.

When her muscles tightened around him, he slipped his finger between them and touched her. One perfect time.

She clung to him and let her climax take over.

Right behind her, he pushed hard and reached his release with a growl and dropped onto her, huffing out breaths and damp from exertion.

Closing her eyes, she inhaled deeply to burn this moment into her brain. She might never have another, but she would always know what it was like to feel this with someone she loved.

Chapter Thirty-Seven

TANNER LAY AWAKE, thinking about the future. His? Hers?

Did *they* have one?

They didn't.

Jin lay cradled in his arms, and he was pretty sure this might be as close to heaven as his sorry ass was ever going to be.

Jin had been awake for a few minutes, but he'd thought she'd gone back to sleep when she asked, "Tell me about your family." She added, "Please."

That seemed to be their code word to share something they normally wouldn't.

He thought about his family that seemed so far away even though they were in Texas, and he was only in California right now. "I have three sisters. Two are grown and have land near my mother's ranch."

Jin's mouth dropped open. "*Ranch.* You really are a cowboy?"

Tanner grinned. "Yes, ma'am." He watched her consider that for a moment, then she said, "What about the other sister?"

"The last one is sixteen and headstrong."

Jin smiled. "This surprises you?"

"Not really. She gets it honestly, just like the rest of us." He wanted to know more about her, too. "What does Soo Jin mean?"

"Treasure. My mother gave me that name because she wanted me to find someone who would treasure me. Silly."

Not really. Tanner stroked his hand along her smooth skin. Her mother was right. Jin deserved to be appreciated.

"Where is home, Tanner?"

"Amarillo, Texas, but different branches of our family are

spread from Amarillo to Midland in what's called the panhandle." And speaking of family, what would he tell his mother and sister if he couldn't fix this mess with the State Department? Martina's mother was going to die any day. The minute she did, his mom would be a mess if he didn't get Martina cleared to be adopted and brought here.

"I studied geography," Jin said, pulling him back to her. "I know that is the part at the top of your state. How long has your family lived there?"

"Since the 1700s."

"That is hard to envision. My family owned nothing even before my mother became ill." She switched topics. "Do you ride horses?"

"As often as I can when I go home."

"I have always wanted to sit on a horse, maybe even ride one."

He asked, "Weren't there any horses where you grew up?"

"I'm sure there were, but I was not around any. I was only allowed to study and practice fighting skills. I told you, my life has never been my choice."

He'd heard something similar from another woman who had claimed she'd had no choices and played on his sympathies. Allie had convinced him that the mess she was in was not her fault. The husband she'd married too young terrified her. She'd said over and over how she'd never gotten a chance to live her life, going from her parents' home to that of her husband's when she was nineteen.

Tanner had thought he was in love with her, but as he looked back it had been nothing more than a high school infatuation. One that had continued for too long and had become too significant in his mind when she'd rejected him to marry someone else.

Eight years later, though, he'd ridden in like a white knight to save her from a brutal marriage, or so she'd made it out to be. Much later, too late, Tanner found out she'd been just as guilty of bed hopping with other men as her husband had been with women. And Allie had been into drugs.

But in spite of what everyone tried to tell him, Tanner had stood by Allie every step of the way to help her get through a divorce that left her financially secure. He'd even paid for rehab—twice—and listened to her plead that there had to be a better way, and that it was too hard with him to help her find another way. All that rehab hadn't stuck, but it had played in her favor in gaining sympathy during the divorce where she was allotted a fat settlement.

The minute she gained her freedom and had a choice of staying with Tanner or moving on, she'd walked away. She'd gutted him. That's when he'd finally realized he'd done all that for her thinking she'd choose him, because she'd toyed with him and teased about how wonderful it would be when they could finally be together.

He brushed his fingers along Jin's arm. How could he trust a woman he barely knew when he'd been fooled by one he grew up with?

"Jin," he said, and waited for her to meet his eyes. "There are hundreds of miles of tunnels below Pyongyang. How did you know which ones to take to get us out of the city?"

"In the time I was not forced to study for the Hunters, I studied maps passed down from friends who would die if they were caught teaching me. I had been working to learn the maps for more than five years, waiting for the time when I could leave to come here. Then when they brought my sister to America, I knew I must get out to save her."

The ocean of difference between Jin and Allie hit Tanner like a pissed-off bull. Allie had been given all the choices a young girl could hope for, far more than Jin had been offered. And yet Jin had grown strong in spite of her struggles. Allie had done just the opposite.

Looking back at his time with Allie, his chest no longer ached over her. And if he had to be completely honest with himself, even at the time, his ego had taken a harder blow than his heart.

Was Jin like Allie? Was she playing him?

He was going with his gut on that one.

Jin curled into him, and he pulled the cover up to keep her warm.

This woman in his arms had a grip on his heart that would rip it in half when he eventually had to give her up.

He kept trying to imagine it, but he couldn't.

One thing he did know. He'd do all in his power to keep her safe and give her the chance to make a choice when this was done. If that didn't include him, he would find a way to live with it.

Chapter Thirty-Eight

"TAKE A DRINK of this." Tanner handed Jin a cup of ginger ale he hoped would settle her stomach and put some color back in her cheeks after the flight from Los Angeles to Ogallala, Nebraska. He was still nursing a cup of coffee and felt bad about finishing off a hefty breakfast when Jin could hardly keep the cold drink down.

"Thank you." Jin sipped the drink, but her eyes were straying to the clock shaped like a chicken. "I am wasting time."

"It's not ten yet, so we're still on schedule. Take a minute and get your stomach settled before we head out." At least the diner they'd found nearby was quiet. Jin needed that after getting off the Bombardier Learjet Sabrina had sent.

A sweet ride for anyone not terrified of flying.

Dingo put his glass of Coke down. "He's right. A few minutes won't make that much diff—"

The clip clop of approaching boot heels on tile floor stole Dingo's attention. His expression rolled into a shocked look a second before a woman said, "Why are you surprised?"

Dingo stared up, dumbfounded, and finally blurted out, "What are you doing here, Val?"

"You said you were in a hurry to find some bad people." A nice pair of legs covered in black tights stepped into view.

Tanner followed those legs up to a cranberry red knit dress with a black belt and gray scarf swiped around her neck. No coat, so the clothes made sense. It was cool outside right now, but the high temperature was expected to be in the upper fifties today. She carried herself like a woman who didn't let something like the weather get in her way. Crazy blonde hair curled in a messy style that worked only on a hot woman.

All that came with a firecracker attitude. She asked Dingo, "Are you going to introduce me and maybe move over or just treat me like you did—"

Dingo cut her off by scooting deeper in the booth as he made introductions. "Val, this is Tanner and Jin. You two, this is Val. She's the one who located the doctors in Chinatown."

"And the list of airports with Gulfstream IVs in this area," Val added, planting herself next to Dingo. "Now you just have to find one like the weather agencies use that's outfitted for flying into storms."

Tanner watched Dingo, who looked like a man in need of a quick exit strategy.

Val dipped her head to look at Jin. "Poor thing. Are you sick?"

Dingo answered, "She doesn't like flying and we just landed."

Val jumped in with a suggestion. "You should take flying lessons once this is over." She waved a hand that encompassed all of them and what Tanner took to mean their mission as *this*.

Jin stared at her as if a three-headed dragon had landed at the table and was giving her tips on how to use utensils.

Did that slow Val down? Not even.

She was an animated person who waved her hands when she spoke. "Really. Flying lessons are a good way to combat your fear of flying. Take control."

Jin shuddered and put her cup on the table.

Tanner waited for Dingo to inform Val that now would not be a good time to push any of Jin's buttons and unleash instant whoop-ass.

When that didn't happen, Tanner sent Dingo's friend a warning glare. "Not helping right now, Val."

"You don't know that. Right, Dingo?"

Dingo mumbled something unintelligible, then took the food the waiter handed him. While Val explained that she'd already eaten but would take a hot tea, Dingo filled his mouth, avoiding taking a side or answering Val.

That was interesting. Nothing ever bothered Dingo, but this woman clearly did.

And now Tanner knew what the woman Dingo had tapped

for information in Los Angeles looked like. She'd also quickly narrowed down a list of airports where Gulfstream IVs leased hangar space after Jin had told them that was the aircraft discussed for seeding operations.

Tanner let Dingo eat in peace, just glad when Jin attempted her soup.

Val finished off her hot tea and stood up, announcing she needed to visit the ladies' room and offered, "Come with me, Jin. You'll feel better if you move around."

"Dingo didn't tell me you were a doctor, too," Tanner quipped.

Val smiled at him. "I might like you in spite of the company you keep." She quickly told Jin, "And I mean the *male* company, not you."

Jin smiled as she stood. "I like you *for* the company you keep."

That brought a sharp smile to Val's face.

Hearing the strength in Jin's voice again, Tanner stopped worrying that a stiff wind would knock her over. He'd struggled not to reach out for her or hover. That's all he'd need in front of Dingo, and now Val.

The two women walked away with Val chatting up a storm about how California was the only place to live in this country, a surfer's paradise.

Tanner tossed his napkin down and stuck his elbows on the table. "What were you thinking bringing her?"

Dingo pushed his dishes aside. "Does it look like I *brought* her?"

"No, but she can't stay."

"Sending her away at this point is more effort than I'm up for."

That had the ring of some seriously screwed up history, but Tanner wasn't one to judge. "Then what're you going to do with her?"

"Me?"

Lifting his hands in a WTF move, Tanner said, "She didn't come all the way here to see *me* and I have my own hands full."

Dingo slumped back and stared at the stained acoustical ceiling for a moment, then leveled an I'm-in-a-corner-here look at Tanner. "She won't breathe a word of anything we do. But I may not be welcome in Atlanta once Sabrina finds out about this and that I kept yet another thing from her."

"We're doing that to protect Sabrina," Tanner reminded Dingo, but he didn't like holding out on her either. That wasn't the way Slye operated.

But this team protected their own, including Sabrina whether she wanted it or not.

"Listen, Tanner. We shouldn't have either one of these women here, but now that Val has shown up, she can find something missing faster than you can sneeze. If what Jin told you was true about the Orion Hunters getting to her anywhere, then she's safer with you. For now."

Tanner had justified all this over and over in his mind already. Dingo was just getting it straight in his.

But Tanner didn't want to hear "for now" and be reminded that any day now he'd have to watch Jin be taken away, maybe as a prisoner. "I know."

Dingo sat up, warming to the subject. "We could bring out four agents who won't accomplish as much as Val will in one day. She's that good and has an uncanny ability when she investigates. She gets paid insane sums to find the impossible for a wealthy clientele."

"Just as long as you can keep her safe," Tanner pointed out.

Dingo swallowed hard and dropped his gaze to the table, hiding his thoughts for a moment, then his mouth twisted with a droll smile. "Val is trained in weapons and hand-to-hand combat. She was one of the best backups I had at one time."

When had that been? Tanner wasn't asking. This whole mission was the longest running FUBAR in history.

He said, "If I thought bringing out the entire Slye organization would find Jin's sister any faster I would, but we might as well put up a billboard saying we're looking for her if too many people come on the scene. We scare this bunch off, we'll lose any chance of stopping them."

Dingo and Tanner had split up an area one hundred miles in diameter. They'd visit every airport to ask about a female pilot. Dingo had intended to pose as an investigative reporter doing a story on Asian-American women in aeronautics, but Val might actually be a better one to play that role.

Tanner and Jin had a different tactic—pretending to search for a hangar where Tanner could park his Gulfstream IV.

Amanda, Sabrina's assistant back at headquarters, was compiling driver's license ID photos for any form of the name Patty Smith starting in the Ogallala, Nebraska area and spreading out geographically from there. Tanner had sent a scan of the photo Jin carried of her sister to Amanda, giving her an age span anywhere from twenty to thirty.

So far, no match had pinged.

That would have been too easy.

Tanner said, "This is going to be like hunting that damn needle in a haystack."

"It wouldn't be if we dangled something they wanted in front of them."

Tanner hit the table with his fist. "No!"

Dingo sat back with a smug look. "It's like that, is it?"

Jin had been used constantly for someone else's benefit. He understood that she loved her mother and believed she'd been handed off for her own welfare, but bottom line, she'd been sold to a dangerous organization who had never even allowed her a life.

Dingo waited for an answer.

"We're not using her." That was all the answer Tanner would give.

The crazy Aussie's eyes twinkled. "Just checking, mate."

"You son of a bitch."

Jin stepped up to the table at that second and frowned at him. "That is not a nice thing to call your friend."

"She's right about that, mate," Dingo said, as Val slid into the booth next to him.

"That actually fits him," Tanner explained to Jin, ignoring Dingo's snicker.

Val smiled. "You two having a bromance moment?"

Dingo and Tanner said, *"No!"*

Jin caught Val's humor and her eyes twinkled with mischief. "What is a bromance?"

"Never mind." Tanner stood up, took one look at Jin and realized she knew exactly what it was. She'd wanted to tease him. Why couldn't they be just two people having a casual afternoon so he could tease her back about how he'd explain later in bed?

Some days he hated this life. "We've wasted enough time here."

Val jumped up. "Oh, I think this was *very* informative." She whispered something in Jin's ear.

Jin busted out laughing.

Tanner shouldn't envy the wild blonde for that, but he did. Jin's smiles were rare and precious. She shouldn't waste them on Val.

Then Jin turned that vibrant smile on him, and he forgot about Val and Dingo even being there. "What?"

"I am feeling better."

"I'm glad." He was not putting her back on an airplane after the hell she went through getting here.

Outside, Tanner handed Jin the keys to their Range Rover and Dingo did the same, handing Val the keys to his Escalade.

Jin climbed in on the passenger side of Tanner's truck.

Val slid behind the wheel of Dingo's ride and cranked the engine.

Dingo shook his head no and Val just smiled in pure defiance.

Tanner chuckled at Dingo's grumble. Once he had Dingo's attention again, Tanner got down to business. "Text me once every two hours and I'll do the same. If I don't get a text, I'll track you by GPS."

"You're the one who has to watch out for Bruce Lee wannabes. Nobody is chasing me or Val, but I'll text you."

A primary reason Tanner set up this two-hour texting check point was in case someone got to Jin, because that would only happen if they came through him, and he didn't make it.

He strode over to his vehicle and slid in, taking a moment to eye Jin. She was nervous again. He smiled at her. "What's wrong?"

"Nothing."

Which translated to "something" in female talk. "I'll wait until you figure out what nothing is."

She cocked her head at him. "Have you always been this stubborn?"

"Pretty much."

She muttered something in Korean, or one of the other twelve or fifty languages she knew, then huffed. "I want to know what you will do if we find my sister."

"When."

Her face softened at that. "Yes. When we find her."

"If she helps us, I'll speak up for her with the State Department, but she has to go in with us voluntarily."

"I will also have to turn myself in. True?"

"Yes." Knowing that was coming up soon was digging a hole in his gut. "But I'll be there with you."

She tried to smile, but it was sad. "I understand."

"Talk to me, Jin. I may not be able to snap my fingers and fix this for you, but I'm going to try very hard to keep you from ending up in the wrong place when this is over."

She picked at her clothes, taking shallow breaths, then raised liquid eyes to him. "I will do what I must, but my time with you has been the closest I have ever been to making my own choices. I have been ... happy."

A tear escaped and ran to the corner of her lip.

She was killing him.

Tanner leaned over and kissed her tear away then kissed the lips he craved with every breath. Sure, he'd loved the feeling of being inside her all last night and waking with her next to him, but Jin was more than amazing sex.

She'd found her way into his heart and set up camp.

No one else would ever unseat her from that position and the idea of not being able to keep her with him tomorrow and the next day and the day after that was physically painful.

He deepened the kiss, and she touched his face with her soft hands. That touch would bring him to his knees if he was standing right now. He'd never wanted a woman, or anything else in this world, the way he wanted Jin.

When he pulled away, she held his face between both hands, stopping him from moving. Her worried gaze roamed over his face. "Promise me you will not come after me if they do capture me."

"No."

"Please, Tanner. I have been willing to risk all to find my sister, but I will not risk you."

He caught her hand in his, turned it and kissed her palm. "Nothing's going to happen to me as long as you don't run into the line of fire. I can do what I need to do as long as you're safe. I know you can handle yourself, but that doesn't mean I'm going to let you fight some nutjob Orion Hunter."

She blew out a stream of air that sizzled with frustration. "You are a stubborn man."

"Yes, ma'am. I like getting my way." He winked at her and settled into the driver's seat to get rolling. His phone chimed with an incoming call. Sabrina's ringtone.

"Tanner."

"Tell me you're not toting around the woman you brought back from North Korea."

Shit. "About that—"

Yelling would have been a better sign than Sabrina's quiet voice. "Do not even think about trying to lie your way out of this. The State Department knows she's in this country. They want her and the other two now."

"How'd they find out about her?"

"It doesn't matter how. We brought her back. They know about it. We hand her over."

Tanner guided the SUV onto the road and pushed it up to speed. "I can't do that."

Chapter Thirty-Nine

IF SILENCE COULD be wielded as a weapon, Sabrina's was deadly.

Tanner said, "Give me a minute to catch you up."

"Oh, that would be nice since my ass is the one on the line for all this."

She was yelling. Better.

Tanner explained everything about Pang and the Orion Hunters, that Har was dead, plus the ambush he and Jin went through yesterday.

He wound it all up and said, "She's here with me now. If we can find her sister before Pang's canister is loaded, we have a chance at catching him and exposing the entire operation. We need Jin to identify her sister and to translate. If I bring her to Atlanta now and you hand her over, we lose any hope of stopping this."

"We'll turn this over to Homeland and bring the FAA in on it."

"Homeland can't get in position fast enough and if the FAA shuts down flights in this area, this bunch will know they've been found. Then they'll go underground for a week, a month, or a year. We'll never see it coming or have any hope of catching them again. Right now, we have the element of surprise. Lose that and the only way we'll know if they've attacked is when millions of people and animals start dying. The damage will be done and irreversible."

Eighty percent of the Bodine clan had farms, ranches and homes sitting in the direct path of the fallout from the Ogallala Aquifer.

He was failing to bring Martina home. The least he could do was protect his family and every other family that would be affected. Once he returned home, he'd have to face his sister, Lydia, and explain how he'd let her down, because this had already gone so far south that the State Department would refuse Martina any chance of coming to the US to be adopted by his mother.

He must have gotten Sabrina's attention with that last statement, so he gave her the rest. "I believe what Jin's told me about the Orion Hunters being in our government and law enforcement. We both know it only takes one person in the right position to be dangerous."

"Like whoever sold us out on the CIA op in the UK two years back."

"Exactly. With a little luck, we'll not only stop this now, but possibly turn up a list of the people in the US who are part of the Orion Hunter network."

Sabrina was tapping a drumbeat on her desktop again. "I'll send out more agents."

"Too many people out here will draw attention."

"If you and Dingo have split up, neither one of you has backup."

Tanner had to give Sabrina something. She, Dingo and Josh were tight as family. Sabrina would be on the next flight out to be Dingo's backup herself and bring someone for Tanner.

"Actually, we both have backup." Tanner hoped Dingo wouldn't take his head for this, but Dingo wouldn't hold back on Sabrina at this point. "Dingo has a friend who helped us find the doctor in Chinatown. He says she's trained and can handle a weapon."

"Tell me her name isn't *Valene*?"

Ah, hell. In for a penny ... "I would, but then I'd have to lie to you."

Cursing boiled from Sabrina's end.

Tanner pulled the phone from his ear until that subsided. "You don't like her, huh?"

"I'd like her just *fine* six feet under." Sabrina tapped some more. "Who's backing you up?"

He glanced over at Jin who was staring straight ahead, clearly worried. "Soo Jin."

Sabrina chuckled and Tanner smiled until her chuckle turned dark and scary. She said, "You've both lost your minds."

A definite possibility but admitting that would not be wise. "Based on what Jin has been able to tell us, Pang needed two days to create the chemical and bond it to silver iodide, then they'll discharge it into a rainstorm. There's a front coming across tomorrow, maybe first thing in the morning. If we locate the airplane they plan to use, then all we have to do is sit on it and wait for the canister to show up."

"And how do you and Dingo plan to locate this airplane?"

"Jin said their plans called for using a modified Gulfstream IV, I'm thinking a similar setup to NOAA's Lockheed Hurricane Hunters. Val came up with a list of seven that are renting hangars in a two-hundred-mile radius."

"What if you don't find them?"

He admitted, "If the four of us don't find this by daylight, then our only other option will be to flag any Gulfstream IVs with flight plans in this airspace as a potential threat. But if we have to do that, this bunch will come back later and succeed because we won't have any idea when or where they'll strike. They may pick another aquifer."

No yelling, cursing or scary quiet voice. Sabrina was thinking.

Tanner asked, "Did Nick make it back?"

"Yes, and he's the next one on my list."

"He was helping me."

"I don't care. None of you should have withheld information."

"You might not like that we did, Sabrina, but we did it to protect you."

"*I don't need your fucking protection!*"

That yelling was not good, because she very rarely cursed.

He failed to pull the phone away fast enough that time. When she quieted, he gave another shot at convincing her why the government couldn't be brought in right now. "The State Department isn't interested in the Orion Hunters, but the Hunters exist, and they've infiltrated our government."

"Do you have proof of that?"

Damn, she had him. "No."

"The State Department issued a deadline of handing over the Koreans here in Atlanta at two tomorrow afternoon. They don't know about Har being dead, yet, or that we've lost a physicist bent on destroying one of the largest aquifers feeding eight states."

"Buy me some time is all I'm asking. I should know something one way or the other in the morning."

"Tanner, we're out of time. I don't know how they found out, but the one thing the State Department does know about is Soo Jin. They want her. If you and Dingo find the seeding airplane by tonight, contact me and I'll let Homeland know about it, but I've sent the jet back out to Ogallala. You, Dingo and Soo Jin are to be onboard for an 8:00 AM departure."

A cold chill settled into Tanner's insides.

If he took Jin to Atlanta tomorrow, she'd be vulnerable to Orion Hunters who were waiting on her to be brought in.

If he didn't, he'd leave Sabrina to face the State Department empty handed.

Chapter Forty

JIN NEVER WANTED to fly again, but she would make a deal with the devil to find the Gulfstream IV that Pang intended to use. The one her sister would fly before they killed her.

Tanner parked at the next-to-the-last airport on his list as the sun dove toward the horizon. It would be dark in another hour. They'd driven over a hundred and fifty miles in a drunken path that wound from Ogallala toward Denver.

Dingo and Val had fared no better, but they still had two airports to check.

Jin climbed out and pulled on the slightly-too-big, light jacket Tanner had bought for her in the last town, but everyone was commenting on the unusually warm temperatures.

Rain was coming just after daylight.

She fell into step with Tanner, who slowed his long strides for her. She asked, "What are you going to do if we don't find the right airplane?"

"I have plan B, but it will only delay their attack and give them the advantage of knowing we're onto them. Until that happens, Pang has no reason to think you knew what he was doing."

Jin lifted the white earbuds attached to an iPod Tanner had gotten for her along with sunglasses. She was pretending to be his daughter. With the loose jacket, and as long as no one saw her eyes, they wouldn't realize she had any Asian blood or that she was a grown woman.

The office for this airport was nicer than the others. Two stories with a tower above the second floor. Large hangars dotted the open space on each side of a dual runway. Small to midsize airplanes were tied down in areas between the hangars.

Tanner held the door for her.

She ducked inside, head down, and immediately started shuffling around like he'd told her to do at every stop while he inquired about a hangar for his Gulfstream IV. So far, everyone had been happy to show him how well their hangar accommodated that specific airplane because they just happened to have one.

None of those had any type of seeding equipment attached to the outside or a vent opening where one might have been inside. Tanner also had his people back in Atlanta running the numbers on every Gulfstream on his list and Dingo's.

Nothing had popped up and none of the parked Gulfstreams had flight plans filed for later in the week. If any of them decided to take off into a storm tomorrow, Tanner said this woman Sabrina would handle getting those flights grounded.

One airport had a vacant hangar, but their Gulfstream customer had flown his family to Costa Rica for a wedding.

While Tanner did his part, Jin scanned the papers and magazines scattered around the waiting area. It would be nice to have the freedom to own any newspaper, magazine, video or other simple entertainment that was not regulated by the government like when she was in North Korea.

Her gaze was drawn to the picture of a smiling couple on the front of a ragged magazine. They were standing in front of an airplane that looked just like the ones she'd seen in the hangars.

Tanner's booming southern voice carried from where he spoke to someone in charge of this airport. "I appreciate it. Here's my card if anything comes available."

Jin's hands shook as she lifted the magazine.

Tanner touched her shoulder. "Come on, hon."

She turned to him, trying to think what to say.

His eyes narrowed when he picked up on her distress. He barely dropped his chin to let her know he understood something was wrong. "Let's get going and find dinner."

She took her time walking beside him from the office to the SUV when she wanted to run. He helped her into the truck then got in on his side and said, "Don't panic, sugar. Dingo and Val still have two locations to check out."

Jin closed her eyes for a moment and prayed she would make

the right choice. She pulled her glasses off and placed them on the dash then turned to him and lifted the magazine for him to see the cover.

He studied it and the man the article was about, then pushed his gaze back to Jin. "That's the right airplane, but that magazine is from California."

"The airplane is not. Take a closer look at Mr. Dearborn's wife."

Tanner did, then his eyebrows shot up to touch the lock of hair that had fallen on his forehead. "Is that—"

"Patty. My sister." Jin's pulse jumped at the possibility of seeing her sister again. "The man identified as her husband is building Dearborn Airfield, a private airport two hundred miles from here where they are customizing the interiors of Gulfstream IVs."

Tanner reached over and grabbed her into his arms. "You are amazing. You found what even Val couldn't."

Now, if Jin could be as fortunate in finding her sister and helping her escape.

Chapter Forty-One

TANNER HAD HIS Bluetooth hooked up so he could speak with Dingo and leave his hands free to react if a wild animal dashed into his path on this pitch-black stretch of highway. "Head back to Ogallala."

"Where are you now?" Dingo asked.

"We're close to Sterling, Colorado. I think we've found the location. I'll check it out, then I'll touch base with you."

"Give me two hours and I'll be there by daylight."

Tanner glanced over for an instant at Jin who was listening intently to his half of the conversation.

Eyes back on the road, he said, "Can't wait that long. We'll be there in forty minutes. If we have the right aircraft and Pang is there, they'll have to take off before daylight to interact with the storm coming in. Based on the weather report we've been monitoring, they may have to take off even sooner."

"You're talking an hour window of time to get there, find Pang and let Sabrina know to bring everyone in on them. I don't like you doing it with just Jin, mate."

Tanner didn't like any of this either, but that hadn't stopped the universe from throwing crap in his way since Pyongyang. "All I have to do is a quick recon to confirm we've found the right place. Sabrina won't have as much time to chew on my ass. She'll bring in everyone from Homeland to the FBI and they'll love her for it. Maybe that'll get her out of the hot seat with the State Department."

Maybe that would buy Tanner enough points to gain Sabrina's help with keeping Jin and her sister from being sucked into the system where they'd be targets of Orion Hunters hidden within the government.

Tanner would never cross Sabrina, but neither would he just hand Jin over. Not now. Not ever.

"I heard from Sabrina, too," Dingo said, letting that sit between them for a moment. "I hate it for you, but I don't see any way to get out of taking Jin in."

Tanner knew she was listening carefully to his side. He didn't want to argue this in front of her, so he said, "I'll let tomorrow take care of itself."

"Call me as soon as you have word on that plane."

"Will do."

Tanner pulled the Bluetooth off and dropped it in the cup holder. Headlights approached then dimmed just long enough to pass them.

Then another stretch of nothing.

Jin said, "Please do not treat me as a fool or a child."

That opening could go nowhere but down. "Meaning?"

"You are going to call in an army of people when you know you have the right location and if Pang is there."

Some lines couldn't be crossed. "I have to, Jin."

"But my sister."

"If I can find her and get her away from the others, I'll take her with us, but she'll be in my custody at that point and she'll have to prove that she wasn't voluntarily helping them."

"She isn't. Give me a chance to prove she's innocent in all this."

He'd avoided this question for two days and the time had come to face it. "What if she's not?"

"She is!"

"She's an Orion Hunter."

Jin whispered, "So am I."

"No, you're a rebel who will not go along with anything you consider morally wrong."

"She is the same," Jin argued.

"How can you be so sure? You haven't seen her in three years. Your sister could have been brainwashed in that time."

Jin was shaking her head, refusing to accept anything other than what she believed. "Patty was sweet and would never hurt anyone. She understood that we had to go along with the Orion

Hunters, because we had no choice. Those were her words the last time we were together. She said, 'Do what you must to survive, Jin. Pretend to be who they want you to be so that we can be together again at some point.' I had to pretend that I liked studying ancient languages and testing artifacts."

Jin paused, staring out at the dark night as she finished explaining. "I had to excel at my studies and my fighting skills, but I would not harm someone for them. And neither would she." She turned to Tanner and swallowed hard. "I fear for what they have planned for her. The night I learned of this mission, one of the Orion Hunters said that my sister would die, and she would never see it coming. I have no idea how they plan to kill her, but I will find a way to stop them."

Tanner admired her loyalty. Jin was an all-in woman when it came to family and love.

She would love without limits. She cared for him. Given some time, she might even love him.

He wanted that. Wanted her. But he wasn't sold on her sister. In fairness to Jin, arguing would only upset her when neither one of them had any hard evidence. "Okay, we'll do our best to find Patty and keep the Hunters from unleashing that toxin."

With only a few hours to do it.

Why hadn't he promised world peace as long as he was making ridiculous commitments?

"I have a confession to make."

Jin had spoken so softly he did a double take. "What confession?"

"It was not intentional, but the problems you had leaving North Korea were my fault."

He'd learned to wait for everything from Jin. Information came in small pieces that had to be snapped together for a complete picture. "What did you do?"

"Do you remember me telling you about Pang's boss, Myong?" When Tanner nodded, she continued. "He had raped a young married woman and she took her life rather than face her husband. Myong hated children, but when an accident—that I do not believe was an accident—killed his sister who was a single mother, he petitioned to bring his thirteen-year-old niece to live with him even though the mother left specific instructions requesting that a close female friend should raise her."

That was fucked up. "What'd you do?"

"I could not leave knowing what he would do to his niece. I left evidence pointing a finger at Myong as a traitor and having knowledge about Pang and Har's escape. The DPRK is full of spies, and someone found the information too soon. That is why the soldiers arrested his boss. So, your problems were my fault, but I was afraid to tell you when we were escaping and other times with your men close by." Her words fell off at the end.

Tanner had to admit that in her shoes he would have done the same thing. He reached over and took her hand in his. When she looked up at him, he told her, "I understand why you did it and my team would, too. Besides, you got us out of there. I'm glad you protected that child."

Her face softened. "Thank you. I will not carry that with me ... any longer."

What bothered him the most about that confession was what Jin *hadn't* said just now. Her relief was palpable.

It didn't take a rocket scientist to figure out that she wanted that off her conscience in case she died.

She had yet to realize that just as she couldn't let that child suffer, neither would Tanner allow anything to happen to Jin. At least, not if he had the power to stop it.

He took the exit for the road to Dearborn Airfield, and five miles down the highway a ten-foot-tall, chain-link fence separating the airport from the road came into view. Security lights shone down on construction equipment parked near a slab that looked like a foundation for the next hangar, in addition to three already standing.

Four light aircraft were situated between the hangars and an impressive two-story complex for a private airport in the middle of nowhere.

Not only that, but lights were blazing inside the building at almost four in the morning.

As he slowed, he could just make out an airplane large enough to be the Gulfstream IV parked in the first hangar.

Hot damn.

And another comparable one in the next hangar.

Well, hell. He'd have to check them both out unless he found a machine for dispersing the silver iodide in the first one.

Jin put a hand on the console and pushed up to look past him, over the steering wheel. "How long will it take to get inside that fence?"

He should be flattered she had no doubt he'd get them inside, but he was too worried about taking her. "I'll go in, check it out and come back to the truck if I see any females there."

"I know that is not your plan. I am not going to stay here when you have no one to watch your back."

"I can watch my own back, Jin."

"I am the only one who can identify my sister. What if you find something written in Korean? How will you know if it is important or not?"

All valid points he wished he didn't have to accept, but he did. Time was racing by. "Then do as I say, when I say."

She cocked her head at him, and amusement danced through her tart words. "Like when you told me to hide in the corner of that building in Chinatown? You should follow *me* this time."

"Not going to happen."

A mile past the airport, he found a rutted dirt road that turned off next to a creek with the only trees growing for miles. He parked, then loaded a backpack with ammo, a wire cutter and lock pick tools.

He held a Glock out to Jin, because that was the lightest and simplest handgun he had.

She stepped back. "No."

"You can't always fight your way out of a situation, and you need this in case anything happens to me."

"I will be with you."

Yes, but what if he was dead? "You need a weapon."

"Give me a knife."

But would she really use it to kill someone attacking her? He handed her a switchblade she could put in her pocket.

Even with him jogging, Jin had no trouble keeping up. They reached the fence line in fifteen minutes and crept around the perimeter until Tanner found a spot to cut through the chain link. He peeled the jagged edges apart for Jin to step through, then he followed.

At the first hangar, he slipped along the side until he reached a locked door on the half-round building. He picked the lock, which took little time since it was more of a deterrent to someone nosy than actual security. This airport was not open to public traffic so the bunch who owned it probably felt they had little reason to worry about theft or vandalism this far off the beaten path. That also explained the lack of security cameras. One bit of luck amid the FUBAR.

Inside the first hangar, small lights at the rear offered enough illumination to study the details of the Gulfstream IV.

Tanner walked silently around the aircraft with his ninja close but had her wait when he found stairs leading to the open cockpit. At the top of the steps, Tanner found a plane in the midst of having a luxury interior installed. Shit.

He returned to the ground and motioned for Jin to follow him to the next hangar.

Same thing there except that Gulfstream's interior wasn't as far along.

Stepping over to the last hangar, his hope was disintegrating since the aircraft in this one was smaller, and the front of the hangar was open. Anyone could walk in.

This one held a Beech 99 aircraft. The kind a professional skydiving group would use.

But with one difference. This Beech had a vent poking down through the undercarriage. Tanner squatted to take a closer look. He was about ninety-nine percent sure that was not standard on a jump plane.

He stood and walked around the wing and gripped the Lexan roll-up jump door where parachutists exited the airplane. Clear horizontal strips ten inches wide were mounted to an aluminum frame that rolled up inside the canopy like the action of an overhead garage door. Once he had an opening he could fit through, Tanner climbed in and raised it the rest of the way, then stood to give Jin a hand up. The space was wide enough for two average adults to fit through.

"What is this?" she whispered.

He was trying to figure that out himself as he took in the hollow fuselage. Black cargo netting that resembled an oversized spider web hung loosely across the aft, turning the rear section into a dark hole.

That left an easy fifteen feet of forward compartment that was empty other than two parachute packs anchored with elastic cords to tie-downs on the starboard side of the floor. One was yellow and the other a drab green.

And a suspicious three-foot-wide machine mounted on the port side.

He leaned down. "This might be our airplane."

Tanner moved up to the machine and knelt where he could shine a tiny LED light over the top. It had lettering that looked like Chinese to him, but he'd bet it was Korean.

Jin dropped down next to him. "This machine is similar to the one on the drawings I saw in Pang's area of the lab." She smiled at Tanner with a cocky tilt to her head. "Now you need me to translate. Good thing you brought me."

He liked this confident side of Jin. "Point taken. Can you open it to see if the canister has been loaded yet?"

"I should be able to, but ... that does not make sense."

"Why? What does it say?"

Jin reached for one of two metal clasps and froze.

A woman's laughter percolated through the silence outside and was followed by a man's voice speaking too low for Tanner to understand his words. They were entering the hangar.

Lights flipped on overhead in the giant space.

Tanner grabbed Jin and dragged her deep into the plane behind the cargo netting where the rear area was cast in dark shadows.

"Pang cut this too close," the woman said, banging a door shut on a metal cabinet. "We should wait for a better window."

Jin grabbed Tanner's hand and squeezed. One look at her face was all it took to confirm that they'd found her sister, Patty.

"We can't, doll," the man said. "Pyongyang wants this operation shut down as soon as we're through today. If *they* say we're compromised, that's enough for me."

Had the Orion Hunters back in North Korea decided their

operation was compromised because one of their Orion people inside the State Department tipped them off? Or was it because Har was dead?

Or because they knew Jin was here?

The sound of them moving around ceased and footsteps headed around the rear of the airplane, toward the jump door.

Tanner cursed to himself. He'd left the damn thing unlatched.

Patty spoke in a brisk tone that had not a speck of Korean accent. "The jump door is open. Who was the last one to touch this, Stan?"

"Pang and Lenny. I'm not busting on Lenny. Poor guy was probably in a hurry to get the canister packed and be done with that prima donna. Pang's lucky that he came up with this formula or someone would have buried him by now."

Stan climbed in through the opening, a fit man in his thirties with short brown hair. He had no accent.

Tanner placed him as Midwestern.

Patty grumbled then told Stan, "I'd be more impressed if the prima donna had developed a chemical that could be shot out like a normal cloud seeding."

"This still works. Once it's released it's so fine that the particles will float, giving us a wider spread for the contamination. It really is genius, but don't tell Pang I said that. Once this toxin is on the ground, all we need is some rain and those babies start expanding and saturating their way down to the water table. Hell, we'll be able to do more damage this way."

Jin covered her face with her hands. Hearing her sister so comfortable with this plan had to be breaking her heart.

Patty groused, "Yes, but I hate to see a fine aircraft abused."

"I'll buy you the newer model when we get settled again, doll."

Patty dragged metal steps into place that she used to step into the fuselage. She turned toward the cockpit too quickly for Tanner to see much, but she had Jin's same height and body shape. A trim five-foot-six, but where Jin's dark brown hair fell to her waist, Patty's had been cut in layers that fell loose and free.

Tanner had to tell Dingo this was not about seeding a cloud, but somehow spraying this over an area. He shielded his phone inside his jacket to text Dingo but ... no tower.

Are you kidding me?

Stan went to the parachutes and started checking them over while Patty took the pilot's seat.

Shit.

The turbo props turned over once and caught.

Jin made a panicked move, but Tanner caught her around the waist and hauled her back next to him. He covered her mouth at the same time. She jerked around and raised terror-filled eyes to his, shaking her head that she could not do this.

The motor noise covered anything he'd say, but he still whispered next to her ear. "I know you're afraid, but he's got a weapon and will kill both of us. Just stay here no matter what I do and don't make a sound. Can you do that?"

She pulled his fingers from her mouth and cupped her trembling hands between her lips and his ear. "We must stop now, or we will all die."

"No, we won't. You stay back here until we land."

Jin kept shaking her head. Stubborn woman.

The airplane was already out of the hangar and headed toward the runway. As Stan closed the jump door and latched it for takeoff, the last blast of wind batted hair around Tanner's face and blew Jin's hoodie off, slapping loose strands everywhere from her ponytail.

The plane made the turn onto the runway and Patty gunned the throttle. Jin clutched at Tanner when the G force pulled her back.

Tanner hooked his arm around her, drawing her to him. With the noise of the motor, Jin's next words were lost. Once he had her hugged up tight, she lunged back to talk next to his ear.

"I could not read all of it, but I saw the word explosive."

Tanner wrenched around to see Stan on the port side now, holding onto a strap anchored to the cabin roof, and tinkering with the machine.

Now Patty's conversation about abusing a fine aircraft and Stan's reply that he'd buy her a new one clicked and made sense.

They intended to put it on autopilot, set the bomb timer and dive away while the aircraft exploded, dispersing the chemical. No one would ever figure it out.

The wind at that altitude would spread a fine mist of chemical for miles.

He had to stop them before they jumped.

Chapter Forty-Two

THE AIRCRAFT HAD leveled off and was cruising at what Tanner estimated to be around fifteen thousand feet above the ground. But the wind ahead of the storm was beating the fuselage, causing the craft to shudder and jerk.

Jin was curled into herself, shaking.

He kissed her and said, "Don't move, no matter what."

Patty unlatched herself from the pilot seat and braced herself on the cabin wall as she stepped around to stand over Stan as he unhooked her parachute from its moorings. He stood and helped her into the yellow harness and loaded the pack onto her back, then unlatched the jump door and rolled it up out of the way.

Wind and engine noise sharpened, and cold air lashed through the fuselage.

Patty caught Stan's arm and yelled, "What about the timer?"

Stan gave her a thumbs up, then turned to reach for the green harness and parachute.

Now or never.

Tanner eased up, hunched over as he unlatched a clip on the heavy-duty cargo netting strung like a web across the rear compartment. He led with his weapon.

Patty had just snapped her helmet strap and turned around to face the jump door when she and Stan noticed Tanner.

Stan dropped the pack and yelled, "What the fuck?"

Tanner said, "Hands up. We know about your plan. It's done."

Patty took a step toward the door.

Tanner shouted, "Freeze or you're dead."

"How could you?" Jin screamed beside Tanner, yanking his attention away from Stan for a second.

Jin clung to the netting, trembling, with tears pouring down her face.

"Put the gun down or she dies," Stan shouted.

That split second Tanner had let his guard down was all Stan needed to draw his Glock and point it at Jin.

Tanner held his weapon on Stan, but he didn't want to kill the one person they probably needed to disarm the thing.

Or risk a stray bullet striking the bomb.

Patty stared at her sister. "What are you doing here? You're helping *him*? An American? You're a disgrace to our people."

Tanner used the time while Patty ranted to figure out his next step, which was *what*? Hell if he knew. If he took his gun off Stan, he risked Jin being hit.

"Me?" Still clutching the swaying net, Jin stood up straighter and grew a steel backbone. "I do not murder people. How can you do this?"

"These are Americans. The man who left us to be sold was American."

"Mother did not sell us."

"Yes, she did, and I thank her spirit for it every day."

Stan warned Patty, "Six minutes. Do something."

She nodded and told Jin, "How can you care about Americans who are not Orion Hunters? They are our only family. The *Korean* Hunters fed and raised us. They educated us and how do you repay them? By betraying all we stand for. You are not my sister. You are nothing more than a wasted sperm."

Jin shouted, "You are not *my* sister."

Stan shouted, "Fine. Nobody is anybody's sister. We're done here, Patty."

The plane hit a patch of turbulence and lurched up and down hard.

Patty bounced against the side once and fell out the jump door.

Tanner flew sideways toward the door but twisted and lunged for the floppy netting that Jin was using to stay upright.

Jin shrieked, "No!" and grabbed his arm, yanking him to her with more strength than he'd have thought possible.

Good thing or he'd have missed the handhold and slid out the door behind Patty.

Stan grabbed his parachute as he tumbled back toward the machine. He stabbed an arm through the shoulder strap and tried to stand at the same time.

The airplane dipped, and he tripped, sliding across the cabin floor then half out the jump door.

Tanner lunged with one hand and grabbed the free strap on Stan's pack, jerking it back.

Stan swung around wild-eyed, gripping the single strap as he fell all the way out the jump door, dragging Tanner with him.

Tanner held onto the strap with one hand and the netting with his other. His shoulders screamed with pain. He prayed the netting wouldn't break.

Wind battered Stan's body. He fought to push a hand up and get a double grip on his side of the pack. His terror-ridden gaze whipped into view just as the plane hit another air pocket and dropped again.

The tension on the pack was slack for a microsecond, then Stan's weight plunged down in a vicious yank on Tanner's muscles.

That broke Stan's hold on the strap.

His scream died in the brutal wind whipping his body through the air. Tanner had lost his HK in all that, but a weapon wasn't going to save him and Jin.

He dragged himself and the parachute backpack over to her and yelled, "Help me put this on."

Her eyes glazed with shock.

Oh, hell. He was not losing her now. He roared, *"Jin!"*

When she snapped out of her daze, he shouted, "Help me put this on." With her hands shaking so hard every effort took twice as long, they managed to get him strapped in.

The airplane leveled off.

Tanner had to get to that machine now. It was on the other side of the jump door. Only a few feet away, but one bump and they'd both slide out the door.

He grabbed Jin's arm and started toward the machine.

"No!" Jin had a death grip on the webbing.

He didn't have time to coax her. "Do you want to die?"

That might have been the wrong question considering she had a look on her face that said she was ready to end this terror. He asked, "Are you willing to let *me* die?"

A strange look came over her face and she finally let go of the webbing. He held her arm in a grip that would probably leave bruises, but if he got tossed out the jump door, she was coming with him.

He pulled her to the machine and lowered her to the floor, keeping her on the cockpit side of him so she couldn't fall out of his reach. "Open this thing up and take out the canister."

"I don't know if I can do it without setting off the detonation."

He'd lost the chance to save Martina and now he was going to have to watch his family and everyone anywhere close to water influenced by the Ogallala Aquifer lose everything.

What had Margaux said? *You can't save them all, cowboy.*

"If we can't take the canister out, then I'm getting you out of here." He started to stand.

Jin gripped his arm, pulling him back down. "I will not live just to let all those people die. You would never forgive yourself if we did not try."

That's how he'd be looking at this if he were alone right now. He'd move his family to save them, but he'd move heaven and earth to protect Jin. "I won't forgive myself if anything happens to you."

"I love you, cowboy."

What a time to find that out. "I love you, too, sweetheart, but I'll love you even more if you'll get moving."

"Let me try to do this." She reached for a latch.

He put his hand on hers before she opened the machine and she smiled at him. "Have a little faith, cowboy."

This was the woman he wanted by his side forever. If he could just keep them both alive. He glanced at the timer. "You have ninety-eight seconds."

Without another word, she turned into the determined ninja he'd fallen in love with. She read the Korean scribble, then unhooked each latch. She continued, reading quickly, and moving her hands just as fast.

She was so precise about every movement that he could feel his heart slamming up against his chest with every second that flew out the jump door.

"Eighty seconds, Jin. We've got to go." They still might not survive the explosion.

She pulled out a silver canister and held it like a newborn. "I have it. Now what?"

"We jump."

Her face fell and she started shaking.

He grabbed her by the shoulders. "Do you trust me?"

She stared up at him with those silver-blue eyes. "Yes."

He stood her up. "I trust you to hold that canister so I can hold you. I won't let you go."

She cupped the canister to her chest. He picked her up beneath her elbows. "Wrap your legs around my waist."

He wrapped his arms tight around her and dove out of the airplane, and her throat-ripping scream split his left eardrum as he let them free-fall to put as much distance between them and—

Ka-boooom!

Yeah, that.

As they fell faster, Tanner buried his face in Jin's shoulder to shield her as the wave of heat and concussion from the explosion knocked him sideways in the air. When he looked up, far beneath the line of thunderheads, a streak of sunlight was trying to peek over the horizon. Tanner had no freaking idea where they would land, but they'd gotten out of the plane in time.

Jin's words popped into his mind. ... *the Orion Hunters said that my sister would die, and she would never see it coming.*

What if they'd planned Stan's death, too, and the parachutes had been sabotaged?

Chapter Forty-Three

DINGO SET HIS duffel bag on the ground near the jet and turned to the footsteps clipping the pavement, coming toward him.

"This has been fun," Val said with her signature snarky tone. "Almost like old times. You know, back when you came to see me for different reasons."

Two days with her had been a blessing and a curse.

She'd made this job easier, found information they had to have fast, and had not wasted a minute of the time negotiating a deal.

The curse had been spending hours so close to her and not being able to touch her.

"Thank you for everything, Val. I mean it."

"I'd say you're welcome, but—" She looked up, tapping her cheek in thought. "*You're* not welcome. *You* don't deserve my help, but your friends do. I like them." Her gaze flitted everywhere as she spoke, except at him.

"Look at me, Val."

That yanked her gorgeous eyes to him.

She had too much pride and backbone to ever let him think he made her uncomfortable or intimidated her. He'd loved that about her. She was strong and gutsy. She wasn't cut out to be a high-maintenance woman. But she'd forgotten that he knew her "tell." She'd look all around when she was on edge.

He took her hand, and she snatched it back, leaning in with a glower. "Nothing has changed between us other than you owe me big time for this."

The last two days had shown him that he couldn't leave things the same way with her any longer, but now wasn't the time to make amends. Not when he had to fly back and face Sabrina first. "I'll give you an email to send your bill to, Val."

"Email isn't safe."

She was screwing with him. He said, "Then I'll snail mail it to you."

"The post office loses my stuff all the time."

He stepped up close, daring her to back away, but his girl never backed away. *His girl?* Not for a long time. Never again. He would not lose his patience and end this on a bad note. "Tell me what you want, and I'll have the money wired to your account."

Her eyes had started flitting about again, but she stabbed a piercing glare at him. "Nothing. I want nothing from you." She turned to walk away.

Fuck patience.

He grabbed her arm, spun her back and cupped her face, kissing her finally. Yes, Jesus, finally he could taste that mouth again and feel that part of his world he'd missed more than he could ever explain to her.

When he finished and stepped back, he took a bit of pride in the awe-filled look on her face.

That lasted the whole five seconds she let him enjoy it. "Nice try, Dingo, but I'm not interested. My price is much higher than something so negligible."

Way to kill the moment and carve out a section of his heart at the same time. He ground his back teeth. "Then what *do* I owe you, Val?"

She found her first real smile. "I'll be in touch."

His stupid brain jumped to a potential clandestine visit when no one would know he was near her. Maybe he could find a way.

He watched the sway of her hips as she walked away from him and all at once, reality crashed in.

She'd just given him the same words he'd left her with seven years ago. The words he'd intended to make good on before the world was yanked out from beneath him and she'd found someone new.

The words she'd just spoken had been an intentional and all-too-clear message.

She would *never* call him again.

And that was the way it should be because he would only bring danger to her door.

He sucked his pain inside where it belonged, picked up his duffel and climbed the steps to enter the cabin of Sabrina's jet. The first thing he noticed was the yellow, leak-proof biohazard container that was twice the size of the deadly seeding canister that it contained. That was thanks to Blade, who'd made a call to have the container delivered.

"You okay, man?" Tanner came walking up to him.

The cowboy had cuts and bruises from a rough parachute landing, but he was alive.

Dingo dug out one of his convincing smiles. "Yeah, I'm right fine, mate. What about you?"

"Just hung up with Sabrina."

"Got any ass left?"

"A little and getting chewed out was nothing compared to everything Sabrina has done." Tanner looked around at Jin who was curled up on one of the sofas with a giant stack of magazines and books, all of which would have been forbidden to possess in North Korea. Before they'd boarded, she'd asked to stop at a newsstand. She'd bought one of everything light and fluffy, including two romance novels, both with cowboys on the cover. She looked up and caught them watching her, then met Tanner's eyes and grinned.

When his attention returned to Dingo, Tanner said, "I'll owe Sabrina for the rest of my life, but I'm happy to pay that debt. She hammered out a deal with the State Department."

"Tell me she came out on top," Dingo said. He could use some good news right now.

Tanner's face lit with the kind of happiness that came from deep inside. "Sabrina agreed to never tell anyone that the United States had contracted to bring terrorists into the country if they agreed to give Jin asylum. Jin's going to tell Sabrina everything she knows about the Orion Hunters and Sabrina's CIA friend is creating Jin a new identity. The State Department could do it, but Sabrina agrees that we don't know who we can trust there right now."

Dingo nodded that he agreed but didn't know if it was wise for Sabrina to ask Gage Laughton for anything. "She find out who set us up at the safe house?"

"No and she's pissed, too. They sent a new guy from the State Department to finalize the details with her. When she asked about her original contact and who would be heading up an investigation to find the leak about her safe house, she was told that he couldn't reveal details of any investigation and her first contact had died last night of a heart attack. No one knew he had a weak heart."

"Weak heart my ass. I bet she *is* pissed, mate. Hell, I'm pissed. That means we can't use him to find out who screwed us. Her contact was probably just a front man for the one pulling the strings." Dingo cursed, shaking his head. "That limits our chances of finding out if there are Orion Hunters in the State Department."

"Exactly, but you know Sabrina. She isn't done with this by a long shot."

"True." Thinking about Orion Hunters living here as sleeper cells, Dingo asked, "So Jin's sister *was* in it the whole time?"

Heartache pulled at Tanner's gaze. "Yep. Her sister paid for trusting the Orion Hunters. Patty's husband had to be in on killing her. Her chute had been sabotaged, but obviously, his worked since we're both still here. I just want to get Jin cleared through headquarters then she'll have time to grieve in private."

"Think the Orion Hunters can find Jin?"

"Not where I'm taking her."

Dingo pulled on his ear, thinking. "What about the little girl your family wanted to adopt?"

Tanner's grin dimmed a bit. "Her mother died last night, but Sabrina wrapped clearing the adoption into the deal. When things were looking bad for cashing in my deal with the State Department, I contacted a former Delta buddy and asked him to go down to Mexico. He's kept an eye on Martina and he's handling the funeral arrangements for me. Once that's done, he'll escort Martina to my mom's home this week."

Dingo found a real smile for that. A sharp pang of jealously punched him in the gut, but Tanner had believed in Jin when no one else did.

He'd earned her.

And from what Dingo had figured out about Jin, she would protect her cowboy whether he liked it or not.

Chapter Forty-Four

CHATTON SAT IN her Lexus rental and watched a jet taxi down the runway for takeoff at the Ogallala airport while she waited on Wayan to come on the cellular call.

"I hope you have news for me," he said when he answered.

"I do." News came in two forms. She doubted he was going to like his. "Har is dead, and Pang was captured and taken into custody during a raid on an Orion Hunter complex."

Wayan's silence slithered around, looking for a victim. "What of the woman?"

"She was on the aircraft sent up to seed toxin-laced silver iodide into a storm. The airplane exploded. The only bodies found were a woman whose chute failed to open and a man who took the dive without a parachute."

Wayan could form his own conclusion about Jin. Chatton watched Sabrina Slye's jet soar into the skies and fly away with Chatton's only hope of fulfilling this deal with Wayan.

Tanner's woman had battled the odds to escape North Korea and saved millions of people. She deserved her freedom, and Wayan had lied to Chatton about Soo Jin's wanting to defect to China.

Wayan finally said, "That is unfortunate, Chatton. This means you have broken our agreement."

"I did what I could, Wayan. I lost, too."

"I do not lose, Chatton. And when someone fails me, they must pay a price."

She lifted her sunglasses and sat them on top of her head, thinking. "Are you threatening me, Wayan? I proved my value to you by keeping an eye on The General, so he doesn't screw you."

"I do not threaten. It is a waste of energy. I make promises. Here is my promise. You will never find the person you are searching for, but *I will*. And once I do, you will regret having disappointed me."

The call ended.

Chatton gripped the steering wheel, admitting she might have made a mistake she'd never thought possible.

She might have underestimated Wayan.

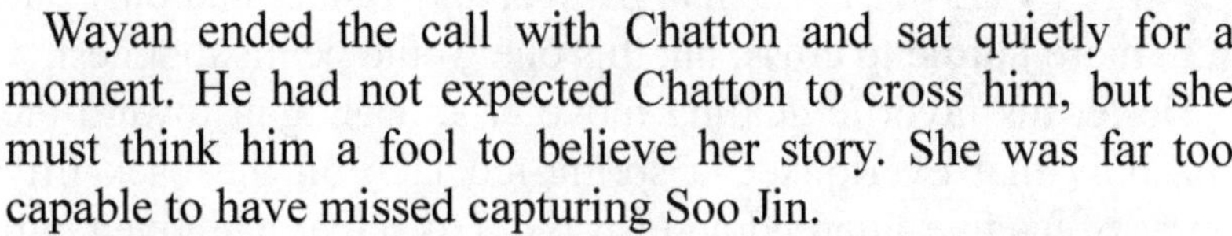

Wayan ended the call with Chatton and sat quietly for a moment. He had not expected Chatton to cross him, but she must think him a fool to believe her story. She was far too capable to have missed capturing Soo Jin.

He pressed a button on the control center built into his onyx desk.

In less than ten seconds, one of his most trusted men entered, dipped a brief bow, and asked, "What might I do for you?"

"Lee, who did you say had located the Orion Hunter doctor in Los Angeles just before the doctor was killed?"

"A woman by the name of Valene Eklund. She is an independent contractor who locates items or people of high value. She is paid very well for her work and considered to be exceptionally skilled."

"I want you to arrange for someone who has no tie to us—and who is American—to contact her on my behalf."

Lee nodded. "What will be the reason for this contact?"

"I have a job for her."

Chapter Forty-Five

TEN INTENSE DAYS had passed, and Tanner had only one more hurdle to cross, but this one would be his toughest.

He let his favorite gelding move at an easy gait toward the meadow that overlooked a spring-fed lake on the back fifty acres of his five-hundred-acre spread. His father had given him this piece when Tanner told him he wanted the spot to build a house on this hill for Mary Lou.

Of course, Mary Lou had been twelve and Tanner had been eleven at the time.

Things changed when she hit high school and football players were more exciting than the cowboys she'd grown up around.

He smiled at the distant memory.

But he wanted that house more than ever now. He just needed someone to want it with him.

Jin had never been given a choice. Once he'd finally convinced her that with her new identity and word leaked that she'd died when the aircraft exploded, her presence was not a danger to him, Tanner had spent the past week looking into possibilities for her while Jin stayed at his mother's house. His mama took a liking to her, but then his mama had always had sound judgment. She'd warned him about Mary Lou and Allie.

He should have taken his mama's advice more often.

But he'd gotten his stubborn attitude honestly from the same woman.

Jin shifted in his arms, taking in everything they passed. "This is beautiful. When can I get my own horse?"

"You can ride this one."

"No, I mean once I learn how to ride by myself."

He'd picked out a sweet mare for her but changed his mind

before he told her about the horse. He didn't want to take even that choice from her. "Just say when you're ready for a riding lesson and to go shopping."

"I'm ready." She twisted around and smiled at him. "Not right this minute. But when we go home. Okay?"

Home. He felt that word deep in his soul. "Okay."

When they reached the meadow, the sun was just peeking over the eastern horizon. He'd taken her riding almost every day for the past week, but they always seemed to end up here. She whispered with reverence, "I love this spot."

"Me, too." He had to get this over with. "I want to talk to you, Jin."

"Yes?"

"You're as safe as you can be out here where a driveway is five miles long. With your new identity as Jennifer, I can help you get set up in a job once you figure out what you'd like to do," he clarified, determined to let her know her future was hers. "And a place to live. You just have to tell me what you want."

She sat so still he might have thought she'd gone to sleep if not for the deep sigh. "Is that what you want me to do?"

"The point is not what I want for you, but what *you* want. I love you and I want you very much. But you've never had a chance to make your own decisions. I'll be around so long as you want to see me." He swallowed. "Just tell me what you want."

She pushed a leg up and started moving like she intended to stand up in the saddle. Tanner grabbed her at the waist. "Where are you going?"

"To see you."

He laughed and lifted her, turning her around until she sat with her legs hanging over his thighs. She sported new blue and white leather boots that she'd squealed over picking out. "Thank you for all the thought you put into what would be good for me. Now, I want to know, what about you?"

"What do you mean?"

"What do *you* want?"

He stared off into the distance at the sun rising further up into the sky above his land. "I plan to keep working with Sabrina, but only domestic jobs. I've had enough of going overseas. I want to build a house on this spot and watch the sun rise and set as often as I can with—" He looked down at her. "The woman I love."

Her eyes smiled back at him. "The course of true love never did run smooth."

"Is that more Shakespeare?"

"Yes."

"What does it mean?"

"That I should like to now tell what I want." Her eyebrows lifted. "Is that all right?"

"Yep. That's what I've been trying to get you to do this whole time." He loved looking into her eyes and seeing love, but he had to give her a chance to stretch her wings. "What do you want, darlin'?"

She lifted her fingers to touch his cheek. "I want to learn what it is like to be free to get up every morning and choose how to spend my day. To go wherever I want and not answer to anyone."

Wasn't that what he wanted for her too? Then why did his chest hurt with the possibility of losing her? He'd done this before. Not that he'd ever compare Jin to Allie again, but this felt too familiar. What was that old saying about setting something free and if it loves you, it'll come back?

He could do this.

Jin stroked his face and he'd miss that as much as everything else about her. Her touch had brought his heart back to life and he feared if he couldn't keep her close the damn thing would shrivel and die completely.

She smiled and her eyes held contentment. "I want to live in a house where I'm happy and with people who love me." She looked around her, then back at him, and tears had pooled in her eyes. Her sister's body had been found with a parachute that failed to open. Jin grieved for her on so many levels. He'd stood with Jin as she'd said goodbye at a private funeral in a cemetery that Sabrina had arranged. It was nowhere near here for Jin's safety. The worst part had been watching her grieve the sister she'd believed in, when the real Patty had been something completely different.

She'd mentioned having a ceremony for her mother, but not when or where. He'd be there for her then, too.

He caught her hand in his and kissed her fingers, talking past a ridiculously huge lump in his throat. Damn he'd fallen so hard for this woman. "Go on."

"I want to have children who will always know they are loved and wanted. I don't know what work I will choose to do, but I want it to benefit others." She took a moment then said, "I want a man I can trust and believe in who I know will stand guard over all he loves. You are that man. I love you, cowboy. I want children with our blue eyes. Will you build me a house here?"

He couldn't speak for a second. "Your mother was right when she named you. You're my treasure. I'll build a house worthy of the one thing I value above all else. Your love."

Then he kissed her as the sun rose on a new beginning.

***

DEAR READER,
This book became very personal for me, and I wanted to give you a little background. I absolutely loved giving Tanner and Jin their story, but this was also one of the toughest stories I've written. There isn't a more difficult place on Earth to research than North Korea, in my opinion. With DECEPTIVE TREASURES, I tried to share a bit of the world I spent so much time in while writing this story so that you could see it through Jin's and Tanner's eyes, but first and foremost my books are to entertain, not to be a news report on international politics. If this story has piqued your interest, I encourage you to do your own research to find out more about North Korea, and please say a prayer for those who are not as fortunate as we are (I speak of the US, since that's my home) to live in a country where we enjoy a level of freedom that some people have no idea even exists.

Thank you for reading my books. If you enjoyed this story, please help other readers find this book by posting a review.

To find out about new releases, sign up for Dianna's private newsletter list (emails are NEVER shared) at
AuthorDiannaLove.com

For SIGNED PRINT copies of Dianna's books visit www.DiannaLoveSignedBooks.com where you can preorder new books.

E-book and international fans:
You can also order a set of signed bookplates for your print books and/or signed cover cards just for the cost of postage at www.DiannaLoveSignedBooks.com (click MORE).

Keep reading for an excerpt of
STOLEN VENGEANCE.

**The Slye Team Black Ops
romantic thriller series is 'completed' (great for binging!)**

Prequel: Last Chance To Run
Book 2: Honeymoon To Die For
Book 3: Kiss The Enemy
Book 4: Deceptive Treasures
Book 5: Stolen Vengeance
Book 6: Fatal Promise

"Love pens a compelling plot, charismatic characters, vivid imagery and a passionate love story that will leave you breathless..." ~~ **Romance Junkies**

STOLEN VENGEANCE

DIANNA LOVE

Chapter 1

DINGO PADDOCK KEPT his head down and his shoulders stooped as he swiped a threadbare sleeve across the sweat running into his eyes. Nighttime heat turned the layers of too-large, secondhand clothes into a furnace, but he'd chosen them as camo, as well as for mobility in a fight. The layers lent him the appearance of the homeless who wore everything they owned.

Plus, the clothes concealed a Chris Reeve knife, ankle-holstered Glock 42, and a Sig Sauer 226 9mm in a shoulder holster.

Atlanta sometimes suffered a brittle cold night this late in June, but not this year. The temps had shot up over ninety earlier in the day.

Being armed to the teeth trumped comfort tonight.

Meeting a snitch wasn't out of the norm for anyone who lived in the shadows of intelligence work like Dingo, but meeting with this *particular* snitch tonight ... it shouldn't happen.

Coming out of hiding lowered this snitch's life expectancy to zero, and hinted that Dingo might have made a mistake the last time they met. Six years ago.

If he had, the fallout would be bloody.

Something was up. He'd used his electronics skills to search for any reason this snitch would return, but there was nothing.

Because there was *supposed* to be nothing–and no one left– from back then.

He took his time walking across a street that ran through the West End. At two in the morning on a Tuesday, most of the city slept. This area had once been a nice place to live, but that was years ago, long before the current transient residents and less fortunate were even born. He shuffled into a space between two ramshackle buildings that offered a false sense of safety to those sleeping beneath blankets of newspapers.

The area reeked of piss, rotted food and the despair of knowing tomorrow would be no better.

A reminder of Dingo's life back when abusive adults had called the shots.

He'd put a stop to that by the time he reached sixteen.

A fire burned in a fifty-gallon drum, and three men hovered around it out of solidarity and for the offer of light. Eight days to Independence Day, but this bunch had nothing to celebrate.

If Dingo closed his eyes, he could see seven-year-old Sabrina's joy at watching her first fireworks display. She'd been so excited until she noticed kids sitting on their dads' shoulders. He hadn't been big enough to carry her on his shoulders yet, and felt lacking as the big brother she considered him.

Stay in the present to stay alive.

One of the men at the fire made a move, shifting in Dingo's direction.

Tall guy who wore a faded flannel shirt rolled up to his elbows and pants sagging on his wiry frame. Lean muscle and prison tattoos on his forearms hinted at risk for anyone tangling with him.

A jagged scar ran south on his cheek.

That only made him ugly, not dangerous.

But the menace peering out of those black slits for eyes said he considered himself the most dangerous beast in this corner of the homeless kingdom.

And it might not be an empty boast.

He was sizing up Dingo as a potential threat in his territory.

Scar Cheek's next move would be to test for a weakness.

Dingo remembered his kind from hard times on the tough streets of Queens, New York, as a twelve-year-old piece of white trash with an Aussie accent to boot. Opening his mouth back then had flagged him as foreign scum, another step below homegrown.

Hadn't taken him long to think twice about speaking if he didn't want to spend more time fighting than eating. First rule of survival was to choose your fights wisely.

How many times had he told Josh and Sabrina that?

Food had been sparse enough for one before he met a punk named Josh and a scrawny hellcat called Sabrina.

He'd taught them that brains could outmaneuver brawn.

Those two had caught on fast. Before Dingo knew it, Sabrina had turned fourteen and promoted herself to the head of their little gang and he'd let it stand. He'd never wanted to run the show and had warned both of them not to get attached to him.

Only fools get attached to anything or anyone. That's what he'd tried to drill into their thick skulls.

Josh and Sabrina might have learned that simple lesson if Dingo hadn't up and marked them as being under his protection.

What'd that make me?

The king of fools, because at thirty-one he'd still step between either of those two and a bullet. They were the closest he'd ever come to having family. Some things *had* changed since then, but not by much. Sabrina now ran covert teams of deadly operatives, which included Dingo and Josh.

As Dingo passed by the drum with flames flickering out the top, Scar Cheek drifted further in Dingo's direction.

This guy thought fresh meat had just wandered in.

Even at twelve, Dingo had been no pushover. Since then, he'd faced off with predators far worse than Scar Cheek and walked away ... okay, limping sometimes, but he had no time to waste proving who was dominant tonight.

Not when he was down to eleven minutes to make his meeting with Bergman, the snitch who shouldn't be in Atlanta again.

Not after what went down all those years ago in California.

Bergman had left this country so fast his shadow had to run to keep up. He shouldn't be back now. And to be honest, Dingo doubted the snitch waiting on him *was* Bergman. More likely, it was someone Bergman allowed to use his identity to get a message to Dingo. But for tonight's discussion, he was Bergman.

If Bergman was truly stateside? That was bad news.

Understatement.

Bad would be holding a pellet gun against an enemy toting a

double barrel shotgun. This kind of news was more like shaking a stick at someone holding a howitzer.

Misery balled in Dingo's gut and banged against his chest.

Just thinking about Bergman reminded Dingo of all he'd lost. Biggest loss of all? Valene Eklund.

He shoved that agonizing memory back deep into its hole. This couldn't be connected to her. Dingo had cut the head off that snake and stomped it to pieces before he'd crawled out of the viper pit half alive.

Valene was safe.

She'd stay that way as long as he never went back.

Jagged pain sawed through him again. Tough shit. He had to accept losing her as the cost of keeping her out of the crosshairs of an insane criminal.

She was fine.

She had to be. He'd stayed out of her world completely for six years now, not even using his world-class skills to check on her from a distance, because ... he did that to hunt down the nastiest humans this world had ever seen.

He'd never use his abilities to snoop on those he respected and cared about, and even if he didn't have his own moral code for how he used his electronics skills, he still wouldn't snoop on Valene.

No point searching for more heartache.

Valene deserved to be happy, but that didn't mean he wanted a front row seat to her joy when it had nothing to do with him. She'd been *more* than fine when he'd seen her a month ago. When she'd turned her back on him.

There was no reason for the ball of dread churning in his belly right now, but good luck convincing his gut.

Footsteps scuffed close behind him.

Dingo sighed. Scar Cheek was not giving up.

If tonight's meeting with Bergman fell apart, the best-case scenario would be a twenty-four-hour delay before Dingo received a second cryptic message with new meet details.

Worst case? No second meeting, because Bergman hadn't made it through the night to see daylight.

From behind Dingo, Scar Cheek cleared his throat.

His next move would be to call Dingo out in three, two, one...

"Hold up, bitch."

At the same instant, Dingo heard a deep voice through the earpiece of his comm unit ask, "Want me to deal with your fan club?"

That would be Tanner Bodine, another member of Sabrina Slye's elite team, who had eyes on Dingo's six from where Tanner perched on a rooftop across the street.

Dingo whispered to Tanner, "When I turn, if I scratch my nose, pop him."

"Roger that."

Dingo tucked his chin against the rags wrapped around his neck and head as a makeshift scarf. Between that and his dark brown hair that had grown out in dense waves, no one would see his earpiece audio receiver unless they got up close and personal. Pivoting slowly, he kept his shoulders tucked to look as non-threatening as possible and lifted his hands waist high, palms out.

He didn't want to hurt any of these guys. "No worries, mate."

With all the Aussies now on commercials, these days his accent actually drew a positive reaction more often than not.

Scar Cheek crossed his arms. "Nobody passes without paying. What you got?"

"Not a thing, just like everyone else here."

"That's too bad, because I don't like your kind."

Seconds were ticking away. "Let me pass and I won't be back."

That drew a mean laugh from Scar Cheek who started forward again. "Hand over the scarf and anything in your pockets."

Fuck it.

Dingo frowned as if he was considering what Scar Cheek said and lifted his finger to his nose then started walking backwards.

Scar Face kept coming. "I'm not joking, fucker–"

Dingo heard the muted pop of Tanner's suppressed shot, but only because he knew it was coming.

Scar Cheek flinched and arched his back, twisting around, trying to see what had hit him.

Dingo backed away as Scar Cheek muttered, "What the

hell…" He jerked his attention back to Dingo and took a step forward then folded at the knees, hitting the ground face first.

The two men still hovering at the drum looked up at the sound of Scar Cheek's body slapping the hard ground. They took him in, then sized up Dingo and went back to attending the fire.

Tanner hadn't killed the guy.

He could have, but Tanner had carried a .300 Blackout Remington 700 sniper rifle. It was suppressed, so the shots were barely audible. An elastic cuff on the buttstock held five tranquilizer rounds–a special new tranq round Sabrina was testing. The tranq wound would hurt like a bad bee sting for the thirty seconds it took the drug to work, but now Scar Cheek would sleep long enough for Dingo to handle his business with Bergman.

In a few steps, Dingo reached a dark opening seventy feet from the men at the drum. It had once been a side entrance to the two-story building. A body-sized lump covered with a soiled blanket slept on the tiny landing between the doorframe and a stairway that *should* go up twenty steps.

That had surely been the plan when they built this place, but after the first two steps, the next eight were missing.

A metal handrail attached to the wall ran all the way up though.

Dingo leaned into the opening to be out of sight, then pulled on his night vision monocular that lit up the dark and changed everything into greenish-gray hues.

Leaping over the body, Dingo landed on the second step, then lunged up to grab as high as he could on the metal handrail. It gave under his weight, but not much. He didn't waste time as he pulled himself up in case the anchor bolts gave out. Swinging his booted foot onto the next metal step, he dragged his weight to a standing position and paused to check down below.

No one could see him up in this black hole even if one of the homeless got curious.

He hurried up the last steps to the top landing where busted wood hung from the doorway on his left. Bits of broken furniture lay scattered everywhere.

Muffled noises erupted halfway down the hall.

Bergman wouldn't have anyone else here. He operated alone.

Or he had at one time.

Dingo had known the snitch for five years before he left the country. The man normally waited so silently in the shadows you'd think you were alone if he was two feet away.

That second person creating noise might be a party crasher. Dingo had to keep Bergman alive or lose intel he desperately wanted. Needed. Just to be damn sure Valene was still safe.

He rushed forward carefully, watching his step so he didn't fall through the rotted floors. What little noise he made would bother him, but it was being covered by Bergman's high-pitched voice that cried out. "Stop. Stop! How many times I gotta tell you? I don't know. If I knew the name, I'd tell you."

"Then you're of no use to me old man. You should be careful who you screw over in the future, but then again ... you have no future."

"*Nooo.*" Then silence.

Shit.

Dingo pulled out his Sig and shoved the door open, banking on the element of surprise.

That might have worked if not for rusty hinges squealing like stuck pigs.

And Bergman's attacker standing just inside the door.

The dark figure spun around and kicked Dingo's gun away, then drove a knife dripping with blood at him.

Dingo sucked back to save his stomach and grabbed the guy's wrist, wrenching it. He slammed the wrist against the doorframe. The knife flew out of sight, but the guy was already swinging wild hits. His fists battered Dingo's ribs in rapid fire.

If the fucker had killed Bergman, then Dingo needed the attacker alive.

Dingo swung away and came back around in time to see a foot flying at his head. He ducked and shoved upright then rammed his shoulder into the attacker, who had four inches of height on Dingo's six-one. He'd given it all he had, knocking the guy into a wall.

The rotten structure shattered and the lack of resistance sent Dingo landing on top of his opponent with wood raining down on them.

A loud creak ripped through the air. The floor threatened to break away.

That body smash should have at least stunned Bruce Lee's evil spawn, but no. He wasn't even at a disadvantage being caught on the bottom of their tangled pile. Sharp strikes hammered Dingo's ribcage again, dammit.

He already felt like he'd been run through a blender inside out.

Tomorrow was going to suck, but not as bad as tonight if he lost this fight.

He'd never learned all those fancy martial arts moves.

Where he came from, the dirtiest fighter won.

Dingo shoved the wood off and pushed to his feet.

With a move straight out of Hollywood, the guy flipped over, landed on his feet and took off down the hallway toward a window opening that had no glass left.

You're not escaping that easily, Kung Fu.

Dingo charged after him, talking to Tanner as he did. "Get to the east end of the building. Chasing someone headed for a window on the second floor."

"Roger that."

But Tanner had to get down off the roof and across the street.

Dingo scooped up what looked like the leg of an old wooden chair that lay in pieces, and flung it for all he was worth. It whacked the crazy guy in the head with a solid thud.

That sent his perp stumbling just short of the window opening.

Dingo came barreling up, jumping over holes in the floor, and lost his footing as he reached the end of the hallway. The bastard staggered, but swung around with a wicked kick aimed at Dingo's head.

This time Dingo was ready, and knocked the leg aside and ducked.

Who hired this guy?

Mercenaries with this level of skill did not come cheap.

In the next second, the son of a bitch made a move that telegraphed his intention to go on attack again, even after taking a hit hard enough to give him a concussion.

What was it going to take to drop this maniac?

As the perp swung around, Dingo cupped a fist with his other hand and jammed an elbow into the guy's throat. He got a boot in his ribs for that and arched face first into the wall. Dammit. That shit hurt.

Fuck it. Dingo came around with a roar and body checked Kung Fu straight on, sending the bastard backwards into the window.

Make that right *through* the window.

Wood disintegrated as Kung Fu's body blasted through the opening and out of sight.

Dingo lunged to grab him, but came up with a handful of nothing. He leaned through the window, fighting to draw air in spite of his battered ribs.

When he looked down, his attacker was sprawled and not moving. "Shit, take your time Tanner. I think he's dead."

"Roger that."

"I'm going back inside to see if my contact is dead, too." Dingo hurried back to the room Kung Fu had come out of, but every breath hurt like a bitch.

Climbing out that window and down the side of this building to get out of here won't be no picnic either.

When he reached the room, his stomach flipped over.

It *was* Bergman.

The snitch's lungs were playing a familiar tune, the death rattle. Kung Fu had gutted Bergman with a quick X across his soft abdomen. Bergman was trying to whisper something.

Dingo dropped onto his knees to get close enough to hear, because they both knew calling an ambulance wouldn't save him. "Why'd you come back, Berg?"

"Had ... no ... choice."

Before Dingo could press him on that, Bergman said, "Three targets." Wheeze, rattle. "Part of ... big plan."

"Where are the targets?" Dingo asked.

"L ..." Gurgle. "They ..." Bergman's eyes rolled up.

Dingo shook him. "Stay with me. L what? Who are the targets? They what?"

Bergman gasped and wheezed, sounding wet. His eyes focused for a moment. "Initials. F.E.P. O... N. C." More wheezing. "P.G

... C. He ... found me. Want you.”

Dingo’s blood ran cold at the only *he* that could have sent Bergman back here, but that wasn’t possible. “*Who* are you talking about?”

“Satan’s ... Garden ... C–”

Bergman gave one last heave and air slipped past his lips in a whistle, then he stopped moving.

Dingo stared at him in disbelief.

Bergman had to be wrong.

Dingo had sacrificed eleven months of his life and most of his soul to destroy Satan’s Garden Club. He’d killed Santori Garcia, the head of that murdering group, and made *sure* he was dead. No rising from the grave for that one to threaten Valene again.

She was safe. He refused to believe otherwise.

This intel had nothing to do with her.

Someone had to be using the Satan’s Garden Club name again, because the only person still left from Garcia’s crew was a nasty buggar who’d been fourth in command. That one had another eighty years in prison, plus he’d never been high enough in the ranks to have been fully in Garcia’s confidence—not enough to know about Valene.

Tanner’s voice cut into Dingo’s thoughts. “You better get down here.”

“Why? What’s up?” Dingo finished searching for any information on Bergman. Wasted effort.

“Your guy’s gone.”

“What?” Dingo stood up.

“I did find something odd.”

“Hold on. I’m coming to the window.” Dingo found his Sig where it had landed in a pile of debris, then limped his way back down the hall. When he got there, the damn body *had* disappeared. “What you got, mate?”

Tanner had a golf bag slung over his shoulder–a way to stash the rifle so it wouldn’t attract attention–and his monocular flipped up on his forehead since the streetlight at the corner of the building gave enough light to see the weed-infested pavement. He looked up at where Dingo stood at the open window and said, "I doubt this shiny gold coin has been here very long."

Dingo cursed. "Can you read anything on it?"

Tanner held the coin to catch the light. "S. G. C."

Satan's Garden Club's calling card. The impossible had happened. Garcia's people were back in business.

Whoever had found Bergman would come for Dingo next.

Or Valene.

✺

Read *Stolen Vengeance* now!
Order your signed and personalized copy at
www.DiannaLoveSignedBooks.com

~~~

The Slye Team Black Ops
romantic thriller series is 'completed' (great for binging!)

Prequel: Last Chance To Run
Book 1: Nowhere Safe
Book 2: Honeymoon To Die For
Book 3: Kiss The Enemy
Book 4: Deceptive Treasures
Book 5: Stolen Vengeance
Book 6: Fatal Promise

Want more romance with suspense?
You might like Dianna's new shifter romance series:

The League of Gallize Shifters books are stand-alone paranormal romances written in an larger urban fantasy style world.
Book 1: Gray Wolf Mate
Book 2: Mating A Grizzly
Book 3: Stalking His Mate
Book 4: Scent of A Mate
Book 5: Wild Wolf Mate

Dianna Love and Mary Buckham created the sci-fi/fantasy, time travel Red Moon Trilogy, stories appropriate for Hunger Games readers.

(You can order signed/personalized print copies at
www.MicahCaidaSignedBooks.com)

Book 1: Time Trap
Book 2: Time Return
Book 3: Time Lock

Author's Bio

New York Times **Bestseller Dianna Love** once dangled over a hundred feet in the air to create unusual marketing projects for Fortune 500 companies. She now writes high-octane romantic thrillers, young adult and urban fantasy. Fans of the bestselling Belador urban fantasy series will be thrilled to know more books are coming after soon with the new Treoir Dragon Chronicles. Dianna's Slye Team Black Ops sexy romantic thriller series wrapped up with Gage and Sabrina's book–Fatal Promise–perfect for bingers! She has new League of Gallize Shifters paranormal romance series. Look for her books in print, e-book and audio. On the rare occasions Dianna is out of her writing cave, she tours the country on her BMW motorcycle searching for new story locations. Dianna lives in the Atlanta, GA area with her husband, who is a motorcycle instructor, and with a tank full of unruly saltwater critters.

Visit her website at *www.AuthorDiannaLove.com*
or *www.DiannaLoveSignedBooks.com*

Acknowledgements

I am blessed to have a team that starts with my amazing husband, Karl. He takes care of so much for both of us every day and throughout the year that allows me to write my stories, plus he teaches motorcycle safety. The world is a better place because of him.

Cassondra Murray is the first to read every story and she sees it more than once. In fact, she's the last one to touch it before I make the final run through. She never fails to surprise me with her insight and how spot on she is with details from one book to the next. I love the opportunities we have to make trips together and readers are always happy to see her with me.

This story started with a discussion I had with Steve Doyle, a former Special Forces soldier who is always willing to be my weapons and operational specialist on the Slye Team Black Ops romantic thriller books. I so appreciate the initial brainstorming he and I did to choose North Korea as the opening setting and suggestions he offered for my black ops team. I am thankful every day for men and women like Steve who keep us safe and free.

Once I have the seed of an idea, my characters and a backbone for the story, USA Today bestselling author Mary Buckham and I brainstorm our books together a couple times a year. That is incredibly valuable to me. The rest of the time, Mary is working on a new *Invisible Recruit* story.

I would be nowhere without my amazing beta readers. Joyce Ann McLaughlin is always ready to read these books during the early "not quite polished" stage and share her feedback. I love her notes and the way she's just as quick to tell me what she loves as what needs a second look. Manuella Robinson is always willing to read anything I ask of her and she's so fast. I appreciate her honest opinion and constant support.

Judy Carney is yet another beta reader when she performs the first copy edit read. Her enthusiasm for the project comes through in everything she notes. It's always a joy to work with her.

Thanks to Kim Killion who designs all the covers for my Slye Team series, which I LOVE! She is so talented!! Thanks also to Jennifer Jakes for running her magic formatting wand over my files every time. I'm always happy to see an email from Kim or Jenn!

Any mistakes made or adjustments for fiction are my own, because every one who helped me went above and beyond the call to give me the best information.

Thanks also to Leiha Mann, Su Walker and the RBLs for supporting all authors! Love and appreciation goes to my amazing Reader Community, who support me all through the year. If you're interested in joining my team, just stop by my Facebook group page.